PENGUIN BOOKS

CASTLE

OF THE

CURSED

T0322228

ALSO BY
ROMINA GARBER

CASTLE OF THE CURSED

ROMINA GARBER

PENGUIN BOOKS

PENGUIN BOOKS

UK | USA | Canada | Ireland | Australia
India | New Zealand | South Africa

Penguin Books is part of the Penguin Random House group of companies
whose addresses can be found at global.penguinrandomhouse.com

www.penguin.co.uk
www.puffin.co.uk
www.ladybird.co.uk

First published in the USA by Wednesday Books, an imprint of St. Martin's Publishing
Group, and in Great Britain by Penguin Books 2024

001

Text copyright © Romina Garber, 2024

The moral right of the author has been asserted

Designed by Jonathan Bennett
Printed and bound in Great Britain by Clays Ltd, Elcograf S.p.A.

The authorized representative in the EEA is Penguin Random House Ireland,
Morrison Chambers, 32 Nassau Street, Dublin D02 YH68

A CIP catalogue record for this book is available from the British Library

ISBN: 978-0-241-70158-4

All correspondence to:
Penguin Books
Penguin Random House Children's
One Embassy Gardens, 8 Viaduct Gardens, London SW11 7BW

To my love, Leo—

A global pandemic brought us to the same city,
and a major radio station hosted the wedding of our dreams.
Our love story has only just begun, and it's already a page-turner.

Dear Reader,

Castle of the Cursed is my darkest story and very different from my other books.

This is a tale about grief. The narrative addresses suicide, mental health issues, death of a parent, sex, and violence. Please be certain you are in the right mindset to read on.

Estela is trapped in a dark place, caught in the shadow of her pain. And yet, in the blackest depths of her despair, she sees stars.

That is humanity's true magic—our unabashed ability to hope.

In the pages ahead, you will read: *No hay luz en Oscuro*. But that's not true.

If you take away one thing from this gothic tale—even if this note is as far as you make it—let it be this:

There is always *light in the dark.*

Que Brálaga los bendiga,

Romina Garber

Do you not think that there are things which you cannot understand, and yet which are; that some people see things that others cannot?

—Bram Stoker, *Dracula*

7 MONTHS AGO

TENDRILS OF BLACK SMOKE COIL around the metal poles of the subway train.

I blink. They're gone.

We lurch forward, and I count twenty-six passengers, including us. Ages range from seventeen (me) to over eighty (old man behind Dad).

My parents and I ride standing, as do two women in crisp suits too clean for the colorless seats. A party of German tourists has taken over one end of the compartment, reeking of beer and tobacco. Four teen girls in pleated uniforms sit on the bench across from me, huddled close and speaking in whispers.

My gaze lingers on the students, and I wonder if I would be happy with their lives. Would I enjoy waking up every day to the same outfit, same routine, same bedroom—?

"Who are they?" asks Dad.

Arching my neck, I spy the names of the textbooks peeking out from a star-studded bag: *Physics, Calculus, U.S. Government.*

"Seniors."

"That's all you got?"

Dad sounds like he wants a challenge, so I stare harder. The students are glued to the same phone screen, which one of them holds vertically, at an awkward viewing angle. I follow the camera's trajectory to the other end of the train, where two people are making out.

"They're recording that couple over there—"

I fall silent as one of the girls looks up and her gaze grazes mine. I'm struck by the darkness of her irises. They're pitch-black.

She keeps looking around, as if searching for an escape route. Unlike her friends, she hasn't adorned herself with jewelry or makeup, and she seems more concerned with the phone than the couple it's recording. The device is an outdated model with a single camera lens.

"They're using the black-eyed girl's phone," I theorize to Dad in a low register, my voice barely audible. "Maybe some kind of social test. Could be the other three haven't accepted her yet."

I glance at Dad to see how I'm doing. One of his bushy brows dips as he winks his approval, and my lips stretch into a grin.

"She comes from a Dominican family," he says under his breath, "and her mother is employed by the school, so it's likely she's worried about getting in trouble." He must see my confusion because he adds, "On the platform, I overheard her speaking with her mother in Spanish on that very cell phone."

I cross my arms, irritation singeing my cheeks. "Rules of the game are *no prior information*, and besides—"

"Train platform counts as part of the scene—"

"You won't teach me Spanish!" I speak over him. "You and Mom just want to keep it as your secret language—!"

"Aren't you too old for this game?" asks Mom. She always shuts me down when I bring up Spanish.

Or Argentina, where she and Dad are from. Or pretty much anything about the past.

"*Too old?*" echoes Dad. "Liv, your daughter still hasn't retired from hide-and-seek, and her list of rules for that game is longer than the Constitution!"

They crack matching smirks, and even though I'm used to their ribbing, today the dig stings.

From the corner of my eye, the black smoke snakes its way through the other passengers again. I open my mouth to say something, but it vanishes as swiftly as before.

Like it's not actually here.

Probably the beginnings of an ocular migraine. I diagnosed myself last week when I started seeing spots in my peripheral vision and looked up the symptoms online. They don't last long, so I just have to ignore it.

I study the four girls. I can't help noting how their uniforms hug their bodies, their nails shimmer with glossy colors, their hairstyles frame their faces. I look down at the end of my own frizzy ponytail, my loose Goodwill sweater, Mom's jeans that are too long on me . . . and I feel a sense of loss for something I can't name.

The old man behind Dad coughs, leaving a spray of red on his clean handkerchief. He rolls it up, darting a glance at the woman beside him, who's too glued to her phone to notice. She looks like she could be his daughter.

"Dad." My brain tingles with new energy, as if more neurons than usual are firing. Dad calls it my investigative instinct. He says I'm a natural.

"What is it, Stela?"

"That man just coughed blood."

Dad follows my gaze. "What other symptoms have you observed?"

"*Raul*," chides Mom. "Don't encourage her."

I focus harder on the elderly man, clocking the way his head lists right, like a partially deflated balloon. Skin sags off him in a way heavier than age, as if he's dropped a lot of weight fast. "Could be cancer," I say, forgetting to keep my voice down. "Or AIDS—"

"Can you save the detective exercises for when we're back at the hotel?" interjects Mom.

"And investigate *what*?" I ask. "The wallpaper pattern?"

Her lips twitch. "So you have to be Sherlock twenty-four seven?"

"Dad's Sherlock. I'm Watson."

Dad smiles, and Mom's right cheek dimples. The power flickers off and on, but my parents' expressions don't dampen.

"Did you see that?" I ask. The air begins to dim, like someone is lowering the lights. Or my vision is waning. "I think I'm having an ocular—"

A blast of smoke overtakes the compartment, burning my words to ashes. I gasp as thick clouds swirl around me, obscuring everything from view.

"DAD? MOM?"

I can barely hear myself over the rushing of air, and I squeeze my eyes shut to protect them, squinching my nose against the acrid scent. Dread knots my stomach at my parents' silence, the oxygen in my lungs thinning as my pulse pummels my chest—

The smoke clears suddenly, and I inhale deeply as I open my eyes to an explosion of silver.

The starry burst is bright enough that I have to shield my gaze, and once it dissipates to gray mist, the subway looks the same.

Literally.

Everyone is frozen in place, like the scene inside a snow globe once the particles have settled.

The students are still huddled around the phone. The sick man is still clutching the handkerchief in his pocket. My parents' lips are still curved up at the ends.

I touch Mom's fingers, but they're limp. I shake Dad's arm, digging my nails in, but he doesn't react.

"What's happening?!" My voice is high and splintering. "*WAKE UP!*"

The train shudders, a warning cry of metal—

And twenty-five bodies crash to the floor.

RAUL'S RULE #1

DON'T THINK;

FEEL.

CHAPTER 1

"ESTELA AMADOR?"

The driver approaches us at the airport with a sign that reads LETICIA GUERRA, my nurse's name, as my own would draw too much attention.

Yet it's my name he calls on his approach, clearly recognizing me from the news.

"Where is Doctora Brálaga?" asks Nurse Leticia in a guarded tone.

"I don't know. I'm with a car service," he says in decent English, with only a slight accent.

He doesn't look like the typical driver. He wears skinny jeans, aviator shades, a blue surgical face mask, and a charcoal zip-up with the hood over his head.

My nurse frowns with uneasiness. She was given a companion ticket to accompany me on the flight to Spain, but this is as far as she comes. Her return trip is in a few hours.

I stick out my hand to her in farewell, so she'll know it's okay to leave.

"Oh, put that down," she says, and my joints stiffen as she reels me into a hug.

My first embrace since—well, in seven months.

"You are so young, Estelita," she whispers in my ear. "Don't give up on the world so soon." Then she retrieves a small pill container from her pocket and offers me my medicine for the final time. I pop the meds into my mouth and take a swig from my water bottle.

"Twenty-five voices were silenced for good," she says, more serious than I've heard her. "*But you still have yours.*"

I wait until I've fallen into step behind the driver to spit out the pills.

The fog rolls in as the castle comes into view.

It's a thin film of mist that makes me feel like I'm entering a dream dimension.

We've been driving through northern Spain for two hours, but it's only now that castillo Brálaga's silhouette burns into the horizon. From here, it looks like nothing more than a dark speck in the corner of my vision.

If only it were farther away.

The last time I rode in a car, I was being shuttled for questioning by the NYPD, FBI, CDC, and a bunch of other acronyms. It was the same script with all of them:

"*My name is Estela Amador. My parents are Olivia and Raul. We're subletting a place in Asheville, but we live on the road. We came to New York City because I begged them to bring me here.*"

I begged.

It's *my* fault.

I feel my pulse slow to a crawl, like my body is losing power and shutting down. I lower the window until it cuts just below my eyes and press my cheekbone to the cool glass, letting the wind whip my face. Its gentle slaps try to revive me . . .

But you can't reawaken a corpse.

"¿Todo bien?"

I stare at the driver in the rearview mirror. I'd nearly forgotten him. For a fragmented instant, I could almost believe I was in the back seat of my parents' ancient Subaru, watching the world from my usual vantage point.

"¿Necesitas algo?" he presses. I don't know what he's saying, but he looks like the Invisible Man with his hood, sunglasses, and surgical face mask on. It's not even sunny out.

"Hay una gasolinera donde voy a llenar el depósito y allí podrá tomar algo, aunque sea un poco de aire."

I nod in assent just so he'll leave me alone. It's annoying that he's speaking in Spanish now, when at the airport he spoke perfect English.

The truth is, I should have spent the past few weeks studying Spanish in preparation for my move here—but if I had, coming to Spain would have felt too much like an actual decision, and I might not have gone through with it.

Outside, the fog is fading, revealing that up ahead the ground grows teeth. Forests serrate rolling hills, and perched on a peak overlooking the tree line is a black dot.

My new home.

I can't see the community of Oscuro yet, but I know from my online search that the colorful patchwork of small houses with sloped rooftops is tucked into the castle's side. The town is so tiny, I had to zoom in as far as possible to reveal its name on the map.

The first result that popped up when I searched for Oscuro was its translation to English—*dark*. I couldn't find a website or any kind of social media presence for the town. It doesn't even have a Wikipedia page.

But the castle does.

Castillo Brálaga

Located in northern Spain, this Gothic construction was built in the late 1200s by a wealthy man about whom everything has been forgotten, except his surname.

The estate has never been sold, only handed down through generations of the Brálaga bloodline. Over the centuries, it has developed a sinister reputation.

The home has been unofficially dubbed "la Sombra" by locals because the town of Oscuro lies in its shadow. It's rumored that bad luck plagues its inhabitants, sparking a superstition that the castle is cursed.

There's only one hyperlinked citation, and the page never loads.

Once, I would have relished unraveling this riddle. *Christie, Chandler, Capote*—Dad and I used to play a game where we'd read the same detective novel and circle the page number where we cracked the case; then we'd swap copies to see who got there first.

But now I'd give anything to exchange my mystery for a choose-your-own-adventure book where someone else could make all my decisions for me.

Your parents are dead.

To remain at the Rainbow Pediatric Mental Health Center in DC, which will kick you out in two weeks when you turn eighteen, turn to page 6. To move to Spain and live with an estranged aunt you've never

heard of, turn to page 23. To jump into a time machine and undo the
past seven months . . .

    Try the science-fiction aisle.

"Ya podrá ver el castillo a lo alto. Es esa sombra lejana en la boca del bosque."

The driver disconcerts me again with his presence. Since it doesn't sound like he's asking a question, this time I don't nod.

I may not be able to see his eyes in the rearview mirror, but I've felt his gaze on me for most of the drive. Nurse Leticia warned me that as the sole survivor of a tragedy that made global headlines—what the media called the Subway 25, for the number of dead—I would draw attention. But that didn't prepare me for the ogling at the airport, or the pointing of phone cameras, or the way strangers on the plane whispered my name like they knew me.

I turn pointedly to the window again, hoping the driver takes the hint that I don't want to talk. I stare out for so long that the castle grows from a black dot to a pointy blob. I saw in the Wikipedia photo that its defining feature is its sole tower—an arrow aimed at the stars.

Given the lack of traffic, we'll probably make it there before sunset. Only I'm not ready for this ride to be over.

Home has never been a destination for me. It's *momentum*.

My earliest memories are riding in the back seat of our car and drinking in the vast blueness of the Pacific Ocean. Mom was a freelance journalist, Dad a private investigator. They were always chasing the next case or story, so we never lingered anywhere long.

The road is as close to a homeland as I have.

I used to believe Mom and Dad were too free-spirited for a conventional life. I figured they wouldn't discuss their parents or pasts with me because they had fallen out with their families and were waiting until I was older to fill in the details.

It wasn't until they died that I learned just how naive I had always been.

CHAPTER 2

"A CAR'S COME FOR YOU, ESTELITA."

I look up from my notepad at Nurse Leticia framed in the doorway.

My first day at the center, the staff greeted me solemnly and with some trepidation, offering me pity and condolences—except Nurse Leticia. Or Lety, as she asks us to call her. *You're less alone than you feel* were her first words, delivered to me with a smile.

My roommate, Bebe, peeks in from behind the nurse. She only comes to our room at night, when she thinks I'm asleep. Works for me, so I can spend my days crying in peace.

Grief is like climate change: the sobbing comes in cycles, bands of storms that roll in with little warning and uproot my thoughts. Little by little, I feel the pain transforming me into someone new.

"Here," says Nurse Leticia, setting down a pair of jeans and a button-down shirt at the edge of my bed. "These should be your size."

"Is it Agent Navarro?" I ask as I reach for the clothes and pull them on under the covers. "Has something happened? Is there news?"

"Ay, Estelita, always with the questions," she says as I work under the sheets to swap my cotton pants for the jeans. "Hurry, and you'll find out for yourself."

Bebe scampers away as the nurse turns to go. She only approached because she didn't want to miss the gossip.

The clothes are smaller than my old ones, so they fit better. I guess I haven't been eating as much as usual. When I get in the black SUV, I'm alone in the back seat. Agent Navarro didn't come.

She was the first FBI agent I spoke to after . . . what happened. She has a temperate warmth about her, like she thinks of her heart as an asset when solving a case and not as something that must be shut off. She reminds me a bit of Dad.

Since I'm a minor, legally my name should have never been released to the press, but a reporter uncovered my identity and printed it. Agent Navarro was so outraged on my behalf that she gave a quote to an outlet calling the journalist in question an *"embarrassment to humanity."*

I've brought my notepad, and my tiny scrawl of case notes takes up every bit of space, the ink running in places where my tears have fallen. The staff at the center have given me limited television privileges to keep up with the news, as long as I show them I can handle it. They say the instant I prove otherwise, I'll get cut off from the investigation.

Through the tinted window, I watch the greenery of residential communities dull into the grays of downtown. The Rainbow Center is a treatment facility for children of the elite, like politicians, celebrities, and the wealthy. It's a place to get professional attention away from the public eye. The government is footing my bill, a sign they want to take care of me as much as they want to keep me close.

"Hey, Estela," says Agent Navarro as soon as I step out of the SUV. She's waiting for me on the street, as are some male faces I remember from a few weeks ago, when they first brought me to this building.

I hoped to prove to them I could be useful on the case by providing detailed accounts of every passenger, the kind of notes Dad would take when surveying a scene. Agent Navarro and the others were riveted by my observations . . . until I brought up the black smoke.

There wasn't a shred of evidence that supported the presence of a fire—nor any hint of a weapon or a culprit. That's when they informed me I was experiencing post-traumatic stress disorder and needed time to recover so I could see things more clearly.

As no family member stepped forth to claim me, I was declared a ward of the state and signed into the Rainbow Pediatric Mental Health Center in Washington, DC.

"Is there news?" I ask by way of greeting. "Do you have a suspect?"

"Let's go inside," she says, and I note a new stiffness in her tone. I follow the agents past security and metal detectors, and this time instead of being welcomed into the director's office as an American hero, I'm ushered into an interrogation room.

My throat goes dry the instant I slide into a chair and Agent Navarro sits across from me. No one else comes in with us.

Her bald mahogany head shines under the fluorescent lighting as she sets a paper bag on the table. "I thought we agreed to trust each other," she begins, and my stomach hardens in anticipation of what this is about. "You help me figure out what happened to your parents, and I try to keep you involved in the case."

"Right," I say, sitting up to catch the curveball she's about to throw.

"Then why did you tell me your dad was a cop in Los Angeles?"

I blink and my mind blanks. I was prepared for her to bring up anything—our nomadic lifestyle, extended family members, even *taxes*—but not this.

"He was," I assert when I find my voice. "For seven years."

"And yet there's no record of him ever being in the LAPD."

I feel the color drain from my face and the air retract from my lungs as the ground slips away from me. My dad's identity as a detective forms part of the foundation upon which I built my own sense of self. The universe can't take this from me, too.

"My dad was a c-cop."

I try to state it firmly, but my chin trembles on the last word.

Agent Navarro's expression cracks with a sympathy that I want to believe is real. "He was," she says, and I feel the breath rushing back into my chest. "Just not in this country. You don't have US residency. Your parents never filed the proper paperwork."

"I don't understand. I was born here." I sound defensive even to myself.

Agent Navarro doesn't answer. She just reaches inside the paper bag and pulls out three passports. They look like they were all issued by the same country.

The letters on the covers bleed together as my vision blurs, so I can't read them.

This can't be happening. My parents and I are—*were*—bonded by trust. We didn't keep secrets. There wasn't space for them in the Subaru.

Except about the past, whispers a small voice in my mind.

"Argentina," I say at last. I sound choked, like there's something caught in my throat.

"No."

"What?" I blink in surprise, spraying my cheeks with tears.

"You're from Spain."

Agent Navarro stands up, abandoning me to my stupor as she goes to confer with unseen agents.

I can barely catch my breath, but I need to corral my thoughts if I'm going to figure out what's going on. Did they bring me in because they suspect my family? Or *me*? That doesn't make sense. What was our weapon? Our motive?

They must be deporting me! I'm no longer the United States's problem—

The door clicks as Agent Navarro comes back in. Seated across from me again, she says, "I believe you didn't know any of this."

"Do I have family left?" I ask, hoping I won't wind up in some Spanish foster care program before I'm thrown out on the street.

"We've reached out to Spanish agencies to try locating relatives," she answers in a lighter tone. "Until we know more, nothing changes. You will remain where you are until the doctors say you're ready to be discharged. This country is the only home you know, and we are not about to abandon you."

I hear my exhale, but I don't suck in new air. She's gone from cold to overly friendly, and the fake charm doesn't work for her, like tasting a saccharine treat. "You want something," I say as it dawns on me.

Agent Navarro's eyebrows arch in surprise, and she sizes me up like she's evaluating me anew.

"What is it?" I ask, impatience getting the best of me.

She links her hands together on the table, her gaze never straying from mine. "We need you to stand at a press conference."

I don't like them, but I stood at plenty of those a couple of weeks ago. Once my identity was released, the government was quick to turn me into the public face of the tragedy. "What do I have to say?"

"Absolutely nothing. You are not to speak."

The instruction makes me a little queasy, but I don't disagree because I prefer not to participate.

Soon after, I'm led into a space where the press is congregated in front of the FBI director and other top figures. I'm steered right to the director's side, and he places a large hand on my shoulder, beaming.

I look around at the gathered reporters and tap into an electric current of anticipation. The government must be making a major announcement.

"One month ago today, twenty-six people boarded a subway train," says the director solemnly. "At 4:06 p.m., something happened in one of the compartments that stopped twenty-five people's hearts at the same time. It happened in New York, but it didn't just happen to New Yorkers. It happened to America. It happened to the world."

He looks down and gives me a solemn nod. His words weave wonder into the air, and the surrounding silence is so thick that camera clicks echo like bombs.

I wait with bated breath like everyone else. It feels like the whole world has been salivating for a villain, somewhere to place the blame for the Subway 25. Last week, Germany publicly offered to send their best investigators to help our law enforcement. As a third of the victims were their citizens, many countries believe them to have a strong claim. Is that why the FBI feels compelled to make an announcement now?

"Today, we can reveal what caused the deaths of those twenty-five passengers."

Gasps erupt across the room, including my own. I can't breathe, blink, think. It's like every part of me just sprouted ears.

"After reviewing the evidence, we can confirm this was *not* a terrorist plot, nor was it an attack at all. The subway line in question is the oldest in operation, and the city of New York has been systematically decommissioning these trains over time, as new ones come in to replace them. This particular train was an older model, and unfortunately one compartment suffered a lethal gas leak."

A gas leak? I don't understand. Then why didn't *I* die?

"It's thanks to Estela's testimony we were able to put it together." The director squeezes my shoulder. "She saw a man cough blood into a handkerchief just moments before everyone became afflicted. Estela suffered some minor hallucinogenic effects, but she did not breathe in enough of the gas for it to be fatal. For now, she is still recovering and under medical supervision, so she will not be taking questions."

He looks down at me again and says, "The whole country—the whole *world*—grieves with you, Estela. We thank you for your help in finding the cause of this tragedy."

I feel my jaw drop open.

I want to shout: *HE'S LYING!*

The government just made up their own version of what happened, based on facts they can fathom. A story they can control. If this version of events is accepted, we're never going to get real answers.

I need to say something.

Agent Navarro's hand grips my shoulder. I want to cry out, shake my head, *speak*. But I'm distracted by the tiny voice in my mind asking: *Are you sure?*

And then there's the question others will invariably ask: *Do you have a better theory?*

Before I can decide what to do, Agent Navarro guides me away. I keep trying to speak, but words won't come.

When the SUV drops me off at the center, the old *me* stays behind.

I abandon everything in that back seat—my notepad, my hope for answers, and my *voice*.

THE VOID

ESTELA STOPS SPEAKING.

And she knits herself a shroud from the silence.

She is told she suffers from PTSD, survivor's guilt, generalized anxiety disorder, clinical depression, and more. They give her drugs that help soften the edges of the world around her, but they don't dampen its colors. Or the past. Or the pain.

The world can't get quiet enough.

Her own face mocks her everywhere. On the nurses' phone screens when they think she isn't looking. On the rec room's television, until the staff spy her and change the channel. On the pages of newspapers and magazines reserved for more privileged patients.

She used to be one of those special people, until she stopped speaking. They say she has "shut down." She is absent, untreatable, a worst-case scenario. She has become an empty shell.

Estela has lost interest in everything. She has shed her form and exists outside of time and space. She can't fathom why her body is still here when she is not.

She wishes to disappear completely into the void of her mind . . . But a venomous voice keeps pulling her out.

"There was another story on your parents today."

The voice belongs to her roommate. Bebe is a teen actress of some note, and she was the center's biggest celebrity until Estela's arrival.

"Did you know they were here illegally?" Bebe prods. "Does that mean you're here illegally?"

Every night, as Estela lies in bed, longing to drift to sleep, Bebe's voice whispers fresh nightmares into the dark.

"Some people say your parents were behind the attack, and they sacrificed themselves on purpose. They think you're radicalized, too, and that's why the government is hiding you. Imagine if they knew you were here."

Once, Bebe brings Estela an artifact from the outside world. It's only a scrap of paper, but it feels like lead in her hand.

The torn piece of newsprint reads:

> Sources say Estela Amador is being treated for severe mental health issues resulting from the gas she inhaled. A government agent who spoke on the condition of anonymity says when she turns eighteen, she will graduate to an adult facility. He doubts she will ever be released.

Estela wants to forget the scrap of paper, but she can't.

Words haunt, but objects exert gravity. They ensnare. Now she can never get lost in her mind's depths. The world will never get quiet enough.

Not without an intervention.

She knows the nurses' schedules. She's memorized the passcode to the drug dispensary. She always marks her escape routes.

Tonight, the world will be as silent as Estela.

She wakes up in a hospital bed.

Estela has been placed on a seventy-two-hour watch. She is given heavy doses of antidepressants.

When she returns to her assigned room, Bebe does not speak to her anymore.

Weeks pass, and Estela keeps up her silent vigil. She watches other patients improve with a regimen of therapy and medication, but no matter how the doctors adjust her dosage, all she feels is brain fog.

And she welcomes it.

In this state, she drifts closer and closer to the void of her mind. Slow and semisedated, she can't focus. She can't make plans. She can't remember.

Then the letter arrives.

CHAPTER 3

TODAY, I HAVEN'T LEFT MY BED.

Little by little, I'm managing to disappear. It's easier now, since everyone stopped paying attention.

"You have a message from Agent Navarro."

It's Nurse Leticia. I don't stir.

"They've managed to locate a family member of yours in Spain. You have an aunt!"

I barely register anything but the word *aunt*. My chin moves, just a fraction, and the nurse shows me an unsealed envelope. From within, she retrieves a folded-up letter.

"I'll read it to you," she offers when I don't reach for it.

> *Querida Estela:*
>
> *Soy su tía Beatríz, la hermana de su madre. Vivo en España, en nuestra residencia familiar, el castillo Brálaga. Si le apetece, la invito a vivir aquí conmigo.*
>
> > *Con cariño,*
> > *Dra. Beatríz Brálaga*

Nurse Leticia waits, but I have no reaction to offer her.

"Do you speak Spanish?"

I stay silent.

"Well, she says she's your mom's sister, and she's inviting you to live with her in Spain at what she refers to as your family's *castle*. The FBI has already vetted her, and they say she's a small-town doctor who runs a local clinic. Agent Navarro believes this Beatríz is equipped to look after you, both medically and financially, but it's your choice what you want to do."

No matter how hard I try to silence the world, my past won't keep quiet.

"I told you, Estelita," whispers Nurse Leticia. "You're not alone."

Before she leaves, Lety places the envelope on the bedspread. I stare at the paper and am reminded of its weight. The way a page's gravity pulls one toward its words.

I hide the envelope under the mattress. I don't pull it out for days. Not until Lety asks me about it. She says I must make a choice.

I open the envelope in the bathroom. I pull out the letter and scan the text, even if I don't speak the language. Then I let the page fall into the toilet bowl.

But before I can drop the envelope, something slips out.

I catch the wisp of paper that's nearly disintegrated. *A photograph.*

BOOM.

I feel a punch to the chest and lean forward from the impact.

BOOM.

It sounds like my heart just awoke from hibernation.

BOOM.

And it desperately wants out of its cage.

It's been so long since I last heard my pulse that I relish the rush of blood, like a parched desert wanderer happening upon a fresh spring.

I recognize Mom's teenage face. The thick eyelashes and right-cheek dimple are her defining features, both of which I inherited. Beside her is another girl who looks to be her sister. She seems a handful of years younger, with the same heavy hair and hourglass frame.

But it's not the *who* affecting me. It's the *where*.

I can almost feel the purple-patterned wallpaper under my fingers and the icy stone floor beneath my feet. My heart's lashes intensify as a small spark ignites in my brain, a candle of what was once a wildfire—and I'm hit with an undeniable realization:

Something impossible happened to me in that purple room.

NOW

WE PULL OFF THE ROAD, but we haven't made it to the castle yet. We're at a gas station by a roadside motel with a restaurant/bar.

. "Solo tardaré un momento."

I don't know what he said, but as soon as the driver opens his door, I swing mine, too. I wasn't expecting the pit stop, but it feels good to straighten my knees and arch my back.

There's a bite in the crisp air that indicates fall's imminent transformation into winter. I smell a medley of trees, including pine and oak and eucalyptus, and I hear the whispering of the woods in the distance ahead.

Yet a large part of me feels separate from the scene. As if this is all a dream, and the real me is back at the center, buried under the blissful blankness of medication.

I walk uphill and cut across a copse behind the station. When the thicket of trees thins, I get my first clear view of castillo Brálaga. Perched at the edge of a cliff and looming over the small village of Oscuro, the black stone castle monopolizes the horizon.

It looks straight out of a gothic storybook, the uneven landscape rising to meet its rocky walls. The highest point of la Sombra is its sole tower, and the asymmetry gives the construction an off-kilter feel. The whole thing looks like a strong gust of wind could send it tumbling down the cliff . . .

And even then, it would sprout bat wings and fly.

"Estela!"

The driver's voice calls out to me, but I ignore him. I consider not returning to the car and just walking into the fading sunlight, seeing how far my feet can take me, and assuming a new identity wherever I land.

But my face is a walking billboard. The world will never let me forget my past.

I study the Gothic construction a little longer, all thin columns and pointed arches. I've traveled the entire United States, and I've never seen anything like it.

After they started medicating me more heavily at the center, I stopped dreaming. Or if I had dreams, I didn't remember them the next morning. That changed with the photograph. After seeing it, I had a nightmare so vivid it felt more like a memory.

I was very young, five years old at most, standing in the purple room.

And I saw the same black smoke as on the subway.

When I awoke, my skin was slick with sweat and my heart raced. I thought I was dying. Only as I kept breathing, I realized it was the opposite.

I was *feeling*.

I wrote down the dream for the medical staff the next morning. They said my aunt's letter had likely surfaced a repressed memory, and the black smoke was a metaphor my childish mind conceived to cope with trauma I experienced at an early age. They even theorized that I must have seen it on the subway because that imagery is how my brain interprets danger.

They said I'd had a breakthrough.

It was then I decided to stop taking their medication. The numbness wasn't enough anymore. I wanted to hear my heart again.

Withdrawal symptoms like lack of appetite and fatigue are easier to handle; it's the amped-up volume of the world, of my thoughts, that's harder to hide.

A car's engine purrs closer, and the driver pops his head out the window. The sun's fiery final flames reflect against his sunglasses.

"¿Lista?" he asks.

I sigh.

To move into a cursed castle, turn the page.

CHAPTER 4

THE CAR COMES TO A stop in front of shut iron gates flanked by twin gargoyles, and the driver whispers something that's either a prayer or a curse. I can't tell.

He springs out of the car and pops the trunk. By the time I click my seat belt and climb out, he's already back inside the vehicle. I find my duffel on the ground.

He books it out of here like he's terrified just being on the castle's property, and I assume my aunt must have prepaid for the service. Is that why the driver kept his face concealed? Did he think he was protecting himself? Does he believe in the castle's curse?

I turn toward the gate, which is shut with a thick chain and heavy lock. I don't see a doorbell or a box to buzz in.

My stomach does a funny flip, and it dawns on me that in this instant I'm freer than I've ever been. I could turn and run and never look back.

Like my parents did.

I stare between the black railings, across a tangled and overgrown garden that reminds me of Miss Havisham's from *Great Expectations*. The foliage is dry and untended, and above it stands the castle, with doors as tall as trees and knockers the size of manatees.

Questions claw at my skin in the voice of old Estela. *Why did Mom keep this place a secret from me? What really happened in the room from the photograph? Who is my aunt and what does she want from me?*

If I leave now, I'll never know.

I pull the duffel strap across my chest and walk alongside the iron bars, stepping on unkempt wild grass. Why did my aunt bother bringing me here if she wasn't even going to let me past the gate?

I spy a handle that nearly blends into the fence and turn it, expecting it to be locked. The door hinges inward.

I cut across a cobblestone path that's been nearly swallowed by weeds, until I reach the giant arching double doors that look twenty feet high. Closer up, I trace the outline of a set of smaller, human-sized doors embedded in the larger pair.

The wooden doors are as jet-black as the stone used on the rest of the construction. Like they were chopped from a tree the color of midnight.

I stare at gargoyle knockers that look like goblins with fangs. Before I can reach up, the door cracks open on its own.

The castle exhales old air. And as I inhale its familiar breath, I'm overcome with bone-deep nostalgia.

The sensation is one no image could hope to capture or convey. It's the musk of something ancient and powerful and *alive*.

Not a shadow castle, but a shadow creature.

The past is more than just a feeling here. It's a *presence*.

The woman who steps out is tall, yet she's dwarfed by the doorframe. She has the same shape as Mom—a narrow hourglass—and similarly sharp features, including high cheekbones and a straight nose. But that's where their similarities end.

Mom was always in jeans, and her favorite tops had vivid colors and asymmetrical patterns. She also preferred to wear her hair loose and untamed, but my aunt keeps her curls corralled in a tight bun that tugs on her face.

Wearing a floor-length, long-sleeved black dress that hugs her figure, Beatríz looks exactly how I would envision the owner of this castle—*a few centuries ago*.

She gives me two kisses, one on each cheek.

"Bienvenida, Estela."

She must see something in my expression because she follows up her Spanish greeting with slightly accented English. "Welcome home at last."

Tension closes in my stomach like a fist. Something about the words feels like more than a greeting. As if this were not just my first home, but my final one.

She looks down at my solitary duffel and studies the area for more bags.

But on the road, you learn to let go of material possessions. They only slow you down.

She surveys the street beyond the iron fence, and I wonder if she's looking for the driver. After a moment, she gestures for me to follow her inside.

There's nothing warm about Beatríz's demeanor, and any hopes of Mom's sister being like her are dashed.

As I step into la Sombra's entrance hall, it takes my eyes a few seconds to adjust to the dimness. Illumination comes from what must be candles bracketed high up on the walls. I can't see if they're real or electric because they're encased in thick crystal that obscures their flames. All that's visible is a red light, waxing and waning in a slower way that makes me think of the vintage lava lamps at a cabin we once rented in Oregon.

"I asked how was your trip?"

Beatríz is staring at me expectantly, as if we've been having a conversation.

"Estela?" She tips her head, concern deepening her voice. She scrutinizes me with the same disappointed look as the doctors at the center. Like I'm a defective model.

"I see they were serious when they said you don't talk."

After another moment's examination of my face, she leads me to the next room, and I nearly gasp.

The red-tinged air brightens as we enter the most majestic space I've ever seen. The high arched ceiling has ribbed vaults that crisscross it like an exoskeleton, as if we're in the heart of the castle, enclosed within its rib cage.

Stained glass windows span the length of the back wall. The main illumination comes from a massive fireplace, and every kind of seating option fills the hall, from velvet armchairs to leather couches. Hanging above the mantel is an elaborate crest that's a deep bloodred color and features an inversely mirrored full moon and black castle.

The fireplace casts shadows across the crest. Its blaze is hidden behind a crystal dome barrier, just like the lights bracketed along the walls. The flames lap around the frame, distorted by the filter, like a sea of blood—

"That's our family escudo," says Beatríz, and I blink, breaking my trance.

"Shield," she amends, like she's just located the right word. "It has hung here since the castle's original construction, eight centuries ago."

The silhouette matches la Sombra's architecture, but I wonder what the significance of the full moon is.

As we pad down another crimson corridor, I'm overcome with the feeling that I'm retracing old steps. Like déjà vu, mixed with a hit of nostalgia. Yet nothing about this castle is familiar. It's hard to synthesize.

I nearly freeze at the sight of a pair of gargantuan gargoyles as we're met by a grand staircase that branches up in a *Y* shape. The gargoyles are on the ground and seem to be guarding the steps, their wings unfurling into swooping banisters that reach up to the next story.

I looked up Gothic architecture and read that gargoyles were used to ward off evil spirits, especially from holy places. They were placed on a construction's exterior to symbolize that demons were without and salvation was within. So seeing these monsters' faces *inside* the house isn't exactly reassuring.

Beatríz keeps us moving past the stairs, and we reach a dining hall with a wooden table that could seat twenty people. Only two places have been set at one end.

"Do you need to wash up? The bathroom is to your right."

I bring my duffel with me, and when I come back out, there's food on the table. I slide into the high-backed seat across from my aunt, in front of a bowl of red soup. Between us are three small plates of olives, cheese, and chorizo slices, alongside a platter of a dozen breaded balls and half a loaf of bread.

"Have you had gazpacho before?"

I nod in assent. My parents loved this Spanish tomato soup, so we had it often.

"It's cold," she says when she sees me blowing on it. I already know that, so I'm not sure why I blew. Must be nerves.

"These small plates are called tapas, and these are croquetas," she says, referring to the breaded balls. "Half are filled with jamón serrano, the other half with setas."

I know *jamón* is ham, but I've no clue what *setas* means. I finish the soup and eat a couple of croquetas to taste both varieties, determining that *setas* means mushrooms.

"I run the local clínica," says Beatríz, waiting until she's finished eating to speak. "It was endowed by our family, and it's more sophisticated than any other business for many kilometers."

She sounds like she's selling me her services, and I note that her job is a source of pride for her. "Your doctor sent me your prescriptions, so I will continue to administer your medication."

She doesn't mention anyone else living here, nor do I see a wedding band on her finger, any sign of service staff, or even a single framed photograph.

"If you're finished, follow me," she says, picking up my glass of water and leading us out.

I grab my bag and trail her back to the gargoyle staircase that branches up in a *Y* shape. This time, she starts climbing, and after a moment's hesitation, I follow.

The gargoyles' eyes seem to trail us. I count ten steps to the middle landing, then twelve more as we go up the right side of the *Y* and cut down another crimson corridor.

"This is the extent of the house that's habitable," she says, stopping at a closed door after twenty-three steps. "Most of the structure is in disrepair and off-limits, so there are rules for living here."

She stares at me grimly, and I flash to the photograph of the purple room. Beatríz looked younger than Mom then, but now she has aged past her older sister.

"Rule number one: You are not to explore the castle beyond where I show you," she says, holding up one finger. "And rule number two"—she raises a second finger—"you are not to invite anyone over. ¿Está claro?"

I nod in agreement because it's the path of least resistance.

"I have arranged for you to receive Spanish tutoring in the mornings. I wasn't sure if you would need it, but I think you do. Afternoons, you will report to the clínica and help me there, then we will come home together to eat. ¿Bueno?"

I want to shake my head in refusal, but it'll be easier to just disappear. So I nod again.

Yet in my mind, I'm already retracing the steps to the front door. I don't have a cell phone, but there will be public phones in town. I can take a cab to the airport and fly back to DC. I'm sure Lety will let me back into the center. I still have a couple of weeks before I turn eighteen. I can figure something else out—

"My room is two doors down," says my aunt, handing back my glass of water. When I reach for it, she holds out something small in her other palm.

I was informed my aunt would have my prescriptions and would continue to administer my doses because I'm not to be trusted with pill bottles after what I did at the center. But this doesn't look like any medication I've ever taken.

The pill is black and shriveled and makes me think of the seed of a sickly tree.

"This is the equivalent of what you're taking," she says, with a bite of impatience.

I don't reach for it.

"Is there a problem?" she probes.

I stare at the seedlike thing in her hand. There's no way that's medicinal. It looks more like poison. I look at her, and I'm not sure if I'm frowning or glaring. Is there a difference? Whatever the name of the expression, I've no doubt she's picking up on my refusal.

"Your doctors weren't sure you could handle this transition," she says, closing her fist. "If that's the case, we'll have to find a new arrangement."

I can't believe it's possible to dislike my mother's sister this much so soon. And yet it's barely been a couple of hours, and I already despise her.

Since I'm going to spit it out anyway, I open my palm to accept her pill. Yet part of me wants to call her bluff and dare her to contact the center. I doubt she would have gone through the trouble of bringing me here just to ship me right back.

I tip the black seed in my mouth and chase it with water. Seeming satisfied, my aunt says, "Buenas noches."

As soon as she shows me to my room, I slip inside and spit the pill into my hand. Then I stuff the seedlike thing into an inner pocket of my duffel for future investigation.

My new bedroom is the size of an apartment and comes complete with its own bathroom and an empty closet that could double as a second bedroom. My parents and I could have lived comfortably together in here.

It's hard to imagine Mom growing up in this castle. It's even harder to imagine that *I* might have grown up here, maybe even in this very room, if not for whatever happened that sent Mom and Dad packing. Their decision changed my nationality, my language, my upbringing . . . and they never even bothered to tell me.

I push those thoughts away and try to focus on something else.

The bathroom has a raven-claw tub and no shower. I twist the brass tap to fill it with hot water. A collection of shampoos, conditioners, body gels, moisturizers, and bath bombs line the porcelain, all of them unopened.

I haven't bathed unsupervised in months, haven't had any privacy at all. It feels surreal to be completely alone like this, to know I could do anything I want without anyone stopping me. I could hold my breath underwater until the last bubble pops.

I dunk my head and wait in muffled silence to be proven wrong.

As the seconds pass, the world gets too quiet. When the absence of sound becomes overwhelming, I wonder if that's what death is, just an earsplitting silence for all eternity. I break the surface, gasping for breath.

When I finish bathing, I towel off and change into black leggings and a hoodie.

Then I break Beatríz's first rule.

I wear socks but no shoes.

Padding across the icy hall, I stay close to furniture and other heavy items, where the floor is more settled and less likely to creak. Once I return to the landing of the Y-shaped stairs, I climb the twelve steps of the left branch.

The darkness feels deeper here, and my steps are muffled by giant mothballs. I use my key chain flashlight—an investigative necessity, according to Dad—to examine the hall's peeling paint and cobwebbed corners. A tingle creeps up the back of my neck that isn't a spiderweb.

I feel like I'm being watched.

I swing my light in a circle around me, but I don't catch the whites of anyone's eyes. Yet as I keep going, peeking into dilapidated bedrooms and bathrooms, the sensation of being followed only grows.

But I hear no footsteps.

Something brushes my cheek—

Sucking in a sharp breath, I spin and flash my light in every direction. The beam flickers, cutting in and out, before shutting off for good.

I toggle the switch, but the device is dead. I can see why the locals believe something is off about this castle.

I should head back to my room, but the bands of fear tightening around my chest excite me. The siren call of my heartbeat is too tempting to ignore.

A monstrous shadow grows sharper as I approach the end of the hall, and once my eyes adjust, I see another gargoyle carved of black stone. Like the ones from the staircase, its expression is grotesque and its eyes follow me closely. Once I manage to look past it, I notice a nondescript door.

I swing it open to a swirl of silver, and I enter a starlit space with a wall of stained glass windows. And I'm reminded of a different silver blaze.

In the early weeks after the subway, before medication drowned my dreams, I used to get the same vision, night after night. It wasn't the twenty-five dead bodies, or the black smoke, or even my parents. It was the blast of silver right before the train came back into focus.

That was how the dream would begin. Then the light would retreat into twin orbs—a pair of eyes.

He had dark hair, chiseled cheekbones, and a starry gaze. I must have made him up to watch over me at night.

I never remembered the details of our time together once I awoke, just the imprint of his face and the way shadows danced around him, reflecting back not a man's shape but a monster's. I thought of him as my nighttime guardian, a gargoyle with an angel's face protecting me from nightmares. I called him my shadow beast.

Yet the silver light in this room comes from the night sky, filtered through stained glass. The windows are cloudy with dust, but I can still make out their original designs: the eight phases of the moon.

This room has a hallowed feel to it, as if it was once a sacred chamber. Like a lunar temple for summoning gods. *Or demons.*

The walls look scratched, and as I approach for a closer inspection, I see that they're covered with words. Even before reading them, I know what they say.

The same line has been etched into the stone, over and over and over again, in different handwritings and to varying degrees of legibility: *No hay luz en Oscuro.*

There's no light in Oscuro.

The words are an incantation, and I'm thrust back in time to the purple room, as a memory overtakes my senses:

> *A black fire blazes through the room, singeing the wallpaper and producing clouds of smoke.*
>
> *A person is screaming, and I see Mom framed in the doorway, her arms outstretched, horror splayed on her face. She looks like she's desperate to reach something in the black flames—*
>
> Me.
>
> *Five-year-old me is being burned alive.*

CHAPTER 5

I RELIVE THE FIRE IN the purple room all night in my dreams.

I need to learn what *really* happened there, without this supernatural filter my mind has thrown over it. Something tells me it's got everything to do with why my parents left this country and never looked back.

In the bathroom, I wet my hair in the sink. It's grown long, hanging lower than my breasts. I find some leave-in conditioner among the bathroom products and comb it through my brown curls with my fingers. I also discover a drawer full of makeup; most of it seems unused and possibly expired. My thick eyelashes always make me look like I'm wearing mascara, just like Mom. She never wore makeup, so I don't, either.

I take my time getting dressed, not looking forward to another morose meal with Beatríz at that mockingly large table. I pull on jeans and a top, zip up my hoodie, and slip into the bulky black shoes I wear everywhere. Dad called them my combat boots.

Remembering that it's cold outside, I loop on a scarf.

Thankfully, Beatríz isn't in the dining hall, nor is the table set. I step through a door at the end of the space and find a spacious kitchen with clear windows that let in an abundance of light. The refrigerator is sleek and silver, its modernity at odds with everything else about this castle. A note has been pinned to it with a magnet, in my aunt's tidy scrawl.

Estela,

I left you pan con tomate in the refrigerator.

I will see you at the clínica at 15:00 hours. Follow the path to the village.

In the morning, visit Libroscuro for Spanish tutoring.

—Beatríz

On the countertop is a large key that must fit the front door, next to a basket with half a loaf of wheat bread. I find a serrated knife beside it.

I approach the blade tentatively, like it's some kind of test. Then I pick it up and bring it close to my face, waiting for someone to spring out and wrest it from my fingers.

I feel an eerie satisfaction imagining the doctors at the center's looks of terror if they saw me right now. Then I think of Nurse Leticia's disappointment, and I pull the knife away from my cheek.

I carefully slice two pieces of bread and place them in the toaster. Next, I open the fridge to find a glass jar with what looks like tomato jam, which I spoon onto the toasts once they pop. The relish smells so fresh that I'm almost hungry.

I tear off a sheet of paper towel and wrap the two slices face-to-face, like a tomato sandwich.

The castle feels different this morning. I thought it might intimidate me less in the daytime, but light casts new shadows, throwing into sharp relief the construction's size and age.

Beyond the dining hall, I spy a windowless crimson corridor that leads into the depths of la Sombra. I study the darkness, and it studies me back.

This castle has eyes.

Venturing through this place on my own, without anyone to hear me scream, feels like a new level of dangerous. So I dart in the other direction, to the front doors, as la Sombra's walls bear down on me like a physical weight. I only slow down once, to take in the grand hall with the ribbed roof and the Brálaga crest, which is even more spectacular in the daytime.

The morning has dawned grayish, and it's much colder outside than I expected. Even with my hoodie and scarf, I'm freezing. But going back inside to get a jacket feels too risky now that I've made it out, so I charge ahead with what little armor I have.

I amble down the overgrown garden to reach the gargoyle-flanked gate, then I follow the cobblestone path to town. From here, it's obvious how la Sombra got its name: the castle's shadow falls over all of Oscuro.

Halfway down the hill, uneven rows of homes spring up around me, all of them on a tilt. Balconies bump against each other, as do sloping ceilings, and there are cars parked on only one side of the street. Some windows are cracked open, and as I whiff roasted coffee beans and oven-baked bread, my stomach rumbles.

I unwrap the paper towel and leave one toast flat in my hand while I bring the other one to my mouth. I didn't know tomatoes could have an aroma, but I'm inhaling it now along with the olive oil—a sweet and grassy medley that compels me to take a crunchy bite. Warmth spreads through my body, and drool pools in the corners of my mouth as I tear into the toast again and again and again, feeling tomato juice drip down my chin.

Only crumbs of my breakfast remain by the time I've made it past the homes to Oscuro's downtown, and I survey what is basically a town square. There's a restaurant, market, convenience store, and secondhand clothing shop that offers tailoring and repairs, as well as a few smaller businesses.

The clínica is easily the most imposing structure, taking up nearly one whole side of the plaza. It looks like it was tacked on after the original construction. The second largest place is called Ayuntamiento de Oscuro. It looks somewhat abandoned, and I wonder if it's the local seat of government.

All four streets face a central fountain that's run dry, featuring an oxidized copper statue of someone holding a pitcher like they're pouring water. It makes me think of the zodiac sign Aquarius. The bluish-green figure looks androgynous, with long hair, large eyes, and a hooded cloak.

An old lady sits on a bench in the statue's shade, throwing seeds at pigeons. The rest of the plaza is deserted. I stroll along the smaller businesses to see what else is here—but I stop walking when I see a storefront with books behind the display glass.

My mood improves as I push open the front door of my favorite place and inhale the thick musk of aging paper.

At last, I breathe easier.

Growing up, the first thing I did whenever we landed somewhere new was visit the local bookshop. Sometimes I had to take a bus or two to get there, but once I arrived, it was always the same: a refuge for homesick bibliophiles.

I imagine libraries are even more special because you have to be part of a community to borrow books. Every time we settled somewhere new for longer than a few weeks, I would consider getting a library card. But just the thought of all those cards adding up in my wallet, an ever-growing collection of non-homes weighing me down over time, was too daunting. Instead, I told myself I'd get a membership the day my parents got us a home of our own.

That way I would know I belonged.

This bookstore is unlike any I've ever visited. The wood used in its crafting has a raw quality that seems prehistoric, like it was cut from trees that had been around since Earth's beginnings. The shelves are so tall they nearly graze the ceiling, blocking much of the light, and as I touch the gnarled wood, I get the sense this store is nearly as old as the castle.

I wind through narrow stacks that feel breathlessly tight, and I'm relieved when I arrive at a clearing with a couple of armchairs and a table. Surveying the pathways around me, I skim the signs to see where each aisle leads: FIC-CIÓN, REFERENCIA, JUVENIL—

"¿Busca algo en particular?"

I still at the guy's husky voice.

Turning around, I see bright amber eyes and a crooked smile. He looks to be about eighteen and wears jeans and a charcoal T-shirt, topped with a slim black blazer. I can only make out the first two words of a partially obscured phrase on his shirt: LA SOMBRA.

"It's you!"

He switches to English upon registering my face, and his eyes flare even brighter. "This is so great! I'm Felipe."

The familiarity in his voice makes me feel like I should know him. Or maybe it's a cultural thing. He moves in like he's going to touch me in greeting, and my stomach twists with discomfort.

I know it's customary to kiss here, but I can't help backing away.

Felipe freezes, and his face falls. "Eh, perdón. *I'm sorry,*" he says, stuffing his hands in his pockets. His arms push back the sides of his blazer, and I read the full phrase on his shirt:

LA SOMBRA DEL VIENTO. It's a famous book by a Spanish author, Carlos Ruíz Zafón. Mom loved that series.

I move deeper into the store, hoping to lose Felipe in the stacks, but I hear his faint footfalls following me. I quicken my pace, eager to run across another customer or bookseller, and I hit the back of the place. Casing my surroundings, I log a door, ladder, wall display—

I don't have to turn around to know Felipe is behind me.

As I strategize an exit, my gaze snags on a sign over the display on the wall. It reads: LEYENDAS LOCALES. An array of books are lined up face out, their covers all bearing images of the same castle.

"You live there."

His husky voice is low but loud. He's too close.

"With la doctora," he adds, now even closer. I'm not sure if he's asking or telling me.

I spin around and take a large side step around Felipe, switching our positions. It's a trick Dad taught me. Now Felipe is the one against the wall.

"It's okay," he says, dark hair falling over his eyes. "This is my family's store. You're here to see me."

I frown in confusion.

"Spanish tutoring? Your aunt said you would be coming."

Libroscuro. The name clicks into place from Beatríz's note. Once I saw books through the window, I was sucked indoors so fast that I missed the sign.

"Let's work in the office," he says, moving toward the ladder. I look up at an opening and glimpse a bright attic with natural light flooding through.

I lived in a remodeled attic with my parents in Durham, North Carolina, while Mom wrote a string of stories on Duke University's women's soccer team and their undefeated season. The space had a small triangular window, and I loved looking through it and watching the wind whisper to the golden treetops, scattering their coppery leaves across the air.

I stare as Felipe is swallowed by the light, and I think of Alice going down the rabbit hole. Except in the real world, girls don't follow strange boys into attics.

I reach for one of the books featured in the Leyendas Locales display. It's glossy and thin. In fact, all of these la Sombra books are brief. They're more accurately *booklets* with hard covers.

I flip through the pages. They feature mainly artistic photographs of the castle's exterior and the town of Oscuro. There's no more information in here than what's in the Wikipedia entry. After centuries of existence, this town has less public history than most new businesses. I feel the ghost of a tickle in my gut as I consider how many secrets that adds up to—

"Are you looking for the *real* history of la Sombra?"

For a moment I wonder if I'm speaking out loud. Then I look at Felipe, and I remember he's not just a strange boy. He's also a *bookseller*.

I nod in assent.

"We have better books, but they aren't for sale. They're my family's private collection. I can show you, but you'll have to come upstairs."

He climbs the ladder again, and the light overhead flickers, like clouds eclipsing the sun. I have the strangest sense of déjà vu, but I shrug it off. Felipe might be my first lead here.

I climb all fifteen rungs, and I see a desk, a couch, a wall of filing cabinets, a kitchenette, and bookshelves crammed with tomes that seem too old and in too much disrepair to sell. Overhead, a skylight illuminates every corner of the attic.

Felipe sinks onto one of two stools at a high table in the kitchen area. There's just a sink, microwave, and fridge. I slide onto the stool next to his and see that a book has already been placed on the table. I don't realize I'm reaching for it until the text is in my hands.

The cover is a faded black, void of text or images. I open it and finger the rough pages. There's no title. No author. No printing or copyright info.

"It's made of leather stretched over wooden binding," says Felipe, and I nod like that means something.

Even though the book seems weakened with age, it doesn't feel fragile. It has a sturdiness, like it was bound in a time when words had more heft.

"We can start our Spanish lessons here if you like," says Felipe, and I set the book back down on the table. "This is the first text of record published about castillo Brálaga. It dates back to the 1600s."

The first few pages are blank, marked only by the yellowing of time. Then the first line of ink appears:

La maldición del castillo

I tap the sentence, waiting for him to translate.

"*The curse of the castle*," he says. "*Maldición* means curse."

I flip the page, and Felipe says: "This is the author's introduction, but they never reveal their name. They write that this book is the result of years of research and interviews, made up of witness accounts, diary excerpts, news articles, and personal correspondence."

We spend hours poring through the opening pages.

Since the Spanish is so archaic, Felipe only stops to point out a word or a phrase now and then, but mostly he's just translating the content. I doubt the outdated language would be relevant today.

At long last, we make it to the first chapter. "*Chapter one,*" he translates. "*The earliest written record I could find appears in a journal approximated to be from the 1300s.* Are you hungry?"

I frown, confused by the author's writing. Then I look up from the page to see Felipe is asking me a question. I shake my head, but my stomach dissents loudly.

He chuckles and grabs a sandwich from the fridge that's already parted in half. He gives me one part and chomps on the other as he scans the next lines and inwardly translates them before speaking.

I stare at the baguette on a small plate in front of me; from what I can see, it has a filling of ham, tomato, and cheese. I inhale, and I'm hungry—but by my exhale, I'm nauseous. It's been like this on and off for so long.

"*The journal describes a black castle*"—Felipe translates, pointing to the page where it says *castillo negro*—"*at the crest of a cliff. There isn't much else until the 1500s,*" he reads, "*when the place became known for flinging its doors open for full moon parties*—fiestas de luna llena—*that would go on for days.*"

Felipe falls silent again as he wolfs down his half in three bites and reads ahead. "*Whatever happened at these parties remains a secret,*" he translates after swallowing, and when he glances at me, I glean a warning from his gaze. "*Anyone rumored to have attended a full moon party was never heard from again.*"

My eyes feel extra dry, and I force myself to blink a few times.

Felipe closes the book. "I think this was the wrong place to start. I have some workbooks—"

I slam my hand down on the book's cover, a little too hard. "Or not," he says, wincing as if I'd just hit him. "Be careful. This is an antique."

I pull back my hand, embarrassed.

He opens back to where we were, and he reads ahead to himself again. But seconds pass, and he doesn't translate out loud.

"After it happened," he says softly, no longer looking down at the book but straight into my eyes, "you were all over the news."

I don't need him to explain what *it* means; I almost appreciate having the worst day of my life compressed to those two letters.

He keeps looking at me, like he's waiting for something, and I'm worried he's going to pressure me into speaking. I nod for him to go on.

"Everyone started whispering about la doctora," he continues, to my relief. "That's when I put together who you were."

His mouth hitches up on one side in a crooked smirk. "And I knew you would come back. I just had to be patient. La Sombra is where you belong."

Like Beatríz, there's something *more* than welcoming about Felipe's greeting. It's almost as if they believe I'm never leaving.

To my own disappointment, I show up to the clínica on time.

"Did it go well with Felipe?" asks Beatríz when I step inside.

I nod in assent, surveying her workplace in all its modernity. Unlike the castle's and the bookstore's narrower and shadowy layouts, this place is open and spacious and bright.

"The clínica was endowed by our family," she says, leading me past the waiting room, which is all white walls and high ceilings. The medical center beyond consists of an office, an operating room, and a wall of patient beds separated by privacy curtains. "Going into medicine is a Brálaga tradition," she informs me. "There's been a doctor in every generation of our family. It runs in our blood."

I guess all traditions come to an end eventually.

I feel her stare, but I don't return it, pretending to be interested in the equipment by one of the patient beds.

"Over here," she says, leading me through a back door, "is our storage area." The temperature plummets as I enter a small space packed with machinery, medications behind locked glass doors, and a metal freezer.

"This is our legacy," she says, chest swelling with pride. "We're a small community here, with a population of 852 . . . 853 with you. The nearest hospital is hours away. Before there was health insurance, one of our ancestors came up with the idea for everyone in Oscuro to pay into a town health care fund. We use it to secure medicines and specialists when they're needed. We have a full operating room and our own private blood bank."

I cock my head, unsure I heard right. *Blood bank?*

"All residents donate a few times a year," she says, yanking open the handle to the freezer. A blast of icy mist hits us, and I peer inside to see rows upon rows of plastic bags filled with crimson liquid.

"As a matter of fact," says my aunt, shutting the freezer, "I'd like to do a full workup to begin your file."

They did workups at the center, so this isn't new to me. Still, Nurse Leticia told me they sent my file to my aunt, which means she must have my most recent report from three weeks ago. Why does she need to run more lab work?

Beatríz guides me back to the relative warmth of the main clinic area and sits me down in a chair near some glass vials. "Roll up your sleeve," she instructs as she pulls on plastic gloves.

She hasn't even hugged me, but she expects to take my blood. It rubs me wrong, and I don't move.

"What is it?" she asks, needle in her hand.

You already have my bloodwork, I want to say.

I wait for the words to make it up my throat to my lips, but they can't seem to scale my tongue.

"I have a patient coming soon," she says, making me feel like a small child. This is a pointless battle to pick, so I roll up my sleeve.

Beatríz grips my elbow, and my hand tenses into a fist at her touch. I barely feel the needle as she jabs it into my arm, as if she's done this millions of times.

"Good," she says as the vial fills up with dark crimson liquid. "Relax your arm, Tela—"

She clears her throat. "*Estela.*"

I feel the stab of pain I was expecting from the needle, only it's from hearing that nickname. As long as I can remember, my parents called me *Stela*. And yet something stirs within me on hearing *Tela,* and I know it was my name once.

Beatríz seals the glass with my blood but doesn't remove the needle from my arm. She reaches for another empty vial—

I yank my arm free.

"What are you doing?!" she shrieks as the needle slides out of my skin, along with some drops of blood.

I get up and back away, until I have a direct line to the front door. If she comes after me, I can beat her to the street.

"You need to calm down!" she says, staring at me through eyes rounded with outrage. "I'm going to store your blood, then you can get to work."

I cross my arms in response.

She takes the vial to the storage room, and when she comes back out, her face is emotionless. "You will be digitizing patient files at that computer."

I follow her gaze to a desk in the middle of the office. The computer is an older model than the sleek-monitored Macs we had at the center, but it still seems more modern than the rest of this town.

She walks to a cabinet and yanks open the first drawer. It's stuffed with colorful folders. "Begin with Ángel, Alberto Castaño Cruz." She pulls out a thick blue file and sits down at the terminal. "The program is already open," she says, and the black monitor brightens with colors. "Click here to start a new patient file, then fill in the fields using the information in the forms."

She types in the first few sections, until I get the hang of it, and then I take her place. I work until early evening, when Beatríz comes out of her office and says, "Time to go." She sets a security alarm using a special key that she taps against a sensor before locking up the clínica, and we walk back to the castle in silence.

Dinner tonight is gambas al ajillo. The aromatic garlic shrimp is served in a ceramic orange bowl. The scent makes my mouth water, and I realize I haven't eaten since the pan con tomate this morning.

I used to love food.

When my parents were alive, I would ask for seconds and thirds, sometimes even fourths. Yet I only eat six shrimp, and my stomach feels bloated. I may still be breathing, but most of me died on that subway—including my appetite.

When Beatríz finishes eating, she stands up, and I rise, too.

"This silence of yours concerns me," she says, holding out the black pill. She watches me chase it with a drink of water.

Then I turn on my heel and head to my room, where I spit out the seed, and it joins its twin from yesterday in my bag's pocket.

Tonight I set off in a new direction.

Wearing socks but no shoes again, I climb down the grand staircase to the main level, then I pad past the dining hall and into the crimson corridor I was too afraid to enter this morning.

The wiring seems weaker here, the candle-like lights producing a duller reddish flame. Why are they on at all? Doesn't Beatríz turn off the lights at night?

The passage bifurcates. I stare at the Y-shaped choice before me, and I choose left.

The corridor is long and narrow, lacking in rooms or décor, and the ground feels like it's tilting up as the hallway spills into a spectacular silver chamber. Moonlight pours in through parallel walls featuring identical rows of stained glass windows, and a sprawling chandelier hangs over a floor that sparkles like it's made of stars.

I can't look down from the chandelier. It hangs at an unnerving angle, its crystal arms reaching for the room's walls like a giant glittering octopus. The whole thing seems dangerously close to plummeting, so I edge toward the windowed wall to avoid getting speared with a tentacle—and I see another girl.

My heart stalls.

She stiffens, too, spotting me at the same time.

My reflection and I spin around slowly in perfect sync, and I realize only *one* wall is windowed—the other one is mirrored. The looking glass runs the length of the chamber, cracked in places and blackened in others. Some corners have even chipped off.

Something flickers in my peripheral vision, and I look up in time to see a crystal teardrop fall from the chandelier. It shatters on the floor, exploding in a starburst of sparkles. I crouch down and look closer at the ground.

The base of the floor is polished stone, but it's been dusted with debris from fallen crystals—and I'm not wearing shoes.

I just have to avoid the pointy pieces.

Moonlight rebounds on the mirror, giving the room enough illumination that I think I can make it across without hurting myself. There's a door at the other end of the chamber, and I want to know where it leads.

I keep my gaze low as I take my first step across the glittering minefield. I stand on tiptoes as much as possible as I weave around sharp shards, but I have to slow down when I get to the middle of the room, where the debris is denser.

The moon's silver light dims, and I wait for the clouds to clear. Yet the air keeps darkening, as if someone is putting out the stars.

I look up as a shadow stretches across the wall of windows.

Blackness spreads through the room like smoke, and air whispers past my ear, heavy with more than just oxygen. It's a *voice*.

"No hay luz en Oscuro."

I'm not sure I actually heard it. I spin around to go back the way I came, but I'm clumsier now, and I feel tiny stabs through my socks every time I step on something sharp.

My dusty reflection chases me in the mirror—as does a second, taller and broader silhouette.

I look behind me, but no one's there.

Yet in the mirror, the large, person-shaped shadow is closing the distance between us.

BOOM.

My pulse swings its hammer, shaking my whole frame. I'm not sure which is more shocking—its presence or the shadow's.

I haven't felt my heart in months, and I was worried it'd stopped beating. Only now it's hammering at its cage, proving me wrong.

BOOM. BOOM. BOOM.

I move faster, and my foot stumbles on the jagged edge of a broken crystal. "*Ah!*" I cry out in pain, the first sound I've heard myself make in months. It sounds more beastly than human.

I stand in flamingo pose to make sure nothing's stuck on the sole of my foot. The cut is shallow, so I can still move.

In the mirror, the shadow is gone. Moonlight breaks through the darkness again, and I study the floor as I weave through the glass rubble toward the exit. I don't dare look back until I'm past the chandelier, and then my jaw drops—

BOOM.

A man of flesh and bone stands in the middle of the room, looking down at something in his hand: the bloodied shard of crystal I stumbled over.

When he lifts his face to meet my stare, the room is blasted with silver starlight.

BOOM.

The face from my dreams.

BOOM.

It's my *shadow beast.*

CHAPTER 6

I SIT UP IN BED after running harder than I ever thought I could.

I hug my knees to my chest, trying to catch my breath and hold on to it. But with every blink, I see those moonlit eyes.

Watching me.

My gaze snaps to the door. Whatever that was, he didn't look human. But is he just in my head?

He will find me again.

The thought comes with the certainty of death. Real or imaginary, that shadow beast didn't look like something I could outrun.

I've already locked the door, but I keep eyeing it. I doubt a wall of wood will be enough to keep such a creature out. I need to reach Nurse Leticia. Maybe I can send her an email from the computer at the clínica. Clearly, I wasn't ready to leave the center.

Unless there's a reason I'm here, says the small voice in my mind that compulsively argues with me. It makes me feel like I'm always playing devil's advocate with myself. Dad called it my instinct to challenge everything. He said it would keep me honest and make me a good investigator.

Raul's Rule #2: A detective's best compass is in their gut.

The phrase flies back to me, as if Dad were whispering it in my ear. I go to my duffel and dig to the bottom, until I pull out a picture frame.

Behind the glass isn't a photograph but a handwritten list titled *Raul's Rules*. They're a dozen things my dad used to say on repeat when he was on a case.

Some of these he said so often, Mom and I would finish the sentence for him. That's why for his thirty-fifth birthday, I picked out a sheet of pretty blue construction paper and wrote out twelve of his most popular sayings.

Whenever we landed somewhere new, he would prop that frame on a surface to designate his work area. He said he liked to keep the list close while working a case. The sight always made me proud, like I was contributing to his investigation in some small way.

I set the rules on the gold-trimmed desk by the window, and my gaze jumps up to the first one: *Don't think; FEEL.*

Whenever he opened a case, Dad's first instinct was to empathize with everyone involved—even the culprit. He insisted the best investigators were humans first, detectives second. *Killers are people, too,* he would say, semi-seriously.

But since my parents' deaths, I haven't wanted to feel. In fact, *feeling* is the last thing I want to do.

I keep going down the list, in hopes Dad has left me a clue what to do next.

Raul's Rule #3: Keep an open mind.

Does that mean I should consider the black fire, the smoke, and the shadow beast could be real? I almost laugh, except there's nothing funny about my life right now. I have no idea how to distinguish what's fiction from what's fact.

I need a librarian for my thoughts.

I read the next line:

Raul's Rule #4: Keep a written record.

That's how Dad would get started—by taking notes. He used to fill up every corner of his notepads with his scribbles. When I asked him why he wrote everything down, he said, *You have a better chance of solving a puzzle if you're holding all the pieces.*

That could have been an honorary thirteenth rule.

Beatríz left me a notepad and pen on the desk, presumably for my Spanish lessons. I sit down in the hard-backed chair and skip about a quarter into the blank booklet, burying the entry so the ink will be hidden deep within the pad.

I press the pen's point to paper, jotting today's date in the corner. Then I fill out my timeline of unexplained occurrences:

- *12 years ago—survived a black fire in a purple room*

- *7 months ago—survived black smoke and a blaze of silver on the subway; later, dreamed of a shadow beast with silver eyes*

- *Tonight—chased by the shadow beast from my dreams*

"I found us a more modern book to read," says Felipe as soon as I step inside the store, and I follow him to the attic.

"This traces the history of Oscuro," he says once we're seated in the same spot as yesterday.

"By the 1700s, la Sombra's parties were over. This is when they began keeping better records." There are colorful page markers sticking out from the text; it's clear Felipe reviewed and annotated the book ahead of time. He's either a very thorough tutor or exceptionally passionate about the subject.

He opens to the first marker and reads: "*De a poco, se fue formando un pueblo a la sombra del castillo.*" I recognize the words *sombra* and *castillo* by now, but not the rest.

"*Slowly, a town began to form in the shadow of the castle,*" he translates. "*Formar* means form, so *formando* means something that is in the process of forming."

Felipe is in full-on tutor mode. As he leafs through the book, he stops after every sentence to define the main vocabulary and review verb conjugations. After years of begging my parents to teach me Spanish, I should be grateful for the language lesson—but right now I'm more eager for information.

I need to know if there's *any* chance the smoke, the black fire, and the shadow beast could be real.

"These are all the real estate records from that time, tracing the town's growth." Felipe has flipped to his next place marker, and I stare down at a ledger of properties.

My gaze snags on *castillo Brálaga*.

In 1712, it belonged to a man named Juan Carlos Fernando Brálaga. In 1733, it was passed on to Rogelio Antonio Brálaga. In 1750, Mauricio Homero Brálaga. I skim along the names of ownership—and a chill races down my spine.

The ominous feeling I got when Beatríz and Felipe welcomed me here makes more sense now. According to historical records, my bloodline binds me to la Sombra. Is this the fate Mom was running from? Is this why Beatríz brought me here now?

Am I the castle's new heir?

Yet it's not just the surname Brálaga that unsettles me; it's the *dates* of inheritance.

Our life spans seem strikingly short.

Felipe's finger draws my focus as he taps on another property: *Calle Nube 32.* Beside it is the date 1705 and the owner's name—*Luis García Sarmiento.* The next entry is a proper five decades later: *1758, Ángelo Cruz Sarmiento.*

1812, Sancho Aurelio Sarmiento.

1860, Romano Héctor Felipe Sarmiento.

This is Felipe's family, I realize. Their life spans are longer, but the surnames are the same. I skim the other properties' ledgers—all of them have been handed down through generations of the same family. This whole town is a relic of the past, perfectly preserved, down to the bloodlines.

"Something else," says Felipe, and while I'm still processing the second page marker, he flips to the third. Before I can see what's there, he covers the page with his hand.

"Have you noticed what Oscuro is missing?" he asks me.

I used to play this game with Dad. He said it was harder to see what's *not* there, so sometimes when we would revisit a place, he'd ask me to identify things that were different from last time.

So what is Oscuro missing? A lot of things. A movie theater, for one. Mom and I used to love going in the middle of the day, while the rest of the world was working or studying. A library, an art gallery, a school—but that's all typical of small towns. Residents visit the nearest bigger town or small city.

What should be here that isn't? I'm usually good at this, but my mind is still jittery from last night, like I'm hopped up on caffeine, and I can't focus on this game. I shrug in hopes Felipe will illuminate me.

He moves his hand away, and at the sight of a cross in a heap of rubble, the answer is obvious.

There's no church.

"I don't know how it is in the United States," he says, "but in Spain, there's a church at the center of every town, especially one with a castle. It was the first thing people built when they settled somewhere."

I didn't grow up with religion, but I remember the small towns we visited in the U.S. having this in common—a place of worship.

"Each of these stickers marks every attempt to build a church in Oscuro." Felipe thumbs through the pages, no longer translating the Spanish to English, but summarizing. "Every construction attempt ended in tragedy."

I'm not sure what frightens me more—Felipe's words or their delivery. The way his amber eyes shine reminds me of how some of the residents at the Rainbow Center would look when they were having an episode.

"La Sombra is by default our most sacred symbol," he says. "It's our holy place."

I narrow my eyes, not loving his choice of words.

"I wasn't sure before," he says, almost whispering, "but after what happened to you, I believe."

I want to leave and not hear his next words, but I'm caught in the beam of his stare.

"I think you're here because *the castle wanted you back.*"

I leave my bedroom as soon as I think Beatríz is asleep.

Felipe's lesson today messed me up. At the clínica, I could barely manage the mindless task of digitizing patient files because I'd seen the last name Ángel in the property ledger. It's hard to fathom that everyone here belongs to a founding family.

Dad's last name—Amador—isn't in the clínica's files, which means he's an outsider. Does that have anything to do with why we moved away?

I approach the Y-shaped passage. Last night, I found the mirror room in the left wing, and as much as I want to know what lies beyond it, I'd rather not slice my feet open. So I take a right turn instead.

I feel my calves tighten as I walk, the passage descending. The air grows mustier and earthier as the crimson corridor spills into a dusty salon void of furniture or adornment. Yet the scratches and punctures on the walls show the space wasn't always this empty.

I keep counting steps as I cut across another room that's been equally hollowed out, and another and another. The barren spaces are echo chambers, doorless and windowless and featuring entryways with pointed arches.

The chilly floor grows thick and warm beneath my feet as I step on an old, prickly rug. The fabric scratches at my socks, even more uncomfortable than the cold stone floor. The crimson rug ends at a wooden door with metal hinges.

When I turn the handle, I see what I can best describe as a windowless cathedral.

The space looks infinite. Rows upon rows of stone pillars blossom into ribbed vaulting. The candle-like fixtures are bracketed high up, leaving the ground in shadow. And as I walk across the floor, the reddish light above me goes out.

I take another step, and the next one shuts off, so I stop walking altogether. All the lights burn out at once.

I hear my intake of breath as blackness blots the air, and while I wait for my vision to adjust, I feel the shadow beast before I see him—a sign he's my own creation.

The small hairs on my skin ripple with his presence, and I break into a run. I keep my arms outstretched in front of me so I don't crash into a column, determined to make it past this room.

My hands flatten against cold stone, and the impact jolts through me. I feel my way along, but it's a wall. This is a dead end.

A flash of silver blasts across the room, blinding me for several seconds. When the brightness dims to a couple of small orbs, I see his shadowy form taking shape.

A gargoyle come to life.

The reddish lights flicker back on, illuminating him. He could be a teen or in his early twenties; and yet, the starry galaxies of his eyes contain universes.

They glimmer and fade like they're powered by their own light source.

He's in a crisp suit that both emphasizes his muscular frame and obscures it, the fabric so inky black that it casts shadows around him. He's either the world's wealthiest man or the Devil himself.

Somehow, my face seems to hold his interest as well because he's studying me back just as intensely. As if he recognizes me, too.

And even though I *know* he can't be real, my heart catapults to my throat.

BOOM.

The silver eyes narrow.

BOOM.

The razor-sharp jawline tilts to a 45-degree angle.

BOOM.

His gaze drops to my chest. Like he can hear my heartbeats.

"Me estás viendo."

Exquisite. I've never used the word before, yet it flies into my mind now, as I hear him speak. As if the flawless face, powerful frame, and expensive clothes weren't enough, his voice is as deep as the earth and as soothing as the ocean's surf.

He's too large to exist. Undoubtedly, he's my greatest creation.

I just wish I knew what he was saying.

"You can see me." This time he speaks English; I guess my wish is his command.

It's not a question, but I nod anyway. The shadow beast's eyebrows quirk up. "You can hear me, too?"

I nod again. Something hardens in his expression, and too late I realize I've answered wrong.

"It was *you*."

An edge sharpens the smoothness of his voice. "I do not know your plan, and I do not care. You have one breath left to end this spell—or I will end you."

I stare at him, my jaw hinging open.

They warned me at the center that the black smoke could progress to other visions, so I'd need to be vigilant. I focus on the calming mantras they taught me: *Don't engage in my mind's games. Concentrate on what I know to be real. The shadow beast is an illusion, and illusions can't touch me—*

"One," he counts off.

I have no idea how to fight—much less defeat—my own mind. I can't move or think, but my heart is raging.

BOOM. BOOM. BOOM.

Calm down, Estela! I inwardly shout at myself. *He's not real, he can't touch me.* I have to slow my pulse, breathe, focus—

The air siphons from my lungs as a steel vise wraps around my neck, caving in my throat. Pain explodes through me as spots darken my view, and I know I won't inhale again, not ever.

With the last gasp of air in my mouth, I blow out my final breath, and I hear a raw, raspy voice I almost recognize whisper-shout:

"WAIT!"

CHAPTER 7

MY THROAT TICKLES. MY TONGUE tingles. Tears wet my lashes.

I spoke.

I'm so shocked that it takes me a moment to process my *other* shock—*I'm still alive.* His hands are no longer around my neck, and there's a few feet of space between us.

He *listened* to me.

"End the spell," says the shadow beast, his beautiful voice at odds with the death it promises.

How is it possible I could feel his touch if he's only in my head? Or have my hallucinations gained so much power they can hoodwink my other senses? He takes a threatening step forward that cuts the distance between us by half.

"What spell?"

My voice comes out creaky and a notch higher than I remember. And despite the doom facing me, my blood floods with relief that I'm still alive.

No, it's more than that. Something I didn't know until this moment—

I *want* to live.

"No more games." The monster's warning comes shrouded in shadow as clouds fill the silver of his eyes. "I know what you are, bruja. Release me or die."

Bruja—I know that word. It means witch.

"I-I'm not." I clear my throat of its cobwebs. "I'm just a girl—"

His shadows expand like smoke, darkening the air. *"Liar."*

His whisper is everywhere, voice blowing through my hair, ears, fingers. I sprint along the wall to the other end of the room—

But he's already there.

His shadows enclose us in a smoky night, his silver eyes our only source of light. "Please," I beg, my heart reverberating in my throat, slowing my speech. "I have no idea . . . what you're saying—"

"Your face has been haunting me. I started to believe I was going mad."

Only in my imagination would this guy be obsessed with me.

"The explanation," he goes on, "must be that you are the bruja responsible for bringing me here."

I have no idea what he means, but given the pain he can cause me, I'd rather play along than piss him off. "I was on the news," I say, my throat smarting with the effort of speaking. "The . . . subway."

A flash of electricity claps in his eyes.

"That is the spell of which I speak," he says, to my bewilderment.

I'm not sure how long I stare at him, immobilized by his words, until the small voice in my mind reminds me: *He's in your head.*

This is some desperate part of my brain reaching for any kind of explanation for what happened to my parents. Only this is *really* a reach. The kind of reach that probably wouldn't be taking place if I had stayed at the center.

It's clear I wasn't ready to leave.

I breathe in the scent of a frigid night, and I'm back in a wooden cabin on an icy mountain in Montana where my parents and I once spent the winter. The snow was so thick that there were no sweet plant notes in the air, nor the earthy scent of the ground, nor the musk of small animals. I remember thinking whatever smell remained must be the scent of the stars.

That's what I inhale now as the shadow beast leans in, and I have to tilt my neck all the way back to keep from breaking his stare.

"I . . . I need time to figure this out," I say, in hopes of putting an end to this encounter. "But kill me, and . . . and the spell becomes unbreakable."

He stares into my eyes, like he's trying to see through my lies. "You have until next nightfall."

His voice is the quiet rumble of the first thunder from an approaching storm.

"Free me or die."

I don't stop running until I reach my room, then I go into my bathroom and yank open the drawer that I filled to the brim with period pads and tampons.

I shove my hand in to pull out the notepad I hid last night, and I bring it to the desk.

I flip to my list of strange occurrences. On the next page, I jot today's date and start a new list, titled: *Shadow beast.*

Then I bullet-point what I know so far:

- *Dreamed him up months ago*

- *Has silver eyes*

- *Seems to command shadows*

- *Says he came to the castle the day of the subway*

- *Claims to be under a spell*

- *Caused me physical pain*

- *Thinks I'm the witch responsible*

Of all the far-fetched things on the list, the most unbelievable to me is the last. *He* doesn't trust *me*. It's almost flattering.

I wake up to golden sunlight, with the notepad open on my chest. The shadow beast's face swims before me as the details of my dreams slip between my fingers, like water.

All I remember is he was in every single one of them, hunting me through the castle, like some twisted game of hide-and-seek. Only every time he found me, the nightmare reset, and a new chase set off.

I still feel the ghost of my pulse as I sit up, and my notepad topples to my lap. I look down at the last thing I wrote last night:

"You don't know what it is to doubt everything, even yourself."

The line is from *Dracula*. I read the novel at the center, and those words found a home in me. I guess I still haven't been able to shake them.

I have to go back on my old meds.

I squeeze my fists as I make the promise, and my nails leave deep crescents in my palms. But I'm *not* taking Beatríz's black seed. I want my usual pills, or I'll reach out to Nurse Leticia and tell her my aunt is not complying with the center's regimen. I hide the journal in my period drawer again before changing and heading out.

"¡Buen día!" says Felipe as soon as I walk into the bookstore.

It's impossible to miss the way he lights up when he sees me. No guy has ever been this openly delighted by my presence, and I feel my mood thawing a little.

"I made you something," he says as I follow him up to the attic. He swipes a small rectangular thing off the desk and hands it to me.

It's a business card that reads LIBRERÍA LIBROSCURO with the store's contact information. Only LIBRERÍA is crossed off and BIBLIOTECA has been typed over it with a typewriter. I look at him in confusion.

"Turn it over," he instructs.

On the other side, I see that my name has been typed in as well, including my mother's maiden name: ESTELA AMADOR BRÁLAGA.

"It's your library card." His mouth hitches up on one side as he flashes me his crooked smirk. "This means you can come over and read any book you want at any time, no charge."

I stare at the card in awe, more moved by the gesture than Felipe can understand. My lips part, and I hear myself say, "Thank you."

His eyes widen with surprise, and my face muscles slacken with relief. Last night, only the shadow beast heard me use my voice, so I couldn't be sure I really spoke until now.

Felipe doesn't say anything for a stretch, which is a first for him so far. "You—you're welcome."

"So, *librería* means bookstore, and *biblioteca* is library?" I ask.

"Así es," he says, beaming.

"It sounds flipped," I say, thinking of the English words. "Like *librería* should be library and *biblioteca* bookstore."

"I'll take that as a sign my lessons are working."

I feel the edges of my mouth pull up. It's been so long since I smiled that the facial movements feel foreign.

"Hoyuelo," whispers Felipe. I don't know what that means, but I notice he's looking at my right cheek. Where Mom's dimple showed up when I smiled.

Today we read from a black book that looks slightly less old than the previous ones. For starters, the cover has images on it—or maybe *etchings* is a better word. A moon, stars, a cross, and a set of jaws with sharp fangs.

"This book is an anthology," Felipe informs me as we sit down at our usual stools. "It's considered fiction now, but these were originally published as true stories."

I open to a table of contents. There are thirteen chapters. "*The Tragedies of the Brálagas of la Sombra*," he translates.

We spend hours reading together. All thirteen families featured in the anthology suffered unnatural deaths—exorcisms gone wrong, deadly blood spells, hauntings, murder-suicides, dealings with devils ("demonios"), attacks by werewolves ("lobizones"), faeries ("hadas"), and other monsters.

The thirteenth tale is Felipe's favorite because it's about a magical Book, with a capital *B*. It was delivered to la Sombra by an enemy of the castle's founder, the original Brálaga, who instructed the family to keep it safe by hiding it outside the walls of the castle—but before anyone had a chance to open its pages, Brálaga's spirit manifested and murdered them all.

Then Brálaga destroyed the Book.

Felipe sets down a platter of bocadillos on the table, and I rip into one of the tiny jamón serrano sandwiches. "Scared yet?" he asks, sitting so close to me that our knees brush.

"Of what?" I ask, folding my legs under me. "None of this is true."

Felipe flinches, like I personally offended him. I wait for him to say something or go get us a new book, but he just traces a drawing with his finger. It's of a man holding the Book from the thirteenth tale, which bears the Brálaga crest on its cover.

"What's wrong?" I ask.

"Nothing," he says with a shrug.

"Are you upset the Book was destroyed before you could read it?" I ask to lighten the air.

"I just didn't expect you to be so suspicious after what you lived through," he says, sounding almost angry.

My gut hardens, and my guard shoots up. "I think you mean *skeptical,* and yes, I am. Sorry if that disappoints you."

"I think you mean it *confuses* me."

"Why?"

"You saw black smoke, and even though there was no evidence, you wanted the world to believe you. What makes your ancestors less trustworthy?"

I open my mouth, but nothing comes out.

It's not just that he makes a valid point—it's also that he *went there.* He poked my rawest wound. I don't think Felipe would have done that if this book weren't so important to him. But he's not a Brálaga, so why does he care so much?

"What do *you* think is the truth?" I ask, trying to ignore the sting from his question. "Do you believe all these supernatural encounters really happened?"

"I don't have answers yet, just ideas," he says, not meeting my eyes. "But I'm not sure you're ready to hear them."

"Tell me," I say, burning a hole in his head with my gaze, until at last he looks at me.

"Before he died," he begins, "my great-grandfather told me something. He didn't have any *evidence*"—Felipe's eyes light up with excitement—"but he never lied to me."

So far, Felipe has shared his knowledge with me freely. Yet *this* secret, he protects. Whatever his great-grandfather told him, there's no doubt Felipe believes it.

"What is it?" I ask.

His throat is so dry I can hear him swallow. "He told me some Brálagas are—*special*." Felipe says it like he's not sure it's the right word. "On the full moon, they can perform magic."

I look at the drawing of the castle's crest on the Book's cover, and he must be having an effect on me because the first thought to cross my mind is, *Maybe that's what the moon represents*.

Either my ancestors and I share a supernatural sensibility, or we suffer from an inherited mental illness. "Do you have a lunar calendar?" I ask, the detective's compass in my gut spinning erratically.

Felipe strides to the desk and riffles through the papers until he finds something. "This calendar uses small black circles for the full moons," he says, bringing it to me.

I flip back seven months . . .

And I see the black dot.

The Subway 25 happened on a full moon.

RAUL'S RULE #5

THERE ARE NO COINCIDENCES, ONLY CLUES.

CHAPTER 8

ON OUR WAY HOME, BEATRÍZ and I stop by the local restaurant to pick up what she says is her standing monthly order of paella.

Tonight, I'm determined to ask my aunt about the purple room. Now that I've found my voice, I intend to question her about everything I want to know.

"I hope tutoring with Felipe is going well," she says from across the table when we're almost finished eating. The seafood-based rice dish is good, but very rich and filling, so I only eat half of what's on my plate.

"Felipe is a good boy, but . . ." She takes a long swig of her wine. "He has a big imagination."

I'm not sure why she's volunteering this information, and I'm intrigued by her use of the word *but*—as if having an imagination is a drawback. I must be frowning because Beatríz answers my unasked question:

"Felipe has had his head in fiction ever since he learned how to read. For one with such an overactive imagination, too much fantasy can be a dangerous drug. I doubt there's any saving him now."

Her gaze grows distant, and I wonder why she's saying this, or what she means by *saving,* or who she's really thinking about. But I have a more pressing question.

I dig my hand into the pocket of my hoodie, and I pull out the photograph she sent me, where teenage versions of her and Mom are posing in the purple room. I set it flat on the table between us.

Beatríz's face puckers, like she's ingested something sour.

I clear my throat and move my tongue to speak five words: *"What happened in that room?"*

I only know I haven't asked the question out loud when Beatríz says, "Your mom was younger than you are now in that picture. Keep it. It's yours."

She pulls my plate toward her, ready to clear the table and end any chance of this conversation happening. I keep trying to force the words out, but my vocal cords won't cooperate. My throat closes, and my jaw stays firmly shut.

Rather than panicking, I flip the photograph over.

Dad said for every interrogation, you should always have a plan B. So on the back, I've written a different four-word question: *Where is this room?*

I keep my eyes on my aunt. I don't even blink so I won't miss any part of her reaction. Her hair is pulled back into such a tight knot that it tugs on her skin, making it hard to read the lines of her face. But the answer is in her eyes.

Raul's Rule #6: The big answers lie in the small details.

Beatríz's eyes widen for a flash, like she fears the secret's revelation, and I know it's true. Something horrible happened in that room.

"As I said to you already, the castle is in disrepair." Beatríz stands up, her chair scraping the floor. "Many parts are no longer accessible."

I spring to my feet, too, unwilling to let her off so easily, but my tongue is glued to the top of my mouth. My aunt takes our plates and silverware and her empty wineglass to the kitchen, leaving me struggling with my speech.

I grab my glass of water and the photograph, and I stomp after her, determined to get answers. When I get to the kitchen, she turns away from the sink to look at me and reaches out a hand.

For one dumbfounded moment, I think she's offering me affection. Until I step forward and see the seedlike black pill in her palm.

I don't take it.

I show her the photo again.

"If you're going to act out like this, I'm sure I can find an in-patient facility that will take you."

That's not concern in her voice. It's a threat.

Since I'm going to spit it out in my room anyway, I take the pill and tuck it under my tongue like I've done the past two nights. Then I swallow some water to top off my performance.

My aunt's bony fingers wring my wrist. She pulls me in so abruptly that I swallow again, hard—and the pill goes down my throat.

She lets me go just as quickly and starts washing the dishes, as if nothing happened.

I press a hand to my chest as the thing makes its way down, and I run up the stairs, a single thought repeating itself, standing out from the jumble of my mind: *My aunt just forcibly drugged me.*

No wonder Mom left this place. Her sister is a monster.

I hurry so I can throw up whatever she just gave me, slamming shut the door to my room—

The shadow beast steps forth from the darkness, like he exists just for me.

Startled, I back up to the wall. My breathing shallows with every step he takes, his presence as intoxicating as it was in my dreams.

"I believe I gave you a choice," he says, his voice as cold and murderous as it was last night. Everything about the shadow beast is blade-sharp, from his cheekbones to his jawline to his gaze.

"End the spell or die. What is your answer?"

After dinner with Beatríz, I'm not sure my voice works. "I—" My throat is rough, and I try to clear it. "I'm not a witch. I'm just a girl."

"Then your life is forfeit."

I'm not going to get any answers by making enemies with my own mind. If this hallucination represents a repressed part of my self, I'll get further as a friend than a foe.

"But I—I think I can help you," I say, my voice trembling as he moves closer. "I have a source who knows a lot about this castle's supernatural history. Tomorrow I can ask him about spells."

The silver eyes are so near, they're all I can see. "Arrogant of you," he murmurs, "to assume you have a tomorrow."

BOOM. BOOM. BOOM. My heart is racing again, and I can't deny there's something inviting about its song.

"W-we should be working together," I say, nerves fraying my voice as his shadows eclipse all the light.

"If something happened to us, to *both* of us, at the same time—that must mean we're connected." I have no idea what I'm saying; my only plan is to keep him talking. "At least tell me your name?"

"What for?" he whispers, his mouth by my hairline.

"So I'll know what to call you. Or at least I'll know who killed me."

I wince as my mind twinges with a spasm of discomfort. Is he going to end my life with a brain aneurism?

"You know well," he says, pulling back to look me in the eye, "my name is Bastian, bruja."

"*I don't know you, and I'm not a witch,*" I insist without breaking his gaze, emphasizing each word. I don't remember ever naming the shadow beast, so I'm not sure where *Bastian* came from. "Is that short for Sebastian?"

"You tell me," he says, still scrutinizing me as hard as I did Beatríz at dinner. "You must know who I am if you brought me here."

Is he admitting he knows I'm manifesting him? "I don't know you, so I'm not going to call you that," I say, refusing to cede more ground to this frustrating figment. "I'm going to call you *Sebastián.*"

I meant to say Sebastian, but for some reason I pronounce it with a Spanish accent. The shadow beast doesn't answer, and my mind twinges again, like someone is wringing my brain's folds dry.

"Stop that!" I say, rubbing my temples. "If you kill me, we're both dead. Your only chance is to work *with* me."

A faint heartbeat begins to sound in my mind, but it's too calm to be my own. I only hear it between every third beat of mine.

"What are you doing to me?" I ask as the overhead light flickers, producing a strobe-like effect. A wave of lightheadedness crashes over me, and I blink away the dizziness.

"I have not yet begun," he says, giving me more space. "What is it? You look green."

"There's something out there." I lunge for the bedroom door and yank it open. The heartbeat sounds louder in the hall.

I follow the pulse and feel Sebastián's presence sticking to me, his shadow darkening the walls as I hurry down the stairs and pass the dining hall. Thankfully, Beatríz isn't there.

The heart's beating is growing louder with every step.

"Where are you going?" asks Sebastián, as the red-tinged lights around us flicker again.

"Are you messing with me?" I ask him.

"Is this real or part of the performance?" he shoots back.

"Don't you see that?"

"See what?"

Either I'm getting played, or I'm the only one seeing something again. Neither option is good.

We reach the fork where the castle bifurcates, and I look from one crimson corridor to the other. The passage that leads to the mirror room is dimly lit, but the one I took last night to the cathedral is flickering.

"What do you see?" asks Sebastián as we cut down the east wing, through the string of barren rooms.

"The lights are flickering." As I say it, the blinking stops.

We're in front of the double doors that open into the windowless cathedral. "They led me here," I say, reaching for the handle.

Sebastián flings the doors open and advances into the cathedral, his shadows darkening the air, until the entire hall is an inky black night. I get the sense he's scanning the whole place at once.

"There is nothing here," he says when he's finished, appearing before me. As the shadows retreat into him, the air brightens back to a dull reddish hue.

"Yet this room holds secrets," he says with a frown.

"Like a hidden door?" I ask, wondering if it's the purple room.

He cocks his head to the side, surveying me. "Why did you bring me here?"

I hear the death lining his voice, and I know my brain isn't big enough for the both of us. The shadow beast and I can't coexist.

"What makes you think I'm the bruja, and not my aunt?" I challenge him.

"She cannot sense me, nor can I touch her. You alone perceive me—so you must be behind the spell."

How convenient; I created a creature only I can see.

Sebastián's viselike grip closes around my neck, and pain shoots through me. *BOOM. BOOM. BOOM.*

Lightning flashes in the silver of his eyes as my pulse picks up speed. He's excited by my fear. "Any last words?" he whispers, our noses nearly brushing.

I inhale his starry scent, and I can almost feel the moonlight of his gaze tickling my skin. This cathedral may be windowless, but the night sky has never felt closer.

"If you're going to kill me," I squeeze out through his grip, "can I at least pick the room?" My mind must have conjured the shadow beast to protect me from the truth, so it's possible he also holds the answers.

I watch his jaw clench before he opens his fist, freeing my neck. "*Where?*"

I massage my throat and take measured breaths. I'm seeing spots, and my head is throbbing, but I use what energy I have left to dig into my pocket and hold out the photograph. "*Here.*"

When he reaches for it, I keep my grip on the paper, so he can't take it. Our fingers rest there, touching.

A shiver runs down my middle when he looks at me. Then he studies the picture.

He stares for so long, and with such focus, that I take him in slowly and uninterrupted. His sculpted face is smooth, sans age markers, not a wrinkle or blemish anywhere. Yet the rest of him is harder to make out.

It's as if his body is cloaked with the night itself. The length of his form is covered in a formfitting fabric so dark that it shades the air around him, shrouding his details. Yet the blackness isn't opaque; there are lights in its depths, and I get the sense that if I look long enough, I might not even notice when his hands close around my neck again.

"No," he says, and I blink, forgetting my question.

"I have explored this castle every night, and I have not seen this room . . . Yet it feels familiar." This last part sounds more muted, like he's thinking out loud.

He stares at me now, with the same quiet intensity. "How did you come to possess this?"

"This picture is what lured me to this castle. I know something happened to me in that room, but I don't know what. I've come to find it."

He watches my lips move as I talk, and an inner warmth spreads down my middle. But being attracted to my own hallucination makes me even more screwed up than I already am, so I close my eyes to shut him out. Yet I still see him against the black of my lids.

When I open my eyes again, he's gone.

Along with my photograph.

I wake up earlier than usual, so I cross paths with Beatríz in the kitchen. "I'll walk with you today," she says, wearing another dark and outdated dress.

I was planning to return to the cathedral first thing to see if I could locate the photograph I lost last night, but now I'll have to wait until later. We walk in stiff and uncomfortable silence the whole way to town, and when we get to the bookstore, she goes inside with me.

"Buen día, Doctora," says Felipe in greeting. He looks more than just surprised. He seems nervous. "¿Cómo la puedo ayudar?"

"Quería asegurarme de que todo iba bien con la tutoría."

"Su sobrina es una estudiante excelente." They both turn to me, and I stare back blankly. Felipe smiles and Beatríz grimaces.

"Bueno," she says, turning back to him, "también te quiero recordar que tienes cita para donar sangre mañana."

"Ahí estaré."

"Nos vemos por la tarde," Beatríz says to me before sweeping out the front door.

"What was that about?" I ask Felipe.

"She wanted to see how tutoring was going. I said you were a quick study," he says, and we both smirk.

I follow him as he climbs the ladder, and he adds over his shoulder, "She also reminded me I have an appointment to donate blood tomorrow."

A chill runs down my left arm as I recall Beatríz drawing my blood. "How often do you do that?"

"Few times a year." He shrugs. "Whenever la doctora says it's time."

Once we're seated at the high table, I ask, "What can you tell me about my family?"

"The Brálagas are the oldest bloodline in Oscuro—"

"No," I cut him off. "I mean my parents. Do you remember anything about when we lived here?"

He looks at me like I asked a trick question. "Do you? Remember anything?"

I frown with annoyance. "I asked you first."

"I don't know. I was young. I don't remember much." He breaks off and seems to be listening deeply for something, possibly the sound of customers.

"But I heard stuff over the years," he goes on, his voice significantly lower. "People say your family are victims of the castle's curse. First, you and your parents disappeared overnight. Then your grandmother died. Soon after, your grandfather. And then . . . the subway."

He doesn't explain further, and I'm glad.

"La doctora was left alone when her parents died, and after firing the castle's staff, they say she's never let another person set foot inside la Sombra again."

He had me until that last part. "That sounds like an exaggeration. The castle is ancient. She must have had to call a repair person at some point to fix the plumbing or wiring or *something*."

"They say la Sombra's power has never gone out, not even in bad snow-storms. And have you seen the condition of the garden? She won't even hire a landscaper."

I think of the kitchen's modern refrigerator; that model didn't exist half a decade ago. "So you're telling me my aunt carried in a state-of-the-art refrigerator on her own?"

He shrugs. "If it's new, it has wheels. Unless—is the kitchen on a different floor?"

"It's not," I say, noting how he logs this scrap of information, the same way I archive evidence in my mind, and it reminds me that Felipe has his own agenda. These past few days, I've been the hungry diner and Felipe has been feeding me intel; but now his own appetite is rising to the surface.

"What about what your great-grandfather said about Brálagas having magic?" I know I'm only indulging my delirium by bringing this up—but what happened to the photograph last night? Did I drop it, or is Sebastián real? I felt his grip around my neck, and today my throat even feels a little sore.

I don't know what to believe, if I can trust my own senses.

Felipe bounds to the desk. He uses a key to unlock a drawer, and he pulls out a pamphlet printed on thick parchment. He holds it gingerly as he brings it over.

The paper has an ancient feel and scent. At the top of the pamphlet is the Brálaga coat of arms: the full moon and la Sombra's silhouette, inversely mirrored, against a bloodred background.

There are only four lines of ink, written in striking calligraphy. Felipe reads them aloud:

> *Disco que asombra,*
> *Río rojo más puro,*
> *Castillo de las sombras,*
> *No hay luz en Oscuro.*

The last line lands in my stomach with a thud. "What does the whole thing mean?"

"Think you can figure it out if I help you?" he asks, activating tutor mode.

I take a stab at the first line. "Disco? Like the dance?"

Felipe snorts. "No, it means disk."

I grin, too. "That makes more sense. So, *disk* that . . . a-sombra? Is that like a shadow?"

He chuckles again. "*Asombra* means astounds or astonishes."

"So . . . *disk that astounds*?" He nods in assent, and I continue. "*Río . . .*

means river?" He nods again, his smile growing. "Red . . . most . . . pure? *Red river most pure?*"

"Yes!" he says proudly. "And the last two lines?"

"*Castle of the shadows . . . there's no light in Oscuro.*" I reread the whole thing, in English: "*Disk that astounds, red river most pure, castle of the shadows, there's no light in Oscuro.*"

I look at him, still confused. "What's it mean?"

"I think it's kind of a riddle."

I used to love those. "*Castle of the shadows* means la Sombra," I say, and I start to pace the attic like I used to when I was in problem-solving mode. "*Red river most pure* . . . could that be blood?"

I stop moving and look at Felipe, who nods in assent. Thinking of the Brálaga crest, I say: "*Disk that astounds* must refer to the moon. So, the answers are: full moon, blood, la Sombra, and . . . *nighttime?*"

His brow arches up. "That was quick."

"But if those are the answers, what's the question?" I ask, resuming my pacing.

"What if it's a spell?"

I freeze, feeling my eyes widening at the word. If—*if*—Sebastián is real, and *if* there's actually a spell, and *if* Brálaga magic exists . . .

"Do you think my aunt can conduct magic?" I ask, answering Felipe's question with another.

The humor fades from his features. It feels like removing the filter of friendly bookseller and seeing his true face underneath.

The hunger I glimpsed earlier was nothing compared to the ravenous way he looks now. He's more than the bright-eyed tutor of the past few days, and I see the danger Beatríz picked up on. Felipe is an investigator in search of a secret he's so desperate to uncover, he's willing to risk everything for it. Even himself.

He reminds me of *me*.

"No one knows what la doctora does inside la Sombra," he says, lowering his voice. "You're the first to get close. If anyone can find out . . . it's you."

"Can I see your calendar again?" I ask.

Felipe grabs it off the desk, and I look down at the tiny black circle for this month. I guess I'll have my answer soon.

The full moon is in three nights.

CHAPTER 9

DINNER IS LEFTOVER PAELLA.

After what Beatríz did and said last night, I can hardly stomach food in her presence. It was easier sharing space at the clínica, where we work in separate areas. Being at the same table is unbearable.

The only sounds are the tines of her fork scraping against the polished porcelain plate. I set down my glass of water, a little too hard. It thumps against the wood, and my aunt raises a quizzical eyebrow at me as she swaps her fork for her wineglass.

As she brings it to her lips, I shatter the silence.

"How much longer are we going to do this?"

The question flies out on its own, bypassing my brain as my body expels it.

"She speaks," says my aunt, setting down her glass. She sounds less pleased to hear my voice than I was expecting.

I guess after last night, she's no longer curious about what I have to say.

"Where's the purple room?" I ask, getting right to the point.

"It's gone," says Beatríz, swallowing another forkful of rice.

"The room ran away, too?" It's a cheap shot, but so are her lies.

"I told you the castle is in disrepair. Some parts are no longer accessible."

"Then why did you send me that picture?"

"To prove my identity."

"Why *that room*? What happened there?"

Beatríz holds my gaze, and now she's the one who's gone silent. I get the sense she's searching me for something, too.

"I've contacted an in-patient facility a few hours away from here, and they have a bed available." Beatríz's subject shift is so swift, it takes me a few seconds to pick up on what she's saying. "Continue this line of questioning, and that will be your next stop."

She drops the black pill on the tabletop in front of me.

"Now take your medicine."

I want to shove that seed up her nostril. But I know better than to strike too early. So I swallow her pill, and I spare her a glower before hurrying to my room.

The halls look even redder tonight as I rush to throw up the seed. I didn't get the chance to last night because Sebastián distracted me. Seems to be what he does best. Tonight, he better not be—

In my room again.

This time he's standing over my desk and reading my journal. I hid it in my period drawer, so he could only have known where to find it if he's inside my head.

He looks up, no trace of shame at breaching my privacy. Between him and my aunt, I'll never find any peace in this house.

"Give me back my photograph."

The words come out of their own volition, same as with Beatríz.

The shadow beast glowers at me. I doubt he appreciates my tone. "What is the black fire?" he asks, holding my notepad open to the page where I made my list of strange occurrences.

"That's enough!" I squeeze my head between my hands, willing him out. "This time I'm giving *you* a choice—show me where the purple room is, or get the hell out of my head!"

"I have told you I do not know. Do you not believe me?"

"Why should I? I don't know anything about you. Where do you come from? Why are you here? *Who are you?*"

"I am Sebastián."

"Hilarious." I'm tired of my mind's games. "I know you're not real, but you obviously have information buried deep in my brain somewhere that I want myself to have, so just spit it out already—*where's the room?*"

His brow furrows, like I've spoken a language he's not fluent in. "You are evidently unwell."

"You catch on quick."

He gapes at me for what feels like a full minute. Then a horrible howl thunders through the room, and Sebastián's features crack with pain, like he's been shot.

I back away as he doubles over. It seems like he can't lift his neck to look at me.

"What is it?" I ask.

He doesn't answer. His eyes are slits and his mouth hangs open. He seems to be in severe agony. Is this what happens when you destroy a hallucination?

"Where does it hurt?" is all I can think to ask.

"Ev-every-where," he manages to get out. His voice isn't breathy. It's more choppy, like a radio station with signal interference, and there's a low-pitched wailing—

"Are you laughing?"

As the wail becomes a howl again, there's no denying it's laughter. "You—" He tries to speak past his guffaws. "You believe—you *made* me?"

I perch at the edge of the bed. I was not prepared for how a merry monster would behave, and now I can see why. It's *insufferable.*

Sebastián is still doubled over, his howls sputtering, and it seems like this embarrassing display is finally coming to an end. I don't care how much pain I earn myself, I'm going off on him. "What the hell is your—?"

But when he raises his chin, and I see his face, the shadow beast's smile is a supernova. The silver galaxies of his eyes are luminous, his skin as fresh as the earth after a storm. The dazzling sight makes me feel as tiny as I hoped to make him feel, and I forget what I was saying.

"You really think quite highly of yourself."

There's a somewhat lighter quality to Sebastián's voice now.

"What does that mean?" I ask.

"You credit yourself as my creator." There's such a smug superiority in his expression that I wish I had a mirror to hold up.

"Prove you're real," I say, crossing my arms, "and that a *spell* is behind everything."

"What sort of proof would satisfy you?" His tone is as dry as a desert. "You do not even believe I am real when I stand before you."

"Then tell me something about yourself," I demand.

"If you are in such a sharing mood, you start."

"Meaning what?"

"Who are *you?*"

He sounds like the caterpillar in *Alice in Wonderland*. "You already know," I say with a hard breath. "You saw me on the news months ago—"

"I know your father did not protect you from a lethal gas."

My spine stiffens at the mention of Dad.

"That was a lie," he says, his voice lower and his manner more menacing. "No human could shield you from brujería."

My gaze swings up as the overhead light flickers.

"It's happening again," I say, and then I open the door and head down the crimson corridor.

Sebastián is already at my side.

He moves like a shadow, not human or even creature-like, but something else altogether. Once more, the flickering lights lead down the right wing to the cathedral.

"*Again?*" he asks, not hiding his annoyance.

"I'm just following the lights. I feel like they're leading me to the purple room."

"What makes you think that?"

"What makes you think the subway was a spell?"

He frowns at me. "What else could have caused an interdimensional disturbance?"

"Interdimensional *what*?"

"Whatever caused those deaths also displaced me from my home realm. Only a powerful bruja could have pulled that off."

"What realm are you from?"

This time he doesn't answer. I guess my mind hasn't gotten around to writing his backstory yet.

Still, I need to shatter this hallucination somehow, and undermining its logic seems like the best way. "You said *bruja*," I point out. "Why do you say that word in Spanish?"

He considers my question before answering. "I read all the books in this castle to learn the languages of your world. Most were in Spanish, so it must be the language I best absorbed."

"You know where the library is?" I ask, brimming with curiosity.

He cocks his head, sizing me up. "You ask a lot of questions. It is now your turn to answer mine—tell me more about these lights."

"There's nothing to tell. They just flicker off and on at a distractingly quick rate."

"Are they flickering now?"

"No," I say, and as I look around the nondescript room that leads to the cathedral, it strikes me that the lights inside that cavernous space never actually flickered.

Does that mean *this* is the right destination?

There's no furniture or windows here. This vacant room looks just like any other . . . except for the red rug. I haven't seen any other carpeting at the castle.

I drop down to touch the rough fabric. When I pull back on a corner, I see only the stone floor below.

Cottoning on, Sebastián yanks up half the rug with one tug. At the center of the floor is a square outline with a metal ring embedded.

It looks like a trapdoor.

Sebastián lifts the ring and pulls open the hatch. Then he melts into shadow. I follow him down the stone steps at my slower pace.

By the time I reach the bottom, we're in a cold basement with walls crafted of stacked gray stones. There's only one light bracketed high up, barely illuminating anything.

I feel like I'm in a trance, following some inner map from my childhood. I remember exactly where the hidden doorway is, the one I thought only I knew about. I run my fingers across the apple-shaped stone that I once believed opened just for me.

A sharpness stabs my finger.

I didn't spy the tiny thornlike spikes because they blend into the rock.

As I smear my blood across the wall, something flashes in Sebastián's gaze. He looks unwell at the sight.

But then excitement takes over his features as the borders between stones begin to darken, the rock physically separating—and the outline of a doorway appears.

I touch the apple-shaped stone again, and the door swings inward. Sebastián beats me through the opening, and I follow him inside.

The room is no longer purple. The wallpaper is blackened and scorched, the scars reaching all the way up to the ceiling.

The fire was real.

A wave of dizziness crashes over me again, only this time it's so intense, I feel nauseous. Shutting my eyes, I'm swept back in time with the tide.

I'm in the center of the room, black flames blazing all around me.

I can see Mom's agonized face as she screams from the doorway. She's looking into the room, her gaze jumping from me to someone else. A third *person.*

Beatríz.

She stands in the far corner, just beyond the fire's reach. Only unlike Mom and me, she doesn't look afraid or horrified.

She looks triumphant.

I open my eyes as the lightheadedness recedes, along with the memory.

"What happened here?" asks Sebastián. He's inspecting a ribbon of wallpaper that's curled away from the wall.

"A black fire," I whisper, "when I was five." I gravitate to the place where I'm standing in the memory. "I was here, in the middle of the flames. Only the fire didn't hurt me."

Just like the black smoke on the subway.

"Beatríz was at the far edge of the room. Watching me."

"The human who lives here?" asks Sebastián, sounding mildly surprised. He drifts to a corner of the room, and I assume he's pacing while he thinks—until he reaches down and pulls up a stone from the ground.

From the hole he retrieves a handful of documents. He reviews them years before I do. When I come over, he hands them to me.

The first three papers are photographs of a small girl.

Me.

In the first, I'm sniffing a purple flower in the garden. In the second, I'm crawling up the staircase. In the third, I'm smiling to someone and baring a small chip in my front milk tooth. Something about this last picture feels off, and I wonder who I'm looking at off camera.

The fourth paper is the only official document. Bile rises up my throat because I've seen this kind of paperwork before, only then it bore my parents' names.

A death certificate.

The text is in Spanish, and I stare at the letters of the name for a long time before I finally read them.

Estela Amador.

Me.

CHAPTER 10

I'VE BEEN DEAD A DOZEN YEARS.

Somehow, it makes sense.

Now I know why the black smoke couldn't touch me. Why I'm having nightly conversations with a shadow beast. Why I didn't die with my parents.

"I don't exist."

A weird laugh escapes my throat.

Since I was a little kid, I've felt like I'm missing a kind of anchoring to the world that others are born with. It wasn't just my parents' lifestyle—my sense of homelessness went deeper than that. I've always felt like a stranger in my age group, in my life, in my own skin.

When I was ten, I read a story about a girl with a hole in her heart that would not heal. Since air kept escaping through it, her feet never touched the ground, and she floated over her life, unable to actually live it.

That's how I've always felt, only now I know why.

This must be the reason Mom and Dad kept me on the run; so no one would get close enough to see the truth.

I'm just like Sebastián—a very lifelike ghost.

"You can't kill me," I taunt him with a weird giggle. "I'm already dead! We're *both* haunting la Sombra!"

"What is happening?" he asks.

"I'm *dead*!"

"You are not dead. Trust me."

"Trust *you*?" My voice hits a hysterical pitch, but I don't care. "*Neither* of us is real!"

"Have you consumed a mind-altering substance? You seem different— *where are you going?*"

I take the photographs and certificate with me as I race back up the steps to ground level. Sebastián shuts the trapdoor and restores the rug in the span of an eyeblink, but I keep running through the castle until I get to my bedroom, where he's already waiting for me.

I didn't get the chance to throw up Beatríz's pill last night or tonight—the exact two instances when I saw the flickering lights. Sebastián is obviously distracting me because I should have made this connection sooner.

I dig into the pocket of my duffel and pull out the pills I didn't take my first two nights. This drug must have led me to the purple room. Maybe there's more it can show me. I toss the seeds into my mouth—

But they don't land on my tongue.

"What are these?" asks Sebastián. He swiped them in midair.

"Medication from my aunt. Give it back!"

"After what you said about the black fire, are you sure you can trust her?"

"How are you not getting this yet? Nothing matters because we don't exist and none of this is real—*you're a figment of my imagination, and I'm* DEAD*!*"

I shriek the final word at the top of my lungs, and Sebastián's icy hand slams on my mouth, pressing against my teeth. The force of his movement shoves me back, and my spine hits the wall, the impact rattling my insides.

I sneak a glance at the door, expecting my aunt to barge in. Sebastián keeps me pinned between the wall and him, and I breathe in through my nose, inhaling the stars that cling to his skin.

"You do not feel dead to me," he murmurs, sliding his fingers off my lips.

But I still feel the brand of his touch on my mouth. The trusty compass in my gut has gone haywire because it's pushing me toward the shadow beast.

Sebastián is still staring at my mouth, and I briefly wonder if it's actually burning. But then he takes a step back, and my lips turn to cinders.

"Give me back my pills!" I snap at him.

"Calm down—"

"GIVE THEM TO ME!" I shout, daring my aunt to hear me.

"You leave me no choice," he says, and before I can register the threat, he yanks up my chin, bringing my face close to his.

For one ridiculous moment, I think he's going to kiss me.

Then pain explodes at my throat, as my skin rips open.

I wheeze as blood rushes to the wound in my neck, my veins like straws feeding Sebastián. My entire body feels like it's being drawn in through his mouth.

My eyes roll to the back of my head, my skin burning like it's on fire. My arms and legs go limp with sleep as black spots overtake my vision, and I remember the ocular migraine I thought I was getting on the subway.

Except it wasn't a headache at all.

Dread churns in my stomach as black smoke spreads through the room, and if I had any oxygen left, I would scream. The dark plumes infect every particle of air, until they swallow the walls, and I'm no longer in la Sombra.

I'm enveloped in an inky night. Nothing else exists, and as I start to wonder if I'm floating in outer space, I see the glimmers of two stars.

A childlike being steps forth from the shadows, his silver eyes cutting through the dark, and I recognize a young Sebastián.

Beside him is a wooden box his exact size. It's rattling, like something inside wants out.

Young Sebastián wrenches it open at once—and out bursts a furry blue beast the size of an adolescent grizzly bear.

Sebastián growls. So does the blue bear. They circle each other.

The beast attacks first. It strikes at Sebastián, but the young shadow is quicker and sinks his fangs into the creature's furry blue arm. The bear cries out and stabs Sebastián's neck with its claws.

"Ah!" Sebastián pulls away, massaging his neck, and the bear limps back, licking the wound in its arm. But before it's gotten far, the shadow boy pins the creature down, and he bites into its hide again, this time to feed—

The scene blinks, and an older Sebastián is wrestling the blue bear, which is still alive and has grown bigger than him.

They quit fighting when an older being who looks like he could be Sebastián's father enters the space. His gaze is frostier than the deadliest snowstorm. "When you did not kill this beast as a child," he says, "I assumed you were waiting for it to grow plump, so the blood in its veins would be richer and its fur would be large enough to fashion yourself a new cloak."

Sebastián doesn't say anything. He is stoic, his expression a mask of neutrality, but his fists clench at his sides.

"It is time for you to prove me right," commands his father. "Drink."

Horror breaks through Sebastián's face, and he takes a step back. "I cannot."

"Then starve."

The scenery blinks, the lights flickering off and on. Sebastián and the blue bear are emaciated now, and they seem sluggish and tired. The older being returns. He studies his son without pity. "You have failed me" is all he says.

In a heartbeat, his arms are around the bear's neck.

"No!"

Mustering all the energy he has left, Sebastián rushes at his father like he can stop him. But he's barely gotten to his feet when he hears the sound of the bear's neck snapping.

"Fail me again," warns his father, "and the consequences will be worse."

The scene blinks again, and now the air is deep purple, cut out with thousands of black silhouettes. It looks like an army of shadow beasts is fighting against beings with tails.

One of the shadow beasts is particularly swift with his meals, disposing of bodies like he's crushing soda cans. He fights in a cloak of blue fur—

The memory cuts out, and my bedroom comes back into focus. Sebastián's jaws have released me.

My knees give in, and I slide to the floor, gasping for oxygen. As the smoke dissipates, I see him clearly.

The shadow beast's incisors have grown into pointy fangs, and they're dripping with my blood. It rolls down the sides of his mouth and smears his chin.

His silver eyes are round and cloudy. "You are alive," he whispers, licking his lips like he's savoring my taste.

My heart pounds, proving his point.

"W-what was that memory?" I ask, my voice raspy.

His eyes widen. "You *saw*?"

I nod, and he doesn't say anything else. Instead, he stumbles toward the door. He looks drunk.

Tonight, he doesn't vanish into shadow.

He walks out. Like a man.

I wake up on the floor.

Lifting my head, I gasp as pain zaps through my neck. I cup the spot where it hurts, and I use my other arm to push myself up. Then I drag myself to the bathroom.

My reflection reveals that dry blood is caked on my neck, throat, chest, and arm. Evidence that Sebastián isn't just a figment of my imagination. He exists.

And he's a *vampire*.

As soon as I think the word, I cringe in the mirror. And yet I can't deny he's real, not after his bite and the memories I glimpsed when he drank my blood.

What does it mean that we were both hit with the same spell across different dimensions? What could our connection be?

I run the faucet to fill the bathtub, then I rest my head against the porcelain, shutting my eyes as I scrub my skin to wash off the blood. "*You are alive,*" I hear Sebastián whisper in my ear . . . then his fangs stab my throat.

My eyelids fly open and my spine stiffens.

I survey the bathroom, but the shadow beast isn't here. I'm alone.

I drain the last of the reddish water. I'll have to keep my neck concealed while it heals so Beatríz doesn't notice.

I still don't get how she didn't rush in after all my screaming last night. Either the walls are soundproof, or she takes a heavy sedative to fall asleep.

I spot the death certificate and the photographs on my bed when I enter my bedroom—and the rest of what happened last night comes flying back to me.

Without thinking, I snatch the papers and march into my aunt's room, wearing only a towel. "*BEATRÍZ!*"

I skip knocking and twist the handle. It's unlocked.

Her room is bigger than mine but more spartan, and she has an old-fashioned phone on her nightstand. Everything is polished dark wood. The four-poster bed is neatly made, the bathroom empty.

I try the kitchen next. She's not there, either.

Back in my room, I pull on a turtleneck, and before leaving, I hide the photographs and death certificate with my notepad in my period drawer.

I go directly to the clínica because my conversation with Beatríz can't wait. I need to know what the death certificate means. If she threatens me again, I'll have to lead the Spanish cops—Dad's former coworkers—to the purple room and let them sort this out for me.

The door to the clínica is locked, and a handwritten note is taped to it.

Me fui a Madrid por un congreso médico. Regresaré en unos días.
                                              —*Dra. Brálaga*

The note is in Spanish. Like she left it for her patients and not for me.

I make out the words *Madrid, medical congress,* and *days.* So last night she was threatening to institutionalize me, and this morning she takes off? Why didn't she tell me she was leaving? And why did she remind Felipe of his appointment to get his blood drawn today?

It doesn't make sense.

I can't help feeling like this has something to do with the purple room. Does she know I found it? Is she afraid I'll go to the authorities? *Will she be back in time for the full moon?*

My mood improves in the librería, when Felipe offers me a mug of steaming hot chocolate topped with frothy cream.

"Your aunt is gone," he says by way of greeting. "She left a note about going to a medical conference in Madrid."

"I know." I blow on the drink, warming my hands against the mug. The first sip scorches my tongue, activating every nerve ending down to my toes.

"Seems kind of last-minute. And she bailed on my appointment to draw blood." When I don't say anything, he asks, "When did she tell you she was leaving?"

"She didn't. I found out from the same note."

His brow rises as I sip some more hot chocolate, the foaminess tickling my top lip. "That's odd," he says.

"That's Beatríz. Or haven't you noticed she's not exactly chatty?"

"Not even with you?"

I shrug, and today I'm the one leading the way to the attic, cradling my hot chocolate. Strange, how this space is where I feel safest in Oscuro. It's the only place where I don't worry about being hunted, or drugged, or judged.

"Thank you," I say to Felipe when we're both upstairs. "For tutoring me. I like coming here."

"Every teacher likes an eager student," he says, flashing his crooked grin.

I feel myself grinning back, even though just days ago the reflex seemed like an obsolete function.

It's been years since I made a friend. When the partings became too painful and the pen pals too plentiful, it got easier to avoid socializing at all. It worried Dad more than Mom. I heard them argue about it once, and Mom said, *She can make friends when she grows up.*

I thought she was calling me immature, so it surprised me that Dad didn't defend me. But now I think of the gravity with which she said *grows up,* and I wonder if she meant it literally.

"I wish what happened hadn't happened," says Felipe, his smile slackening into a more intimate expression, "but I'm happy you're here, too."

It's refreshing not to have to doubt he means what he says. Felipe's face is easier to translate than Spanish, which is what makes him so easy to be around.

"Where did you grow up?" he asks me, his voice as soft as his gaze.

"The United States."

"Which state?"

"All of them," I say, sitting down on the aged leather couch. I realize my mistake at once as it nestles every part of my body. I doubt I'll ever get back up.

Felipe drops onto the cushion next to me. "We don't have to talk about it if you don't want to."

"I don't mind," I say with a shrug. "I grew up on the road. My parents and I lived everywhere, from condos in big cities to cabins in the wild."

"Your parents didn't work?"

"Mom was a journalist and Dad a private detective."

"And school?"

"I was homeschooled." I'm struck by the irony of the term, since I've never had a home. "That means my parents taught me," I clarify when I see his confusion.

"What about friends?"

"I stopped making friends because I got tired of leaving them behind." I sound almost angry, and I flash to the four girls on the subway and the longing I felt when I saw what they shared. A chance to grow up together.

Instead, they died right in front of me.

"Toda mi vida," says Felipe, "tuve la atención completa de mis padres." I look at him, and he says, "Now you say it."

"What's it mean?"

"Work it out as you go. Try it."

"Toda mi vida . . ." I say, the only part I remember.

Felipe goes to the desk, and when he comes back, he hands me a piece of paper. "Read it out loud."

"Toda mi vida," I say, "*all my life.*" Felipe nods in approval. "Tuve la atención completa de mis padres . . . *complete attention . . . my parents.*" I look at Felipe and translate the full thing: "My whole life I had the complete attention of my parents."

The hole in my chest widens as I say it, and my heart holds its next beat.

"Good," he says of my translation.

"But even with their full attention," I say, "I was still missing something. I used to think it was a room of my own. But now that I have that, the hole is still there. It's only . . . only when I'm *here* that I feel better."

My cheeks warm as I admit that last part. Felipe's face heats with color, too.

"Estela," he says, and a cold fear spikes the warmth as it occurs to me that he may want more than friendship.

"Can I visit you at the castle in two days?"

I'm relieved that's all he wants. "Why two days?" I ask, thinking of the full moon.

"It's my day off."

Beatríz said I'm not to bring anyone to the castle, but if she's going to take off without warning, I'm not going to follow her rules. Besides, if Felipe won't be at the bookstore, I'll have nowhere to go during the day. And I'd rather not be alone.

"Sure," I say after a beat.

Today, he adopts a more traditional tutoring approach, opting to teach me from a workbook, and we don't say another word about la Sombra.

I want to ask him about vampires, but I can't bring myself to form the question. Knowing I'll be completely alone with Sebastián in a few hours is exciting and terrifying in equal measure. Part of me never wants to go back to la Sombra. Part of me wishes the clock would move faster.

My skin craves the shadow beast like a new drug. I shouldn't want his fangs anywhere near me—and yet, I've been fantasizing about his bite all day, as if it had been a kiss. I'd rather not think too hard on how wrong that sounds.

This is the first time I've ever felt this way about anyone, like a pull that's impossible to resist. Returning to Sebastián's orbit feels as inevitable as gravity.

I *want* him to touch me.

I *want* him.

I *want*.

"Closing time," says Felipe, snapping me out of my reverie. A million moths flutter in my belly as I stand up to return to the castle.

I follow Felipe downstairs, and I see someone else in the store. A man in a tweed coat who walks with a cane. "Hola, Estela, soy el padre de Felipe. Me llamo Arturo Sarmiento."

I stick out my hand and greet Felipe's father with a firm shake. "Hola."

"Tu tía me ha pedido que me asegure de que tienes donde comer, así que estás invitada a comer con nosotros."

I look to Felipe to translate, even though I understood the last part. I'm just buying myself time to react.

"You're invited over to dinner tonight," he says, beaming.

"My wife is already cooking," says Arturo in a thick accent. He smiles, and it's clear his son inherited his father's crooked smirk.

I'd rather return to the castle, but I can't come up with a good way out of this. So I just smile and nod in assent, and after father and son lock up the store, the three of us climb the road uphill, toward the residences of Oscuro.

La Sombra looms over the pueblo, blacker than the night itself, its lone tower stabbing the sky. Overhead, the moon is just a sliver shy of full. In two nights, la luna llena will begin—but will Beatríz be back in time to test Felipe's great-grandfather's theory?

"You're going to pass our street!" calls Felipe, and I realize I'm so deep in my thoughts that I've marched too far ahead.

I wait for the guys to catch up. Felipe is moving slower to match his dad's pace with his cane, and it strikes me what a big help it is for their family that Felipe runs the bookstore.

"Ya no corro carreras," says a smiling Arturo.

I look at Felipe, and this time I take a stab at translating: "*I don't run races anymore?*"

"Excellent," says an approving Felipe. I smile back, equally pleased with my Spanish progress.

"Aquí estamos," says Arturo when we arrive at a house that's buzzing with noise. It sounds like the whole town is crammed inside.

Felipe casts me an apologetic look as the door opens, and I'm swept in by a tiny mob.

"Bienvenida, Estela. Soy Lucía, la mamá de Felipe," says a squat and curvy woman with bright red nail polish and half-moon eyeglasses. She pulls me into a hug before I have a chance to extend my hand for a shake.

The next few hours are a blur of faces and names and double kisses, each person blending in with the next, forming a tapestry, all of them inextricable from one another. I think of the ledger in Felipe's book tracing everyone's ancestral properties. The residents of Oscuro are so deeply planted here that they seem impossible to uproot—and yet, *something* sent Mom packing.

The Sarmientos' home is wooden-floored, with a warm fireplace and sloping ceilings. In stark contrast to my aunt's house, photographs line most flat surfaces, including the walls, featuring many of the faces here tonight. I do a double take when I see that la Sombra's crest hangs over the hearth. Beneath it, on the mantel, are candles and a single framed photo. I move closer to be sure it's who I think it is—

Beatríz.

"Estela, esta es mi abuela," says Felipe's mom, and I turn to see the old woman who feeds the birds in the plaza. "Se llama Gloria."

"Hola, Gloria," I say, greeting Felipe's great-grandmother.

I move in for the customary kisses, and she says, "Angelito"—*little angel*—and presses a hand to my cheek. "Te quemaron."

What did she say? Doesn't *quemaron* mean burn?

"¿Qué?" I ask.

"Está cansada," says Felipe's mom with a strained smile. *She's tired.*

"What's she talking about?" I ask.

"I get her to bed," says Lucía in choppy English, flashing me a too-large smile.

"¿Cómo estás?" asks Arturo, swapping in for his wife almost instantly.

"¿Conocían a mis padres?" I ask if they knew my parents.

"No," he says, shaking his head a tad too effusively.

"¿Por qué la foto de Beatríz?" I hope I asked him why they have Beatríz's photo framed.

"Es nuestra alcalde," he says.

"No entiendo." I have no idea what *alcalde* means.

"*Mayor,*" says Felipe, coming over with two glasses of soda. Arturo smiles and takes off, looking almost relieved to leave me with his son. "Beatríz is the town's mayor."

I stare at Felipe, speechless. He holds out a glass to me, and I take it. "Want to see my room?" he offers.

"Yes, please," I say, eager for a moment of quiet. There are so many people here that they've spilled out into the backyard and front lawn. They've been rotating indoors to meet me, and I think my head is going to explode.

We slip to the back of the house, where a set of narrow stairs leads to a basement. Picturing the attic of Libroscuro, I'm eager to enter another of Felipe's cozy, book-lined spaces. I hurry down the steps, but halfway, I freeze.

Every inch of wall space is papered, forming a collage of images that comes together to form a fragmented picture.

La Sombra. This whole place is a shrine to the castle.

"What is this?" I ask.

"Art. *I hope.*"

I stare into his eyes so he'll see I'm being serious. "Why did you make your room look like la Sombra?"

His smile falls away. "Remember the thirteenth tale about the magical Book?" he asks, and I nod. "*It's real.*"

"What do you mean?"

"It's *us.* My family." His eyes are shiny with moisture. "*We are the keepers of the Book.*"

CHAPTER 11

"WHAT ARE YOU TALKING ABOUT?" I ask, trying and failing to process Felipe's newest revelation.

"My great-grandfather told me," he insists. "You're invited to come in, you know."

I realize I'm still standing on the last rung of the stairs, and my skin crawls as I step down. All four walls of his room make up a mural composed of images whose edges don't quite match, forging a twisted version of la Sombra.

It's like being inside a pop-up book castle.

"If you're its keepers, then where is the Book?" I challenge.

"I don't know yet," he says dismissively, like that's not the important part. "But I will know *someday*. The secret is mine to inherit, just like Libroscuro."

"Did your great-grandfather tell you anything else, like what's in the Book?"

Felipe shakes his head. "He said it can't be read except by a Brálaga."

"So it's a Book from a story that can't be read or found." I wish I sounded less skeptical, but I can't help it. "Do you have any older siblings who might know more?"

"My older brother left town years ago."

"Did you have a falling-out?" Seeing his bemusement, I prod, "Was it a fight?"

He shakes his head. "It's hard to explain, but you'll see that people here belong to one of two groups—the nicknames are Oscurianos and Noscurianos. Oscurianos are lifers, and Noscurianos leave as soon as they can. They rarely return."

"Why not?"

He shrugs like he doesn't know or care.

"Aren't you curious what else is out there?" I ask, gesturing to the walls of his room. "Beyond this town?"

"I travel," he says, almost defensively. "But Oscuro is my home."

I sense there's more he's not saying. And yet I'm almost jealous of Felipe's single-mindedness about la Sombra and the librería and his place in the world. It must be so much easier to know where you belong and not have to question it.

"Why didn't you mention that my aunt is the mayor?" I ask.

"Politics isn't a big deal here. Besides, it's always a Brálaga in charge."

"What do you mean? Aren't there elections?"

"You don't get it," he says with a sigh, shaking his head like he's tired. He walks to the bed, its bloodred covers the only spot of color in the room. He sits down and taps the spot next to him.

When I sit, he says in a low voice, "Your family runs this town. They finance everything."

"I definitely don't get it," I say, agreeing with his first statement.

He twists his body on the mattress to face me. "Families own their property because it gets handed down through the generations, just like the castle. But there are still taxes and utilities and other services that have to get paid. Your family handles that for everyone, including our health care."

"I thought households paid into a health fund," I say, recalling my aunt's words.

"Not with money. We pay with our blood. By donating a few times a year to make sure there's enough of each type."

"How can Beatríz afford that?" I ask.

"Estela, your family is more than old money—you're *ancient* money. You will never have to worry about anything again."

"Except surviving," I say ominously. "We Brálagas have a short life expectancy."

"Maybe . . . or maybe la Sombra holds more secrets than we know."

I search his face for a smile before asking, "What do you mean by that?"

"Isn't it obvious after everything we read?" he asks, his eyes ablaze like a bonfire was just kindled. "Your Brálaga ancestor who built the castle wasn't human. That's why your family can interact with the supernatural."

Beatríz wasn't exaggerating when she alluded to Felipe's outsize imagination. "You should be a writer," is all I can think to say.

"I am! I'm working on my own book about la Sombra." His gaze lingers on mine, laden with whatever else he's not saying, and I realize I must be part of the story.

The thought pisses me off. I hated being tabloid fodder, and I definitely don't want to star in a book.

"What about you?" he asks. "What's your plan?"

The question makes me wish we were back out in the crowded living room and not in here where it's spacious and quiet and every breath can be heard.

"I—I don't have one."

"Yeah, you do," he says with bold assertiveness. "Your aunt brought you here to inherit her estate and her mayorship and her practice—"

"Whoa, slow down—"

"It's a good thing! You've come here to take her place."

It's the same thought I've been circling, but hearing him say it out loud rips the fear from my mind and gives it form. I leap to my feet, the food I ate tonight jostling in my stomach. "I never said I was staying in this ridiculous town!"

Felipe looks so crushed all of a sudden that under other circumstances it might be comical. But right now, I'm not finding anything funny.

"Why wouldn't you stay?" he asks.

"I haven't decided anything yet," I say, crossing my arms. "I just got here."

"Where would you even go?" He springs to his feet, too. "You don't have anything left in the United States, not a house or parents—"

"Felipe?"

His mother stands above, calling down. "¿Todo bien?"

"I was just leaving!" I call back to her, my eyes burning as I climb the steps as fast as I can.

"Estela se va," she announces to the living room, and I'm sucked into a sea of farewells that extends to the front lawn.

When I finally make it to the street, cold air buffets my face and the stark emptiness of the night soothes me. I hear footsteps behind me, and the creaking of tiny wheels, and I turn to see Felipe rolling a cart filled with Tupperware.

"This is for you," he says. It looks like everybody brought me a dish to take home. This is enough food to sustain me for at least six months.

"I got it," I say, reaching for the handle.

"I'll walk you."

"I can manage—"

"Parental orders." He starts rolling the cart uphill toward la Sombra, and I have no choice but to follow.

We're quiet the whole way. I lag a few steps behind to make the point that I'm not interested in his company. The only sounds come from the occasional hoot of an owl and homes where people are still finishing dinner or watching television. They're eating a lot later than Beatríz and I do.

When we reach the end of the residences, all that's left is the steep slope up to the castle gates. "I can go alone the rest of the way."

Felipe ignores me and keeps walking, without slowing. He goes right to the hidden door in the gargoyle-guarded gate and opens it, wheeling the cart through, then he holds it for me. I start to get a creeping sensation he's not going to turn around at the front door. Especially since he knows I'm alone tonight.

Well, *technically*. He doesn't know about Sebastián.

At the thought of the shadow beast, my stomach does a small flip. I don't know what worries me more—that I'm about to see him, or that he won't be there.

Especially since we'll be alone.

As Felipe lugs the cart up the sloping garden, I say, "Thanks for walking me, but you can go now."

Ignoring me, he cuts across the overgrown foliage and up to the massive doors with the gargoyle knockers. I hang back on the grass with my arms crossed, unwilling to produce the key until he leaves.

He blows out a loud breath. "I'm sorry, Estela. I know I went too far tonight. It's just the thought of losing you is unbearable."

"The only way you'll lose my friendship is by saying the things you said in your room. That crossed a line."

"You're right, and I'm sorry." He steps away from the cart and comes down to where I'm standing. "I hate to leave when you're mad. Let me come in and help you put the food away—"

BANG.

Before I can turn him down, the door rattles in its frame, like a gargoyle is knocking from inside.

Felipe turns to me with wide eyes. "What was that?"

BANG.

The gargoyle knocks again.

"Castle's cursed, remember?" I bite my lip to avoid laughing as I step up to the door, which quits quaking as soon as I fit the key into the lock.

"Buenas noches!" I call back, pulling the cart inside. "I'll get this back to you tomorrow."

I shut the door behind me and look for Sebastián, barely repressing my laughter—but my humor evaporates when I realize he's not here.

A solitary candle burns on the floor, in the middle of the entrance hall.

I spot another one farther down, and the glow of more candles in the distance. My heart starts to beat a different melody, gentler than the heavy bass drum of fear.

I'm not sure what I was expecting after last night, but it wasn't *this*. I pull the cart along as I follow the golden trail, blowing out each light as I go. I've seen enough of Dad's arson investigations to know that too many house fires start with an innocent candle.

I leave the food in the kitchen to sort later, and I keep following the lighted path. It ends just beyond the dining hall, at a bookshelf built into the wall of a crimson corridor.

The final candle is on the middle shelf. I pick it up to illuminate the furniture's details, trying to find a clue as to what's next. I spot a small hole in the side of the wood, like the indent of a missing screw, and I press my fingertip in. There's a click, and the bookshelf unhinges from the wall, like a door.

On the other side, a single candle illuminates a crumbling wing of the castle. There's no furniture, the paint is soiled with bruises, and pieces of wood and stone litter the floor. If the doorless rooms in the east wing look like they've been abandoned for a decade, this wing might not have been touched for a century.

The construction is either unfinished, or it's fallen apart.

"Sebastián?" I call out as I see another candle farther down.

There are cracks in the walls and strange house sounds. I recall what Beatríz said about the castle being in disrepair and some parts being unsafe. It feels like the ground is tilting downhill, but I can't be sure.

"Sebastián, where are you?" I call, after blowing out what by my count is the 198th candle.

Nothing about this gesture is feeling remotely romantic anymore. The darker the air gets, the chillier I feel. Until finally, there are no more candles.

"What's going on?" I ask, my voice trembling.

The darkness cradles me like a quilt. Something brushes my shoulder and I spin around, inhaling sharply. "Sebastián?"

Nobody's there.

"Cut this out!" I say, crossing my arms to keep them from shaking. "Either show yourself, or I'm leaving—"

A candle blazes on in the blackness.

As I move toward the glow, I realize it's illuminating a wall. This is a dead end.

I pick up the flame and turn in a circle, confused, until I lower it and study the floor. There's a *red rug*.

Holding the candle in one hand, I yank back the edge of the rug with the other. A trapdoor, just like the one that leads to the purple room.

Pulling up on the wooden hatch, I see a set of stairs and little illumination. Nothing about this feels safe or smart. I'm not even sure why I would consider going down there when I don't know Sebastián's motives.

All I know is that when he bit me, I saw the black smoke for the first time since the subway.

I need to know *why*.

Using the candle as a torch, I climb down. The steps end in a basement so large that the tiny flame does little to illuminate it. I spot the familiar crimson-tinged lights bracketed high up on the walls, but they too fail to lift much of the darkness.

I have to walk the room and look at it up close to really see it.

The first thing I come across is what appears to be a metal cage. When my vision adjusts to the dimness, I make out that linked to the bars are chains that end in handcuffs.

My mouth goes dry. Why did the shadow beast lead me here?

I step up to a wooden beam, and when I raise my candle, I make out an altar of sorts. It looks like the start to a game of hangman.

Where am I? A dungeon?

"Sebastián!" I call out. "Talk to me!"

A scarred wall looms ahead, and as I hold up my candle, I see that it's a board with slices everywhere, like it's been stabbed with thousands of blades—

"AHHH!"

I scream as a dagger thwacks into the board, so close to me I can feel its trail of heat by my eye. The board rattles, and I drop the candle.

The light snuffs out.

BOOM. BOOM. BOOM.

My heart is racing out of control. "What's wrong with you?" I shout at the air. "*Coward!* If you want to kill me, show your face!"

Sebastián manifests in front of me, shadows licking his skin like smoky snakes.

"Is that your last request?" He sounds different, like he's slipped into a lower register. "You want my face to be the last thing you see?"

There's something new in his expression tonight. A fiery blaze in his wintry eyes that must have been ignited when he drank my blood. Tasting me has changed him.

"Why?" I whisper.

"You reminded me of what I am." There's nothing luminous about his smile now. His mirthless mouth promises only death.

I don't see when he reaches for the second blade.

"AAHHH!"

My scream stings against my sore throat. This time, the dagger lops off one of my curls and pins it to the board.

Sebastián already has a third blade in his hand, so I run.

I can't see where I'm going very well, but I find a wooden device with a shelf underneath that's big enough for me to squeeze inside. "I am astounded I let you live this long," I hear him say as he searches for me.

My pulse echoes in my head, so I know he hears it. My heart is a homing beacon.

"Earth must be softening me," he says, his voice moving in my direction. He's going to find me, and I've trapped myself. I need a better hiding place. I used to be so much better at this game.

I crawl out and dart for cover again behind a rack of whips.

"I should have finished you off last night," he says, and I can't tell anymore if he's talking to me or to himself. "I am even more certain now that killing you will break this spell."

What makes him *more certain now,* I wonder? Did he see the black smoke, too? I flatten myself against a narrow bed that's been bolted to a large, spinning wheel.

His silence is more terrifying than his words, so I taunt, "You couldn't even kill a baby blue bear—"

The shadow beast appears in front of me, and I know at once he could have ended me at any point tonight, or the past five nights.

But Sebastián prefers to play with his food . . . Until the food plays back.

"You should not have said that." He doesn't seem angry or bloodthirsty. He looks *hurt.*

His eyes lock on my throat, and I raise my hands to cover it.

"Why didn't you finish the job last night?" I ask him. "Why all the candles?"

"I wanted to make it special for you," he says, but it's clear this has nothing to do with me. It's about his own pleasure.

I'm backed against the upright bed and have nowhere to go. I can't side-step Sebastián the way I did Felipe when we first met, nor can I outrun or outthink him. My fingers stay locked on my throat, like they can protect me from his fangs.

"If it is any consolation to you," he says, his icy hands closing around both of mine, "it was always going to end this way."

He pushes down on my arms, ever so slowly. "You had to know that once I had a taste"—I gasp as he tears open the turtleneck of my sweater, exposing my skin down to the tops of my breasts—"I would want more."

There's nothing I can do to protect myself. We both know he's in complete control.

Goose bumps ripple across my body as his mouth hovers over mine, no breath blowing from his lips. There's something so alluring about his starry gaze, his hypnotic voice, his fatal fangs that promise escape from pain and eternal sleep. All of these things must be part of his power because I almost want to feel his bite again.

Except . . . he isn't striking.

And his daggers missed me. If the shadow beast wanted me dead, I'd be dead. This is something else . . . He's *manipulating* me.

Sebastián is trying to seduce some kind of confession, which means he still overestimates me—but maybe I can use that to my advantage.

"Or this could all be part of a test," I say, infusing my voice with as much confidence as I can, and the shadow beast's brow wings up in surprise.

"What sort of test?" he asks, and I hear the suspicion surfacing in his tone.

"I mean that you are in a cursed castle," I say, "and if fairy tales have taught me anything, it's that curses happen to bad princes who misbehave and must be taught a lesson."

I'm being facetious, but something about what I said hits a mark because he frowns with too much interest in my words. "If we are both in a cursed castle, what are you being punished for?" he asks.

For a moment I forget how to breathe.

"My dad is—*was*—a detective. A good one. I learned from him how to investigate, and I'm here to figure out what happened to my parents on the subway. If it's a spell, like you say, maybe we can work together. Under one condition."

"*You* are setting the terms—?"

"You don't touch me again without my consent." I say it in a rush, unsure I'll be able to get the words out. "Deal?"

"No deal," he growls, and I get the sense he's not used to taking orders.

"So you won't work with me, and you won't kill me," I say. "What do you want from me then?"

"The truth."

"I wish I had that!" I snap. "I have no idea why you're here, or why my parents died, or if my aunt is really the one responsible—"

"None of that is what I want to know from you," he says, cutting me off before I spiral. "The biggest mystery about the subway is not how everyone died. It is how you survived."

I have no idea what to say to that.

"You . . . think I have magical powers?" I ask blankly.

"Not exactly." He looks like he's evaluating something in my expression as he speaks. "Have you considered the possibility the black fire could have been a protective spell performed on you when you were young?"

His question blows my mind. As I consider his theory that the smoke is *protecting* me, I realize it tracks: I saw it on the subway, and again last night, when Sebastián bit me.

"But why didn't I see it now when you threw the daggers?"

He nods like he's already contemplated this. "I believe it means intent matters. Only true life-or-death danger triggers the spell's protection."

It takes me nearly a minute to pick up on what he's saying. "You mean you didn't *intend* to kill me tonight?"

Sebastián moves toward me again, only this time he bends down so he can look straight into my eyes. His gaze is pure steel.

"If I had intended to kill you, Estela, you would be dead."

I force myself not to shrink from his intensity. "Then why aren't I?"

I don't mean for the question to sound so dramatic, but I feel it on many levels. *Why aren't I dead?*

After a prolonged silence, he says, "I was certain I would kill you tonight."

Shivers race down both my arms. My knees bend as I wonder if there's a point in attempting to outrun him—

"And yet, here you remain," he goes on. "I have no explanation for my choices. Nor can I guarantee they will not change in the future."

Here I remain.

Even a starving vampire with no other source of sustenance can't kill me. Maybe he's right that the black smoke is protecting me because how else can this be explained?

Sebastián believes the spell gets activated if I'm in true danger. It was also danger that prompted me to speak for the first time in months a few nights ago. I thought the impulse was a sign I wanted to live . . . but maybe I was just acting on instinct.

I try reverse-engineering Sebastián's logic: If the black smoke only shows up in case of an actual threat, can it reveal whether a threat is legitimate? Does its presence expose a person's true intentions?

The only thing tethering me to life right now is my desire to know the truth about the Subway 25 and my parents' and my past in Oscuro. But what's left for me on Earth after these mysteries are solved?

Felipe said it himself: a lifetime in this castle with my awful aunt. So what am I even holding on to? Who cares if I stay or go? I don't have parents anymore.

The tears race each other down as I see Mom's right dimple and Dad's bushy brows. It's amazing how fast the world ends: one instant your parents are alive, the next they're dead.

I'm nothing more than a ghost with unfinished business.

Like Sebastián, I might as well do whatever it takes to get answers. Otherwise, what's the point?

"I'm tired," I say, walking away from him as calmly as I can.

But my heart echoes through my body as I pass the crate of daggers, betraying me.

BOOM. BOOM. BOOM.

I know Sebastián hears the beating. I have no idea how my body will react once the blade is in my hand, if I'll be able to go through with it . . . But it's now or never.

So before the shadow beast can figure out what I'm doing, I yank out a hilt—

And drive the dagger into my heart.

CHAPTER 12

PRESSURE BUILDS IN MY CHEST, and I can't feel the blade or see Sebastián or hear what's happening. Just like on the subway, the darkness around me is opaque and all-consuming.

But is it black smoke? Or have I blacked out?

A young girl is giggling and counting off in Spanish. "*Uno, dos, tres, cuatro, cinco, seis, siete—*"

I can't see her, but I know she's me, back when I lived in this castle.

Young me is playing hide-and-seek. My parents said it was my favorite game as a child. Win or lose, that was never the point; I cared about the challenge. Dad used to make fun of how upset I'd get whenever he or Mom didn't choose a difficult enough hiding spot.

I roll my head into a muscled chest, and I know it's Sebastián when I inhale a snowy night. His scent fills my lungs with breath, and I cough out the bad air.

As the fumes fade, the dungeon blinks back into focus. The shadow beast is so close, I can see every smooth pane of his face.

The pressure in my chest is still there, and I look down. Sebastián's hand is between the blade and my breast. The dagger's point hasn't even broken his skin.

"Why did you do that?" His voice is thinner than I've heard it.

My heart rattles the walls of its cage. "You said intention mattered."

"*So you want to die?*"

I flinch from both the words and the force of their delivery. He steps away from me, and even though he produces no body heat, I feel colder without his touch.

Neither of us says anything for a few breaths.

"What do you want, Estela?"

When he says my name, a small bud inside me flowers.

"I want the same thing you want from me," I say. "The truth."

I cross my arms, hugging myself to cover my exposed bra from when he ripped my turtleneck—and also because I need it after what just happened.

I can't slow down to think about what I did, or I'll break.

Tears burn in the corners of my eyes.

"What do you want to know?" he asks at last.

I force back the wave of emotion threatening to overtake me and start with what I hope is an easy question: "Where do you go in the daytime?"

He doesn't immediately answer. "I do not know."

"I can't with you!" I say, throwing my arms in the air.

"I am telling you the truth," he says, as I cross my arms again to cover myself. "I do not know where I go when the sun comes up." His voice is heavy with gravity, like he's confessing to criminal behavior. "I only come to at nightfall."

I think of the vampire myth, how they sleep in coffins during the day, and I wonder if there's a grain of truth there. "So you appear in the castle at night and disappear at sunrise?"

"Yes."

"Why didn't you tell me that before?" I ask, and when he doesn't answer, I do it for him: "You don't trust me, do you?"

He doesn't deny it.

"I cannot trust anything about this castle until I know why I am here and who is behind this enchantment," he says. "For all we know, we are being watched."

"What?" I blurt. "*Who*—?"

"I do not want to frighten you any more than you already are, not when you are so near to giving up."

His description of me hits hard.

Is that how he sees me? Is that why he doesn't want to be partners with me in this investigation—he's worried I can't handle it?

"I can stomach whatever monsters are lurking in the dark," I tell him. "It's *you* I want to know about. Tell me *something* about yourself."

"You still fear I am a creation of your mind?"

"Even an imaginary partner would be better than no partner."

I don't break our stare, and I know this is it. The moment that determines everything between us. Whatever he says next will decide if I can trust him.

"I do not recall the exact instant I woke up here."

It takes me a second to realize he's spoken. The shadow beast's voice sounds so far away, it's almost small.

"It felt like my existence was coming in and out . . . *flickering,* how you described the lights."

I sit down on an edge of a wooden beam while he speaks.

"Once I managed to get a firm grip on this dimension, I knew something was off. Yet I could not figure it out; it was as if I could not access my full range of thoughts. Then I caught the scent of human blood."

Sebastián's gaze drifts from mine, enough that he's not looking me in the eye. "I did not have to think to make that kill. I acted on pure instinct. I yanked her head back by the hair and ripped into her throat, crushing her windpipe in one quick bite—or I should have."

"What happened?" I whisper, breathless.

"She went right through me. I thought she must be a ghost. Until I realized she had not reacted to my presence at all. She was glued to the news being broadcast of an attack on a train with a sole survivor, a teen girl. *I* was the ghost."

"And I was the teen girl."

He nods in assent. "I remember humans coming to the door every evening to drop off food, each new visit a fresh torture because none of them entered the house. I could not even attempt to taste them. Even more infuriating, they could not see me when I would get near the doorway."

Then it's true that only *I* can see him. Just like the black smoke. What does that mean?

"After listening to the news and reading through every book here, I learned that I found myself on a planet *Earth,* in a dimension that deems itself *reality,* where there is no such thing as magic. Or *monsters.*"

"Where are you from?" I chance, even though every time I've asked he's refused to answer.

"I do not know."

My gut hardens with distrust. "Sebastián—"

"My first memories are of this castle. I cannot remember anything before I appeared here. I know my past is within me, behind a spelled lock; I simply lack the key."

I don't know what to think. He claims to know nothing, not about his past, nor where he goes in the daytime. Either he's admitting the truth, or he's clinging to his secrets.

Or he and Beatríz are playing me.

"What about the memory of the blue bear?" I ask it in a whisper, but he snaps his gaze to me so fast that I know I struck a nerve.

"There are flickers of moments," he says after a beat. "I have had flashes of another place, a world more savage than this one. I believe my memories are still within me, simply repressed by the spell. Yet I cannot trust anything, not even myself, because I cannot remember."

He almost sounds tired. "If even I am not trustworthy, how can I trust anyone else?" he asks.

The question pierces my heart, encapsulating everything I'm feeling. I thought the shadow beast impenetrable and wholly unrelatable—but it turns out he's the only being in the worlds who understands me.

"Then am I alive because of the protective spell, or because you want me around?" I ask.

Something like warmth softens his gaze, and he says, "You are alive because I hope to stave off madness."

His silver gaze dips to my cheek, and I know he's looking at my dimple. The warmth spreads to the rest of his expression, shifting the atmosphere between us. I flash to the way I felt when I saw him laugh, and I think this is the first time he's made me smile.

It's more likely he wants to stave off starvation, says the small, argumentative voice in my mind. It's true that as long as I'm around, Sebastián has a blood source.

"I . . ." His voice drops out, and he closes his mouth, still staring at me in that softer way, a slight glaze in his eyes. As if he's been hit in the head and left dazed. He seems unsure what he wants to say.

"I accept your offer of partnership," he says at last, and I bite my lip to keep from gasping.

"And I vow not to touch you again without your consent."

I check Beatríz's room as soon as I wake up, but I don't see any signs that she's back.

Felipe's family's food cart stands empty in the kitchen. I open the fridge to find that everything has been stowed inside in a wall of colorful plastic containers that vary in shape and size. It reminds me of Tetris.

Seeing this gesture of Sebastián's makes me feel more taken care of than anything my aunt has done until this point. If I couldn't get the shadow beast out of my head before, he now consumes my every brain cell.

Even though I now believe him to be real, he still feels like mine. Especially since I first saw him in my dreams, and I'm the only person who can perceive him—plus, he's trapped in this castle with me.

I've never had a boyfriend or a best friend or even a *pet,* and I wonder if this sense of emotional possession is part of what makes someone feel *yours*.

We're just partners on the same case, the small voice reminds me, and my mind flits to Dad's dozen axioms. *Raul's Rule #8: Whatever you do,* never *make a case personal.*

As I pluck my last clean sweatshirt, I note that I'm going to need to do laundry soon. The top feels a little loose on me, and I realize it's the one Nurse Leticia gave me to use the last time I visited FBI Headquarters. At the thought of her, I feel the dagger's hilt in my grip as I drove it into my chest—

I squeeze my eyes shut, as if that will blind me to the memory. Lety would be horrified by what I did.

I'm horrified.

Last night, it didn't feel real. I was so sure that Sebastián would save me. But in the light of day, I'm terrified of myself, what I did, what I might be capable of.

I don't want to be alone right now. What I really need is a friend.

Even though I saw a side of Felipe I didn't like, he's still my friend. My experience with the concept may only come from books and television, but I know that friendship means accepting a person as they are, flaws and all.

When I get to the bookstore, Felipe looks beyond relieved to see me. Purple bags betray his lack of sleep, and I'm overcome with guilt.

"Here's your cart back," I say before he can speak, wheeling it forward to him.

"Are you okay?" he asks, his eyes bouncing across my face like an anxious parent's.

"Of course!" I say, waving off his worry. "The banging was a wind tunnel effect that sometimes happens at night. I think it's why people assume the place is haunted." I pluck the excuse from a winter we spent in Hanover, New

Hampshire, where the wind howled so much that it would slam shut all the doors.

"But there wasn't any wind—"

"Please thank your parents for everything," I press on. "I had a really nice time . . . for the most part."

He cringes with guilt, and I know the subject change worked. "Sorry again for what I said about you not having anywhere else to go."

"Don't say it again, and we're fine," I say, even though there's more to it than that. Felipe may not have outright expressed his feelings for me, but his reaction last night to the possibility of my leaving makes me worry they've become more than friendly.

We head to the back of the store and climb the ladder to the attic. "What would you like to read about today?" he asks.

"I'm curious about la Sombra's history with supernatural creatures . . . like, have there ever been any *vampires*?"

"Oh—I have the *perfect* book!" Felipe's voice quivers with the same excitement every bibliophile gets when they're asked to recommend the right read at the right time, and I'm glad he doesn't pry into my choice of subject.

We settle on the stools, and he sets a large white tome on the high table. "This book's author was a Brálaga. They catalogued la Sombra's brushes with the supernatural over the centuries and gathered information to create this almanac of magical creatures and potions."

Felipe opens it to the index, then he flips to a page near the end with the heading *Vampiros*.

"*Vampires come from another realm,*" he translates, and I recall that Sebastián referred to the subway as an *interdimensional* attack. "*They're made of dark energy . . . and they survive by sucking the life force of other creatures.* In other words, *blood.*"

"If they're in this book, does that mean vampires have been in la Sombra before?" I ask.

"Not necessarily. It could also be that another being familiar with vampires provided this information. The author doesn't cite their sources, and this book was published in the early 1900s, so we can't know."

"Does it say anything about how a vampire would cross over, if they could?" I press.

Felipe frowns, and I know I need to back off, or he's going to start asking questions. He skims the text for a few seconds, then he says, "According to this, the only way a vampire could enter our reality is by making a pact with a witch."

I feel my face paling. This is all fitting a little too neatly with the narrative Sebastián has fed me. And yet the word *pact* implies he would be in on the spell.

Is that the real reason he won't tell me anything about himself? Are he and Beatríz working together?

"Okay, you're worrying me," says Felipe, studying my expression. "You've gone from *skeptic*"—he emphasizes the word, like he's proud to use it correctly—"to believer in no time."

"I'm not a believer *yet*. You'll have to keep reading to fascinate me."

He reviews the text again. "It says here . . . a vampire can't manifest at full power in our realm. They will be limited by the spell that brings them here."

I have to blink a few times. "*Full power?* What does that mean?"

He shrugs. "It doesn't go into detail."

I pull the book closer. "Show me."

He leans in, and I feel his breath on my shoulder as he points to the last line on the page. I wait for him to translate, but he doesn't say anything.

I read to myself: *Si un vampiro cruza a la realidad de la Tierra, será limitado por la magia de sangre que lo transportó.* When I look up at Felipe, he's nodding at me encouragingly, so I sigh and try to work it out for myself.

When I was younger, I struggled to read. If I stumbled on a hard word, Dad would cover it up with a ruler, revealing just one syllable at a time, until I managed to pronounce the whole thing. It was one of the first things he taught me: when a problem feels too big, break it down into its smallest possible parts.

So I focus on the first half of the sentence and start with the words I recognize: *Vampiro* is vampire; *realidad* is reality, *Tierra* is Earth. From the context, I gather *cruza* must mean cross, and I say, "*If a vampire crosses into Earth's reality . . . ?*"

By Felipe's face-splitting grin, I know I'm on the right path.

The second part of the sentence reads: *será limitado por la magia de sangre que lo transportó.* I think *limitado* must mean limited, *magia* is magic, and *sangre* is . . . *blood.*

I stare at the Spanish term for *blood magic* for so long that I don't react until I hear Felipe's voice: "*If a vampire crosses into Earth's reality, they will be bound by the blood magic that transported them.*"

I turn the page for more, but there's a new heading: *Venenos.*

"Venoms," Felipe translates.

That's it for the vampire section. I shut the book in frustration. *Bound by blood magic.* If Beatríz is behind the spell, it follows that Sebastián would be anchored to the castle.

I inhale sharply as Felipe's finger brushes a stray curl away from my face. "Your hair was by your eye," he says, dropping his hand quickly.

I snap to my feet. "*Why,* though?" I ask, pacing the attic, looking everywhere but at Felipe. "Why does a Brálaga have to live at la Sombra? Why hasn't anyone sold the castle yet?"

I wait for him to speak and provide an answer, or at least point to a new book, but he stays quiet. So I meet his gaze.

Only he's not watching me. He's staring at the closed white book on the table.

"What is it?" I ask.

Felipe stands, too. "You're looking for facts when all this town has are stories."

"Okay, then," I say, crossing my arms. "Tell me a story."

He turns to the bookshelf, and I wait for him to pick a text. "We don't have religion here. We have la Sombra." He surveys the spines as he speaks. "The Oscurianos, those of us who choose to stay, we believe we are here for a purpose. But you won't find that purpose in any of these books. It's old knowledge, the kind that gets passed down not in ink, but blood."

He seems different as he says this. Older. "It's not just the Brálaga line that remains unbroken," he goes on. "I showed you the property records. Every bloodline is loyal to this town. To la Sombra."

"But *why*?" I insist.

"Some of us believe . . . *I* believe . . . the original Brálaga hailed from another realm," he says, picking up on what he was telling me in his room. "We call it Otro. *Other.* We think by opening a gateway, he's made us vulnerable to that dimension, and he had to seal the opening with blood magic. As long as Oscuro's founders' bloodlines remain planted in this soil, the gateway to Otro stays sealed."

"What happens if it opens?"

The light in Felipe's eyes dulls. "La Sombra would swallow our world."

CHAPTER 13

THE SUN SETS EARLIER AS winter nears, so it's night out when I get back to the castle. My heart thunders the whole way because I'm about to see Sebastián.

I left the bookstore a little before closing so Felipe wouldn't try walking me home. The emotions that surfaced when we argued in his room won't sink back down, and a new energy has wedged itself between us that feels prickly against my skin.

More and more, I feel like in coming to Oscuro, I've stepped onto a game board without knowing I am one of the pieces. This town runs on an ancient superstition about my bloodline, and those who stay are the ones who believe it to be true.

I head straight to the kitchen to check for signs that Beatríz is back, and I see movement by the dining hall.

"Beatríz?" I call out.

"No," says Sebastián as I approach, and I have to blink a few times to be sure of what I'm seeing.

The wooden table is weighted down with a feast of godly proportions, and the shadow beast is standing behind a chair. He slides it out for me, and I'm beyond speechless—I'm stunned.

"As your aunt is not here to do it, I thought I would present your dinner."

It's the melody of his voice that motivates my legs to move, and I somehow make it to the chair. Before me is a sprawling three-dimensional mural of food that extends the full table, featuring everything I brought back from Felipe's.

Everything.

It takes me a moment to assess my options because Sebastián has created what could be an exhibit at a culinary art museum. An eclectic forest of knotted, bread-trunked trees with crowns of spaghetti, gnocchi, and angel hair is planted in a field of paella, beneath an elaborate full moon. By the trees is a residential area with rows of houses built with walls of manchego and topped with slanted roofs of jamón ibérico. There's even a recreation of la Sombra, but I can't see what Sebastián used for its construction because the whole thing is coated with coffee grounds to make it look black, adorned with streaks of red that's either ketchup or hot sauce.

"See anything you like?" he asks.

I bite down to keep my mouth from betraying me.

"Is something wrong?"

I shake my head and attempt to serve myself *anything* from this table. What looks easiest to pluck is a hard-boiled egg that's part of a spiral design replicating the full moon.

"Um, how did you cook these?" I ask, the egg cold and light in my hand.

"*Cook?*" he echoes.

Now the laughter bursts out of me, and I can't hold back. When I see the befuddlement on his face, my cackles intensify, and I realize how funny I must have seemed to him the night I told him he was a hallucination. "I'm sorry," I say between breaths. "This is the sweetest thing, but it's . . . it's not . . . *edible.*"

"What do you mean? This is all human food."

"Eggs have to be boiled, bread has to be sliced, hot sauce doesn't go on coffee grounds—" I notice a wineglass by me that's filled with a dark red drink. "What is *that*?"

"Tomato juice."

I bring it close to my nose and sniff. *Gazpacho.*

"Cheers!" I say, and take a big swig. Sebastián slides into Beatríz's seat across from me, his face fallen with disappointment.

"I guess you don't know *everything*," I gloat, still smirking.

This appears to be the wrong thing to say because his frown lines only deepen. "I should have watched more carefully, but I lost interest when the human went into the kitchen."

"*Beatríz,*" I say. "On Earth, humans use names to make it easier to communicate."

He keeps his gaze lowered like he's ashamed, and I feel bad, so I say, "Thank you for doing this."

"You are malnourished," he says gruffly. "Is *any* of this edible?"

I pick up a ham and cheese house-wich. I collapse the construction, flattening the jamón ibérico against the manchego, and I take a bite. The sharpness of the cheese is tempered by the smokiness of the ham, and I finish the breadless bocadito in two bites.

"Have you learned anything from your source today?" he asks after I've eaten a second house-wich.

I don't want to admit I spent the day investigating *him,* so I say, "I learned the townspeople believe this castle hides a gateway to another realm they call Otro, and that's why they stay in Oscuro through the generations. They believe as long as the bloodlines remain, the gate stays closed."

I still don't know what to believe, but I keep my tone neutral and study Sebastián for a reaction. "Where is it?" he asks me. "How does it open?"

His hunger for the information throws me off. "I don't know. If it's real, wouldn't you have traveled through it to get here?"

He frowns. "I already told you I do not remember. After our last conversation, you still refuse to believe me?"

"It's not that," I say cautiously, unsure how he's going to take my next question. "But has it occurred to you that since you're missing your memories, it's possible you made a deal with the so-called bruja that brought you here? Like a *pact?*"

"I have considered it, and it is possible," he says. "I still want to know for certain."

I nod in agreement. "Good. There's something else—my source believes Brálagas can perform magic on the full moon. Which is *tomorrow*. If Beatríz is really a bruja, she could have taken off to gather ingredients for a spell."

He frowns, plunging deep into thought. "Strange. I have seen no signs of magic from her. What about the castle lights?" he asks, focusing back on me. "Have they not flickered again?"

"Not since you took those pills from me. Maybe if you give them back, we could find more answers."

"The pills given to you by the one you believe to be responsible for our situation?"

We stare at each other, neither one willing to give ground. I definitely get the sense he's not being fully transparent, but then again, neither am I. There can never be full trust between us. Does that mean we can't work together?

He reaches across the table and crushes a house-wich for me in his hand. Then he sets it down on my plate, like he expects me to eat it.

"You need your strength," he says, making me feel eight years old.

My gaze drops to his lips. His sharp fangs are hidden, but I can almost feel them piercing my skin. His bite was the furthest thing from a kiss, and yet I can't quit fantasizing about the rush of pain and pleasure.

It's probably just because no one has touched me in so long.

Yet when Felipe got close, I shirked at his touch, says the small, devil's advocate impulse in my mind.

What if Sebastián is right about me not caring if I live or die? What if it's not him that I crave but the death he offers?

His gaze flicks to my neck, and my pulse canters—which probably only makes my blood more tempting to him. "You went to such an effort for me tonight," I say, "but you have nothing for yourself."

I tug down on the necktie I looped around my neck so Felipe wouldn't see the fading puncture marks. "You can drink from me if you want."

Lightning flashes in Sebastián's eyes, and he looks as primal and lethal as the first night we met. There's a sharpening of his expression, the way a predator looks when it's cornered its prey, and I think he's pleased.

One, two, three, four, five, six, seven . . .

I count off my heartbeats as I wait for his answer, trying not to think of what it says about me that I want him to accept. My need to feel his touch outweighs my instinct for self-preservation.

I'm at beat twenty-eight when he says, "As I have failed you tonight, it would not be fair for me to feed."

He looks down at the table, his voice slightly strained. "And you need more time to recover from my last bite."

I don't know why the rejection stings. I should be grateful he isn't trying to kill me, but instead I'm hurt the shadow beast won't use me to sate his thirst. *I just gave him consent to drink my blood, and he's turning me down?*

"I'm not hungry," I say, pushing away from the plate with the untouched house-wich. "I'm going to bed."

But as soon as I stand up, Sebastián is there, like a gentleman pulling out a chair for a lady. Only he's blocking my exit.

"What is wrong?" he asks.

"Nothing." I shove the chair back and try to sidestep him, but he's in my way again. There's a foot of air between us, and I inhale night-blooming jasmine.

"Have I offended you?" he asks in a murmur.

"You've tried to kill me every night, and now you're worried you've *offended* me? Make up your mind!" I'm aware my tone is flirting with hysteria.

"If I drink from you, it upsets you, and if I refuse to drink, it also upsets you." He sounds like he's losing his patience, too. "How about *you* make up your mind?"

"I swear, if Felipe hadn't heard you banging against the door of the castle yesterday, I would still be questioning my sanity!"

"Believe me, I have questioned my own sanity plenty of times since meeting you!" As the frustration builds in him, he seems almost human. "I have no idea why I am trying to feed you, or why I am bothering to keep you alive, especially when you do not even care to live—"

I cut him off by shoving my tongue down his throat.

I feel feral and out of control, like I'm trying to inflict pain and not pleasure with my kiss. Yet as soon as his tongue touches mine, I'm transported.

Sebastián's mouth is an explosion of flavors. Black cherries, dark chocolate, roasted coffee—

He pulls away. "Estela—"

But I can't let him go. That felt so good, and I've been alone for so long, that I throw myself against him, drawing his tongue into another dance.

This time I'm the predator, and I don't care. I just want more of how he makes me feel. *Alive.*

When he pulls away again, he puts at least ten feet of space between us. "You are right," he says, the silver of his eyes as bright as moonlit oceans. "You should go to bed."

"Wait—"

"Good night."

Sebastián infests my dreams.

I've had nightmares of him before, hunting me, chasing me, biting me. But this was different. Last night, *I* was the predator.

I kept showing up from the shadows and cornering the shadow beast, no matter where in the castle he sought refuge. It was like we'd traded roles, and I physically overpowered him.

Each time I brought my lips to his, he would warn me that this was a bad idea. But I would drown his words with my tongue until he gave in—then I'd wake up, appalled. Over and over and over again.

I get out of bed.

It's brighter out than usual, so I must have slept in, but I'm not rested. Sebastián's presence feels more pronounced after those dreams, like he's infected my bloodstream.

I check Beatríz's room first thing, as is my new routine, but it's still untouched. The full moon is tonight, and she's not back.

What if she's never returning? asks the small voice in my mind. What if she lured me here to take her place at la Sombra, so she could finally be free?

There must be clues somewhere, something to tell me what she's really up to. I've gone through her things a few times already, but I haven't done an in-depth search of her actual space.

In her nightstand is a ring of keys, probably all duplicates, including an alarm key I've seen her use to lock up the clínica. I pocket it. I open every single drawer and box I see, but I don't find a passport or checkbook or cash.

Either it's all well-hidden, or she's taken everything important with her.

I knock on the floor and walls, but I don't sense a secret compartment like the one in the purple room with my photos and death certificate. I do a thorough inspection of the bathroom and come up empty. That just leaves the closet.

In size and organization, it could be a boutique clothing shop, with extra sections for shoes, handbags, and luggage. The racks and shelves are packed with fashions for both men and women, including ruffly and frilly dresses, ancient-looking frocks made of fur and wool, and accessories like hats and canes. It seems like this closet has been accruing articles of clothing over the generations.

I search everywhere for a false wall, or a hidden hatch, or somewhere to stow secrets, but I find nothing. I'm about to leave when a piece of luggage catches my eye. It's a rolling suitcase, and it's made of denim, just like the matching set Mom, Dad, and I shared. Only this one is a darker wash, and someone has written with marker all over it.

I pull it out from its place in the suitcase lineup, and I try to read what's been written on it. *Propiedad de Olivia Brálaga.*

This was Mom's.

I set it flat on the floor and unzip it. The breath that's released is a ghost of

Mom's scent, and for a moment I feel her *here*. I close my eyes to hold on to her presence for longer, then I open them again and look at her things.

It's mostly clothing. Sweaters, shirts, pants, socks, underwear, even a white dress for some reason. Some things look like they might fit me, others could be a little big—but I'm keeping it all. Before wheeling the bag back to my room, I feel around for anything harder than fabric, and I touch a flat, semi-hard surface.

A book.

I pull out a journal with a brown leather cover that looks old and weathered. Dad used to love this kind of journal for taking notes because of its sturdiness. I wonder if this one was his. I open it eagerly, but the pages are blank and unlined.

I drop off the suitcase in my room, then I pull on my coat and sling my empty denim duffel over my chest on the way out.

The village is quiet as usual as I approach the clínica. Beatríz's note is still pinned to the door. I try inserting a few keys until I find the right one, and the handle clicks. I hurry to press the alarm key to the sensor so it doesn't go off, but there's no beep or flash of light. Like it wasn't armed.

"Beatríz?" I call out. Did she forget to set it, or did somebody turn it off?

One of the patient beds is unmade. I poke my head in my aunt's office, but it's empty.

I enter the back storage area and open the freezer. It was brimming with what must have been a few hundred blood bags the last time Beatríz showed it to me. Now it looks like there are barely one hundred left.

I grab ten plastic pouches and drop them into my duffel. I can't show up to the bookstore loaded with blood bags, so I head to the castle first to drop them off. But as I'm cutting across the plaza, I see movement.

I'm not alone.

Felipe's great-grandmother Gloria is feeding the birds. She's talking to them, and hearing her gravelly voice, I remember how Felipe's parents seemed worried about what she might say in my presence.

Gloria is whistling to a dove as I approach, and I watch as it lands on her wrist and eats the birdseed from her palm. "Hola, angelito."

I think she's speaking to the bird, until she looks up at me, and I realize she's greeting *me* as little angel. That's what she called me at Felipe's house, too.

"Hola," I say, hating how round the *o* sounds in my voice.

She gestures for me to sit, and I perch on the lip of the fountain. "Qué lindo volver a verte," she says. *How nice to see you again.*

Since I lack the vocabulary to communicate everything I want in Spanish, I weigh my words carefully. "¿Usted me conocía de bebé?" I ask if she knew me as a baby.

"Claro," she says genially. "En este pueblito, todos nos conocemos." *In this town, we all know each other.*

Raul's Rule #7 is *Consult the experts,* which is what I thought I was doing with my research at the bookstore. Yet it strikes me now that Gloria is an expert as well. She's an Oscurian time capsule.

"¿Por qué mis padres se fueron?" I lack the fluency to finesse my inquiry, so I ask her point-blank why my parents left Oscuro.

"Ay, tus padres," she says with a pitying sigh, obviously thinking of their passing. Her face pulls together, tears welling in her eyes, and she grabs my arm, her long nails digging in like claws. "Pobrecitos."

"It's okay," I say, wishing she would let go.

"Pobrecita tú," she goes on, shifting her pity from my parents to me. "Condenada a la oscuridad."

Did she just say I'm *doomed to darkness*? I ask for clarification: "¿Qué quiere decir—?"

Her bony hand pulls me in so close that I can see every wrinkle of her face, and I flash to the sand dunes of Arizona. "Por siempre serás nuestro angelito sobreviviente." *You'll always be our surviving little angel.*

"Pero antes que eso," I insist, urging her to think back before the subway, to when my parents and I lived here. "¿Qué pasó aquí?" *What happened here?*

She blinks her glassy eyes, looking lost, like a computer hard drive crashing. I wait for what feels like a few minutes for her brain to reboot, but she just keeps holding on to me in silence.

"Bueno," I say, wresting my shoulder free. "Adiós—"

"Parecía que todo el castillo estaba envuelto en llamas," she says softly, looking up at la Sombra.

I don't know what that means. Something about the castle and *llamas*?

"No entiendo," I say, frustrated.

Actual tears are dripping from Gloria's eyes, and I'm not sure what to do. I shouldn't have bothered her with this. "¿Está bien?" I ask, checking if she's okay.

She stares up at the sky above the castle. "El fuego era negro."

The fire was black.

"Creí que el castillo se derretía." *I thought the castle was melting.*

It's only when I swallow that I realize my mouth is hanging open. My throat is dry as I ask, "¿El fuego estaba *afuera?*" *The fire was outside?*

She nods, eyes wide, like she's seeing it now. How could the flames have reached the outer walls of the castle when the purple room is in the basement and nothing else was scorched? It doesn't make sense.

"Y luego—" Gloria snaps her fingers, jolting me back to attention—"se apagó. Así, sin más. Y el castillo quedó intacto. Ni una marca." *The fire went out and the castle was intact* is all I get from that.

"Esa misma noche, tus padres desaparecieron." *Your parents disappeared that night.*

"¿Qué pasó después?" *What happened next?*

"Tus abuelos no duraron mucho más en este mundo. Imagínate cómo sufrieron. Fue un golpe muy fuerte para ellos." She's talking faster now, making it harder for me to follow. *My grandparents suffered and weren't long for this world—?*

"Tu tía Beatríz nunca fue la misma. Decidió seguir la carrera de medicina y se dedicó a sus estudios." *Beatríz was never the same and became a doctor.*

"Espera," I say so Gloria will slow down. "Más despacio—"

"Pero el culpable fue *él.*"

I freeze when I hear that pronoun.

He.

"¿Quién?" I ask in desperation. "*Who set the fire?*"

She stares at me in silence, her eyes frosty like crystal orbs.

"Corre, angelito," she whispers. *Run, little angel.*

"El diablo aún no ha terminado contigo."

The devil isn't finished with you yet.

CHAPTER 14

WHO IS *HE*?

The question runs through my mind the whole way back to the castle.

I store the blood in the fridge, which is significantly less packed today. I salvaged what I could of the meal last night, but I had to toss out most of the food.

For once, I'm relieved it's daytime because shame still scorches my cheeks over how badly I misread the situation with Sebastián. I can't believe I attacked him the way I did.

As much as I could use the distraction of the bookstore, I'm going to skip it today, since it's the full moon and Beatríz could show up any moment. I want to confront her as soon as she returns. Besides, I can't let her find ten bags of blood in the fridge.

I have so many questions for her—about the fire, the death certificate, the mysterious *he* Gloria referenced. I thought my aunt would be back by now. Where did she run off to so suddenly? Why didn't she leave a phone number to reach her?

Because she isn't coming back.

The thought keeps nipping at the nape of my neck, like a biting breeze. Maybe Beatríz brought me here as her immediate replacement.

My brain feels like it's boiling over with questions and doubts and suspects. I need to organize my thoughts. Now that I have a proper journal—*Dad's*—I'm going to use it instead of the notepad. I make my way to my room—

BANG. BANG. BANG.

I'm starting up the stairs when someone knocks at the front door. My back stiffens—who could it be? Beatríz has keys. Unless this is someone with news about her . . .

Panicked, I race to the entrance and call across the wooden door: "Who is it?"

"Felipe!"

Relief floods my veins, and I swing it open. "Hey!" I say in surprise.

"Hi!" He holds up a wicker basket. "I brought lunch."

"Oh! Thank you," I say, reaching out for it.

"You do remember we made plans, right?"

Today is his day off! I completely forgot that I told him he could come to the castle.

My gut twists, inner compass spinning out of control with warning. My aunt could be back any moment, and I really want to confront her about the death certificate and the black fire without Felipe present. "Can we do this another day—?"

"I'm already here, and I have the food," he says, frowning and holding up the basket like an exhibit at a trial.

"Fine," I say, but my gut still refuses to let me open the door. As much as I want to break Beatríz's rules as punishment for her abandoning me, something is telling me this is a bad idea. My aunt seemed dead set against letting anyone visit la Sombra, and remembering the full moon parties, I say, "Let's picnic in the front garden."

Felipe's smile wilts into a pucker. "You mean this plant cemetery? No way. I want to go inside."

"I'm—I'm not sure it's a good idea. Beatríz told me I'm not allowed visitors."

"We made this plan *days* ago," he argues. "Why are you changing your mind?"

"It's just that—after everything we've been reading, I can't help thinking—what if there's a *real* reason Beatríz doesn't get any visitors? Aside from her charming personality?"

Felipe's expression turns into a full-faced frown. "You said I could come. Now you're going back on your word?"

"I'm just not sure—"

"Are you seriously doing this to me?" he says, for the first time sounding truly angry. "I opened up to you more than anyone else in my life—you know how much it means to me to finally see inside la Sombra! You don't even care about this town or this castle, but I thought you at least cared about me."

"I do—!"

"Then *why* would you screw with me like this?"

"I'm not—!"

He drops the basket on the cobblestones. "Here. Have your picnic alone. I'll see you at the bookstore when *you* need something. I guess that's how this friendship works."

He turns and marches down the dead garden toward the gate.

"Felipe, wait—*you can come in!*" I blurt.

He spins around and hurries back, like he's afraid the offer could expire. The bad mood has already melted off his features as he stares at me in anticipation, basket back in hand.

"So, how does this work—do you move, or do I swing you open?"

I force myself to take one step back, then another, and he rushes inside eagerly, as if la Sombra were a chocolate factory and not a cursed castle.

Felipe's neck swivels as he takes in the entrance hall from every angle, and his silent awe is so thick that it almost feels holy, and I have to break it. "Any books in there?" I ask, pointing to the basket he's carrying.

"Maybe," he says, his gaze soaring up the walls to the red glow of the candle-like lamps. He's never seemed less interested in reading. His eyes glow brighter here than even at Libroscuro, despite the fact that this castle has only a sliver of the attic's light.

"Most areas are off-limits. A lot of repair work needs to be done." I cringe at hearing myself. I sound like my aunt.

"I want to see the tower," says Felipe.

"Um . . ."

"Don't tell me you haven't been there yet?" he asks, reading my expression as easily as I read his.

"I . . . haven't." I can't believe I've spent a week here and haven't even thought of searching for the tower.

"Let's find it together!" He looks like he's approaching enlightenment.

I really hope I didn't make the wrong decision letting him in, but it felt cruel to refuse him when he's spent his whole life longing to see this place.

"Okay, fine," I say, since now that he's brought up the tower, all I want to do is find it.

"From its outer geography," he says, a wrinkle forming between his eyebrows, "we know it's on the west side of the castle."

I visualize the long corridor that leads to the mirror room with the chandelier. Now that I think of it, the ground even felt like it was ascending when I took that path.

"I know where to go!" I say, hurrying ahead at a quick clip. Since it's daytime, and we're wearing shoes, it should be easier to navigate the mirror room's minefield of a floor.

I'm eager to see if I'm right about the tower's location, but Felipe might as well be wading through water, moving slow enough to absorb every square foot of la Sombra. He stops walking altogether when we reach the grand hall with the exoskeleton ceiling. Cutting to the center of the space, he rotates to take it all in.

"There are no photographs of the inside of la Sombra," he says as he admires the crest hanging over the fireplace. "I had no idea what to expect."

"What do you think so far?"

He doesn't answer me.

As we approach the gargoyle-flanked grand staircase, Felipe looks up in awe and wordlessly starts to climb.

"Not there," I say. "Those are the bedrooms. There's only one cool space there, and I'll take you after we find the tower."

He joins me back on the ground floor, and I show him the dining hall, along with the sunny kitchen. "We can leave the basket here if you want," I offer.

"Nah, we'll find a better spot to eat," he says, looking less impressed with this room than the others. "The kitchens were probably on a lower level, originally," he says, frowning at the modern appliances. "The staff would come up to serve the meals. This must have been remodeled in the past century."

He makes a good point. The windows here aren't stained glass but clear, which is why it's so much more luminous than any other part of the castle. Not to mention the tiled walls and stainless-steel appliances all point to recent modifications.

"There's that refrigerator you mentioned," he says, grinning.

Terror grips my gut that he's going to open it and find bags of blood, so I say, "Why don't we take a break? We can sit in the dining hall and dig into the food—"

"No, no, no, we're going to picnic in the tower," insists Felipe, and I'm relieved when he shoots out of the kitchen.

We stride past the bookshelf that's an entrance to the secret wing with the dungeon. But I'm not taking him there, nor to the purple room. No trap- or trick doors. It's bad enough that I let him into the castle.

"There are two paths," says Felipe as we approach the bifurcating corridor.

"I've been down the right wing three times, and the tower isn't there. But I haven't seen all of the left. I think that has to be it."

Felipe looks at the other passage like he longs to check out *both* wings, but he doesn't argue and follows me down the narrow path. "Whoa," he says when we arrive at the mirror room.

"We need to be careful—" I start to say, but the debris on the floor is gone. Someone must have swept it because the ground is glossy and spotless. *Sebastián?*

Felipe is still absorbing the chandelier, walking under it slowly, his chin tilted up. But the falling fixture creeps me out, and I walk a little faster, eager to try the door at the other end of the chamber.

It opens to a round stairwell with spiraling steps embedded into the wall. "It has to be the tower," I say when Felipe joins me.

We climb in silence, our breathing labored. When we reach the top, there's a small landing with a single door.

I try pulling it open, but it's heavy, so I have to use both hands. Once it swings out, I realize why—the door is as tall as the ceiling, and on its other side is a soaring bookshelf packed with texts.

The library is in the tower, I realize.

Actually, the library *is* the tower. A rolling ladder orbits the room, which is lined with floor-to-ceiling shelves brimming with books. A thick band of stained glass circles the top of the space, a buffer between the shelves and the ceiling, letting in sunrays and spotlighting the dust floating in the air.

"The ceiling is flat," says Felipe. "But the tower is pointy." He looks at me with excitement brightening his eyes. "Maybe there's a way up. I've read that castles like this one were built with secret rooms and passages."

He really has done his research.

We survey the book spines around us and pull out texts at random to see if they open trick doors, taking turns using the ladder to reach the higher levels. "What's that?" he asks me, and I come over to see where he's pointing: a solitary book is shelved face out.

No, not a book.

A *tablet*.

I reach up and try to pry it off the wood, but it's been affixed there. "It doesn't come out," I say.

"Let me try," says Felipe, and I move back while he runs his hand across the dark screen, then attempts to twist it like a door handle. But nothing happens.

"Maybe it's dead and needs to be charged," I say.

He inspects the tablet's sides. "I don't see anywhere to plug in."

I look up at the top of the wheeled ladder, to the window that wraps around the ceiling. I can't shake Felipe's notion that there could be a secret room up there. "I have an idea. When I get to the top, roll me around."

I climb to the topmost rung, so that my head and shoulders are facing the stained glass. This must be how the service staff used to reach the windows to clean them—but judging by the dust, no one has been up here in a while.

"Okay, move me!" I call down.

Felipe starts to roll the ladder slowly, and I survey the glass as I revolve round the room, looking for hinges or any kind of opening mechanism. I've nearly traveled full circle when I find it.

"Stop!" I say, and once the ladder is stationary, I reach for the latch on the side of the window. When I unhook it, I swing open the sooty stained glass and reveal an outdoor balcony.

"Come!" I wave Felipe up. "And bring the food!"

He climbs the steps with the basket, which he hands to me, and I pass it through the open window, then I hold on to the frame to pull myself up. Felipe joins me outside.

The balcony is barely big enough for the both of us, and I could probably slip between the wide gapped iron bars that enclose it. But it's got the best view I've ever seen.

The green countryside, the thicket of woods, the tiny town of Oscuro, the mountains on the horizon . . . The world looks so vast from up here, the sky so infinite—and yet, la Sombra looms larger than everything.

Somehow, it's not hard to believe this castle could be a black hole powerful enough to swallow us all.

We sit down, and Felipe sets out a row of crackers and small plastic containers. He spoons some olive tapenade on a cracker and hands it to me, then he makes one for himself. The crunchy seediness against the bitter saltiness of the spread makes for a tasty combination, and I finish it in two bites.

"Your aunt doesn't like me very much," he admits as he hands me a cracker layered with a different spread.

"What makes you say so?" I ask, curious to hear what he thinks about that.

"I used to hang around the castle a lot, hoping she would need help carrying something so that I could have an excuse to come inside. I only stopped because she called my parents and told them I was stalking her." He chuckles and crunches on a cracker.

My laugh turns into a *mmm* of appreciation as I taste a delicious whipped spread that smells like truffles.

"What do you remember about your childhood?" Felipe asks as he plucks a loaf of bread from the basket and rips off a piece. He tears the chunk in half and lathers the creamy spread onto both sides, then cracks some pepper and hands me one of the halves.

"My first memories are of snow," I say, staring at the bread's whipped white surface with its dusting of black stars. "I remember a wooden cabin and a red sled and a puffy purple jacket. When I was young, we moved through Montana and Wyoming and Colorado. I was around ten when I asked my parents if we could try a warmer climate, so I spent most of my teens in Arizona and Texas and Florida."

I take a bite of bread and think about how diametrically opposed Felipe's and my upbringings have been. He's lived in the same home his whole life and plans to remain there, forever—while I've spent my life everywhere *but* my own home. Until now.

"What were they like?" asks Felipe between bites of his own bread. "Your parents?"

My gut hardens, threatening to cut off my appetite. I don't want to talk about them . . . but if I stop, they'll be gone for good. "We used to say Mom had wings."

"*¿Alas?*" asks Felipe, miming flying with his arms.

"I don't mean it literally. It's just how Dad and I used to describe her. She was always soaring ahead of us. She'd wake up first and set the coordinates for the day."

"Were you closer to her or your dad?"

"The three of us were our own world," I say after a moment. "We were all we had. I think Mom was more of a loner at heart. She liked to venture out on her own a lot, so I probably spent more time with Dad."

My voice catches, and I clear my throat. I want to stop talking, but to speak of Mom and leave out Dad feels like too deep a betrayal.

"I wanted to be just like him," I say, the admission dislodging something in my throat, and even if I wanted to stop now, I couldn't. "Ever since I was a kid, he would let me help with his work. He taught me how to read, how to drive, how to play poker."

That's why I have to find out who killed him and Mom. Because this time, he's not here to close the case himself.

"You said you might have brought a book?" I ask, eager to change the subject. I lean over to peek inside the basket.

"Oh, right." His voice is muffled as he chews. Swallowing, he says, "After the tour."

"Then let's keep moving," I say, and we pack everything inside the basket.

Beatríz could be back any moment, and if I want to get answers from her, the first thing I do probably shouldn't be to piss her off. "You should head home soon, before my aunt gets back," I say to Felipe as we're cutting across the mirror room.

"The tour isn't over yet," he complains, and when we approach the fork to the east wing, he turns in that direction. I walk through the string of empty rooms to the windowless cathedral for the fourth time, and I wonder if Felipe will say anything about the red rug that conceals the trapdoor to the purple room . . . but he doesn't mention it.

"There's nothing more to see," I say. "I *really* think you should go before—"

"Catch me!"

Felipe breaks into a sprint, and after a moment's shock, I dart after him. "*Felipe!*"

He cuts down the crimson corridor toward the front of the castle. "Stop!" I call to him.

As he races past the dining hall, his hand digs into the basket.

"Felipe!"

He starts up the grand staircase, and when I follow him, a cracker strikes my head. He laughs, and I shout, "Are you serious?"

I dodge another cracker as I chase him up the left side that leads to the moon temple. As we're running down the hall, he grabs a handful of grapes to lob at me.

"Don't you *dare*!" I shout, but the fruits slip from his fingers, and he steps on them, sliding forward in a funny dance and falling on the basket.

I crack up so hard that I fall to the floor, too, and we're both cackling in the dim lighting. When we calm down and get up, I say, "There is a room here worth seeing before you go."

I lead him to the moon temple with the stained glass windows. As soon as we step inside, Felipe falls into a deeper, more reverent kind of silence than even the library. He approaches the wall and touches the words carved there.

"From the spell," he says to me, his eyes wide and sparkly. "*No hay luz en Oscuro.*"

I don't like the way he's looking at me, and I regret showing him this room almost instantly. "Time to go," I say, hanging by the entrance and not moving any closer.

"Do you remember anything about your childhood in Oscuro?" he asks, walking over to me, and I'm glad he's moving in the exit's direction.

"Like what?" I ask, wondering if this is what he was getting at earlier, when he asked about my childhood memories.

"Like me."

I want to work my legs, but I can't. "*What?*"

"We met," he says, standing just a couple of feet away from me. "When we were little."

"But—*what*?" I sputter. "Why didn't you mention it—?"

"My earliest memory is of this castle," he says, his voice so low that despite his proximity, I strain to hear him. "I remember running toward it, until my father caught me in his arms and carried me away. I don't know how old I was, or if the memory is even real. I just know I've been trying to get here my whole life."

He turns from me and starts pacing the room, his fingers trailing along the wall, touching the words etched there.

"I was five when I tried again. I ran from our front yard. I made it all the way up the castle's front garden. That's when I saw you."

"Did I see you?" I ask, my legs still leaden.

"You did," he says, his tone growing tender. "You came up to me, and you gave me a flower." He flashes me his crooked smirk, and I feel my own features softening to learn how far back my connection to Felipe goes.

I just hope he knows it's a *friendly* connection and nothing more.

"I managed to come to the castle a few more times," he says, approaching me. "But I only found you in the garden again once. Do you remember?"

As he asks the question, I see the flicker of an answer. Wild green grass, a rock, and a young me talking to a boy with the biggest and brightest eyes I've ever seen.

And *blood*.

I look down at my palm, and then at Felipe. He's standing before me now, grinning to see that I've made the connection. The glow of his amber eyes is warmer than ever, like it's been spiked with a new emotion.

He shows me his palm. There's no physical scar on his or mine, but I *remember*.

We sliced our skin with a stone and mixed our blood. I don't know why.

"I will never forget," he says. "I told you I wanted to live in la Sombra, and you said I had to be of your blood. So you offered to help."

I don't recall the details yet, but I know it happened.

"I knew then," he goes on, inching closer to me, "that one day we would share this castle together."

The new, uncomfortable energy between us is back.

"Felipe, we're *friends*—"

"Can't you see we're each other's best match?" The light in his eyes is becoming *too* bright, and I can barely look at him directly.

He moves in, and too late I realize I've backed myself into a wall.

"As soon as I saw you on the news," he says, speaking eagerly, with a frenetic energy, "I knew you'd come home. So I started learning English. I'd studied it at school, but for months I drilled the language into my brain, watching movies and reading books until I could speak it *perfectly*. Just so there would be no obstacles between us."

"You've known me for like a week—"

"No," he says, taking my hand. "I've been waiting for you over a dozen years."

This was what Beatríz meant about Felipe consuming too much fantasy. He's spent so much time reading fiction that he believes he's starring in his own epic romance.

"Felipe, listen to me," I say, freeing my fingers from his and looking him in the eye. "I care about you a lot, but as a friend. I don't want anything more."

"Don't say that," he urges. I try to sidestep him, but his hands hook onto my hips, and he presses me into the wall.

"Come on," he pleads, "give me one chance." Now I see the brightness in his eyes for what it's always been—not fascination, but *fanaticism*.

I shove against him, but he doesn't budge. "Stop, *please*—!"

Felipe's tongue cuts me off, forcing its way into my mouth. I can't fight him off, and when I try twisting my neck, his hands clamp around my face.

I struggle against him until spots cloud my vision, as if I'm about to pass out. I feel a strong gust of air blow from my mouth into his, but not in a way that robs me of oxygen, and all of a sudden I know what's happening—

Black smoke blankets my view.

Felipe's fingers go limp, and I scramble away from him.

I can't see a thing through the fumes, so I cling to the wall, dragging myself in the direction of the exit, until the air clears.

I look wildly around me. Felipe is exactly where I left him. He looks paused, like my parents on the subway.

"F-Felipe?" I say, my voice trembling.

He turns to me, and my heart rams my chest when I see his eyes.

They're made of black smoke.

His whole frame begins to shake, and his mouth falls open. I cover my face with my hands to keep from screaming.

"Estela," says Felipe, speaking in a deadened tone unlike his lively voice. "If you want answers, come to the woods at midnight."

CHAPTER 15

MY FINGERS ARE PRUNES BY the time I stop shivering.

I've been soaking in a hot bath since Felipe left. I barely managed to drag myself up the stairs and into the tub from how violently I was trembling.

That wasn't Felipe telling me to meet him in the forest—it was the *black smoke*.

It seemed to possess him, and after delivering its message, Felipe's eyes went back to their usual amber. Then he booked it out of here as quickly as the driver who first dropped me off at la Sombra's gate.

It *was* Felipe, though, and not the black smoke, who kissed me against my will.

I thought he and I were friends with adjacent obsessions, but it turns out he wanted something from me this whole time. He's been trying to seduce me because he thinks I'm his path to becoming a Brálaga. I was so desperate for a friend, I overlooked the red flags—his fixation on the castle, Beatríz's warning, my own gut instinct.

Still, I really thought Felipe and I were friends. I can't believe he would forcefully kiss me like that . . .

Then again, didn't I just do the same thing to Sebastián?

I guess you don't need to be a monster to do monstrous things.

I open Mom's denim suitcase because I'm officially out of clean clothing. I pull on a pair of charcoal leggings and a knitted gray sweater that's not my style, but it makes me feel warm and cozy and like my parents are close.

Nightfall is an hour or two away, and since I don't want Sebastián to remind me I'm malnourished, I head to the kitchen for dinner. As I'm climbing down the stairs, I see the grapes and crackers on the center landing, and I remember Felipe's basket.

I dart up the other leg of stairs, and I don't slow until I reach the moon temple. There, I find the basket and lift the lid. Alongside the bread, crackers, and spreads is a Ziploc bag with a small red book.

I collect all the food off the floor and bring everything with me to the kitchen. Then I sit on a stool at the large center island, as if I were in the attic of Libroscuro. I rest the book on the stone countertop in the dying daylight, poised to read it, which feels more daunting without Felipe here to translate.

The title page reads: *Hijos de la noche*. Children of the night. Or, since *hijo* is the masculine version of child, it could mean *Sons of the night*.

When I open it, I know why Felipe wanted to share this tome with me—it has pictures. They seem to have been drawn in pencil, but they are as detailed as photographs.

I flip through the pages until I get to the section on *Vampiros*. In the first set of illustrations, they look more like large bats and have nothing in common with Sebastián. I flip ahead to the next part, where the vampires look like winged demons with humanlike faces and fangs. I turn the pages faster, until at last I arrive at some lines of text, and I read:

Los vampiros están en guerra perpetua por el trono.

All I understand is *vampiros* and *guerra,* which means war. So the vampires are at war . . . *perpetua,* is that perpetually? For the *trono*—thunder?

No, that's *trueno.* Trono is . . . *throne*! The vampires are at perpetual war for the throne.

I read on: *El rey dirige el ejército y el príncipe gobierna desde el castillo en la sombra de su padre.*

After rereading the line a few times, I work out that it says: *The king leads the army, and the prince governs from the castle in his father's shadow.*

I turn the page to see a construction that eclipses la Sombra and spans the entire spread. The castle seems to have been built inside a massive mountain, but the rocky walls are so intricately carved they look like papier-mâché.

Across the next spread of pages are grids of comic-like boxes with drawings of the goings-on at the vampire castle. There's no text, but the depictions are so detailed that the subtext is clear to make out.

The figures are drawn as black silhouettes, but the king and the prince stand out by the crowns hovering over their heads. There's a third crowned figure, but they are slain in the first box by shadowy beings when the prince is still a tiny speck of ink. I suspect it was the queen, his mom.

The king goes to war, leaving a thick ring of guards around the prince to protect him. Battle after battle make the king more and more bloodthirsty; meanwhile, the prince's training at the castle seems exhaustive and unending. Until one day, the king takes his son to the field of battle because they are facing an old enemy—the beings who killed his mother.

The prince is ruthless, tearing through the ranks like Death itself. It is here that he gains his name and reputation, and a solitary line of text hovers over his crown: *el Príncipe de Hierro*.

The Iron Prince.

Following his triumph, the prince is locked away at the castle, and the king has him more protected than before. As word spreads of his son's strength, more enemies come to test it. The king and his military keep protecting the boundaries of their realm, going to war with army after army, while the prince continues his studies at the castle, in preparation to rule.

Yet the longer he's caged, the greater the prince's discontent grows. Thought bubbles show that while he sits on the throne, he dreams of being out on the field of battle. His heart hardens to everyone around him, until he loses interest in everything. The last frame is a drawing of the prince's silhouette in a white box, surrounded by emptiness.

I turn the page.

This new spread has fewer boxes, so the pictures are bigger, and there's a line of text at the bottom. The drawings show a series of figures being brought before the prince to face his ruling on various disputes—the details aren't spelled out, but that doesn't matter. Not a single subject leaves the castle with their head.

The text reads:

El príncipe es más temido que el rey. Él es responsable por tantas muertes y mutilaciones en su reino como su padre en el campo de guerra.

I work out the translation quicker than I expected: *The prince is even more feared than the king. He is responsible for as many deaths and mutilations in his kingdom as his father on the field of war.*

I flip the page.

A detailed portrait of el Príncipe de Hierro takes up the whole paper. My eyes trace over the dark hair, deep eyes, and flawless features many times before my brain registers the meaning.

I've met the Iron Prince.

I call him *Sebastián*.

My hands and nails are caked with dirt when I return to the castle.

I open the door to find Sebastián waiting for me in the entryway, and I stumble back, startled by the sight of him.

"What happened?" he asks, studying my fingers.

My pulse quickens. *Does he know?* my heart seems to be asking. *He can't know,* answers my mind. Night hadn't yet fallen when I left the castle.

Still, I flash to the drawings of the subjects he beheaded when he was Prince Bastian, and I know I should be honest. If he learns what I'm keeping from him, he'll kill me for sure . . .

And yet. Sebastián doesn't remember that version of himself, and I intend for it to stay that way.

So instead, I push back thoughts of the Iron Prince and all the violence he's inflicted and say, "I—I tripped." Then I stride past him to wash my hands in the closest bathroom.

"It is the full moon, and your aunt is not back." He seems too preoccupied by that to pick up on my new secret. "You should not be venturing out after dark until this lunar phase has passed."

I think I'll wait to tell him about the black smoke's invitation to meet at the woods at midnight.

"I've been thinking," I say as I dry my hands on a towel, "that just like we studied the limits of the black smoke, we should also study the spell's limits on you. That might help us see something we're missing."

Plus, I need to know your exact limitations, in case your memory returns and you become a threat to me, is what I don't add.

"How do you propose we do that?" he asks as I step out of the bathroom.

"Let me just get my journal—"

Sebastián disappears and reappears in the span of a breath. He moves so fast, it's dizzying. Then he hands me my pen and Dad's leather journal.

I haven't had a chance to write in it yet, and I open the blank book to a random page, bring it to my nose, and take a deep whiff. The papery musk hits my head with a rush, like a drug.

"Should I leave you two alone?" he asks.

"Let's start with the front door," I say, turning away to hide my grin. Who knew the shadow beast could be funny?

"What would happen if you tried to walk outside right now?" I ask once we're in front of the entrance again.

Sebastián complies by turning the handle, but it doesn't budge. He melts into shadow to go through the wood, but nothing happens. I twist the handle myself, swinging the door open, and he materializes on the threshold, staring out into the night.

At first, I think he's in a trance. Then I realize he's trying to break out of an invisible hold; it's as if a barrier is keeping him indoors.

I flip to the beginning of the journal and start a list:

Sebastián's Limitations

1. *He cannot leave la Sombra through the front door.*

"I have another idea," I say. "Come with me."

I hurry in the direction of the tower, and as we cut across the mirror room, he says, "I know where you are taking me. I have read all those books, and none of them holds any answers."

"But have you tried going out to the balcony?" I ask, and from his frown I know he hasn't seen it. When we reach the library, I point up to the window that opens, the ladder still positioned beneath it. Sebastián sweeps up the steps, and when he unlatches the stained glass window, he tries to go through it.

Again, he comes up against an invisible wall.

2. *He cannot go out onto the tower's balcony.*

When he meets me back on the ground, he says, "We can continue later. You need to eat."

That had been my original plan hours ago, before I discovered the Iron Prince. On our way to the kitchen, I recount everything we know about his condition. "Okay, so you appear at night and disappear when the sun comes out, correct?"

"Yes," says Sebastián.

"And I'm the only person who can see you. So far."

"That is right."

Sebastián opens the fridge, and he pulls out a blood bag in surprise. Then he looks at me.

"I appreciate you making sure I'm fed," I say with a shrug. "Just wanted to return the favor."

"*Thank you*," he says, his manners seeming to take even him by surprise, and he buries his face back in the fridge, busying himself with taking out plastic containers and setting them on the stone counter.

I reach behind me with my arms and pull myself onto the countertop, resting the open journal on my lap so I can add two more limitations to the list:

3. He disappears during the day.

4. Only I can see him.

I open a container with cold croquetas and bite into one. "So, you've lost your memory, but you still know your name and that you come from another realm," I say after swallowing, fishing for information. "What else do you remember?"

"I know that I do not hail from your reality. I know I feel a sense of urgency to get home. Yet I am missing the why, where, and how." He hands me a glass of water to wash down the breaded ball.

"You also know about witches because you accused me of being a bruja," I point out before sampling another croqueta.

"I know of all species, including your kind," he says, scrutinizing my expression as I chew, "and I know something is up. You have barely met my eyes tonight. What are you not telling me?"

I can't help wondering if it wouldn't be best to come clean now, while I still have the breath to speak. If he ever finds out I buried the book that contains his identity outside, where he can never reach it, he may not give me time to explain myself.

I swallow, hard.

"We're partners," I say, stating the obvious as my mind races to decide what I should do. "We have to be able to trust each other."

My heart pounds harder, and I keep speaking over it, worried the tempo shift will give me away. "But the truth is, I-I've broken that trust," I admit, and when he frowns with suspicion, I blurt, "by touching you without your consent. And I want to apologize for breaking your boundaries."

He looks stumped for a blink, and then he bursts into laughter, his dazzling smile radiating light like a sunburst. "Shall I apologize for my numerous attempts to eat you?"

I try forcing a chuckle, but his words make my heart go cold. He has no idea how many killings he's committed in his lifetime.

"Is that really all this is about?" he prods.

I don't meet his gaze as I nod in assent, and I know I'm going to have to sell this better. "Today, I was on the other end of what I did to you," I say softly, "and I didn't like it. So I want you to know I'm sorry, and it won't happen again."

I feel him leaning into the counter, and without looking up, I know his face is just a couple of feet from mine. "What do you mean?"

"Felipe came over," I say, closing my eyes so Sebastián won't glean more than what I choose to share.

"What happened?" There's no hint of a smile in his voice anymore.

"I saw the black smoke."

"Describe it." He sounds even closer, but I keep my eyes shut.

I flash to Felipe grabbing me, forcing his tongue—"It happened when Felipe kissed me," I say, blinking my eyes open to keep tears from forming.

Sebastián's face is just inches away, his intense stare locked onto mine, and I have to remind myself to breathe.

"I think you're probably right about a spell protecting me," I go on, because I need to keep talking so I won't break my vow not to touch him. "The black smoke took over everything, like on the subway, then it receded into Felipe's eyes—"

"Did he hurt you?"

Sebastián's voice is quieter now, and more lethal.

"He didn't get to."

Sebastián doesn't move away, nor does his stare break with mine. He's the *Iron Prince,* supernatural royalty with a penchant for bloodshed, and every instinct in my mind is telling me to stay away from him.

But I can't.

He's intoxicating. The Vampire Prince belongs to another world, but the shadow beast is all mine, and I don't want to share him.

"Every time I am about to see you," he says after a stretch of silence, "I wonder if this will be the night I take what I want and leave you a bloodless corpse."

I swallow, my heart sputtering. *Are we really back to the subject of my murder—?*

"And yet," he murmurs, a softness coming over his silver gaze, "every night, when I am with you, I feel . . . *content.*"

He frowns, like that's wrong, and both my breath and heartbeat seem to hinge on what he says next.

"I am not sure if that is the word," he says, "but it makes me want to have you around."

Warmth spreads through me, until I hear, "Yet I know there is more you are not telling me."

I feel the dirt crusting my nails, even though I washed my hands clean. I know I should tell him who he is, but as soon as I do, I'll be awakening Prince Bastian and killing Sebastián. And I can't bring myself to do that.

"I have a new lead," I say, over the renewed racing of my heart. "Remember how I told you the smoke receded into Felipe's eyes? Well, then he spoke to me, only I don't think it was him. His voice sounded different, and he said: *If you want answers, come to the woods at midnight.*" I swallow, hard. "I'm going to check it out."

"Comedy is not your thing."

"I'm not joking."

"Then this is the worst idea you ever had."

We disagree, yet our faces lean in. The closer he gets, the harder it is to keep my lips to myself. "We'll find out," I say through gritted teeth.

"No." Sebastián's grimace turns into a glower. "*You are not going.*"

His body is an immovable wall blocking my way.

"You don't tell me what to do," I say, squaring my shoulders and pulling away from him.

Thunder rumbles, low and lingering, the storm forming in the back of his throat. "*Try me,*" he warns.

"What's that mean?" The impulse to throttle him grows as strong as the one to kiss him, and I move toward him again. My whole being feels like it's at war: my head resists the pull of my attraction, while my body begs me to let go of the reins.

"I will not let you risk your life like this."

"You mean you won't let my blood go to waste?"

I don't know why I say it, but he looks at me like I've injured him. "We had an agreement," he reminds me. "We are supposed to be partners in this investigation. It is selfish of you to risk your life and squander my chances of getting home."

The last word is a kill shot. I don't know why it defeats me, but I wish I was still as numb as the day I got here, so I wouldn't have to feel this chasm opening in my chest.

Sebastián would rather return to a home he can't remember than stay with me.

I want to find a way to empathize, to believe that in his shoes I would feel the same way—but it's only now I realize it's too late for such generosity. Sebastián is the only person I have left in the world. He's *all* I have.

Besides, no one has ever been mine before. Not like Sebastián is right now.

"I'm going," I say, my voice low and even. "If you do anything to stop me, you might as well kill me because our partnership will be over."

I slide to the left on the counter, and he doesn't move. So I jump down and head to my room to change. When I step back out, he's waiting for me in the crimson corridor.

"Estela, please. I cannot protect you out there. Do you understand there is a dangerous spellcaster targeting us, and nighttime is when magic is best conducted, *especially* on a full moon?"

I ignore him as I stride down the stairs.

"Don't go. Please," he says, following me. "Stay here, where I can protect you—"

"You can't protect me," I say without looking back. "You're a ghost."

I walk to the forest, even though I'm early. I couldn't risk staying any longer in the castle in case Sebastián tried to stop me.

I keep my head bent low against the chill as I approach the woods. At least the full moon lifts some of the darkness.

Sebastián was right about the black smoke—it's tied to me somehow. It appeared on the subway, in the castle, and earlier I felt something pass from me to Felipe when he kissed me. If I'm its carrier, then it could be a spell like Sebastián says.

But does that mean it protected me on the subway, or was it the culprit—?

The sight of the black smoke cuts off my next thought, breath, heartbeat. I stare in frozen fright as a smoky tendril reaches ahead of me, like it's leading me into the woods.

The smoke originated from my direction, further cementing it's bound to me in some way. Am I now just going to follow it into the forest in the middle of the night to meet its caster? Sebastián was right—this is a horrible idea.

And yet, isn't he desperate to break the spell keeping him here? If he were in my shoes, he wouldn't cower—he would march into the woods and seize what he wants. So I try to channel some of the Iron Prince's entitlement as I plunge into the foliage.

The trees are tight-packed, and I'm nearly tripping every other step on a raised root or loose rock. Only a few minutes in, I'm completely disoriented. I don't like lacking an escape route, and right now I am severely out of my comfort zone. I'm no good at counting steps or gauging my direction out here.

I severely regret not searching for a flashlight before leaving. I meant to find one, but I left in too much of a hurry. Sebastián is definitely a distraction, and he's hurting my investigation.

The forest is too dark to see much, but somehow the black smoke remains visible, a silvery aura making it stand out.

Something flickers in the distance ahead, and I inhale the smoky notes of a bonfire. An odd humming fills the air, and after a moment, I spy a clearing.

Red flames lick the sky.

I creep closer, and the humming grows louder. I bite back my urge to scream as I see a hooded figure facing the fire—

A hand clamps over my mouth.

I kick my legs and reach back with my fingers to fight off my attacker—

"Shh, it's me," says a familiar voice in my ear, and I stop fighting, so he lets me go.

I take a giant leap away as I turn to face Felipe. "What are you doing here?" I snap at him.

"The castle told us to come," he whispers, lowering his hand to indicate I should keep my voice down.

The castle? The black smoke is *la Sombra*? "What do you mean?" I whisper back. "What do you remember?"

His face is shaded by the night, but the flames' red light reflects in his irises, making his amber eyes glow like embers. "Something happened . . . and a voice spoke through me."

"It was a message for *me*. Not you."

"Well, it showed me a picture of where to go, a spot in the woods I know well. *Here.*"

I don't say anything, and I wonder if he's been playing me this whole time. Is he working with Beatríz? Or whoever this hooded figure is?

"Who is that?" I ask, indicating the person humming by the fire.

"I'm sorry for what I did, Estela," says Felipe, either ignoring or avoiding my question. "I just thought—maybe if I kissed you, you'd feel it, too. But then once I started, it was like I couldn't pull away. Some force seemed to go through me."

I felt it, so I know what he means. And yet his eyes won't meet mine. Like he's still hiding something.

"Estela, you need to go."

"You want me to trust you after today?"

"I'll explain once we're safe—"

"Tell me now."

The hooded figure doesn't move or stop humming, but I have the creepy sensation they know we're here. I keep them in my peripheral vision while I argue with Felipe.

"Start speaking, or I'll scream," I warn.

"H-he told me to meet you here." Felipe sounds terrified. "He said if I did well, he would give us his blessing, and I could move into the castle."

"*Who—?*"

I flick my gaze to the fire again. The hooded figure is gone.

"Where'd they go?" I ask.

Felipe looks horrified. "There's no water in the fountain," he mumbles.

"What are you talking about—?" My question is barely out when black smoke blankets the air, and I can't see a thing.

"Felipe!" I call out, reaching for him.

Before I make contact, a set of fingers interlocks with mine, too rough to be his.

"Let me go!" I yell, struggling against the viselike grip.

When the hand unclenches, I dart away, arms outstretched so I won't run into a tree. And as the smoke dissipates, I find myself in the clearing.

The bonfire's warmth presses into me, its light revealing a stone bench and a clay bowl with strange etchings.

The hooded figure is here. They're standing over something long lying on the grass.

A body in a leather jacket.

Felipe.

RAUL'S RULE #9

YOU CAN'T SAVE EVERYONE.

CHAPTER 16

"FELIPE!"

The hooded figure backs away, and I sprint over. I drop to the ground by Felipe's fallen body, his clothes covered with dirt and twigs. I grab his wrist to check his pulse—

And I flash to lifting Mom's limp arm.

Heaving, I rip open Felipe's jacket and press my ear to his chest. The world shifts orientation, and I remember pushing a woman's leg off Dad's shoulder so I could listen to his heart. His chest was as silent as the train.

I gave Dad CPR first.

I trusted him to save Mom. He would know what to do, I was sure of it. I needed his help.

But I couldn't revive him.

What if I'd chosen Mom first? asks the tiny voice for the thousandth time. *What if I could have saved her—?*

A faint beating sounds in my ear.

It's weak, but I hear it.

"He's alive," says a man's voice, confirming it. "But not awake. He dreams . . . even in waking life. He believes he's destined to be one of us."

One of us.

I snap to my feet and stare at the hooded man. I recognize his accented voice. "The driver," I say. "You brought me here from the airport."

The man pulls his hood back. He has a buzz cut, piercings on both brows, and tattoos creeping up his neck—but I can still make out Beatríz's identical nose and jawline.

"I'm Mateo," he says, "but you used to call me Tío Teo."

"You're *twins,*" I say in awe.

"I'm sorry I couldn't introduce myself before. I wasn't ready for my sister to know I was here."

"You've been sleeping in the clínica," I say, thinking of the unmade patient bed.

"Only since Beatríz left town."

"Which I'm guessing you had a hand in," I surmise, my mind making connections at breakneck speed.

"I may have led her to believe I'd disappeared and was in danger. I've been sending her on a wild chase through Spain."

"Because you needed her away tonight," I finish. "For the full moon."

"You really inherited your mother's smarts, didn't you?" He moves toward me, and I walk around the bonfire, keeping a good distance between us.

"My *dad* taught me to investigate," I correct him.

He cranes his head, exposing the largest ink on his neck: a long black tower. It's la Sombra's library.

"Let's play a game—" he begins.

"I'm not playing with you."

"Are you sure?" Teo brandishes a blade from within his coat, and I barely have time to leap back when he lunges.

I shriek, darting away—and too late, I realize he's not chasing me.

Teo crouches on the ground, next to Felipe's inert body, holding the blade to his throat.

"What are you doing?" I cry out, running back.

"*Playing.* So what's it going to be: Truth or dare?"

"I'm not playing—"

A droplet of blood trickles down Felipe's throat, and I shout, "*Truth!*"

My uncle smirks, and unlike the solar power unleashed in Sebastián's smile, Teo's grin is a starless night. "*Is it true* that you will do what I ask to save your friend's life?"

My heart is racing so fast that I can't believe only a week ago I couldn't hear its beat. "Yes."

"Then remove your coat and lie back on that bench." He points to the stone slab.

"I'll freeze—"

"There's a fire."

"I didn't choose *dare*. And besides, it's your turn—"

"Pity," he says, yanking back on Felipe's hair to better expose his throat. "I thought you wanted to save his life."

I pull off my coat.

The rocky bench looks like a sacrificial altar, and as I approach, I see that there is an identical clay bowl on the other side.

"Sit down and lie back," commands Teo, and I repeat to myself: *The black smoke will protect me.* Even though I know it's not true. If the smoke were on my side, why would it have led me here?

"Roll up your sleeves."

I roll up my left sleeve and ask, "Did you kill my parents with a spell?"

"You flatter me," he says, gripping my wrist. "But I lack the power to—"

I swing my neck up to headbutt him—but Teo leaps back before I make contact, and he knocks me down with an elbow to the chest.

My skull thuds against the stone bench, and I squeeze my eyes shut as pain shoots through me, followed by dizziness and nausea.

"Seems like you don't care much for your friend's life," he says, grabbing my left arm and positioning it so my forearm hangs off the stone and over the clay bowl.

"What . . . do you want?" I ask, fighting down my dinner of cold croquetas.

I feel a pinch and cry out, my arm burning. Teo inserted a needle with a plastic tube attachment.

"*Stop!*" I want it to be a shout, but it's barely more than a whimper. He twists my elbow, and as the tubing fills with my blood, it snakes down and drips into the clay bowl.

"Hold still, or your friend dies," he reminds me.

Even if I wanted to fight, my bones feel too heavy to lift. Sebastián was right that I'm not eating enough. I've lost most of my strength. He was also right that I was being selfish. Now I'm going to die, and he doesn't even get a meal out of me. What a waste of my blood.

Pain rips through me again as Teo bleeds my other arm. He sorely lacks his twin's finesse inserting the needle.

"Y-you killed my parents for this?" I ask, my mouth dry.

"I'm not a murderer."

The defensive way he says it tells me he's insisted on that before.

"Then let Felipe go. You don't need him."

"You've grown up so much." Teo's face softens, and for an instant he actually looks the part of a proud uncle. "You remind me of both of them, Oli and Bea. You're everything they could have hoped you'd become."

Under different circumstances, these words, his smile, the warmth in his voice would have delighted me. His hand reaches for my face, and I turn my head away. Still, I feel his finger stroke my cheek, wiping my tears.

"What do you need my blood for?" I ask without looking at him.

"You'll know soon enough," he says, almost gently.

It feels like my body is deflating, and soon I'll disappear. Even my brain is crumpling into itself, everything shutting down as the blood drips drips drips away . . .

"I take it you haven't found the journals yet," he says by my ear.

I turn my head to face him, but my vision is fading. "What journals?"

"I bet she likes you," he murmurs. "You have the same chispa. *Spark.*"

"What journals?" I whisper, my eyelids flickering.

"Shh," he says, shutting my eyes for me with his fingers. "Buenas noches, Tela."

As blackness overtakes me, I hear him resume his humming. Only that's not what it is—he's *chanting.* It's the same phrase, over and over and over again . . .

That's the spell, I realize, visualizing the ancient parchment Felipe shared with me. Blood drawn under a full moon in the shadow of the castle—only the last line wasn't referring to nighttime. It was a chant.

> *No hay luz en Oscuro.*
> *No hay luz en Oscuro.*
> *No hay luz en Oscuro.*

I open my eyes to the sun.

There's an earthy sweetness in the air. My back and neck are stiff, and I'm on the ground, my coat draped over me like a blanket.

I'm shivering and can barely move from weakness. Did Teo leave me in the forest overnight? *What about Felipe?*

At the thought of him, I force my knees to bend. My arm hurts as I lean on my elbow to sit up and survey my surroundings. The town of Oscuro sprawls below, along with the forest . . . and twisting my neck, I look up to see la Sombra looming over me.

Teo must have carried me back to the castle. Strange that he didn't cross the gate, even though his sister isn't home. *Is it possible he knows about Sebastián?*

There are Band-Aids on both my arms, and twin bruises are already forming where he inserted the needles. I wince with pain as I stand up, head pulsing.

Miraculously, the key to the castle is still zipped inside my hoodie's pocket. Once indoors, I go straight to the kitchen and tear into a loaf of bread with my teeth. I drink as much water as I can, finish the gazpacho, and stack crackers with jamón serrano, cheese, and olives until I'm fit to burst.

I don't see any signs of Beatríz being back. I should call the cops and tell them about Felipe and my uncle and urge them to locate my aunt. Instead, I call Libroscuro.

I dig out the business-turned-library card, and I go into Beatríz's room because it has the only phone I've seen in the castle. I dial the number and hope someone picks up.

"Buen día, se ha comunicado con Libroscuro, ¿con qué le puedo ayudar?"

It's Felipe's father. "Arturo? Soy Estela."

"Ah, Estela, how-are-you?" he asks, making each word sound like its own sentence.

"¿Dónde está Felipe?"

"Ayer se fue a Oviedo a visitar unos amigos. Vuelve en unos días." *He's visiting friends in Oviedo.*

"¿Cuándo habló con él?" I ask Arturo when he last spoke with his son.

"Tempranito esta mañana. Me llamó desde ahí." Felipe called him early this morning.

Relief comes first, followed by confusion. After what happened last night, Felipe just took off? He didn't bother to check on me, or tell the authorities what happened?

"¿Quieres que le pase algún mensaje?" prods Arturo after a few seconds of silence.

"No, gracias," is all I manage to get out before hanging up. I have no message for Felipe because I have no words.

I desperately need to take a bath, but I can barely keep my eyes open. The loss of blood, the lack of energy, all the food I just scarfed down . . . it's too much, and I'm overcome with sleep.

I barely make it to my bed before passing out.

I awaken to twin full moons. Sebastián's eyes.

"You did not return before sunup," he says, his voice low and measured. He is seated at my side, in an armchair he's moved closer to the bed. "You have lost a lot of blood."

His tone is more melodic today, like it's spiked with something I can't identify, but at least I don't hear hints of hostility anymore. "What happened?" he asks.

"Beatríz has a twin brother," I say, sitting up gingerly. "Teo is the brujo behind the black smoke. Felipe was just the messenger—he met me at the woods and tried talking me out of going. But then the black smoke spread, and next thing I knew, I was facing my uncle, and Felipe had been knocked out."

"You encountered the brujo?" asks Sebastián, his tone still hard to pin down. His voice has shifted into an even less familiar register, like a musician reaching for a new note.

"He bled me from both arms under the full moon, chanting *No hay luz en Oscuro*." I say it quickly like that will help me not hear it.

Sebastián's gaze jumps to my arms. "May I?" he murmurs.

My belly flips when I nod. His cold fingers are gentle as he takes my left arm and pulls back my long sleeve, revealing an ugly bruise where Teo drew my blood. Sebastián doesn't say anything, and his head is dipped down, so I can't see his eyes.

"This must be why the brujo has not risked approaching the castle." His hands pull away from mine.

"What do you mean?"

"He knows if he comes here, I will kill him."

His voice is pure winter, and I feel like I'm seeing the Iron Prince. "But you can't touch Beatríz," I say, "so what makes Teo different?"

"If he is the spell's caster, we are bound to each other. Even if he has found a way to protect himself, I do not need to touch him to throw a blade through his heart."

Hearing Sebastián speak so coolly about murder makes my gut clench.

"How did you get out alive?" he asks me, and I think I hear a flicker of suspicion.

"I woke up this morning outside the castle," I say, squaring my chest in anticipation of having to battle Sebastián's distrust again.

But there's no coldness in his expression. If anything, what's throwing me off is his newfound concern.

"Most likely the brujo still wants something from you." As he says this, Sebastián looks almost *worried*.

"What more could he want from me?" I ask, my exhale shaky.

"From *us*," he amends. "There must be a reason we were brought together."

Brought together. I hate how much I love the sound of that.

I nod in assent, but I can't imagine any reason in any universe that would require bringing me together with el Príncipe de Hierro.

"I will gather some dinner for you," he says.

"No—I want to get up. I'll come with you."

He's patient with my slow movements, and when we get to the kitchen, I heat up some paella that was given to me at Felipe's. Then I slide onto the countertop and start eating.

"I do not think I have ever seen you eat this much, or this heartily," he says, sounding pleased as I devour the food.

"That's because you didn't see me this morning," I say, covering my mouth as I finish chewing. "I was like a wild animal foraging for food in the fridge."

Parched, I take a drink of the water he set down for me. When I finish, Sebastián collects everything, and I slide off the counter. The dishes are clean in seconds, and it's quite breathtaking to watch.

Even with a full belly, a biting chill seeps under my skin, and I turn around to see if a window is open. Yet it's not the weather without that's icy, but the climate within.

My parents are gone, Beatríz is gone, Felipe is gone, and, soon, Sebastián will be gone. After all, he's a future king.

My curse is to be alone.

Sebastián comes over and inspects my face. I wish he would slide a finger under my chin and tip my mouth back to meet his, like in the movies—but he keeps a buffer of space between us.

"You are not alone," he whispers, and I'm reminded of the first words Lety spoke to me.

"Everyone abandons me," I breathe, wincing because it's true. "You will, too." Everything about Sebastián lures me in. His moonlight gaze, his starry musk, his chiseled features . . .

He keeps staring at me, like he's processing what I've said, and I hate that he doesn't jump to deny it.

"Estela."

The way he says my name makes my knees weak.

"These new feelings you awaken in me are more terrifying than not knowing who I am."

I'm not sure I heard him right.

"I may not remember my past, but I do know that the delicate things of this world, like *flowers,* do not grow where I am from. We do not have a word that is the equivalent to *nurture.* I am certain I have never kept anything alive, for I am a creature designed for death.

"Yet last night, when you left to the woods, I fell into a dark mood that was not borne of greed or rage or bloodthirst, but *fear.* I was powerless to protect you . . . my favorite flower."

Sebastián seems to be stripping himself of armor as he speaks, and I can't even think.

"It was not until I found you alive and asleep that my fear abated," he goes on, "and a new sensation swept over me. All at once, I felt relieved, content, and safe."

"You *care,*" I say, bewildered. "For *me.*" My high pitch of disbelief is almost comical.

"This *caring,*" says Sebastián, dipping his head so we're eye to eye, "it feels connected to something greater. A force stronger than any magic."

I nod. "It leads to love."

"*Love,*" he repeats. "May I try something that will require touching you?"

"Um, sure."

He opens his arms and moves toward me, then he links his hands around my back, embracing me. Resting my head against his chest, I hear crickets and owls and the ocean's surf.

We don't speak as he holds me. The longer we hug, the more my stiff joints loosen, until even breathing feels easier than it has in a long time.

"I have tried so hard to resist my attraction to you," he says when we pull apart. "May I kiss you?"

"Ye—"

His mouth consumes mine.

There's nothing cold about him anymore as our tongues tangle, and heat blazes up my middle. I feel his hands grip my waist, and suddenly I'm seated on the counter, closer to his height.

As we kiss, his fingers graze up and down my sides, making me tingle all over. His featherlight strokes grow longer, traveling down my hip bone and scaling the rungs of my rib cage. His caresses stop when they reach the bottom of my bra and the waistband of my pants.

It's like my entire range of physical sensation has narrowed to his touch. Wherever his fingers are, goose bumps grow.

We kiss until my mouth goes numb. And for the first time since my parents died, I don't feel alone.

I'll do whatever it takes to hold on to Sebastián and keep Prince Bastian from returning.

I feel different in the morning. Like I've shed my old skin, exposing a fresh layer that's still sensitive and raw to the world.

A small smile tugs on my lips as I think of Sebastián, and I arch into a stretch as a massive balloon swells in my chest—

Pain flashes through my arms, and I remember Teo. The balloon pops.

I jump out of bed and head to Beatríz's room—*still untouched*. Teo said he led her away from here, but how could she not have left me a cell number to reach her? She has a landline in her room, so she could at least call from a public phone to check in.

I dart downstairs to check the kitchen. "Beatríz?" I call out as I search.

When I don't see any sign of her, I head back to my room. I need to take notes on everything that's happened if I'm going to work this out, so I go to my bathroom to retrieve Dad's leather journal from my period drawer—

I take it you haven't found the journals yet.

Teo's words come flying back to me, and I still on the staircase landing.

What did he mean? What journals?

My hunger for breakfast battles my thirst for knowledge, but since I don't know where to start my search, food wins. I make myself pan con tomate while I consider where to begin.

The most obvious location is the library, since it's where texts are shelved. And Felipe made a good point about the ceiling being flat when the tower is arched, so there's solid *secret room* potential. I review other possibilities in my mind: Beatríz's bedroom (already searched), the secret wing with the dungeon (where I'm not eager to go back), the purple room (didn't seem to be anything left to find) . . . but my mind keeps jumping back to the library.

It's the most logical answer, and yet it almost feels *too* simple—until I remember the tattoo on Teo's neck.

His most prominent ink happens to be of the tower. Could be coincidence . . . but Dad had another word for those: *clues*.

By the time I make it up the tower stairs, I have to catch my breath. I rest in an armchair in the tower as I survey the spines surrounding me. Sebastián said he read every book here; if he'd seen those journals, he would have told me, right?

So, what could he have missed?

My eyes land on the only modern device here, the tablet. And I wonder if it's not broken. Maybe it just needs to be unlocked.

There's a nail poking out where the tablet is affixed to the shelf. Remembering the way I accessed the purple room, I prick my finger until blood trickles out, then I press my hand to the screen.

I jump back as the wall starts to tremble, then I laugh out loud. This is la Sombra, after all—when in doubt, Brálaga blood is always the key.

My chest swells with excitement as two shelves slide apart, and books rattle against each other as a narrow stairwell is revealed.

Oh, no. *More stairs.*

When I've climbed up the last step, I pass through a small opening in the wall into a round attic with a cone-shaped ceiling. Felipe was right: I'm at the peak of the tower.

Bookshelves are built into the curved walls, stuffed with journals. It would probably take years to read them all, and I might have no idea where to begin, except there's a letter on the only furniture here: a small table and a chair.

It's almost like this room has been waiting for me, and I wonder if maybe it's not supposed to stay hidden. Maybe it's meant to be found.

I sit down. The message has been inked in a cursive so perfect, it could be a computer font. It's in Spanish, but as I focus on the words, they morph into English in my mind, as if I were viewing them through a phone camera's translation app.

This is the castle's doing, not mine.

Dear Grandchild,

If you are reading these words, you are my descendant.

I leave you these books so you may fill their pages with your stories and spells, to be preserved and passed down for posterity.

My power will be inherited only by those born with a living reflection: the identical twins. Brálaga magic comes in pairs, with each sibling keeping the other in balance.

Remember that great power comes only with great sacrifice. For those who dare to pursue greatness, there is a spell enclosed in a red book that provides passage to the other castle, my home, for a child of no more than five years of age. The other twin must remain as an anchor.

I prophesize that one day, one of these children will become the first Earth-born supernatural being. When that happens, Brálaga blood will be the building block of magic on Earth.

This is our legacy.

> *Your grandfather,*
> *Brálaga*

My palms are itchy, my breaths are shallow, my heart is racing.

BOOM. BOOM. BOOM.

I see the black flames again, consuming the purple wallpaper, and if I weren't already sitting down, I would fall.

Now I know why I never felt the fire's burn in my memories. I could see it, but I couldn't feel it. The perspective was wrong: I was *watching* the scene, not experiencing it.

And not because I was disassociating—but because I was *witnessing*.

I think of the photos and the death certificate in the purple room. My expression in the smiling picture has been bothering me since I saw it. I thought it had to do with the person behind the lens, but now I know why my smile felt wrong: I never had a chip in my front milk tooth.

I wasn't the girl in the black fire.

She was my twin.

12 YEARS AGO

"*UNO, DOS, TRES, CUATRO, CINCO, seis . . .*" *I count off in a game of hide-and-seek.* "*¡Siete, ocho, nueve, diez!*"

I turn around when I get to ten, my vantage point lower than usual.

"*Lista o no, ¡aquí voy!*" *I say, to the tune of* Ready or not, here I come!

I dart down a crimson corridor and pop out by the dining hall. I look under the long table, but no one's there. The aroma of garlic and onions frying in oil invades my nostrils, and I slip into the kitchen, where two women in uniform are dicing vegetables on the counter while something bakes in the oven.

"*La señora said to keep el señor's meal salt-free.*"

"*I know. The chocolate cake is almost ready.*"

They're speaking in Spanish, but I understand every word. I'm tempted to glide a pinkie across the chocolate icing when I glance out the window and see something that makes me run from the castle.

The heavy front door is already open, and I rush to the garden. It's vibrant and healthy and well-tended. I approach a plant with floppy leaves. "*Outside doesn't count,*" *I say in Spanish.*

A voice identical to mine floats out from the foliage. "*You said you wanted a real challenge for a change.*"

The leaves shake, and a girl steps out from the plant. She looks exactly like me, except her front tooth is broken.

"*But without rules, it's not a game,*" *I say.*

"*Breaking the rules doesn't matter, as long as you win.*"

"*That's not fair,*" *I argue.*

We step back inside the castle, and a crimson-tinged light in the entryway blinks over our heads. We both look up as a second light begins to blink in the entrance hall, then a third farther down, and a fourth in the distance.

"What is that?" asks my twin.

The lights continue to flicker, almost insistently. "I don't know," I say, and we sprint in their direction.

Until a shadow falls across us, blocking our path.

"What's going on? What's with the running?" asks one of the women from the kitchen.

"Nela thought that—" I start.

"Tela needs to exercise—" my sister cuts in.

"But I prefer to be inside—"

"So I'm training her."

My sister and I trade grins.

"Well walk then. You know the rules: No running."

When she leaves, we look up at the lights, but they've stopped flashing.

Nela turns to me. "See? Rules ruined the magic."

CHAPTER 17

I CAN'T PROCESS. OR THINK. Or breathe.

I need to get out of here. I try to bring the letter with me, but every time I leave the room, the paper vanishes from my grip and reappears on the table. Like it's spellbound to this location.

Just like Sebastián is spellbound to the castle.

Leaving the letter behind, I race downstairs to the library, then down more stairs, until I've left the tower. Running alongside my reflection in the mirror room, I can't help imagining it's my sister.

The girl in the glass starts to slow down, my reflection lagging behind me. I blink, and the illusion melts away.

My pulse is pounding in my head, sure to set off a migraine—but I freeze by the gargoyle staircase when I see someone coming down the steps.

Beatríz.

If I look half-dead, she's half-decomposed. Her skin has a grayish cast, and the whites of her eyes are streaked with red. Smudged black liner raccoons her gaze and stray curls break free of her bun. She looks like she's aged five decades in five days.

She stares at me like she's seen a ghost. Then I realize I'm wearing Mom's hot-pink sweater.

"Are you all right?" she asks at last.

I shake my head. I have never felt further from *all right*. "I have a *sister*."

My voice breaks on the word, and I suck in a ragged inhale. I refuse to cry when I need to speak.

Beatríz says nothing. She stares down at her fingers, and I'm reminded of Lady Macbeth and her bloodstained hands.

"How could they keep this from me?" The question comes out a whisper, and I can't stop the tears from streaking down my cheeks.

I'm *enraged* with my parents.

I wish they were here mostly to scream at them and call them out for the liars they've been. The salty water falls more forcefully, and I have to dig my nails deep into my palms to keep the dam from breaking.

"How"—a sob escapes my throat—"how could I forget I have a twin? *Where is she?*"

"Let's sit down," says Beatríz at last, her voice as thin as mine. "You look like a corpse."

Look who's talking.

I want to defy her, but she starts moving toward the dining hall, and I have to follow if I want answers. Once she enters the kitchen, I drop into a chair at the long table. It feels like the hole in my chest is widening, letting out all my oxygen. I can't make it any farther.

My aunt comes back with two glasses of water, and this time she sits next to me, not across the table. There's just a couple of feet of air between us.

After a while, I realize she isn't going to speak first. So I start at the beginning. "I know about the fire," I say, my throat dry even after drinking from the glass. "I found the purple room. And my *death certificate.*"

I take another gulp of water before I ask, "Is it my sister's? Was Estela *her* name?"

Beatríz shakes her head, but her lips stay sealed, almost pursed together. Like a lock.

"Then the certificate is mine?" My hand trembles on the table as I say it.

Beatríz stares at my fingers as she says, "It's a fake."

"I don't understand."

"Your mother sent it after she disappeared. I believe your father forged it."

"But *why?*"

Today I can make out the small lines in my aunt's face. It feels like her mask is finally cracking. Yet as the silent seconds march past, I realize she still can't talk about it.

"Why revisit the past?" she whispers. "There's nothing good to be found there."

"*Everything* good is there," I say, the words slicing me on their way out. "The past is all I have."

My aunt's hands reach out to grip mine. They are nearly as cold as Sebastián's, but her breath feels warm on my face as she leans in.

"That's not true, Estela. You still have your whole life ahead of you."

This is the first sign of affection she's shown me, but her warmth means nothing if she's not going to tell me the truth. "Everyone around me dies. What kind of life is that?"

Beatríz shakes her head, her eyes round with horror. "It's . . . it's my fault."

"Yours?"

"*Ours.* My brother's and mine."

"I don't understand," I say for the second time.

She shakes her head like she doesn't want to explain.

When I was little, Dad would take me with him to meet with sources at public places like parks and shopping malls, because he said a child's presence lowers a person's guard. I remember he didn't let any silences creep into those meetings.

If a source stopped speaking, Dad jumped in and moved things along with his own theories, no matter how unformed they were—in fact, the more off base, the more likely the source was to start talking again.

"The fire was Teo's idea," I say, studying Beatríz, whose fingers go limp in mine. "It was a spell to send my sister to the other castle, where the original Brálaga lives. And you went along with it."

Beatríz pulls her hands away, and I think she's going to take off again. "We were teens," she says, staying seated, "younger than you are now, when we found the journals."

"What exactly are the journals?" I ask.

"*Spells.* The magical compositions of our twin ancestors, the ones who managed to pull something off. They recorded the successful spells for posterity. Only some of our ancestors warned that the power came at a price. They said once they opened the door to magic, they couldn't close it. They called it a *curse.*

"At first, Teo and I were thrilled. We had always felt there was something special about this castle, about *us.* It made sense that we were destined for power, and the first thing he wanted to try was the spell for crossing to the other castle. He didn't care that the letter specified age *five*. We tried igniting the black fire again and again, but it never worked for my brother. I thought it meant the other realm wasn't real, but Teo was sure it was real and we were just too old. He was devastated."

Beatríz squints, like she can almost see the past from here. "He lost interest in everything. He dropped out of school and disappeared into drugs for years, until . . ." She blinks, and her eyes meet mine. "Olivia said she was pregnant. With *twins*."

Goose bumps race down my arms, and I realize that moment sealed my sister's and my fates.

"My brother convinced me that since twins weren't born into our parents' generation, we'd missed our birthright, but it wasn't fair for you and your sister to miss yours. I still didn't believe in the other castle, but I loved Teo more than anything. I was born a few seconds after him, and the joke in our family was that I was his Sombrita—*little shadow*. Whatever he did, I did."

She exhales long, like she's letting out old fumes along with the words, her eyes shimmering with moisture.

"He had changed so much since we discovered those journals, but with the birth of you girls, we all felt we were seeing the old Teo again. Energetic, excited, hopeful. I didn't want us to lose him. I figured we'd just go through the motions, that's all—that nothing would really happen."

Her voice grows rough, and she clears her throat. "When the full moon rose, you girls were playing hide-and-seek. You were the one hiding. You were always so good at that game."

The tears brim over her eyes.

"So we took *Antonela*."

Hearing my twin's name, I feel something restored to me. It fills the hole in my heart that had burrowed too deep for anyone to reach, buried beneath tissue and wounds and walls.

"Antonela," I whisper, and gasp at the familiarity of the word on my tongue. A muscle memory.

"Your mother was inconsolable," Beatríz goes on. "She tried having us arrested, but all traces of the spell had vanished, and there was no evidence beyond the blackened walls. There was no *body*."

She finally drops her hands to her lap. Her cheeks are slick with tears.

"Only Teo believed we could bring her home. He assured Oli that we needed to do another spell, but it required your blood. Olivia panicked and disappeared overnight."

The air between us has hardened so much, it's difficult to draw breath. "D-did he do a spell," I whisper, "on the day of the subway—?"

"*Impossible,*" she says so quickly that I know she's already considered it, too. "He isn't anywhere near that powerful."

"Then what killed my parents?"

"The *curse*!" She hisses the word, like it tastes foul. "After your sister died, Oli ran off with you, Teo went to a dark place again, and our parents' health began to suffer. They died soon after, and I took over the clínica. I finally had to get Teo professional help, which left me alone here. We never should have set that fire. We cursed ourselves."

Part of me wants to forgive her and recover some of the family I lost, but I can't. She's still lying. "You left me for five days, without a note or checking in. That wasn't the curse. It was your choice."

Her expression hardens, and she doesn't meet my gaze. "My brother called me five days ago and said he was in trouble, that the curse was bearing down on him and I would likely never see him again. He told me he would be gone by morning, so I was in too much of a rush to be rational. I stopped at the clínica to pick up syringes in case he needed to be sedated, and I realized I forgot to leave you a note, so I wrote a message on the door."

"Why didn't you call?"

"I lost my cell phone the second day."

"Why didn't you try me from a public phone to the line in your bedroom? Or to the bookstore?"

"I don't know!" She springs to her feet, and I jump to mine, too, blocking her exit.

"I do! Because you didn't know if you were coming back," I answer for her. "I had taken your place at the castle, and you were going to ask your brother to run away with you and leave the Brálaga legacy behind. But since you couldn't be sure I wouldn't call the cops, you had to ditch your cell phone to avoid being tracked. So you communicated with him on a disposable phone instead."

Her eyes grow wide with shock. She doesn't say anything, and I know I'm right.

"But something drew you back to Oscuro," I go on. "And it had to be the same thing that lured you away—*your brother.*"

"Have you seen him?" she asks, confirming my theory.

"He must want us both here for something," I continue, thinking out loud. "Another spell?"

"Stop it! I won't have you talking like him under my roof—"

"You weren't even coming back to this roof!"

"I never said that—"

"You didn't have to. I could read it on your face."

"*I wasn't sure what I was going to do!*" she shouts, and we both go quiet. It's the first time she's told me the truth, and we both hear it.

She sits back down, and so do I. Now that she's being honest, I ask, "Why don't I remember Antonela?"

"We think those memories must have been destroyed by the spell that sent her to the other castle. Along with your birth language."

"What?"

"After Antonela disappeared, you stopped speaking. Nor did you ask about her. It was like you had become a blank slate. I don't know what happened next because you all took off. I'm guessing that since your parents had spent time in the U.S. and were both fluent in English—they used to have private conversations that we couldn't follow because they spoke so fast—they must have raised you with the language."

"So my past was just lost?" I ask incredulously.

"Your parents probably never brought up your sister again to keep from reopening a wound that had magically sealed itself. They chose to carry the grief for you."

I don't have the headspace to look at things from their perspective yet— I'm barely processing my own. But one particular word stands out from what she said. *Grief.*

"Then are you saying—?" I can't finish the question, and I try again. "Is Antonela—?"

I swallow, trying to control the emotions rising up my throat as I form the words: "Is she *dead*?"

Beatríz's face crumples, and I feel mine falling, too. I have my answer. *My aunt and uncle killed my sister.*

"How do you know?" I ask, my voice growing heated. "Maybe she's in the other castle with Brálaga, and she has magical powers by now, and as long as I'm alive in this world to anchor her, she will live on in the other . . ."

I trail off because what I'm describing sounds a lot like a story we tell our-selves about a loved one when they die.

"You have every right to hate me," says my aunt. "I hate me, too. I've regretted my actions every day. It's why I devote myself to this castle and this town—to make up for the life I took."

I feel a knot the size of a baseball rising up my chest. "Why bring me here if you knew how much danger I'd be in?"

"After the subway, I realized you wouldn't be safe anywhere. I thought I could make amends to my sister by at least attempting to protect you."

"More like you needed someone to replace you here." The ball of emotion is at my throat, making the words come out squeezed.

"That's not true!" she says defiantly. But she seems to catch herself because she exhales and adds, more calmly, "It crossed my mind that I could save my brother. I wasn't planning on abandoning you here forever"—her words gather speed—"but I wanted to give myself the chance to disappear even for a little while, just to remember what it's like to be a normal person because I'm tired of being a prisoner chained to this place and feeling so completely *alone*!"

Her hands cover her face, fingers forming a cage as her cries burst out, like a volcano erupting. Her shoulders shake as she fights against her sobs.

The sound is a trigger that takes me back to the center. I know exactly how that loneliness feels.

Night after night, I would tell myself I knew the truth, remembering the black smoke, trying to hold on to myself until I realized I had no one to hold on for, wondering what if something really was wrong with my brain, and most of all wishing my parents hadn't left me behind. When she's calmer, I ask, "Why did you wait so long to find me?"

"I tried to, for months," she says from behind her hands. "I presented myself at the American embassy, but they lumped me in with all the fanatics. I went through every piece of news, until I read somewhere that you had been institutionalized. I called the center, but as no family was listed for you, they never put me through. The letter was a last resort."

Her hands finally come down. She looks more like Mom now, messy and raw, not uptight and distant. "Give me a chance, Estela. Por favor."

"How do I know you didn't help your brother with the subway spell, just like you did the black fire?"

"I told you, the subway *wasn't a spell*," she says with a bite of impatience.

"How do you know—?"

"Because I've refused to do magic since Antonela died," she says in a rush.

"Teo needs his twin to perform spells. He hates me for keeping magic from him, but I thought it was for the best."

"That's not true because he did magic two nights ago," I say. "He took my blood using your equipment, out in the woods, under the full moon. Felipe was there."

She shoots up so fast, she knocks over her glass of water, and the liquid pools across the wooden tabletop. "When were you going to tell me this?" she demands, ignoring the spill.

"How am I supposed to trust you when you were forcibly drugging me days ago?"

"That's not—" She sighs and shakes her head. "I'll explain later. Right now, we need to find my brother. Maybe we should search the castle, then the woods—"

"No need," I say, cutting her off. "I know where he's been staying."

Beatríz bundles me up like we're going to the North Pole.

As we walk together to town, my gaze darts to every corner, expecting Teo to jump out at us. I catch Beatríz doing the same thing, so I know I'm not alone in my alertness.

"We should stop by the bookstore to check on Felipe," I say.

"You said Arturo told you he went out of town."

"But what if Teo—?"

"Felipe must have panicked after what happened in the woods, and he went to stay with friends out of town to avoid questioning."

"If you knew Felipe," I argue, "you'd know that *anything* to do with la Sombra can only draw him closer."

Beatríz doesn't answer me, but when we get to the town plaza, she swings open the door to Libroscuro. "Hola, doctora!" says a smiling Arturo. "Veo que ha vuelto del congreso. Muy bien."

"Gracias," says Beatríz, and I smile from her side, grateful she's here to do the talking. "¿Está disponible Felipe para darle clases a mi sobrina?"

"No, sigue de viaje el chaval," he says with an apologetic smile. "Por una vez que se toma un descanso, no se lo iba a negar."

"Seguro. Bueno, hasta luego."

When we're outside, Beatríz asks me, "What did you get from that?"

"He's still traveling, and Arturo didn't want to deny him a longer break?"

"Good," she says, sounding pleased with my translation. We reach the clínica, and she unlocks the door. Tension tightens my muscles.

We search the whole place in moments, but Teo is not here anymore. It's only when we regroup by my computer that we find the five-word message he left us, on a sticky note he stuck to the monitor:

Help me bring Antonela home.

12 YEARS AGO

"*LET'S GO," SAYS MY SISTER* in Spanish.

She's shaking me awake in bed.

"Now?" I ask, my throat thick with sleep.

"Look."

I pop open an eye. "What?"

She tilts her head back, and I stare at the ceiling. The lights are flashing on and off.

I sit up. "Let's go."

We open the door slowly, so its creaking won't give us away. Out in the crimson corridor, the lights are blinking, calling to us.

We follow the trail down the stairs and deeper into the castle. We pass through the string of doorless rooms leading to the windowless cathedral, only now the walls are adorned with artwork and the spaces are appointed with furniture. It's only when we reach the spot with the trapdoor to the purple room that the blinking stops.

Then the lights turn up to full blast, illuminating the hall.

"Now what?" asks Antonela.

"Maybe we wait here."

"Or maybe there's something hidden we have to find."

By the way her eyes grow round, I know this is the version we're going with—which suits me fine because I love mysteries. So we begin to look around, inspecting every corner we can reach and casting a close eye along the rug, which looks much brighter and cleaner.

There's a coffee table at the center of the rug, and I jump in a wide circle around it to see if the floor feels loose anywhere.

"Just pull it back," says Antonela, grabbing the edge. I join her, and we fold it over together.

Our wide eyes meet. Wow, we mouth at the same time as we spot part of the outline of a trapdoor.

It takes our joint effort to lift the coffee table and open the trapdoor. We climb down a set of steps to a basement where all we see is an empty hall of rocky walls, and I blow out a frustrated breath.

"There's nothing here!"

Yet Antonela doesn't seem upset. She gets close to the wall, as if she hears something on the other side. "It's like a heartbeat," she says vaguely. Then she reaches up and touches the stone that activates the hidden door.

"Ow!" Blood trickles out from her finger onto the rock.

"Are you okay?" I ask, coming over.

A rectangular outline expands across the stones. "Look!" she says, her voice high-pitched with excitement.

Together, we open the door a sliver, enough for our tiny bodies to squeeze through.

"Purple!" we squeal in unison. It's our favorite color.

We giggle madly and hold hands as we dance round and round and round, high on the castle revealing this secret just to us, a buried room where we can hide without anyone finding us, and we drop to the floor in a bundle of laughter.

"This room is our secret," Antonela says to me once we've calmed down.

"Our secret sister space," I say in agreement.

"Forever," she says.

"Forever."

We pinkie swear, and then we spring up and go back to dancing. Like we truly have forever.

CHAPTER 18

"BUT WHAT IF IT'S TRUE?" I ask yet again, as we climb the overgrown garden to the castle doors.

"I already told you, I'm a physician," says Beatríz, carrying a fabric bag that she didn't have with her earlier. "You can't revive the dead. *Especially* when there isn't even a corpse."

"But you didn't believe the spell to send her to the other castle was real, and it worked!"

"It doesn't take magic to ki—to make a person disappear," she says, choosing different words. "*Magic* would be reviving them!"

It's clear where she stands on this, so I switch subjects. "I met Teo my first day here. He was the driver who picked me up from the airport."

She looks at me in shock. "*That's* why the driver didn't wait for me to pay! I called the company the next day, and they told me the trip had been canceled. I just assumed the center in DC had arranged your transportation so you didn't meet my driver." She shakes her head in a kind of awe. "He must have been keeping watch over me ever since the subway, expecting you would come home eventually."

We reach the front doors of la Sombra, and Bea slips the key in the lock and looks at me. "Be ready."

"You think he's here?" I whisper.

"Just in case." She shows me what's inside the fabric bag, and I see a dozen syringes. They're the sedatives I saw on my tour of the clínica the first day.

Holding one up to demonstrate, she removes the plastic cap over the needle and says, "Stab him with the pointy end, then press in to inject."

She hands me one. "Put it in your coat pocket."

My eyes feel like they take up my whole face as I accept. This still doesn't feel like real life, and I ask her, "Why aren't we calling the police—?"

"Shh," says Beatríz, opening the door.

We search the front part of the castle together, our bedrooms, the grand hall, the kitchen—but there's no sign of him. "Should we check the hidden rooms, like in the basement and the tower?" I ask.

She shakes her head. "I was being cautious, but I think since he left us a note, he wants us to come to him. He's waiting for an answer."

I follow Beatríz to the kitchen, where she washes her hands before pulling out a pan and eggs. "I'm going to make you a Spanish staple," she says, reaching into a cupboard for a bag of potatoes. "Tortilla de papas."

"I'm going to get comfortable," I say, and this is the first time I'm actually looking forward to a meal with my aunt. "I'll be back." When I get to my room, I call out, "Sebastián?"

He isn't here. I hide the blood bags I just stole from the clínica under my bed, since I can't put them in the fridge. Then after pulling on my sweats, a top, and my hoodie, I head back downstairs.

"Can I help?" I ask, joining my aunt in the kitchen.

"Sure. Whisk eight eggs." She plucks a bowl from the cabinet.

I open the fridge, and while she starts peeling potatoes over the sink, I start cracking eggs. "Was your mom—my grandmother—a big cook?" I ask.

Beatríz lets out a yelp of a laugh that startles us both, and I drop half a shell into the bowl. "My mother did *not* cook," she says as I fish it out with the whisk. "She had a household staff for that. It was the same with her mother, and her mother's mother. You and I are breaking with tradition. ¡Salud!"

She holds out the potato peeler, and I clink it with my yolky whisk, smirking. "Dad was always the cook in our family," I say. "Mom was allergic to the kitchen."

Smiling, my aunt looks so much like Mom that just breathing hurts. "Your mother wasn't *allowed* in this kitchen after she snuck in early one morning when she was nine and tried to make breakfast," says Beatríz, some color returning to her face. "It was as bad as you're imagining. After that, she was banned, so whenever she wanted a snack, I had to go in and get it for her."

I whisk the eggs, wondering more about Mom's childhood. "What was Mom's favorite part of the castle?"

"The library. She was a born writer. Her little hands always reached for pens and crayons, and she'd leave her markings everywhere."

I bring the bowl to Beatríz, who is still peeling potatoes. "What was Antonela like?" I ask in a lower register.

My aunt's hands stop working. She doesn't look at me, but her chest rises and falls faster.

"She was an explorer. You liked to sit still, like your dad, but she had more of your mom's restlessness. She loved to play outside and didn't mind things like dirt and bugs."

A blade slices through a potato, and after Beatríz finishes chopping, she instructs me, "Cut these two the same way." Then she turns on the heat and drizzles olive oil into a pan.

By the time we sit to eat, it's dark out, and I need to decide what to do. As soon as Sebastián sees Beatríz, he's going to have a reaction. I just hope it won't be to kill her on sight.

"What do you think?" she asks me.

"Of what?"

"The tortilla española."

"Oh!" I look down and realize I've scarfed down my slice. "Delicious," I say honestly.

I tried it at Felipe's house, but it wasn't as good as this one. That night, I remember being hungry and having to wait a while before the food started circling. "Do Spaniards eat late?" I ask.

Beatríz nods, glass of water in her hand. "Our biggest meal is la comida, in the afternoon, and then la cena is late at night, a few hours after your usual dinnertime. But your doctors asked me to stick to your usual schedule so you wouldn't feel a disruption." She takes a sip of her water. "Speaking of meals, it's your birthday in three days."

I've been actively avoiding thinking of it. The first birthday I'll celebrate without my parents.

Mom and I had my present picked out for when I turned eighteen. It was a promise we made to each other years ago. But it's impossible now.

"I'm sorry," says Bea, reading the sadness on my face. "If you don't want to celebrate, I understand, but I'd like to at least make you something you like. Maybe you can tell me your favorite food?"

Movement flickers in my side vision as Sebastián materializes.

He looks from Beatríz to me and frowns questioningly. I shake my head slightly to signal him not to do anything. "Um, sure, I'll think about it," I say, standing up. "I'm really tired. I'm going to head upstairs—"

My aunt places the black pill on the table in front of me. Before Sebastián has a chance to swipe it and bewilder Beatríz, I ask, "What is it?"

She rises, too. "I think it's time I show you."

I follow Beatríz down the east wing of the castle, where the purple room is buried.

Sebastián's shadow darkens the wall, but my aunt seems oblivious to his presence. We cut across the red rug, and she opens the door into the windowless cathedral. Sebastián appears in physical form beside me, and we exchange curious glances.

My aunt pads across the hall, and at the back wall, she presses her hand to a nondescript stone. Sebastián stiffens; she must have pricked her skin, and he scents the blood.

The stone lights up and slides out. Beatríz twists, and a door swings open, just like the secret one that leads to the purple room.

We step into a dimly lit shed. It smells musty and dank, and all around me are gardening tools and gear.

"Put these on," she says, handing me rain boots.

"Are you certain you can trust her?" Sebastián asks me.

As certain as I can trust you, I mouth. When he grimaces, I know he understood me.

She grabs a pair of gloves before reaching for another door. As she twists the knob, I spy something—*thorns*. Another blood-print check.

As soon as she opens the door, Sebastián goes ahead of us and stops at the threshold.

He's hit a barrier, I think.

But then he steps forward, only slowly; and when I look around, I see why.

We've entered the strangest space I've ever seen. I'm not even sure if we're outdoors or underground.

It looks like a garden made of body limbs. To my left are plants that resemble legs and arms with toe-like flowers, and to my right are tiny trees with bone-like trunks and tonguelike leaves.

"What is this?" I ask, revolted.

"Blood," says Sebastián, his voice low with awe. "It is everywhere."

I have no idea what he's talking about, but then I see Beatríz raise what looks like a watering canister, only the liquid inside is red.

"This castle runs on blood," says my aunt. "That's the real reason we established the blood bank. This is a jardín de sangre." *Blood garden.*

Sebastián and I exchange stunned stares.

It's hard not to be creeped out by the plants that look like body parts growing in the ground, but Sebastián walks around the foliage fascinated, like he sees a beautiful garden and not a grotesque display. I remember my first impression of la Sombra was not of a shadow castle but a shadow creature . . . I guess I wasn't far off the mark.

"So, the lights and the fireplace—?"

"Fuego de sangre," she answers. *Blood flames.*

"You mean there's no electricity?" I ask quizzically.

"The soil this castle was constructed on isn't wholly of this Earth. As there is no magic here, it must be nourished by our blood, which contains our ancestral power. In the earliest days, neighbors were sacrificed. The original owner used to host wild parties to feed the castle, but as civilization matured over time, mass murder became harder to pull off."

The full moon parties. They were real. I can hardly believe it, and I suddenly wish I could tell Felipe.

"Over the generations," she goes on, "our ancestors found a more *civilized* method: collecting blood from residents to feed the castle. That is what we are doing when we tend this garden."

The soil seems to be a mix of dirt and blood, and I notice dark droppings in places. When I look closer, I see they're the black pills.

"The seeds of these plants can be eaten," Bea explains, following my gaze. "They have supernatural healing and nutritional properties, and I've been continuing the work of our ancestors by cataloguing the effects of each plant. I prescribe them as homeopathic remedies for my patients. We take care of la Sombra, and la Sombra takes care of us."

I don't know what to say. Or think. Or feel.

"The seed I gave you is the most potent plant here," she goes on, "which our family uses when introducing a new family member to the castle."

"What do you mean?" I ask.

"When it comes to spouses or hired help, we introduce their blood to this garden first, in higher and higher doses, until it's safe for them to start visiting and eventually move in. We also give them these seeds to ingest so that the castle recognizes them as part of its family. That's how it worked for your father."

"That's why you wanted to draw Felipe's blood the other day," I say, remembering how she reminded him of his appointment.

"I figured it was only a matter of time before he got in here," she says. "I wanted to give him some extra protection."

I can hardly believe it. This castle really is a creature. And like all beings of this world, it's been named by others: *la Sombra*.

"I should've never let Felipe in. I put him in danger." I feel Sebastián's comforting hand squeeze my shoulder.

"You didn't know he was working with your uncle," says Beatríz. "Nor did the boy know what he was getting into." She sighs and sets down the canister.

I still hold her responsible for what she did to Antonela, but I do believe that Beatríz has changed. I don't think she and her brother are the same. She's stepped out from his shadow; she's not his *sombrita* anymore.

"I'll take the pill now," I say, swallowing it sans water.

I think Sebastián bends down and scoops some seeds, but it's too quick to tell.

"How often do you water—er, *blood* these plants?" I ask.

"Once a week." She approaches a metal chamber, and I know it's a freezer by the exhale of icy mist when she opens it. "I fed the castle a big meal before leaving, but I think Teo has been getting into my stores at the clínica," she says, and I look away guiltily. "I wonder what he's doing."

Sebastián lingers by the freezer while Beatríz and I head back into the shed. I hope he doesn't finish *all* the bags in there.

I left you some under my bed, I mouth to him.

"I already found them," he says, baring his fangs in a scary smile.

I keep my aunt company as she washes the dishes. She looks so exhausted that her eyelids are drooping, and I wonder when the last time she truly slept was.

"Let's go to bed, it's been a long day," I say. She doesn't argue and lets me steer her upstairs.

It's only once I'm alone in my room that Sebastián and I can properly speak. "I take it she is not involved in her brother's plans?" he asks.

I shake my head. "I found another room today with journals of spells my ancestors attempted. And I learned something."

"What is it?" he asks, and I know he feels the gravity of my news because concern colors his gaze.

"I had a sister. A twin."

He stares at me with wide eyes, wordless.

"They killed her," I say, my voice breaking. "In the black fire."

Sebastián pulls me into his chest, and I inhale night's cologne. "I am sorry," he murmurs.

How is it possible to miss someone I only learned about hours ago? After becoming an orphan, I didn't think I had anything left to lose. But the world just keeps on taking.

"Your uncle will pay for all he has done," Sebastián vows into my hair.

I flash to the book I buried in the garden, and my stomach roils with guilt. Am I just as bad as the rest of my family, using lies and deceit to get what I want?

"What if it turns out you're with someone where you're from?" I ask, the anxiety eating at me. "Or if you have a family or important responsibilities or *power*—?"

"What if you had died in the woods?" he asks, cutting me off. "I was so consumed with the fear of losing you that I could not produce another thought."

"You only have access to seven months' worth of memories," I argue. "How can you know you really feel this way about me?"

"I can only describe it as I feel the pain of breaking-in muscles I did not know I had," he says, and his silver gaze no longer holds any coldness. "You are cultivating a gentleness in me I never had cause to develop. I do not want to lose these new pieces of myself any more than I want to lose you."

Everything he says is perfect, and yet I don't deserve it. I am keeping his identity from him, just as my family did to me.

But I can't lose him.

Our lips meet, and his tongue flips a switch that makes every inch of me tingle.

I barely feel the floor beneath my feet as he guides us to my bed. As we move, Sebastián zips down my hoodie and pulls off my shirt, letting the layers fall behind me like flower petals.

I'm trembling as he pulls down my pants, his starry gaze glued to mine, like he's daring me to say *stop*.

I'm only in a bra and underwear as he slides me onto the bed. We're both sitting up as he kisses my neck and draws a path to my chest with his tongue. I boldly reach back and unhook my bra. The straps sling off my shoulders and the whole thing rolls down, exposing my breasts.

I've never been naked in front of someone like this, and I feel a sear of heat flush my cheeks. I want to ask him if he's going to remove his shirt, too, but I can't make my tongue form the words.

"You are beautiful," he says, running a finger across my jawline, his cold finger leaving a trail of heat on my skin. "We can move slower if this is too fast."

I chuckle nervously. "Must be the opposite for you. This must feel like slow motion."

"*Time* is a concept with which I have only recently become acquainted," he says. "What I know of it can be summed up in a line from a book I read in this library: *Being with you and not being with you is the only way I have to measure time.*"

All my organs seem to be melting. Only a week ago, the shadow beast seemed a sadistic monster with no heart, and now he is the most romantic being I have ever known.

"It is better in the original Spanish," he says, his gaze so soft, it looks like a silver sea. "*Estar contigo o no estar contigo es la medida de mi tiempo.*"

His voice sounds deeper in Spanish, and I remember noting the way my parents' pitch would also shift when they switched languages. Without breaking our stare, he rakes his fingers through my hair, pulling the curls back, and his other hand closes around my neck, his thumb pressing into my chin.

"You say when to stop," he tells me, then his hand drops from my face to my collarbone, and then lower still, to my breasts.

Sebastián's caresses make me moan, and I feel an engine deep within me revving to life. His hand trails down my rib cage, and in with my waist, and as it keeps moving south, I fall back onto the bed. His fingers stay on the outside of my underwear, but the cotton is too thin to be much of a barrier.

I can't keep my eyes from rolling back as numbness spreads through me, a relaxing sensation that overtakes every muscle and makes my mind too dizzy to form a complete thought.

"I want to," I mumble, "stay awake."

I'd rather not miss more time with him, but this sense of release is making me sleepy. I'm sad about my sister and hopeful about Beatríz and overwhelmed by Sebastián—and the cocktail is emotionally draining.

"Sleep, Estela," he whispers in my ear. "You will need it for what lies ahead." As blackness overtakes my mind, the last thing I hear him say is: "We have no idea what your uncle is plotting."

12 YEARS AGO

"*UNO, DOS, TRES, CUATRO, CINCO . . .*"

I'm counting, and Antonela is hiding.

This time, I start my search outside. I run to the front door, and when I see that it's open, my worst suspicions about my sister are confirmed. I open my mouth to yell at Antonela that I'm not going to play with her anymore if she keeps breaking the rules, but I forget the game altogether when I spot her.

Antonela isn't hiding, nor is she alone.

A boy is approaching her.

He sticks out his hand, and I see her rest something on it. A rock.

There's blood on her hand as she gives it to him. Then he cuts his own palm open.

The lights in the foyer flicker on and off, on and off, on and off.

Like a warning.

I don't like that the castle is talking to me when Nela isn't around, nor that Nela is talking to a boy when I'm not around. We're supposed to do everything together.

This feels like a bad sign of things to come.

CHAPTER 19

MY DREAMS ARE ALL OF ANTONELA.

Probably because of the black seed, a memory dam broke overnight, and I've started to recall things from when we were five, like us playing hide-and-seek, and discovering the purple room, and me spying on her blood pact with Felipe. He and I didn't meet as kids; he met my twin.

I wake up missing her as much as I miss Mom and Dad. This morning, I accompany Bea to the clínica, but Teo isn't there, and there are no new messages from him. At the bookstore, Arturo tells us that Felipe is coming back tonight.

I have no idea how I'm going to handle seeing him again. I know friends are supposed to forgive each other, but I'm not sure what he did is forgivable. As much as I'll miss our sessions in the attic, I will never be able to trust him again. Can you have friendship without trust?

"I'm going to the castle," I say to Bea. "I'll come back to the clínica in the afternoon."

"Are you sure?" she asks, studying me like I might be coming down with something.

"I didn't sleep well," I lie, before she jumps to take my temperature and oxygen levels.

"Do you have your—?" She mimics firing a gun, but I know she means injecting a syringe.

I reach into my jacket pocket. "Locked and loaded."

"Don't let anyone in."

"I know," I assure her. "I won't be breaking that rule anytime soon. Or *ever,*" I amend when her eyes narrow.

"Good," she says. "See you back here in four hours for la comida."

I prick my finger and press my blood to the tablet.

The bookshelves slide apart, and I climb to the secret room at the peak of the tower, where everything is exactly as I last saw it.

Ignoring Brálaga's letter, I go straight to the journals and open them at random. They all feature a pair of names on the inside cover, and as I flip through the pages, the words translate themselves, same as yesterday.

I skim ingredients, instructions, and diagrams for various potions and spells that claim to do everything from growing a plentiful garden, to invoking prophetic dreams, to producing a truth-telling tea. The last one has a postscript that notes the tea only works on members of the Brálaga family, and only within the bounds of la Sombra.

After skimming a handful of these, I see that Beatríz is right—both twins are needed to produce magic. So how did Teo pull it off on his own the other night?

I open a new journal and read the names scribbled on the inside cover: *Matilda y Josefina.* As I flip through it, I see there's only one page of writing, and the rest of the book is blank.

I read the entry:

> *The bad luck began when I was sixteen.*
>
> *Small explosions around the castle, like energy bursts. One killed Grandfather. When the police and reporters started coming, more people began to disappear. Ironically, the vanishings only drew more crowds.*
>
> *Dad had always been withdrawn. He and his twin brother had a mournful air about them.*
>
> *Only now, he became strangely talkative. It was a nervous chatter, the roundabout kind that usually circles back toward a shameful admission. That's how I learned about Josefina.*
>
> *My twin.*
>
> *My dad and his brother sent her to the other castle when she was four. They were convinced her spirit had returned and was now haunting us for failing to bring her home.*

It wasn't long before Dad killed himself.

I write this as a warning: Keep away from these books. Do not send anyone to the other castle. Let the curse sleep.

I'm so distracted by the journals that I'm late to meet Bea.

Not good. No doubt she's going to fear the worst. I dart downstairs to head out—

BANG BANG BANG.

The gargoyle knockers echo around me in the entrance chamber, and I bring my hands to my ears to muffle the noise.

BOOM. BOOM. BOOM. My pulse chimes in with its own beat.

My aunt wouldn't knock. Maybe if I don't make any noise, they'll think no one's home.

I hear a faint ringing in the distance. Either Beatríz is dialing the phone in her room, or the ringing is from permanent damage to my eardrums from my proximity to the knockers.

"Estela?"

I gasp. "*Felipe?*"

"Estela!" he cries, voice choked with emotion. "Open the door!"

He sounds terrified, but I don't reach for the handle. "Why?" I call through the thick wood. "What happened? Where did you go?"

"Your uncle took me! I escaped, but he's still after me—my parents will never believe me, they idolize your family! No one will understand but you. Let me in!"

My fingers tremble, and I tuck my hands under my elbows. I don't know what Felipe is capable of anymore, so I have no idea if he's telling the truth. "I-I'm not allowed," I call back. "My aunt returned. She says it's dangerous to let people into the castle—look at what happened to you last time!"

"Are you serious? I know you're mad at me, but *he's going to kill me!*"

"He's not," I say, mouth dry because I don't know what's true anymore. "He doesn't need anything from you." I can't tell if I'm trying to convince Felipe or myself.

"Then why did I just break out of the abandoned shack where he's been keeping me?"

What would Teo want with Felipe? "Just—go home!" I shout. "Or go to the clínica, and Bea can look at you, okay?"

"I can't go to town, or he'll find me! He's probably tracking me right now, and if you don't let me in, he's going to kill me, and it'll be *your* fault!"

I feel the tears forming in my eyes. "You're right. I'm cursed, Felipe. Stay away from me."

"I'm already caught in your curse! Don't you get it? He's going to kill me—but I guess you can live with that."

"You can't come in here," I insist, making my voice firm. "But if you're that afraid, I'll walk you to the clínica—"

"Don't bother!" he shouts at me. "I'm going to the police, and I'm telling them *everything*! They'll come here searching for answers, and you can explain your curse to *them*—"

I swing open the door. "I'll walk with you, and we can tell my aunt what's happening," I say, and since the key is in my pocket, I shut the door behind me.

Before the lock clicks, Felipe shoves past me, shouldering the door open. "Hey!" I shout as he knocks me into the doorframe on his way inside.

"*Felipe!*" I call after him, but he doesn't turn or slow down. My heart plummets as I realize I've made the same mistake twice.

Bea is never going to trust me after this.

"Felipe, wait!" I follow him into the grand hall with the ribbed ceiling and ask, "What does my uncle want with you?"

The guy who meets my gaze is not the Felipe I know.

He looks sickly, as if his skin would be sticky to touch, and his gaze darts everywhere, like he's searching for something. Or someone.

"First tell me what happened," he says, leaning against the back of a leather couch.

"When?"

"After I passed out." He's breathing heavier than usual.

"Let's sit," I say, and he looks around, like this might be a trap. But once I drop onto a cushion, he comes around and joins me, his face relaxing as his body rests.

"My uncle bled me from both arms until I passed out," I say. "I woke up on the ground outside la Sombra the next morning. What do *you* remember?"

"Waking up in an empty shack." He swallows, and his throat sounds parched. "It's where your uncle has been staying. He only moves at night, so no one sees him. He took me back to the same spot in the forest two nights ago, tied me up, and blindfolded me, but I could hear him chanting the same words over and over again."

"*No hay luz en Oscuro,*" I supply, and he nods. "Did he use my blood?" I ask.

"I don't know. I woke up in that shack yesterday. I've been feeling sick ever since, and your uncle has been tending to me, but today I felt fine enough to escape once he fell asleep."

"But your dad," I say, frowning. "He said he spoke to you on the phone—"

The castle's front door thuds shut. Felipe and I stiffen, and I don't even breathe until I hear Bea's voice.

"Estela?"

"I'm here!" I call out, and I say to Felipe, "*Wait here.*" I need to do some explaining before she sees him.

I meet my aunt in the hallway.

"You never came," she says, syringe cocked in her hand like it's a loaded gun. "I got worried—"

"I'm fine, but I need to tell you something," I say hurriedly, reaching for her arms so she'll lower her weapon and stop walking. "Felipe's here."

Her gaze narrows with anger. "I *told* you no visitors!"

"Teo was holding him hostage, and he managed to escape," I say quickly, letting go of her arms. "I think he needs medical attention."

"He needs to go home, and his family needs to take him to a doctor far from here," she says, syringe still in hand.

"*You're* a doctor!"

She blows out a hard breath and starts marching ahead to meet Felipe. "Haven't you realized yet?" she asks over her shoulder as she rounds the corner. "He isn't safe with us! No one is—*ahhh!*"

"Beatríz!"

I rush forward as she collapses, but I freeze when I see Felipe. He's caught her before she hits the floor, and the syringe clatters away.

"She should be more careful," he says, setting her down.

"What just happened?" I ask. "Did—did you do that?" I back away a few paces.

"She injected herself—"

"You pushed her hand!"

My heart's pounding shakes my frame. I never should have let him in.

He moves toward me, and I keep walking backward. "Why are you here?" I ask, my voice quavering.

"I may have rewritten some details of my story." His crooked smirk is now more of a leer, his once-handsome face sagging with illness. "When I woke up in your uncle's shed the morning after he drew your blood, I wasn't tied up. Teo gave me a choice: I could go home, or I could make a new home in la Sombra."

I slip my hands inside my hoodie's pocket, and my fingers close around my own syringe, since Bea warned me to be armed at all times. If Felipe reaches for me, he's going down.

"So, what do you think I chose?" he asks, still marching closer. "I tried to resist. I wanted so much to be good for you. But he offered me something I could never refuse." His glassy eyes begin to shimmer, and I see that actual tears are forming.

"Being a Brálaga is all I ever wanted. I hoped to do it by marrying you, but you turned me down. You left me no other choice."

I scramble back, toward the front door, trying to keep out of his reach. "What did my uncle mean? How could you become a Brálaga?"

"He told me I could marry into the family if I did one thing for him."

I feel the blood abandoning my face. "It's your fault if you thought I was his to offer!"

"I didn't say I'd be marrying *you*."

"I don't think you're Bea's type—"

But when Felipe's confidence doesn't crack, I realize who he means, and I gasp. "You can't actually think—"

"I do," he says. "He's promised me your sister's hand when she returns."

"My uncle is sick!" I shout at him. "And my sister is dead!"

"He's going to bring her back." Felipe's face lights up with manic faith. "But first, he needs me to deliver a message."

The brightness of his gaze has hardened to glass, and I break into a run. He looks so ill that I'm hoping I can make it out the front door in time—

I duck as he lunges for me.

Felipe crashes against the door, and I spin away. Careening deeper into the castle, I hope I've bought myself enough time to outrun him. If I can just make it to one of the secret rooms, he won't be able to follow me.

I cut toward the tower, but I hear Felipe's footsteps gaining ground. His breaths grow louder, and I grip the syringe. When he's too close, I swing around—

He bats my arm away, and the needle goes flying. We both dive for it, and I jab my elbow into his eye.

"Ow!"

I reach the syringe first and spring to my feet. Felipe yanks on my ankle, knocking me down.

"Let go!"

He pulls on my leg to slide me toward him, and I arch up to stab him with the needle—but he rolls out of my reach.

A shadow falls over us, and we both look up at Sebastián, whose menacing glare is focused on Felipe. *Is it nighttime already?*

I have just enough time to register that Felipe can *see* the shadow beast, before I realize what's going to happen. "*Sebastián, don't!*"

But he's already got Felipe in his grip, eyes wide on discovering he can touch him.

"Please!" I beg, grabbing Sebastián's arm so he'll let Felipe go. But he might as well be made of steel.

"Who are you?" the shadow beast demands.

"A messenger."

"I don't want your message!" I shout, still tugging on Sebastián's arm. "I want you to go!"

"My message isn't for you," says Felipe, his eyes on the shadow beast.

I feel myself going slack-jawed. How does Felipe know about him?

"Go on," says Sebastián.

"You want to know who you are?" Felipe twists his neck to look at me. "Ask *her*."

My whole body goes cold, and I wish I were anywhere but here.

"What do you mean?" asks Sebastián.

"Estela has a book about you. I gave it to her."

I back away from them both. I consider stabbing myself with the syringe to avoid this moment as Sebastián turns to look at me, shock in his eyes.

"Not that you need the book," Felipe goes on. "If you truly want your memories back, all you have to do is drink. They're stored in Estela's blood."

I feel my eyes grow bigger than my face, yet I don't see renewed shock in the silver galaxies of Sebastián's gaze. He couldn't have known this whole time that my blood was the key to unlocking his past . . . *could he?*

"Don't blame me," says Felipe, and too late I clock the predatory shift in Sebastián's expression. He's staring at him dangerously. "Like I said, I'm just the messenger."

"Yet your message is not in your words."

I've seen that look.

I squeeze Sebastián's arm with all the strength my muscles can muster. "Sebastián, *please*! DON'T—"

But he's already ripped Felipe's throat open and started to drink.

RAUL'S RULE #10

SUSPECTS ARE OFTEN CLOSER THAN THEY APPEAR.

CHAPTER 20

THE BLACK SMOKE IS EVERYWHERE.

"*Sebastián!*" I call into the dark, but I hear nothing back. "*Felipe!*"

The silence is as thick as the fumes—and when the air finally clears, the scene looks frozen in time. Felipe lies limp in Sebastián's arms.

I sob.

The sound fractures the silent tableau, and Sebastián's gaze snaps up. Felipe's blood smears his mouth and chin.

His silver eyes have darkened to a deeper shade, making his gaze weightier. I wonder if I'll be the next corpse in his arms.

"We need to talk," he says. Even his voice sounds heavier, more measured.

"I have to get Bea on the couch," I say, unable to look at his face, which is coated with Felipe's death.

The shadow beast reappears at Bea's side, his mouth by her neck as he reaches for her. "Stop!" I shriek, but his arms go right through her body, and I realize he was trying to carry my aunt, not kill her.

And yet how will I ever know the difference?

I focus on Bea's body as I slide my arms under her back and thighs, then try to lift. But I'm too weak.

Useless, stupid tears form in the corners of my eyes, and I bite down on my inner lip until I taste blood to keep from crying. After dragging Bea by the shoulders to the sofa, I manage to roll her up onto the cushions. I spend a lot of time adjusting the pillows, and when at last I can't avoid him anymore, I look up.

But the shadow beast isn't here.

I return to the corridor where Felipe's corpse lies, but he's gone, too. A shadow darkens the wall, and Sebastián steps out from it. He's cleaned the blood off his face, but he can't lighten his eyes as easily.

"Where's Felipe?" I ask, my voice creaky.

"I buried him in the jardín de sangre. Your aunt will know what to do."

I'm too numb to answer. I have no idea how to tell Bea that Felipe is dead because my boyfriend ate him.

Sebastián holds out a hand to me. Inside is a black seed.

I take it and swallow the pill, my throat so dry I feel its progression.

"I need air," I whisper.

Sebastián lifts me in his arms without warning, and I gasp as the castle blurs around me, and our surroundings settle into the graying twilit sky.

As he sets me down on my feet, I look around in awe. We're standing on the balcony tower.

"I thought you couldn't come here," I say, aghast.

"I could not. Nor was it nightfall yet when I appeared."

"How then?" I ask.

"I believe it is your aunt's pills. They are affecting the parameters of the spell."

I keep my expression neutral, but I'm sure he can hear the speeding of my heart as I wonder what else these seeds could change. What happens if Sebastián gets free of his chains and can roam the planet?

If a shark bites a bleeding swimmer, is the shark a murderer, or is it just obeying its nature?

Sebastián stares up at the stars, and I wonder when he's going to ask me to tell him who he is and where I've hidden the book. Or maybe he'll skip talking altogether and suck the answers from my blood.

After all, he's the Iron Prince other monsters fear, and he's been stuck playing house with a human. A human liar who discovered his identity and withheld it from him. I don't imagine I'll make it through the night.

And maybe I don't deserve to.

"I remember," he murmurs. "*Everything.*"

I trade one gray horizon for another as I look at him. "What are you talking about?"

"There was something off about Felipe's scent." It might be the first time he's used Felipe's name. "It was being masked by the rotting odor of death coming from his condition. When he called himself a *messenger*, I understood. The same thing that made it possible for me to interact with him was what was killing him—*your blood.*"

"*What?*" I ask, breathless.

"Your uncle performed blood magic. He dosed Felipe with your blood, which contained my memories. Your friend was already dying when he got here, even if he did not know it."

"Are you sure?" My voice is barely audible, but Sebastián hears me clearly.

"I used his blood to access the jardín de sangre." It's decisive proof Felipe was dosed with Brálaga blood.

I breathe in deeply a few times, tasting winter's early chill in the air. *Felipe was already dying*. And my uncle denies being a murderer.

Every part of me is shaking. "Why do this?"

"That is a question for your uncle." His voice is colder, a little more like the shadow beast from the first night. "How long have you known who I am?"

"Three days," I admit.

"Since I kissed you."

Guilt twists my gut, and I nod.

"Why did you keep it from me?"

There's no point in holding back now. "I didn't want to let you go."

He looks unmoved, and I rebound the question. "How long did *you* know?"

"Know what?"

"That your memories were in my blood." His expression doesn't soften, but his chin tips up just a little in surprise. "That's why you haven't fed on me again since the first time, isn't it?" I press.

"I suspected it."

"Why?"

"When I drank from you, we both saw memories from my childhood. I only had access to that information through your blood." His eyes darken as the shadows deepen around him. "Yet I sensed that if I recovered those memories, the unburdened version of me—the one you named *Sebastián*—would cease to be. Like any creature, I was only trying to survive."

I want to ask if that's what's happened now, if Sebastián has *ceased to be*, but I can't stomach the answer. So instead I say, "I'm sorry I lied to you."

"I am too much of a monster not to forgive you."

Yet his expression and tone don't lighten. This new way he speaks and the heaviness in his gaze are hard to take. Even the particles of air seem to exert weight on his shoulders.

This isn't my Sebastián. This is Prince Bastian.

"You know what they call me?" he asks.

"The Iron Prince."

His lips curve up in a cold imitation of his old smile, only this one offers no light. "Then you know I come from a world even your most darkly imaginative artists could not conceive. *Sebastián* was a lie that could only exist as long as I did not bear the burden of my past."

"That's not true," I whisper. "You can *choose* to be different."

"You speak of me as if I were human and capable of your full range of emotions. I am the future king of my kind. I crave power, blood, violence. I do not sacrifice for others—I only sacrifice others."

"And still you've been taking care of me—"

"Because it was in my best interest. But if you are expecting me to do the right thing, I will let you down."

I sigh in exasperation. "So this is it then? You're going home and leaving me here?"

"I do not know how to break the spell," he says, and I wait for him to add that he doesn't want to leave because I'm here.

But he doesn't.

Obviously.

"What do you remember?" I ask, trying to speak over the cracking of my heart so he won't hear it. "Of your home?"

"That I am as trapped there as I am here," he says, the edge in his voice growing sharper. "All the knowledge I hold, all the worlds I know, every great battle, I have learned it all from afar. I am always entangled in others' games. Even here, with you. I am an inmate shuffled from one prison to another, without any say in where I go."

"Fight back then," I whisper.

"What?"

My heart pounds in my chest. "Against all odds, you and I have met. We come from literally different worlds, and yet our paths have crossed. Against all odds, you didn't kill me on our first meeting. Our entire relationship has been *impossible,* but it's happening. We can change things—"

"Not anymore," he says. "This is over."

"*No,*" I breathe, and then I can't say more because the rest of my frame is splintering. The slightest movement will shatter the illusion that I'm whole, and I'll crumble into a million broken pieces.

"Go rest," he says, surveying the view, his back to me. "I will keep watch for your uncle."

Daylight makes everything more gruesome.

Bea and I stand in the jardín de sangre, where Felipe's corpse is buried, and I can't understand how we got here. Felipe wasn't perfect, but he didn't deserve a death sentence.

"How did this happen?" she whispers.

"Teo did a blood spell on Felipe using the blood he took from me, after promising him Antonela's hand in marriage—"

"Antonela's—?"

"Yes. All Felipe had to do was carry a message for . . . Sebastián."

"Who?"

The shadow beast may have broken up with me, but as long as he's stuck haunting this place, it's going to be hard to keep him hidden from Beatríz. "Someone else has been living in this castle."

My aunt's gaze grows murderously grave. "Did you invite a friend—?"

"No, he's not human. Besides, he was here when I arrived, but you can't see him."

She blinks, and the hardness is gone from her face, replaced by a concern I recognize well.

"It's not like *that,* either," I hasten to say. "I'm not imagining him."

"Let's start with who is *he*?" she asks, adopting a neutral tone.

This is already not going well.

I sigh and let it out: "He's a vampire from another realm who only appears at night. He arrived the day of the subway attack, so he's part of the spell that killed my parents, and I'm the only one who can see him."

She doesn't say anything.

I'm not sure she's even blinked.

"I named him Sebastián because he lost his memories in the spell," I go on, "but he's really Prince Bastian, future ruler of the vampires. We think Teo brought him here, but we don't know why."

I keep hoping that giving her more details will prove I'm telling the truth, but I can hear that it's sounding less and less believable.

"Estela, forgive me for asking, but if you're the only one who can see him, how can you be sure he exists?" Beatríz cringes like it causes her discomfort to ask the question, but I can't blame her. I was questioning the same thing a few days ago.

"Let him prove his existence to you tonight," I say. "Okay?"

She nods in assent. "So, what exactly happened? This *Sebastián* killed Felipe?"

"No, Sebastián said Felipe was already dying, and he could smell my blood from the spell Teo performed. Then he drank Felipe's blood—which was spiked with mine—and that's how he got his memories back." I look around for a shovel just to turn away from her horrified expression. "What if we dig up the body and you can see the puncture marks?"

Beatríz has a hand pressed to her chest. She looks nauseated. "No" is all she says.

"What do we tell Felipe's parents?" I ask, thinking of Felipe's loud, happy family, and their colorful faces fade to gray as I picture them receiving this news.

Even though things soured between us by the end, I feel a deep sadness that I won't share any more attic sessions with him, or see his crooked smirk when I get something right, or watch his eyes light up with excitement over a book.

"They can't know Felipe died here," says Beatríz. "If this place becomes a crime scene investigation, the castle could assume it's a blood offering, like in the old days." Chills race down my spine at her words. "And with you involved, the sole survivor of the Subway Twenty-Five, the news would be all over it—"

"Felipe's dead?"

Bea and I spin around at the sound of the new voice.

Teo has joined us in the blood garden, blocking our path back to the shed. I look to my aunt in alarm, but she's locked into a staring contest with her brother.

Even though they're silent, unspoken conversation zaps between them, the air charged with emotion. They're the same height, and beneath Teo's piercings and tattoos and facial hair, their features are mirror images.

"Así que estabas aquí," she says to him. *So you were here.*

"English, for our niece," he says in an ironic show of chivalry. "I came when I learned you were having a family reunion and didn't invite me."

"You're making a mistake, Teo," she says to him, ice in her words.

"That's all I've ever heard from everyone. And yet you've gone along with so many of those *mistakes*."

"I'm making amends. You should try it."

"Looks like it's going great. Did you bury the dead boy here?"

Bea approaches her brother slowly, hand in her pocket, probably grasping the syringe. "What did you do to him, Teo? Did you attempt to transfuse Estela's blood? What equipment did you use?"

Once she's within a foot of him, she strikes—but Teo's hand juts out, shoving her arm back into her pocket.

"Don't even try it, Sombrita. If I go down, so do you. And this time there is a body."

She seems stricken, and he looks past her, to me. "Poor Felipe," he says in a mock mournful tone. "He didn't have to die."

"Why are you doing this?" I ask.

"I just want to bring your sister back. Don't you?"

"She's *dead*. You killed her."

"Is she? Only one person can find out for sure." I frown at him questioningly, and he says, "As her twin, you share all the key components."

"That's enough!" snaps Bea.

But she's too late. I'm already hooked. "What do you mean?"

"There's a spell—"

"The last thing she needs are more of your spells!" Bea stands between Teo and me, as if her body is a wall that can protect me from his reach.

"If she doesn't do this, Nela's story will be lost forever," he argues with his sister. "Is that what you want?"

"How dare you put this on Estela when it's our fault Antonela's gone!"

"Is she, though?" he asks, eyes overbright, and I'm so reminded of Felipe that I understand why Bea never warmed to him. It must've felt like seeing the ghost of her brother.

"Stop," warns my aunt. "I won't let you traumatize the girl any further."

"What do you think happened to Oli and Raul?" he whispers, and every part of me stills at the mention of my parents.

"You tell me," she threatens, narrowing her gaze like a detective zeroing in on a suspect.

"I thought it had to be the curse," he admits, all traces of humor gone from his face. "But what if we're wrong?" The spark is back in his gaze and blazing brighter than before. "What if Nela is trying to come home to us, but some-one won't let her cross over? If there's something we can do, if she needs us, *we owe it to her to find out.*"

I don't bother looking to my aunt to see if my uncle's words have worked on her. Because they've already worked on me.

"I'll do it."

"No!" cries Bea, her face drawn in despair as Teo's splits into a smile.

I can feel the hardness in my chest that tells me I'm not going to budge. I came to la Sombra to close my parents' case, and even if the castle's curse is what doomed them, there still has to be an identifiable culprit, weapon, and motive. If Teo wasn't the brujo behind the Subway 25 spell, who was?

And why did they do it?

Felipe is dead, and Sebastián has abandoned me. Prince Bastian is back, and he's made his priorities clear: he wants to break the spell.

Teo's methods may be *out-there,* but he knows a lot more about Brálaga magic than the rest of us, and if he's not a suspect, then he's my best source. I couldn't save my parents, but if there's even a minuscule chance that Teo is right that Antonela is alive and possibly in danger and we have the chance to do something, then I need to act.

To hell with caution and rules.

"She was my sister," I tell my aunt, knowing she will understand after everything she's done for her brother. "I need to know."

"Let's get to the mirror." Teo is already springing into action, and as he strides out of the garden, I follow him.

"How do you know the spell we need to use?" I ask, without waiting for Bea.

"I found it in the journals long ago," he says. "I have just been waiting for you to return to the castle to try it."

"But I thought Brálagas could only do magic under the full moon."

"That's for big outdoor spells," he says. "The rules are different in the castle because la Sombra is fueled by our blood."

He's really read through the journals carefully. "Who restocks the journals when they run out?" I venture.

He looks at me with a wry smile. "Now you're asking the right kind of question."

"What's the right kind?" I ask as we cut through the string of doorless rooms.

"The ones without answers."

I roll my eyes. "I bet you've tried stealing journals from the attic."

"I have, but they're impossible to remove. I even tried photographing them, or tracing them over, but the pictures came out blank, as did the ink in my pen and the lead in my pencils. So I settled for reading through all of them, some over and over again until I memorized as much as I could."

"Why did you kill Felipe?" I ask when we reach the fork in the road.

Teo stops moving. "I'm not a murderer."

There's a harder edge to the declaration now, which only makes him sound guiltier.

"Aren't you?" I ask, forging ahead of him to the mirror room.

I have to wait a few seconds for him to join me, and he's back to all-business. "This glass can be used to channel Antonela's memories," he says, facing the mirror. "*If* she made it to the other castle. You won't get everything, but enough to know she lived."

Bea enters the room and looks at me pleadingly. "Are you sure you want to do this?"

I nod in assent, nauseated with anticipation. "What do I have to do?"

"Look in the mirror, and wherever your reflection leads, follow it," says Teo. "Think of it as a high-security vault. You're the only one who can access your twin's memories because you share the same DNA, so the lock can't differentiate between you two."

He holds out his hands to his sister, who grudgingly joins her fingers with his. Then they begin to chant in low voices, like they're praying: "*No hay luz en Oscuro, no hay luz en Oscuro, no hay luz en Oscuro . . .*"

I look deep into my own eyes, wondering if this will work. How might it feel to see my face on someone else's body and hear my voice come out of someone else's mouth? Will she speak like me? Move like me?

I blink when I realize my reflection is waving me forward. I touch the mirror, and the texture is watery. When my fingers slide through the glass, I press my nose in to test if I can breathe—

And the mirror sucks me inside.

My surroundings shift to utter darkness, and my aunt and uncle are gone. I'm in a vacuum of space, floating.

"Hello?"

My greeting is soundless. I lost either my voice or my hearing or both. I look down at my hands, and they don't seem substantial. I'm a ghost.

I gasp as the scenery begins to fill in.

I see myself at various stages of childhood and adolescence, hundreds of memories jostling for space in the air, all of them unfolding simultaneously.

Only I don't remember any of these moments.

Teo was right.

Antonela made it to the other side.

THE OTHER CASTLE

CHAPTER 21

I SEE A MILLION VERSIONS of my sister, all overlapping, like a timeline splintering into a collage.

And I'm reminded of "El Aleph," a short story by Dad's favorite Argentine writer, Jorge Luis Borges. The Aleph is a point in space that contains all of existence, a window to the universe that's unfiltered and undistorted. It feels like I'm looking into it now.

Antonela is a little kid in some scenes and a preteen in others. I try focusing on a single iteration, and my mind hones in on a specific memory.

Antonela is joined by other young beings who appear to be of different species, yet they all wear the same gray cloaks. This seems to be some sort of school.

I would barely be able to keep my greedy eyes off my sister, except that she and the others are packed in a gathering hall that can best be described as *alive*.

The walls are bloodred and sentient, like a body organ. Black veins branch across them, seemingly connecting the castle's various chambers.

There is a palpable excitement in the air, and I hear some of the whispers.

"I cannot believe we are going to meet Grandparent!"

"Our lessons have *never* been disrupted for *anything*."

"What do you think is happening?"

I understand it all as if they were speaking English, but something tells me I'm tuning in to la Sombra's magical audio setting and not the original language.

A tall hooded being sweeps onto the stage in a black cloak.

They say nothing, and yet the entire hall quiets, the being onstage commanding every molecule of air in the room. Their face is concealed, but their energy is boundless, and even I can feel the electricity they produce. It's like standing in the presence of a being so powerful that gravity warps around them.

And without explanation, I know who this is—

Brálaga.

"It does me good to see you, my grandchildren."

Their voice is hard to describe. It is even more otherworldly than Sebastián's and defies all labels and classifications. It is a voice that belongs to the ocean and the sky.

"Your faces filling this hall brings me great satisfaction. You have made me proud with your efforts in your training, and now I am honored to announce that your *graduation* approaches."

Whispers break out, and it's clear none of the students have heard this word or concept before.

"This castle exists outside of time and space," says Brálaga, and as I look from Antonela to the others, their confusion seems to only deepen. "You are unfamiliar with these concepts because this castle is all you know, and you have been following the same routines your whole lives. This is your world, and none of you knows what it looks like from the outside. You have never breached its walls."

I have never seen a more silent or confused audience in my life. Everyone seems dazed, as if they did not know there was such a thing as *before* or *after*—just an infinite present.

"I built my home as an interdimensional haven for my descendants," Brálaga explains. "You have seen how outsiders are constantly trying to break in. When a foot or a fist or a tail punches through the beating walls of our home, we wrestle it back. That is why you, my grandchildren, must train and make yourselves strong. Yet a few of you, the best of you, will be chosen for a different mission. You will join me beyond the castle walls."

The silence reaches a deeper volume, and the room grows quieter and louder at once. As I study Antonela and the others, I can tell that until now, this castle was everything. Nowhere and nothing else existed.

Now—just like that—everyone feels the pressure and hope of chasing a goal.

This is their first experience of *time*.

"Those who are chosen will no longer go by *grandchild*," says Brálaga. "They shall be given their own name."

Talking breaks out, and when I look back at the stage, Brálaga is gone.

A classmate with fiery crimson hair and feathery wings that stick out from their cloak leans toward my sister and says, "No way you get chosen."

"They could get chosen," says a boulder-like being with one panoramic eyeball. "As the worst Brálaga grandchild of all."

The two of them snicker. I hate them already, but I can't deny that my sister's human body isn't all that impressive compared to the others here. All she has that looks dangerous is her jagged front tooth. She's even physically smaller than her classmates, giving off runt-of-the-litter vibes.

Despite all this, Antonela puffs out her chest and says, "My blood is the same as yours."

Red glowers. "You do not belong here."

My sister seems to have heard this taunt before because she doesn't appear hurt. If anything, she looks *intrigued*.

Almost like after hearing this insult too many times, she started tuning it out. But with Brálaga's announcement, the words hit different.

Less insulting and more promising. And I can almost read the question on Antonela's mind—*What if I don't belong here?*

In the next scene, my sister is with a couple dozen kids, all of them bigger than her. They're in a round room with mirrored walls, staring at their reflections.

Her classmates have similar physiologies to humans, but with otherworldly features that Antonela lacks. Beyond the fact that some have wings or scaly skin or horns, everything from their expressions to their movements to the way they speak gives off more savage vibes, like Sebastián.

As they stare into the mirrors, the students' reflections begin to morph. Red turns their tresses into black vipers, while Cyclops grows a second eyeball on their head. Their physical bodies don't change, just their reflections.

"Is that your glamour?" asks a tall hooded figure who towers over everyone. They wear a black cloak, but they keep their hood up, veiling their face. I assume they're the instructor.

I only realize they're referring to my sister because everyone else is staring at her, too. In the mirror, my sister's reflection has barely changed.

All she's managed to do is fix her chipped front tooth. She looks like *me*.

"I can help," says Red. With a flick of their hand, a gash slices across my sister's cheek in her reflection.

Antonela gasps, lifting her palm to her face. When she pulls it away, there's blood on her fingers. *The redhead actually cut her.*

"I can help, too," says Cyclops. With a tilt of their head, a horrible snapping sound fills the air, as Antonela's right knee bends at a painful angle. She cries out in agony and falls to the floor.

"Stop!" I shout, running over to shield my sister with my body, but no one can see or hear me.

Another student shears off her hair, while someone else blinds her in one eye, turning the brown iris white.

I look to the hooded figure in desperation, but the instructor watches stoically, as if this is part of the lesson.

I have to turn away from my sister's suffering because standing powerless as she's tortured is more than I can stand. I'm going to tear my eyeballs out if I don't get out of here right now. I don't want to see more. I want this to end—

"That is enough."

The students disperse, and the instructor approaches Antonela, who's writhing on the floor, bloodied and bruised and bald. As they move their hand across my sister, she begins to heal and revert to her original form.

"You are not a naturally gifted spellcaster," says the instructor. "I would advise you to focus your energies on perfecting *one* technique. It is better than being terrible at everything."

Antonela stays on the ground, her breaths shallow, eyes wide from the trauma.

"It was for your own good, you know," adds the instructor in a lower register, without helping my sister up. "We must cure you of your humanity before it kills you."

I don't want to see anything else. I don't need to watch more scenes like these to get the picture. I want to end the spell and leave this place as soon as possible.

But if I do, I'll never know the rest of Antonela's history.

After what she's endured, the least she deserves is for someone to bear witness. As her twin, I owe her this much.

So I kneel beside her. Even if this isn't happening right now and she can't sense me, I don't want to leave her alone. I search her eyes, expecting to find her expression distant and defeated—but to my surprise, she seems focused and determined.

She looks like me when I've found a new lead.

My sister begins staking out a particular door that I learn is a place called the Atrium.

It seems to be off-limits to students, since only larger beings in black hooded cloaks ever go through the door.

Her hood over her head, Antonela stands in front of a thick black vein that cuts across the fleshy red wall, her gray cloak almost blending in with the background. She watches as instructors come in and out of the Atrium.

She waits until the hall has completely emptied, then she peels away from the wall and steps into the open. It looks like she's going to try the Atrium door—

There's a flutter of movement nearby, and Antonela freezes.

Someone else is here, and they seem to have materialized from thin air, like they were concealing themselves with a glamour. Antonela ducks, and I hope she hasn't been spotted.

Not one but *two* someone elses step up to the Atrium door—Red and Cyclops. They approach quickly, like they're attempting the same break-in as my sister.

Cyclops grabs the doorknob. When they twist, blood drips down their hand. The door doesn't budge.

"My turn," says Red. Their blood joins their friend's on the doorknob, but again it does not twist.

"What are you doing here?"

We all stiffen at the instructor's voice, even me, and I'm not technically here.

"Nothing," says Red quickly.

"Only full-fledged casters can open this door, and as talented as you may be, you have more to learn," says the instructor. "Now go!"

My sister waits until the hall is empty to take off. Yet as she peels away from the wall, the wall pulls her back.

A pair of hairless arms wrap around Antonela's torso. An outsider trying to break into the castle.

She sucks in her lips to keep from shouting as she summons her strength to break free. I see the effort on her face as she struggles, yet she is not as strong as the others, and her body is starting to go through the fleshy wall—

My sister bites down on one of the arms, and blood squirts out, her pointy tooth breaking through the skin. As the grip around her loosens, she wrestles her way free, then she breaks into a run.

Red and Cyclops are right that Antonela will never be chosen.

My sister is aware of this, too. I know her thoughts as clearly as I do my own. The only way she's getting out of here is through the Atrium—and for that, she will need an instructor's blood.

Antonela and her classmates are with their hooded instructor in a forest of limb-like foliage. In lieu of flowers and leaves, they sport mushroomlike growths that look like tumors and teeth. The forest is a vast and wild version of the jardín de sangre.

My sister is the first to shoot into the foliage, escaping the pack as quickly as she can. She knows exactly where to go, navigating the woods like it's a neighborhood she has visited many times.

Antonela slows down when she approaches a small bush made of fingerlike plants studded with flowerlike black mouths. She extends her hand slowly toward one of the black bulbs, and when she is close enough to touch, the black lips part and bite down on her index finger.

Blood trickles from her skin, and as the mouth sucks it, like a mosquito, Antonela uses her other hand to snap it off the vine. Then she grips the black lips and twists them shut, sealing in the ball of blood.

I know what she's thinking: now she just needs a way to get close enough to an instructor to get a sample of their blood. That way she can use it to open the Atrium door.

Antonela drops the bloated mouth, and it bursts on the ground. She approaches the same plant again, and this time she catches a mouth-flower unawares, before it can bite. She stuffs it into her cloak pocket, where it can't cause any damage.

As she spins to leave, she comes face-to-face with Red.

Cyclops is there, too, along with the rest of their friends. "Where were you so eager to go?" asks Red.

Antonela shrugs and tries to go around them, but Red's entourage blocks the way.

"Show me," Red insists.

My sister takes a step back, and from the way her gaze darts around, it's clear she's going to run—

Two classmates come up from behind and grab her arms, so she can't move. She struggles against them. "Let me go!"

Red smiles as they reach into Antonela's cloak. "Let us see . . . what are you hiding in— *Ow!*"

They fling the black mouth off their finger, blood squirting the air, and it lands out of sight. Red rounds on my sister, glowering and revealing pointy fangs.

"You did that on purpose!"

Antonela gets blasted into the air like a rocket.

Her classmates cheer, and as she cries for them to stop, they divide into teams and toss her between them like a ball. Red's team "misses" and she crashes on the ground.

Before she can catch her breath, my sister is flung back into the air and tossed again and again and again.

Until she loses consciousness.

Antonela awakens in a recovery room in what looks like an open coffin.

She sits up, registering where she is and what is happening. Her body is bruised and bandaged, but still she rises.

She leaves the room and makes for the Atrium again, only this time, she does not hide. She openly stares at the door, like she is past caring about getting caught.

Antonela reaches for the doorknob. She does not even flinch as thorns break the skin of her hand, blood trickling out as she twists . . .

And the door opens.

CHAPTER 22

THE AIR IN THE ATRIUM is a textured gray, like the clouds that clot the sky before a storm. There are no visible walls, and the floor looks like it's made of crushed black diamonds.

I have no idea what this space is—it could exist outside the other castle, outside the other side, outside everything.

As Antonela walks onward, shadowy doors begin to spring up on either side of her. There are no handles or textures, and they look like rectangular black holes, each with its own distinctive pull.

Antonela keeps moving, like she's trying to find the door that calls to her loudest of all. Her attention is drawn to a door that isn't black like all the others but bloodred. The red smoke billows less like air and more like a sea of blood. Right as my sister takes a step toward it, something happens to the adjacent door.

Black smoke starts to puff from the door-shaped black hole, and my sister freezes at the sounds of others approaching.

She looks around desperately for a hiding place, and when she doesn't see one, she raises her hood to cover her face.

At first, I think she's given up—then her cloak darkens to black and she shoots up two feet in height, until she's the same size as the three instructors now approaching.

She's casting a *glamour*. Seems she took her instructor's advice and chose to work on one technique.

Antonela joins the other administrators' ranks, pretending to be one of them. As they gather round the burning doorway, smoke billows out until it blankets everything. Once it clears, a child with black eyeballs steps through.

The others are quick to carry the new student away, but Antonela hangs back, staring after them. She must be wondering the same thing I am—*Is that how she looked when she crossed over?*

She reverts to her original form and keeps walking until walls bloom around her, and she enters a majestic golden chamber with a dozen windows and a domed ceiling. I look up at a ring of designs that makes me think of the twelve constellations. Each drawing has a different word embedded that lines up with a window, giving the impression of a clockface.

Antonela walks ahead, and she stops at one of the windows. She looks out for so long that I go over to see what view has captured her attention.

It's not a window. It's a *mirror*.

Yet the glass is empty, like my sister casts no reflection. I look up and see the word overhead: *Caidoz.*

She walks ahead to the next mirror, which doesn't register her, either. Overhead, I read: *Siranul.*

She walks past the next glass, barely giving it a glance—then she does a double take.

This time, she reflects.

I look up: *Earth.*

Antonela stares at herself. She approaches the mirror, reaching a hand toward the surface. As soon as her finger touches the glass, her body stiffens and her eyes roll to the back of her head.

She begins to seize, her whole body shaking violently. I look around for help, but I don't see anyone else here, and each second of Antonela's seizure seems torturous—

Then at last, it stops.

And my sister is sucked into the mirror.

I follow her through the glass, into a small room with the same sentient red walls as the castle. I barely bother taking in my surroundings because I'm distracted by the sight of Antonela curled on the floor, trembling.

I think she's seizing again, but then she sits up, and I see a change in her expression. There's an intensity in her gaze that wasn't there until now.

Looking around, I don't see anything in this cave other than a large hourglass. Nearly all the sand has already funneled through the top chamber to the lower one. The grains are dropping slowly, but time will be up soon.

Antonela approaches the hourglass, transfixed. She touches the glass gently, but nothing happens.

An idea flashes in her eyes, and she raises her other hand, pushing against the timer like she plans to tip it over—

"I would not do that."

My sister spins around. A hooded being has followed us through the mirror.

She watches them with dread, likely anticipating pain or punishment or both. Yet this instructor stays silent and still.

"Why not?" she dares to ask.

It's the first spark of boldness I've seen in her, but I don't know if it's borne of defiance or defeat. She could simply be past caring what happens anymore.

"*Time* is an uncurable curse, of which you are afflicted," says the hooded figure. "You cannot kill time, nor can you stop or control it. This hourglass is your only aid. It strips time of its invisibility, so it cannot sneak up on you."

There's something familiar about this instructor's voice.

"Who are you?" asks my sister, like she hears it, too.

They take a step forward, and Antonela backs up, tensing, like a bird poised to fly. Then they throw their hood back.

The face that's revealed is otherworldly yet familiar. They have long silver hair, and their eyes seem to contain every color. I'm reminded of Sebastián, but I get the impression this being could be even more ancient.

"Brálaga," says Antonela, recognizing them at the same time I do.

As I take in their features, I realize I've seen them before—the Aquarius-like water fountain in Oscuro's plaza.

"What—what is happening to me?" asks Antonela, her voice thick.

"You were hit with what I call an Earth vaccination," says Brálaga. "Your mind was overcome with images and concepts and emotions from your home world. The ocean, the sun, the moon, the stars. Parents, friends, family, siblings, children. Love, laughter, grief, rage, hope, sex—everything was fed into your brain, all at once. This inoculation is a fail-safe, should you make it this far, meant to prevent you from going into catatonic shock if you make it back."

It's clear from Antonela's face that she registered none of that. She looks distressed. "I . . . feel something. It is inside me," she says, scratching at her chest. "I cannot describe it . . . like a new organ."

"Try to describe it," encourages Brálaga.

"I . . . need. I *want*?"

"What is it you want?"

"I want . . . to experience it. All of it. I want to go *home*."

"Of course you do," says Brálaga. "Now that you've had a taste, you are ravenous for more. It was my intention to awaken your appetite. That is why I made an exception for your kind, giving you access to the Atrium."

"My *kind*?"

"You are a human of Earth," they inform her, and it's clear from her blank reaction that this doesn't mean much. "Tell me, what made you so eager to access the Atrium?"

"Something an instructor said. That they meant to cure me of my *humanity*. It made me think I might not belong here."

"You are right," says Brálaga matter-of-factly. "The doorways you saw all lead to different worlds, universes, dimensions, whatever you choose to call them. All my grandchildren arrive here through one of those doors."

"So—so other places exist, besides the castle?"

My sister's question sounds so innocent, and I'm overwhelmed with pity for her. All she has ever known in life is this Hell.

"Too many to count, child. These doors lead only to the worlds I know about."

"And one of them goes to Earth?"

"No," says Brálaga, and my twin's chest deflates with defeat. "That door only opens when this countdown ends."

She shakes her head. "I do not understand."

"You are just as unlikely to understand the explanation, but I will still provide it. This castle is my fail-safe. I have established a foothold in many universes, and should I ever need a secure hideout, this castle is in a dimension I alone control that is built on my blood. Yet maintaining this realm requires an energy source. There must constantly be new blood cycling through from across many dimensions for the castle to remain self-sustaining. That is why you and your cousins are here."

I have about a million questions, and I hope Antonela asks some of them.

"What is *graduation*?" she asks instead.

Brálaga frowns with a grim displeasure. "You are familiar with the beings who reach into the castle from beyond, through the walls?" She nods in assent, cringing as she darts a glance at the fleshy red walls. "They are not outsiders, nor are they attacking us," says Brálaga. "They are your predecessors."

Antonela's face slackens with a bewilderment that seems to rob her of speech.

"I am not proud of this," Brálaga explains, "but most—if not all—of your classmates will perish here. We pump their blood to run this world, and as their bodies wear out, we must cycle in a new generation of children. Graduation means your class will soon be swept into the walls."

Antonela looks as horrified as I feel. I stare, transfixed, at the sentient flesh surrounding us. The walls contract subtly at a steady rate, hardly noticeable, almost like they're breathing. It makes me wonder if the other castle exists in the belly of a living creature.

"Why are you admitting all this to me?" asks Antonela, and my own muscles contract in fear for her fate.

"Because this is not your path," says Brálaga. "Humans are something of a special project of mine. You are young evolutionarily. You do not yet have interdimensional travel, and as your world is ruled by matter, it is not hospitable to many species. Yet humans' greatest asset is also their greatest flaw— their outsize emotions."

Antonela presses a hand to her heart, like she's pointing to where she *feels*.

"Exactly," they say. "That is why at school we aim to stamp it out of you. The affliction of emotions is not exclusive to humans, yet the ailment is more prevalent among your kind because you do not possess magic. There is no counterbalance to the power of feelings."

As if to illustrate, my sister's face sours. "Why am I here if I was never cut out for casting?"

From her defiance, I know her classmates and this castle have not broken her. Not yet.

"Because I am betting on you."

Brálaga's voice deepens, and on hearing that note of pride again, I wonder if they realize they've also succumbed to this affliction of outsize emotions. "You lack power because magic requires *sacrifice*. You risk nothing because you believe you have nothing to lose. Until now, you never *wanted*."

Antonela looks confused, and I don't blame her. This is all overwhelming. She's gone from lifelong numbness to experiencing every feeling possible.

"At first, I scorned and pitied humans," Brálaga goes on, like they're conversing with a friend. "I could not believe such a weak species had not been destroyed. Yet I watched them for so long that something happened which I did not anticipate . . . I fell in love with the fools."

Brálaga smiles again, and I spy Mom's and my solitary dimple.

"So my bloodline was born. Yet before abandoning the dimension, I left a way for my most gifted descendants to cross over."

"Why would you want humans here at all if we are so weak and ill-suited for magic?" Antonela seems to be reading my thoughts.

"You are here because *I want* something as well," says Brálaga. "My goal is for my blood to become the building block of magic on Earth. For that to happen, I must keep waiting for one of you to make it back."

"What do you mean by *one of you*?"

"My dear," says Brálaga with a pitying look. "Not a single human caster has ever survived."

CHAPTER 23

THE ALEPH OF MEMORIES IS back, and in every window, Antonela is either studying or training.

One of the windows grows larger, and I see my sister reading from a very small collection of tomes. Now that she knows what she is and where she comes from, she must have a sense of where to look.

She finds the journals of other descendants who hailed from Earth. None of their stories are complete, but one thing is clear across all of them—to make it back, one must locate their bloodline on Earth and establish a connection.

I watch my sister in a corner alone, sitting in a meditative pose. Eyes closed and lids flickering, she's chanting something under her breath. A spell.

She pulls back the sleeve of her cloak and looks at the inside of her wrist. There's a tattoo I never noticed: a circle made up of twelve black moons, only the twelfth one is fading.

It must be a gift from Brálaga so she can track how long she has left.

Time swirls around us, splitting everything into more windows where Antonela is spending all her time meditating to retrieve her memories and studying solutions in what must be the library. All the while, the moons keep fading from her skin.

When the next scene grows larger, half the moons are already gone.

Antonela is chanting, working on her memory spell, when she conjures something. Images manifest in the air, and she opens her eyes to a film playing out before us.

My heart hurts.

It's Mom and Dad.

They're at la Sombra, and my aunt and uncle are there, too. I see older people who must be my grandparents. They all look so happy and unburdened. I can hardly believe this is my family.

Antonela gasps when she spots me, and I realize she's just discovered she has a twin.

It's surreal to be watching a memory of my sister watching memories of us, and yet it's also weirdly comforting to share this moment with her. I see the two of us running through the crimson corridors of la Sombra. I see Mom and Dad trying to dress us while we wriggle around in bed. I see us playing hide-and-seek.

Antonela seems to find real solace in these memories. She's still constantly bullied in her classes, so she resorts to these spells more and more. She lingers a lot on Mom and Dad, and I'm sad she will never get to meet them.

When she's studying, she focuses on finding an interdimensional shell that she can use to make the crossing home. Her predecessors tried all kinds of protective spells, yet Brálaga said none of them succeeded. Still, they didn't mention *how* these predecessors failed, whether it was the crossing or their reassimilation on Earth.

Antonela keeps racking her brain for better ideas as the moons continue to fade, one by one. She spends more and more time in the company of memories, and together we watch younger versions of ourselves exploring the castle.

In one memory, a younger Bea and Teo approach my sister while she's got her eyes covered. She's counting off: "*Uno, dos, tres, cuatro, cinco—*"

"*Do you want to go to magic school?*" asks Teo, who looks to be in his twenties.

"*Yes!*" answers Antonela at once. "*Can Tela come, too?*"

"*No, this is just for you,*" says Bea. "*It's something that will be only yours. Would you like that?*"

Antonela looks like she isn't sure. She frowns at our aunt and uncle, deep in doubt.

"*I told you Nela was the wrong one for magic school,*" Teo says to Bea. "*Tela is the better choice.*"

"*Nuh-uh!*" says my sister. "*I want to go!*"

"*Then prove it.*"

An obedient Antonela stands in the middle of the purple room. Teo and Bea take turns hugging her. "Be good at magic school," says Bea.

"*Learn everything you can*," says Teo. Tears are sparkling in his eyes.

Antonela looks from one to the other, probably wondering why our aunt and uncle are so good at playing make-believe. Then they walk to opposite ends of the room and begin to chant.

My twin looks uneasy. "*What are you saying?*" she asks, but they ignore her and keep chanting.

She looks like she's trying to move, but she's frozen. She can't speak, can't squirm, can't scream—

Then black flames spring to life all around her.

When the memory ends, Antonela is breathing heavily, her expression more horrified than even when she was being bullied.

She's *devastated*.

She looks like she's just discovered that she was our family's sacrifice.

Antonela is in the library, reviewing texts. There are only two moons left on her wrist. I look over her shoulder to see what she's reading and gasp—

It's the portrait of Sebastián from the book I buried.

"What are you doing in here?"

Antonela snaps her head up, and I spin around. Red struts over with Cyclops.

"*A Bleeder can cross into any dimension*," Red reads out loud. "*Their blood is the most powerful magical ingredient in all the realms. Yet it must be given willingly, which also makes it the rarest*—why are you reading this? You think Bleeder blood will make you a real caster?" They laugh and toss the book to Cyclops.

The panoramic-eyed giant smirks and flips through the pages while Red hones in on my sister.

"We saw you." Their lips spread into a too-wide smile.

"I-I do not know what you are talking about," says my sister. But nerves undercut her voice, and Red's smug smirk takes over their entire face.

"How did you do it? How did you unlock the Atrium door?"

"I did not," says Antonela.

"You got our instructor's blood," says Red, narrowing their gaze. "How did *you* pull it off?"

"I did *not*," she says again. "The school must have judged me more worthy."

Red's smugness hardens into anger. "*We* will be Chosen," they say in a low growl, pointing to themselves and Cyclops. "And *you* will stay behind."

"We will see," says Antonela, showing more backbone than I expected.

"You think a *human* could ever pose a threat?" asks Red, reveling in revealing to Antonela that they possess this information. "Yes, I found out what you are. I cannot fathom how one of your kind has made it this far."

"Did you say *human*?"

Red glances at Cyclops, annoyed by their interruption. "I did, so what?"

Their panoramic eye looks back down at the book they took from Antonela. "*Human blood is a Bleeder delicacy*," Cyclops reads out loud. "*It is the only offering that will gain* any *being an audience with their sovereign*." They look up from the book at Red, eyebrow nearly at their hairline. "We could trade the human for *Bleeder blood*. You were worried about what would happen if we were to run away—but if we become more powerful than any caster, we will not need to live in fear!"

"You cannot," says my sister, voice cracking as she turns from Cyclops to Red, whose face looks like a match that caught fire. "There is no need, since you are likely to be Chosen!"

Red looks like they're considering their friend's plan, and it's clear their bravado is as hollow as their heart. They are just as terrified as anyone else about not getting Chosen, enough that they're willing to risk everything.

"How would we get there?" Red asks Cyclops.

"Someone wrote it here in the margins," they answer, and Antonela's face falls. "A red door in the Atrium."

They both look to my sister, who's blanching. "Y-you cannot do this—"

Red yanks my sister's hand and slices a line across her palm with their sharp nails. "If your blood really opens the Atrium door, you might be graduating from this place after all."

"Help! Let me out!" Antonela screams. She pounds against the wooden walls of her tight confinement. "Please! I need to stay at the school! This is important!"

All I can see is the darkness around her. I think of the grains of sand falling in the hourglass, like drum hits beating in tune with my heart. My sister is running out of time.

After a while, she gives up shouting and slips a hand inside her cloak, retrieving something too small to see. She maneuvers her arm up to her neck in the confined space, and she winces, but the cloak veils whatever she's doing.

When the lid pops off, I see that Antonela is in a coffin. Rough hands reach down for her.

She's heaving, like she can't breathe, and Cyclops shoves a face mask over her mouth and nose. It's blue and flutters like it's producing oxygen.

As I look around at where we are, my mouth falls open. We're on the rocky edge of a mountain that I have seen before. It was in a drawing in Felipe's vampire book.

This is Prince Bastian's castle.

Red and Cyclops stand unmasked and gawk at the view, in as much awe as Antonela. The air is pitch-black, and there are no lights, no moon, no stars.

A door opens into the mountain, and seven fanged men with silver eyes like Sebastián's file out. They seem to be guards.

One of them sniffs the air. "Casters are forbidden here."

"We have brought a gift for—"

"It does not matter what you have brought," says one of the guards as Red pushes my sister forward. "Casters are not permitted inside. Go now, or your lives are forfeit."

"This is a *human*," says Red. "We bring them as an offering to your ruler."

Now the vampires' attention turns to Antonela.

The one who spoke steps closer, and Cyclops shoves my sister. She stumbles toward the guard, who sniffs at her. His silver eyes flash with light, and he turns to the others, who take turns sniffing her.

The energy changes entirely.

"What do you want in exchange?" asks the Bleeder, showing the casters more respect as my sister is handed down the line. She looks back at Red and Cyclops, face aghast, like she can't believe they're going through with this.

"Please!" Antonela calls back to them, her voice coming out clearly despite the breathing mask. But they don't even glance her way.

"Bleeder blood," says Cyclops to the guard, and I don't know what else happens because now I'm following my sister through shadows in the walls, until we reach some kind of antechamber.

"He is not seeing anybody," says a vampire larger than the others.

"This is nobody," says the guard. "It is a gift. A *human* for his majesty."

"His majesty is fighting the wars—"

"For his majesty's *heir* and acting sovereign is what I meant," clarifies the Bleeder, sounding like he's losing his patience.

The gigantic vampire leans down and sniffs my sister's hair. His eyes do the same flashy thing as the others, and a stomach-churning smile twists his lips. "His Highness will be pleased."

The guard who brought her takes off, and the giant now deposits my sister like she's a doll inside a room that's pitch-black.

Without a word, he leaves.

I wait for my eyes to adjust, but I can't see a thing, so she probably can't, either. "Hello?" she calls out.

The mask inflates in and out as she steps forward into the darkness, toward near-certain death.

Something zooms past her, and she gasps as she nearly loses her balance. "Your Highness?" she ventures.

I can't see, but I can feel what Antonela feels, as something large and hard like a wall presses against her. I distinctly hear a sniff, like someone is smelling her.

My sister doesn't speak or react.

She keeps walking.

"Mmmmm," whispers a voice. "You have a tantalizing aroma."

She spins and swipes her arm, like they're right behind her. But it's just empty air.

She keeps moving forward, eyes narrowed with caution and hands angled out in front of her, less trusting of the dark.

Cold fingers close around her throat, and she reaches for an inhale as a second hand grips the top of her left breast. "That instrument in your chest produces some lovely music."

The hands vanish, but Antonela stays frozen in place, breathing in and out, in and out, in and out.

Then she stiffens her spine and steps forward again.

Without slowing her pace, she keeps moving through the chamber. She even closes her eyes, like it's a test of faith.

"Courageous," whispers the voice, "or foolish."

Their fingers are back at her throat, their other hand closing around her waist, holding her against their frame. "I would keep you around to entertain me longer, but I have plans . . . and I am far too curious to know your taste."

The shadows around them fade just enough to reveal Prince Bastian's face.

Even though I knew it was him, my heart still canters at the sight of the shadow beast. I recognize the hungry look in his eyes, and I know what's coming next.

He grabs Antonela by the hair, exposing her neck.

"*NO!*" I cry, as his fangs bear down.

This can't be! Sebastián killed my sister—

But he shoves her to the floor instead of biting her skin.

"What is this?" he demands, as my twin scrambles back. The shadows retreat, and as the lights brighten, I see that we are in a chamber made of sleek stone. "Why have you carved *CASTER* on your neck?"

"Because that is what I am," she says from behind the oxygen mask, her voice shaky. I spot the blood and move closer to see that Antonela has sloppily cut the word into her skin, probably while she was in the coffin.

"Humans cannot be casters," he says dismissively. "And my guard would not have let you in if you were one."

"Well, why would they think I am one if humans cannot be casters?"

He frowns but there's a flicker of interest in his silver eyes. It's strange to think that in so little time, I already know him well enough to read his expressions. Like picking up a new language and finding out you're fluent.

"Prove what you say is true," he commands.

Antonela isn't fazed, so I assume she expected this kind of reaction. She closes her eyes in concentration, then she shoots up in height, until even Sebastián has to tilt his neck back to look at her.

It's a strategic move because her proof of magic doubles as a show of intimidation, which is the language the vampire speaks best.

Her power move works; she's still breathing.

When she shrinks back down to size, the blue mask pulses faster than before, like it's producing double the oxygen. The spell must have worn her out, or she would have remained in that form, since it gave her an advantage.

I don't see how she's going to be the first Brálaga to make it back when she's not exactly Merlin.

"I was the one who orchestrated the events that brought me before you," she declares, and I'm taken aback by the steadiness of her voice. If she's still breathless, she doesn't show it.

"I knew I could not make it here on my own, as I lack wings or strength, so I got my classmates to transport me. I came to meet you because I seek to make you an offer."

My sister squares her shoulders, and I know that I've underestimated her. *Everyone* has.

She baited Red and Cyclops with what they love most—bullying her—

and left open the book about Bleeders so they would take her where she needed to go. She risked everything . . . just as Brálaga instructed.

Sebastián moves closer now that Antonela is small again, swallowing her in his shadow. "You have nothing to offer me, human caster," he says, his voice as even as a heart flatlining, "except blood."

His hand closes around my sister's neck again, and her face turns purple in moments—

"*Your Highness?*" asks a voice outside the door.

He grunts and eases his grip. "Yet you may entertain me a little longer."

"*Prince—?*"

"I hear you!" he growls at the door, making my bones shake.

Antonela looks down at the final moon on her wrist. Time is nearly up. "Please," she whispers, "listen to me—"

But before she can say another word, she's swallowed by shadows.

CHAPTER 24

MY SISTER IS SUSPENDED FROM the ceiling in a cage made of shadows.

From here, she watches Prince Bastian on a massive stone throne that sits atop an elevated dais, as two hooded beings are brought before him. Their hands are bound in front of them in black stone cuffs. An entire array of guards accompanies the prisoners.

A pair of Bleeders pull back the prisoners' hoods, and Antonela's eyes grow wide as she sees Red and Cyclops.

"Why are they bound? Why are you here?" Bastian demands of the guards. "You know I prefer to hunt my food."

"This is to cancel their magic," says the Bleeder who escorted my sister to the prince's giant bodyguard. "They are casters."

The prince stares at the prisoners' bound hands. "It is a violation of the treaty—"

"We have permission," says that same guard. "They brought the human here in exchange for blood. We reached out to the casters to confirm their story, and we were informed that murdering a being of Brálaga blood carries the penalty of death—even if the perpetrators are Brálagas, too."

Bastian smirks and looks up at where he knows my sister is watching. "You may go," he says to the guards.

"Respectfully, we cannot risk their magic—"

"I can handle two bound and powerless prisoners," snaps the Iron Prince. "Just like I can handle an entire squad of you." His gaze trails along the line, staring every guard down. "You may go."

This time, they obey.

Still, it's clear Bastian's safety trumps his own authority.

Once he's alone with them, Red kneels and says, "Please, Prince Bastian, we brought you that delicious human because we thought you would enjoy it."

Cyclops drops to their knees, too. "We truly meant no disrespect."

The prince waits them out as they beg for their lives, and when they finish, he waits even longer, until his silence is louder than their words.

"So," he says at last, and both Red and Cyclops jump to their feet. "Shall I kill them?"

"No!"

"Please!"

"I was not asking either of you," he says, and they trade confused glances. Bastian looks up, and the prisoners gasp as they notice the cage and Antonela within it.

"What do you think?" he asks my sister.

She looks down, pressing her face to the shadowy bars of the cage. "No," she says. "Do not hurt them."

Even I'm confused. They just tried to have her murdered. "They sold you to me as a meal," says the prince, putting it more colorfully.

Antonela lifts her chin. "So they get to turn me into a monster?"

He frowns, but Red and Cyclops stare at my sister in awe, like they've never seen a creature like her.

"Pick one," the Bleeder commands her.

"For what?" asks my sister.

"Pick one, or it's both."

My sister points to Cyclops.

Red screams, their face splattered with blood, as Bastian rips out Cyclops's throat and takes a deep drink.

When he's finished, his face is smeared with blood. He looks up at my sister. "Congratulations. Your first kill."

My sister looks on, horrified and speechless.

The prince laughs, but no light shines from his face. "Good news, human caster!" he calls up. "I got you a roommate!"

Red materializes through the shadowy bars almost instantaneously, locked in the same cage as Antonela.

"Your guests are here," says the giant bodyguard from the doorway.

"See you soon," says Bastian before walking out, the blood still staining his face.

"The Bleeder called you *human caster*," says Red once they're alone. "Why are you not cuffed?" They don't even look the least bit affected by their companion's death.

My sister shakes her head. "I do not know."

"Can you summon any magic to spell us out of here?"

Antonela shakes her head.

"They must have sensed you have little power," says Red. "You know we will die next, right?"

"I have a plan. But I cannot do it alone."

"What is it?"

"I am going to convince him to bring us back to school. I found a doorway to Earth in the tower, and I will promise to take him there so he can drink all the humans he wants."

"The school is the last place I am going to! They sentenced me to death."

"I will tell them our one-eyed cousin forced us *both* to come. And in exchange, you will stop torturing me and make sure I graduate."

Red's shock only lasts a moment. Then they nod in assent, willing to betray the memory of their best companion. "It is a *pact*."

The cage is on the floor now. It's locked shut, and Red is asleep, while Antonela lies wide awake.

A hand opens the gate, and Prince Bastian waves my sister out.

He seals it closed behind her, then shadows engulf it. Antonela follows him to the dais.

He sits on his throne and pats his lap for her to join him.

She holds her ground in front of him. "I will stand."

"Tell me what you wanted to say, human caster."

"I have come with an irresistible offer. You could drink me now and sate your thirst but a little . . . or you could drain as many humans as you want on Earth, where blood is limitless and of every variety—"

"There is no way to Earth," he interrupts, "so I will settle for you—"

"I have a way! I can get you to Earth," she says quickly, likely spotting the predatory shift in his eyes and realizing she has only seconds left to plead for her life. "Besides being a feast for you, it also happens to be beyond the reach of nearly every realm, including this one. You would be completely free!"

Prince Bastian stares at my sister. He's already underestimated her once, and I doubt he's in the habit of making the same mistake twice.

"Even if you could pull this off," he says carefully, "I cannot leave my castle. The king is fighting a war, and I am his heir, protected above all Bleeders. Whereas you are a human with minimal power who does not stand a chance against my guard."

My sister's expression hardens with offense. "I did not expect you to be a coward."

The Bleeder springs up, fury flashing on his face, and before I can blink, he snaps off Antonela's oxygen mask. "Goodbye, human caster."

"How can you stand being locked up here?" asks my sister, using her final breaths to taunt him.

His stare and stance remain stoic as he watches her run out of air before him.

"You are royalty. You should live large, have adventures, be worthy of your title. Drink all the human blood you want on Earth, and come back without anyone knowing . . ."

Antonela sounds like air leaving a balloon, and her words come out in a final burst: "Why obey like . . . lowliest Bleeder . . . when you . . . are . . . ?"

She falls forward, into his chest, her skin turning as blue as the mask, which Bastian now shoves back onto her face. Antonela takes in raking gasps of air.

"If I get caught violating my father's rules again, they will confine me to my coffin," he says in her ear, his voice low and muffled by her heavy breathing. He probably doesn't want other Bleeders to hear him. "Do you understand?"

"You will not get in trouble," says Antonela, cottoning on and speaking in a barely audible whisper. "You will say I hexed you. The ones responsible are your guards for letting in a caster to see you. Once you return, you will say you had to hunt down and kill me to break the spell so you could make it back to your throne. You will be hailed a hero. They will add *defeating a caster* to your list of accolades."

Bastian scrutinizes my sister like he's considering her offer. "What are you getting out of this?"

"I need a ride, and Bleeders are among the rare beings with bodies strong enough to cross the barrier into Earth's dimension and survive. I am your one-time ticket to this blood-rich world that is nearly impossible to access because I alone can get us through the gateway—and you are my only transport. So, if your answer is *no,* you might as well kill me now."

The prince looks like he has no idea what to make of Antonela. "What about your classmate?" He gestures with his chin at the cage. "Why save them?"

"We need them to lead us to the gateway back to Brálaga's castle, as I was in a coffin when we crossed over. After that," she adds with a shrug, "I figured you might want a snack."

My mouth goes dry. I underestimated her *again.*

The prince sits back down on his throne, and there's less hunger and more curiosity in his gaze when he looks at Antonela. Like he's more interested in her brain than her blood.

"We must go *now,*" she insists, "or we will miss our chance." She holds up her wrist to show him. "The last moon is already gone."

"What does that mean?"

"That the door is open," she says, her voice as low as his. "We have to go through before it closes."

He looks like he is on the brink of a decision.

"Forget your crown," she says. "Forget you are Prince Bastian. Allow yourself this breath of freedom before the kingship and war consume your existence. Unburden yourself. While you are away, you can even change your name. You can simply be . . . *Bast.*"

Their eyes connect in a way that tells me she's hooked him. "I've never had a meal nickname me before," he says, but he sounds more flirty than threatening.

"You will not know your full power until you have sacrificed it all." She sounds like Brálaga. "What do you say, Bast?"

I can't believe Antonela just went from a lifetime of being beaten and bullied to owning her bullies and allying herself with the prince of the Bleeders. Bastian seems to be thinking the same thing, and I don't like the admiring way he's looking at her.

"I say you are fearless." His mouth curls up on one side.

"I know." Antonela steps toward him, and right now she's the coolest, most intimidating person I've ever seen. I can't believe we're twins.

"The question is," she says, sliding onto his lap, "are *you?*"

CHAPTER 25

"*ESTELA?* ESTELA, SAY SOMETHING!"

It's Beatríz's voice.

I pry my eyes open, and Antonela's blurry face swims before me. No, not Antonela's—*mine*.

I'm standing in front of the mirror, staring at my reflection. I look dazed.

"What did you see?" urges my uncle over my left shoulder.

"Are you okay?" asks my aunt on my right, her features drawn with worry.

"She made it," I say, blinking my dry eyes. "She lived."

I barely register Bea's shocked gasp or Teo's gleeful laugh. All I think about is Sebastián. If he got his memories back last night, he must remember my sister and the pact they made. Why didn't he say anything about her when we spoke on the balcony?

He's never forgotten Antonela, the small voice in my mind reminds me.

One of the first things the shadow beast said to me was that my face and voice were familiar to him. Some part of his brain must have recognized Antonela through the amnesia. So did he like me for me, or for *her*?

"What else did you see?" prods my uncle.

"Um, she was going to cross over with Sebastián, but I don't know if they ever made it. He didn't even mention her to me—how can I see the rest?"

"There's a spell," says Teo, tapping the tower tattoo on his neck. "Let's go."

"*Don't!*" warns my aunt, but my uncle is already blasting through the door that leads up to the tower.

Once he's gone, I turn to her. "Leave some of your blood for Sebastián to find so he can follow us there."

"Are you serious—?"

"Just in case. Please."

I'm pretty sure she's not convinced Sebastián is real, but I hope she trusts me enough to do as I ask. When I make it to the journal room, my uncle is pulling out a red book.

"I've opened it before," I say. "It's blank."

"Not this time."

"What happens this time?"

"My hope is we will be able to reach Antonela, wherever she is, and find a way to bring her home."

"How do you know so much?" I ask, a switch flipping inside me as my investigative instinct kicks in. "You know how to bring back my sister, you knew about Sebastián and that his memories were stored in my blood—*how*?"

"You want answers," he says. "So do I. But your sister is running out of time. First bring her home, then I'll answer your questions."

Bea bursts in, breathless from the stairs. "What have you done?" she asks her brother right off the bat.

"Nothing yet," I answer for him. "He hasn't explained how it works."

"Just open the book," says Teo. "Otherwise, Antonela will be trapped there forever, just beyond our reach. Is that what you want?"

"I don't trust him," says Bea. "He's got that fanatic look on his face. He wants this too much."

She's right.

But then again, so do I.

I know why Beatríz is worried, but I need to see what happened to my sister. Felipe already gave his life for these answers. The same answers I came here to find. Antonela was willing to face the Iron Prince just for the chance to come back to us; I can't fail to bring her home now.

Besides, it's just a book—how much harm can it cause?

I open the red cover and flip through the pages. They're still blank.

My shoulders sag with disappointment—

"*Ow!* Paper cut."

My blood trails on the white canvas, and the text falls from my hands as black smoke whirs forth from the pages, overtaking the full space. When it clears, we're no longer in the journal room.

We're in a hall lined with mirrors.

"Where are we?" I whisper.

"I'm not sure," says Teo, turning in a circle to take in every angle of our situation. "My best guess is this is as close to us as Antonela has been able to get, and she's stuck in this dimension."

"How do we get back home?" asks Bea, nerves fraying her voice.

"I don't know," he says, and it strikes me that I'm no longer holding the red book in my hands. "Antonela will help us when we find her."

I start walking, and so do infinite versions of me on either side of the hall. It's dizzying.

"How do we find her?" I ask once my aunt and uncle catch up.

"I don't know," says Teo. "Maybe she finds us."

There doesn't seem to be an end to this hall. We alternately speed up and slow down, until we're all breathing heavily from how long we've been at it. "This isn't working," says Bea.

"We must be doing something wrong," says Teo. He stops walking, and I lean against a mirrored wall for support.

"Look!" says Bea, and I turn to see the surface of the glass rippling out, like it's made of water.

When my reflection refocuses, my eyes look different. They're pure black. Like they're made of smoke.

"Antonela?" I whisper.

The fumes leave her eyes, and I step back as the black smoke enters the physical space we're in. It pulls together into a shadow with features that match my shape and profile.

Antonela is the black smoke.

She sniffs at me. Her movements are sharp and quick, awkward and feral.

In memories, she seemed so weak compared to the other casters. Yet among us, she's terrifyingly inhuman.

My sister's gaze lands on our aunt and uncle. Bea is wide-eyed, her face bloodless with shock, but Teo is on his knees, neck bent, like she's a holy figure.

Antonela raises an arm, as if she's going to strike them down—

"Please!" I say, and she spins to face me. "I-I'm sorry, and they're sorry, for everything you've been through. I had no idea you existed. I only just saw your memories in a spell. Did you see mine in a spell, too?"

She keeps staring at me, but she doesn't speak. Maybe she can't understand English.

"We're sisters," I say, smiling so she knows I don't mean her harm. "Twins, to be exact. We were born together."

She flicks her gaze to our aunt and uncle.

"Bea is really sorry for what happened, but we can deal with them later," I say quickly. "Right now, we want to help you."

She takes her time surveying every inch of me. "Sister," she says in my voice, like she's testing the word.

"Yes!" I say, grinning at her. I can't believe she's actually here, and I haven't lost her. For a moment, I'm almost giddy with glee. "I'm Estela, your *sister*! I've come to help you."

"Help me," she says, the evenness of her tone unnerving. "Yes, you can help me."

There's a hardening in my gut, like a warning system activating. Ignoring my instincts, I ask, "What do you need?"

Without hesitation, she answers: "*Your body.*"

Time holds its breath and pauses Earth's rotation.

I don't know how I didn't see this coming. Or maybe I did, but I didn't want to.

The whole time I was experiencing my sister's memories, I got the sense there were moments missing. I thought it had to do with the nature of the memory magic, but now I wonder if there were things she didn't want me to know. Things I should have worked out for myself . . . Like how once she made it back to Earth, she would need a flesh-and-blood body of her own.

Antonela's physical form burned in the spell that transported her to the other castle. And as Brálaga said, Earth is a dimension ruled by matter—so she can't return without a shell.

And the perfect genetic match stands before her.

"No!"

Bea's voice kicks the planet back into rotation. She comes between us and says, "There must be another way—"

"There is not," says my sister, no trace of emotion in her voice.

"So this was your plan?" I ask Antonela, my voice funereal compared to the unbridled joy I felt seconds ago. "When you hitched a ride with Sebastián? You intended to move into my body?"

"You are my only match," she says matter-of-factly.

This is why Sebastián thought the black smoke was protecting me. Antonela wants my body intact.

After all the work from the past couple of weeks of dredging up my heart from the depths to which it had drowned, it's now sinking within me once more, back into a sea of numbness. If this is how it feels to *feel,* then I don't want any part of it.

"You were freed when Sebastián bit me," I say, going into detective mode and piecing together a timeline because it's the only way I know how to process this. I remember it was then that I saw the black smoke again.

"*Released,*" she corrects me. "Not *free.* I was still trapped in this castle until the boy came, and I sent him to deliver a message to *him.*" She gestures to Teo, who's still on his knees.

That's how he knew. He wouldn't tell me himself because he wanted me to follow through with his plan. "You told Teo to cast the blood spell," I say. "Does that mean you *possessed* Felipe?"

"No. If I had, I could not have used him for the spell to return Bast's memories. My possession would have killed him."

"Why did you want to return *Sebastián's* memories?" I ask, correcting her on his name.

"His amnesia was an unforeseen side effect, and I had to remind him of our pact."

I blink. "*Pact?*"

"When he bit you, I was released, but there was a second part to breaking the spell, which he did not complete. That is the reason he is still here, and why I remain bodiless."

I review what I already know: Antonela needs my body unharmed. That means she also needs a way to get rid of me without causing her new shell any damage. I feel my neurons firing as the connections come through, and I remember how Dad described the rush of getting to this point in a case, when the pieces puzzle together with ease.

"You weren't just hitching a ride to Earth," I say, my heart lashing my chest as I solve the riddle of why Sebastián is still here. "*You brought the Bleeder to kill me.*"

Antonela's approving smile doesn't make me proud. It makes me sad and more than a little sick.

"Exsanguination by a Bleeder kills you without destroying your shell," she says, talking about violence as easily as Prince Bastian. "As it is a supernatural death on Earth—in other words, *magic*—I can use a spell to revive your body. There was just one ingredient missing."

"My *blood*," I say, because it's always the answer in la Sombra. It's the key to unlocking everything from secret rooms to Sebastián's memories.

"When I crossed over to Earth," she says, "my magic was drawn to your blood, for it was mine, too. Yet as you were not at la Sombra, the spell was not contained . . . so it killed everyone around you."

I hear Bea's gasp, but I'm too choked by my own guilt to make a sound. *My fault my fault my fault my fault my fault my fault my fault.* It's all I can hear after Antonela stops speaking. I'm not just the sole survivor—I'm the reason everyone died.

I'm responsible for the Subway 25.

"The truth is," says my twin, "I only meant to kill two people."

Two people. Bea and all her reflections scramble away from Antonela in horror.

"*You killed our parents.*" I sound like I've been shot because I can't catch my breath.

"Once Bast gave me his blood to seal our pact, I knew I could pull off any spell I wanted," says Antonela, not noticing that I've gone catatonic. "Yet the magic I need to cast to regenerate my blood after Bastian drains you requires something more. The ultimate sacrifice. What I wanted most of all—to meet my creators."

"You killed them," I say again, still unable to swallow the words. It's a truth too horrible to stomach.

"After Bastian drains you," she goes on, unaffected, "he will return to his realm, and I will be released into your body. Then the same spell that took our parents' lifeblood will return it to me, and once I am alive again, I will take up my throne in la Sombra. I will feed the castle all the blood it desires, and we will grow in power until we control this entire planet. I will be the human bruja Brálaga prophesied. *They* are my true creator."

Now I know I've strayed far from reality and deep into some twisted fantasy. The culprit I have been seeking, the murderer of my parents—of the Subway 25—is my twin sister. And she plans to destroy the whole world, starting with me.

Worst of all, her plan doesn't seem that far out of reach. In fact, she's nearly succeeded—except . . .

I'm still alive.

"Sebastián hasn't killed me," I say, finding the hitch in her plans.

"I cannot understand why, but Bast was enjoying playing human with you."

"That's because you've never felt love before," I say, and as much as I want to hate her for what she's done, I also want to help her heal from what she's endured. "Neither had Sebastián, but if he's capable of caring about me, so are you." I move closer to her. "We're *twins,* Antonela. We shared the same womb!"

Maybe it's because she's in shadow form, but I don't see any emotion in her gaze when she looks at me. "Now that he remembers you are the key to his shackles, I doubt he will resist the temptation to end this game."

"I'm not giving you my body, and Sebastián isn't going to kill me. I'm going to help you find another way."

"You really believe he feels for you?" she taunts me. "How did he react after regaining his memories? Did he renounce his previous life and pledge himself yours? Or did he pull away in anticipation of what he knows he must do?"

I try to think of something cutting to say. I want to come up with some way of hurting her, but all she's ever known is suffering, so I doubt it would make a difference. I wish I could *despise* her, but all I feel is heartbreak.

"You are alone, Estela," she says, picking up on my defeat. "If you want to be sisters, let me lift this burden off your shoulders. Let me take over."

I wonder why I'm even bothering to resist. Isn't Antonela the escape route I've been seeking? Isn't Sebastián right that I'm ambivalent about life? Haven't I come to Oscuro to deliver myself to the past?

At least now, I'll be sacrificing myself for something that matters. I'll be giving my sister a chance at life.

"You know I am right," Antonela says to me. "Do you even have anything here worth fighting for?"

Everything she says feels plucked from the dark side of my mind. My aunt and uncle destroyed our family. My parents lied. My sister murdered them. And then, on her orders, my uncle killed Felipe.

Sebastián hid the truth and broke up with me. Now the last thing Antonela needs is my death, and her path to becoming ruler of the world is clear.

I have no way to stop her. I have no one left. I have nothing.

Except myself.

I have *me.*

I got myself through the past seven months. I survived the worst moment of my life. I lost my parents. I moved to a new country. I fell in love.

I solved the case of the Subway 25 when no other investigator in the world could do it.

I consider all that Antonela has done and endured for just the chance of a future on Earth. How could I be so quick to throw mine away?

What would my parents think if I gave up now? How would they feel if they learned one of their daughters murdered the other? I can't let that be their legacy. Nor my sister's and my fates.

"*You're wrong,*" says a new voice.

I feel a hand grip my shoulder, and I look up to see my aunt. "Estela is not alone," she says. "She has me."

I swallow and stare into Antonela's black eyes, emboldened by Bea's support. "We are going to find another way," I insist.

"I do not expect convincing you will be easy," says Antonela. "Yet now that you have manifested me in this dimension, I have other options available."

Her words settle into my stomach with a thud. "What do you mean?"

"I cannot return to Earth without a body. As I cannot take yours without Sebastián first taking your life, I will have to commandeer a temporary one."

"I knew this was a trick!" says Bea, rounding on Teo. "What have you done?"

One look at my uncle's face says he already knew this spell would require a sacrifice. "I'm sorry," he says to his sister, and for the first time, he sounds it.

Antonela faces Bea and Teo. "But which one to pick?"

"You're not using their bodies, either!" I say.

"My possession will kill you," Antonela goes on, addressing Bea and Teo, "but at least your deaths will be instant."

"Don't touch them," I say, my heart in my mouth.

She turns to me. "So wasteful, but it must be done. I cannot exist on your plane without a shell. You and I are already bound, so I cannot touch your body while you are alive."

"Please don't do this," I beg. "I saw your life at the other castle. You deserve so much better. Give us a chance. Let's be a family. We will help you. We can work together, find another way—"

"I am going to teach you the most important lesson Grandparent taught me," she says, as her body expands into a blanket of black smoke. "Only when you sacrifice everything will you have nothing to lose."

"NO!" I cry out as the smoke spreads over my aunt and uncle, like a storm cloud.

"I offer myself to you," says Teo, falling to his knees and closing his eyes. "Antonela, use me—"

"Stop that!" says Bea, shaking her brother. "What are you doing?"

"Antonela, please!" I shout up at the smoke. "Don't do this!"

The smoke swirls into a funnel over our heads.

"Get up!" says Bea to Teo, but he stays on his knees, keeping his eyes shut.

"It's what I want!" he insists to her. "Let me go!"

The smoke strikes down, like a hurricane touching land, and I scream—

"Bea!"

My aunt is struck by the smoke, and her neck falls back, her body convulsing.

"No!" shouts Teo.

I grip Bea's arms, trying to shake my sister loose from her body. My aunt looks at me, terrified, her mouth opening and closing as her frame keeps shaking.

"Don't do this, Antonela!" I beg. "Not her, please!"

Bea's eyes roll up, and I cry, "Fight! Don't give in!"

Teo looks frozen as he watches me try to keep his sister alive. Her body is heating up like she's fighting off an infection—and I gasp as black spots sprout in her corneas, the smoke spiraling inward . . .

"Please, Bea, resist!"

The black reaches her irises.

I squeeze my aunt's body as if I could drain my sister out of her—and watch helplessly as smoke consumes every fleck of brown.

GET INSIDE THE SUSPECT'S MIND, BUT DON'T LET THEM INSIDE YOURS.

CHAPTER 26

I'M BACK ON THE JOURNAL room floor. I blink a few times, disoriented.

"Hello, sister."

I scramble backward as the body that was once Beatríz rises as Antonela.

"What have you done?" I ask, my voice breaking.

"Spared you. That is what you like, right? For someone to die in your stead?"

The emotionless expression belongs to a soulless creature. I thought Bea was cold when we met, but this is the face of true winter.

"If Bast does not hold up his end, the whole world will die for you," threatens Antonela. "I will draw everyone here. La Sombra will be unable to resist the temptation of such a blood feast."

She looks to my uncle. "Leave now," she commands him. "I will catch up."

"Don't go with her," I tell Teo. "She just killed Bea!"

Teo locks his gaze on mine, and I know that it doesn't matter that my sister just murdered his—he's already made his choice to serve Antonela. "Your sister has sacrificed more than any of us," he says. "It's our turn now."

"*You* sacrificed her! How many deaths can you bear on your conscience?" I dig my hand into my pocket for the syringe. "Felipe's? Your sister's? Mine? All in an attempt to justify what you did to Antonela twelve years ago—to avoid being her killer, you've become a mass murderer!"

He lunges at me, and I pull out the syringe to strike—but he ducks and elbows me in the side.

I gasp for breath, bending forward, and the needle slips from my fingers.

"*Go,*" Antonela says to him again, and Teo obediently leaves the tower.

Alone with my sister, I am overcome with regret as I stare into my aunt's face. If I had never let Felipe into la Sombra in the first place, if I had just followed Bea's two simple rules, none of this would be happening. If I had listened to her about not trusting my uncle, I wouldn't have manifested Antonela, and my aunt would still be alive.

"I am sorry this is the extent of our reunion," says my sister, though she doesn't sound one drop remorseful. "I trust Bast remembers our pact and is ready to do his part, yet should he hesitate, you will make sure he goes through with it . . . for your world's sake."

She turns toward the stairs, like she's going to leave.

"Where are you going?" I call. "Don't you want to greet your prince? Why not wait and deliver your message?"

"I doubt he will be happy to see me. Nor do I wish to distract him from finishing his task."

She truly *is* indifferent. To everyone.

The room darkens again, and I think it's Antonela turning into black smoke, until I see the flash of silver. Bea must have done as I asked and left blood for Sebastián so he could access the journal room.

"A man is outside," he says to me, barely glancing at Beatríz as he sweeps into the room. "Is it the brujo?"

"You mean *caster,*" says Antonela from under my aunt's skin. "No, he is not."

The shadow beast spins around and stares at Beatríz in surprise. "You can see me?"

"But can *you* see *me*?" asks my sister softly, moving closer to him. "Do your part, and you can go home. I did not lie about that. Goodbye, Bast."

In the fraction of a second it takes Sebastián to work out what's happening, Antonela has already dashed out. She moves at superhuman speed, like him.

Sebastián chases after her.

I run down the stairs, trying to see what's happening, sliding and grabbing the wall. I race past my reflection in the mirror room, and when Sebastián finds me, I'm wheezing in the corridor by the dining hall.

"She is gone!" he says, nearly growling with frustration. "What happened?"

I feel the same hollowness I experienced after my parents died. That sense of emptiness that comes from nothing mattering because all the people you love and who loved you are gone and you're just drifting.

I was supposed to be an anchor, and yet I am unanchored.

"You knew," I say, turning my back to him because I can't stand to look at Sebastián and see Prince Bastian. "Last night, when you got your memories back, you knew about my sister. And you said nothing."

"Our conversation was difficult enough. I did not want to overwhelm you."

"My tiny human brain couldn't handle more."

"I am not sure it could," he says, my sarcasm falling flat.

"Well, it doesn't matter. You're going to kill me. So just get on with it."

I know the brave thing would be to face my fate head-on, but I can't look at him. I can't let the last thing I see in life be him murdering me.

He doesn't say anything, and I appreciate that he doesn't bother denying the facts. The seconds drag past in unbearable silence, knowing every breath could be my last.

"I want," he says softly, "to thank you. For showing me *joy*." He says it like it's a new vocabulary word, and he's trying it out in a sentence. "As Prince Bastian, I was cruel, greedy, unyielding. I believed my heart was truly made of iron, and that is why I did not bother with the pursuit of anything other than power."

By the volume of his voice, it sounds like he's moving closer.

"Yet you found my fracture lines," he says, and I feel him standing over me. "You showed me the strength of softer emotions is they are malleable enough to sneak in through crevices too tiny to be perceived. That is why I did not notice your grip on me until I was already yours."

My heart is ramming my chest, and I have no idea how to feel. Most of me wants to turn around and look at his expression while he's speaking, but to what end? Why is he saying things to make me fall in love with him right as he's about to kill me?

"I don't need all this sweet talk, Sebastián. You can't sugarcoat murder, so just get on with it."

"I am not going to kill you, Estela."

He sounds farther away now, and I turn around slowly, anticipating a trick. "Yesterday you wanted to break the spell," I say. "You said you were over me—"

"I am not over you. I am beneath you."

He drops to his knees, and it's the last thing I expected from the future king of the vampires. "By your world's standards, I am a murderous monster. You were right about cursed castles being for evil princes. I do not deserve you."

After Felipe's betrayal, Antonela's villainy, and Bea's murder, I can hardly believe Sebastián is the one who is still here, sticking by my side. And as I search his eyes, it dawns on me that Beatríz wasn't the one who made this castle a home for me.

That feeling started long before she and I connected.

It's not la Sombra I belong to—it's Sebastián.

A cracking sound reverberates in my chest, like I've been splintered in two, and I collapse into myself. Yet before I hit the ground, I land in his arms.

I let myself break, and he holds me while I shatter. Everything is gone, slipped through my fingers, *again*. And once more, I've been left behind.

"You are not alone," he says, and I realize he's been saying it for a while now, repeating it to me like a mantra.

"But I am," I say. "You will have to go back home one day to sit on your throne—and even if we find a way to get you there that doesn't require killing me, what would be left for me here? A future as la Sombra's new caretaker, cursed to be alone like my aunt was?"

His brow furrows, and he's silent for so long that I worry about what he's going to say.

"I have been thinking of something you said, about how we should fight our fates. I think you are right. *We are impossible*—and that proves anything is possible." He chuckles at himself, and I'm relieved to spy some light in his eyes.

He's not the heavy-eyed Prince Bastian, nor is he the less burdened Sebastián. He's someone new.

"I have spent my entire existence caged in a castle," he says. "If that is to be both our fates, I would rather be locked away together than apart."

"What are you saying?" I ask, and it's like I suddenly don't understand the English language.

"I am not leaving you," he says, those five words changing everything. "I will keep you company for the rest of your long, *long* life. I choose you over . . . over everything."

I can hardly breathe as he rises and holds out a hand to help me up. "What if I live to be a hundred?" I ask as he pulls me closer.

"Time is not a factor where I am from, so it will not matter when I return." His lips meet mine, but the kiss is too brief. "Yet if you plan on living that long," he says, and I groan in complaint as he steps back, "then we must prepare for your sister. Your uncle was waiting for her outside, and she collapsed into his arms. Corporealizing consumes a great deal of energy, so she will need to recharge. No doubt that is why she needed his help to get somewhere safe."

"The clínica," I say. "Looking like Beatríz, no one will question Antonela."

"It is likely she will send your uncle here during the day, when I am not around, to check if you remain alive. I think you should get some sleep now, and leave at sunrise to hide. Do not return until nightfall, when I can protect you—"

"Or," I say, hating his idea, "I can stay here and catch him. My uncle seems to know a lot about Brálaga magic, and I'd like to ask him some questions."

"How will you overpower him?"

I dig into my pocket, but the syringe isn't there.

"I won't have to," I say. "I'll pretend to be dead, and when he comes close enough to check my pulse, I'll stab him with one of my aunt's syringes."

I expect Sebastián to dismiss my idea for fear of my safety, but this new version of him considers my words. "You will need to tie him up. Do you want me to show you how?"

I nod in assent, and he disappears.

"What happened after you made the pact with Antonela to cross over?" I ask as he returns with ropes bundled in his arms. I assume they're from the dungeon.

"That was before I knew you," he says, casting his gaze around the space. "You will want to tie his wrists, ankles, and waist to something like . . . the stairs."

"I'm just asking," I say as we walk toward the gargoyle banister.

"I would prefer not to add to the rift between you two. Is it not enough that I choose you?"

"Can't you tell me what the pact was?"

"She betrayed me. She told me I would be able to feast all I wanted on Earth, and when I was ready to return, I just had to find her double. *You.* She told me once I drank enough of your blood, the spell would break, sending me back home. She did not tell me I would lose my memories, or that I would be trapped in this castle. Now, let's learn some knots."

He loops a rope around the iron banister, then he twists it around, showing me a simple knot. He does it a few times, until I memorize the steps, and then I try it.

"Good work," he says. "I brought a thinner rope for his wrists because you want to minimize the chance of him squeezing a hand out."

He loops the rope around my wrists to show me a way to handcuff my uncle, then he lifts my bound hands, hinging the rope on the gargoyle's wing above me. I am nearly on my tiptoes, and I tug down on my arms, but they're tied up tight.

"You want to make sure your suspect is helpless," he says, and as he stares at me, a change glazes over his eyes. "Then you want to show them you are the one in control."

He grabs the zipper of my hoodie and tugs it down slowly, revealing my tank top.

"What's next?" I ask breathily, every part of me growing excited.

"Next, you expose your suspect for who they are *underneath*."

I gasp as he pulls down my pants, leaving me in my underwear. Then he lifts my hips and cradles my legs in the gargoyle's arms, spreading them open. As he stands between my thighs, I finally work up the nerve to ask, "Does your shirt come off?"

A beat later, Sebastián is only in pants. His torso might have been carved from actual rock, every line and ripple perfectly symmetrical. My fingers fidget overhead, itching to touch him.

His lips find my neck. I feel his mouth brushing along a vein, and I brace myself for the stab of sharp fangs—

But it's his warm tongue that strikes. As he draws designs down my throat, his fingers caress up the insides of my thighs, and the temperature rises about a hundred degrees.

I grow sensitive and lightweight as his strokes inch higher, until he slips beneath the cotton of my underwear.

My spine digs into the metal banister, and I gasp, my gaze blurring with pleasure. I moan as his touch intensifies, my body throbbing like a pulse, until the stirrings of release shoot through me. "You're . . . spectacular," I whisper.

"I hope to always make you feel this good, Estela," he murmurs into my ear, as he unhooks my arms from the gargoyle's wing. After untying the ropes binding my wrists, he sweeps me off my feet, and by my next breath I'm lying on my bed.

"I will bring you—"

"I don't want to eat," I say, cutting him off. My stomach is too full of emotions to digest anything else at the moment.

Bea is dead. Antonela is a monster. Sebastián is mine. As much as my brain tries to process these facts, it doesn't seem to be working as fast as my heart. "Can we just lie down for a little?" I ask him.

He joins me on the bed, and I snuggle into his side. His arm closes around me, and neither of us says anything for a while, my breaths the only sound in the room.

After Mom and Dad died, I didn't think I would ever recover any sense of family, but in the past couple of days with Bea, I had hope for the first time. That hope grew exponentially in the seconds when I thought I might actually recover my sister.

So much hope extinguished in a single meeting.

I think of Antonela growing up in the other castle, and Beatríz growing older in la Sombra, and Sebastián being trained for leadership in his mountain throne—and it occurs to me that all three of them have been trapped in a castle that doubles as a cage.

I have been so much freer than them, and yet I have always longed for a home.

My mind drifts to the four girls on the subway train. I used to try not to think of them because their fate seemed too cruel. Yet now that I have seen other horrors, I can complete the thought that began over seven months ago, when Dad caught me staring at them.

I wasn't just curious about the girls' lives.

I was *jealous*.

I craved what they had, but I was terrified of my parents seeing that I wanted a more traditional life. It felt like a betrayal to them to desire what we didn't—or maybe *couldn't*—have. I didn't know about our residency issues, but I was aware we didn't have a lot of money.

"College."

As soon as I say the word, it feels like I've dislodged something that got caught in my throat years ago.

Sebastián rolls onto his side, giving me his full attention.

"I was going to take my GED," I say, staring at the ceiling, feeling like someone else has taken control of my vocal cords. "My parents never brought up the next step after that, but it was all I could think about. We were subletting a place in Asheville, and I hid the college brochures in the boxes of my morning cereal because my parents didn't eat that stuff."

I haven't thought of us in that Asheville place in so long that I feel a pang in my chest.

"I didn't want to break up our trio, but I dreamed of going to college and moving into a dorm. I'd have my own room, and friends, and access to a school library. I could finally stand still and feel rooted somewhere. I guess the lesson is be careful what you wish for," I add, my voice dropping out.

Sebastián presses a kiss to my wrist. "Thank you. For sharing that with me."

"What about you?" I ask. "Is there anything you wanted for yourself back home?"

After a moment, he says, "*Blue bear*," so soft I'm not sure I heard it.

"Before you, I had only cared for one being," he says, "whom you called *blue bear*. All young Bleeders get one as our first kill. He is our first meal once we begin to hunt our own blood, only I chose to keep mine alive. Whatever instinct impelled me do that, my father made sure to strangle it. There is no room for softness in my world, especially not among royalty. It is a weakness I was born with that I was sure had been crushed. I never dared want anything for myself again."

"I'm sorry," I whisper.

"My father's will is the only one that matters where I am from. He has been pressuring me to find a mate and perform the blood-bond, but with someone of his choosing. That is the real reason I accepted your sister's offer. I could handle loneliness alone, but to share it with a stranger sounded insufferable."

"What's the blood-bond?" I ask.

"An exchange of blood between mates that serves as the basis for procreation among my kind. Bleeder offspring are rare, and conception depends on the strength of the connection."

"So only Bleeders who are in love can get pregnant?"

He chuckles. "*Love* has nothing to do with it. There is a special sac in which we must deposit our blood, and then we bury it in fertile soil where we regularly feed it more of our blood. Only the most powerful blood-bonds can produce a child strong enough to climb out from the ground."

"That's so bizarre," I say, trying to picture it. "I hate the thought of you being blood-bonded or whatever to some amazing Bleeder and forgetting all about me."

He shakes his head. "If blue bear taught me anything, it is that when you care for someone, they stay with you forever. Even if all we get together is one hundred Earth years, I will carry the eternal heartache of your loss, and I will still be better off for having known you."

I curl more tightly into him, wishing I could pause life and stay like this for as long as possible; but after what feels like only a minute, he says, "Estela . . . it is almost time."

"No," I groan, but I can feel that the blackness has lifted, and sunrise is near, which means Sebastián will soon be gone.

"I want to make sure you are ready for today," he says. "Your uncle could show at any moment."

We get up, and after I use the bathroom, we stand together in front of the window. Gray light streams into the room.

"I'm eighteen today," I murmur, mostly to myself.

"It is the day of your birth," says Sebastián. "I have read that humans celebrate this occasion."

"I don't feel much like celebrating," I say with a shrug.

"We will have to change that when I see you tonight," he says with a smirk, even though the silver of his eyes swirls like a storm. "You remember how to tie the knots, right?"

I nod. The gray sky is giving way to blue, and there's no denying the sun is rising. Sebastián is going to vanish into thin air, and now that I have just seconds left, I don't want to lose a single one.

He seems to have the same idea because we begin to make out like the world is ending and any moment an asteroid will take us out. His kisses taste like blackberries and chocolate and minty ice cream.

I feel the first ray of light warm my face. Day has come, and Sebastián is going to disappear . . .

But we're still making out.

We pull apart and stare at each other in the brightening air. It's early morning, and he's still here.

"The black seeds," he says in awe.

I laugh in open delight. This is the *perfect* birthday gift.

Thank you, Bea.

CHAPTER 27

WHEN I OPEN MY EYES, Sebastián is the first thing I see.

I've never woken up next to someone who wasn't my parents, and it feels more intimate than I expected. There's a kind of vulnerability to seeing each other in the morning light.

"I can't believe you're still here," I say, reaching up to touch his cheek. I'm used to seeing him haloed in silver, not in the warmth of day. He looks younger in the gold-tinged air.

"I watched you sleep all morning," he says, "and it has become my definition of peace."

I feel my cheeks flushing. Once we accepted that he wasn't going to disappear, he offered for me to sleep longer while he kept watch for my family members.

"Are you hungr—?"

Sebastián's voice drops out, his expression changing completely as his head angles away from me. Then he says, "Someone is coming."

I get dressed in a rush, while he disappears.

My mouth is parched, and I can't catch my breath. I'm not ready to fight my uncle or my sister yet. Not ready to remember I lost what was left of my family last night. Not ready to *wake up*—

"It is not them," says Sebastián, startling me as I come out of the bathroom. "It is an older man. He walks with an aid. He is now approaching the front doors."

"*Felipe's father,*" I say, my heart falling with dismay. "Should I answer?"

"If you do not, and your aunt disappears, too, more people will come knocking. Eventually, you will have to answer."

"But what do I say to him? You want me to lie to a man to his face about his dead son, and in a language I barely speak?"

BANG. BANG. BANG.

"If you care about keeping this castle's bloodthirst at bay," says Sebastián, "then take it from another bloodthirsty beast—the best thing you can do is communicate to this man in the language he best understands that he must stay away from here."

Sebastián is right that I don't want cops showing up, nor do I want to draw more attention to this place. So I open the front door.

The man on the other side looks aged with worry, and my soul hurts for him. His heart fears he's lost his son, but his brain isn't aware of the facts yet. Right now, Arturo is caught in the despair of not knowing.

Maybe I can spare him some pain.

"Hola, Estela," he says, nodding in greeting. "¿Está tu tía?"

I shake my head. My aunt is not home.

"No la he visto en la clínica," he adds. *I didn't see her at the clinic.*

I shrug and try to summon actual words, but he barrels on before I can open my mouth. "No importa, he venido a verte a ti." *I have come to see you.*

"¿A mí?" I ask. Today, I have no trouble with Spanish. In fact, I even feel more comfortable pronouncing the words.

"¿Sabes dónde está Felipe? No ha regresado de su viaje, y hablé con su amigo Sergio, a quien iba a visitar, y me dijo que no lo ha visto en meses. Pensé que como ustedes han estado tan unidos, a lo mejor te ha confiado algo."

I understand everything he says—it's as if in recovering Antonela, I've unlocked my access to Spanish. Arturo is asking where his son is because his friend Sergio hasn't seen him. Arturo is here because he hopes Felipe confided in me what his real plans were.

I picture Felipe's room with all its posters of la Sombra from every angle, the dark shrine he built for its worship. I think of the attic in Libroscuro, with its ancient books about the castle and the town and its ties to the supernatural. I remember the way Bea's photo sits on the mantel at the Sarmientos' home, just beneath la Sombra's crest. And I flash to Felipe saying his family are the keepers of the Book.

There is no police station in Oscuro, but there is a bookstore, and this castle, and a clínica run by a Brálaga. In my digitizing work for Bea, I barely got through the first last name in the clínica's files because there are so many people of the same family here. Oscuro's residents stay for generations. Mom used to say populations remain firmly entrenched in a place due to culture or poverty. In this case, I think it's superstition.

The people who remain here, the Oscurianos, were raised to fear this castle, to be in awe of it, to watch it from the shadows. They adhere to a higher power than law enforcement or religion.

Above all, they believe in *la Sombra*.

"Felipe told me he received a mission," I say, trying to channel his fierce conviction. "I don't know where he went. I don't even know what he meant. But I believe him."

Arturo's eyes have gone wide. He stares at me for a long moment, and I get the impression of a man whose faith is being tested when he asks, "The fire that took your sister . . . it is true?"

His accent is rough, but I understand him. I nod in assent.

"And—Felipe—he's gone to the same place?"

"Yes," I say, unsure what the fallout will be—if I should expect the cops or a mob next. "Bea chose to go with him," I add, hoping Arturo doesn't run into her. "My sister is guiding them."

Now Arturo's expression slackens a bit, slightly eased. "Pensé que la doctora no quería a Felipe." *I thought la doctora didn't care for Felipe.*

"I think seeing how close he and I got changed her mind."

He nods, his eyes dazed with the shock he's just been dealt. "I wish I could understand," he says. "Pero Felipe creía en el poder de la Sombra. Siempre fue su sueño pertenecer al castillo." *Felipe believed in the power of la Sombra. It was always his dream to belong to the castle.*

"I don't understand, either, but I believe," I say, and we look at each other, in the shadow of our grief.

When Arturo has gone and I'm alone again with Sebastián, he leads me to the kitchen. I feel nauseous from my lies. I refuse the glass of water he holds out to me, and he pulls me into him, pressing a kiss to my head. "You did the man a great kindness."

"I lied."

"You are carrying the weight of the truth for him because you know there is no fixing what is broken."

"I'm continuing my family's manipulation of the people here."

"You are giving him a place to store his grief," he says, and I remember what

Bea said about why my parents kept Antonela's existence from me: *They chose to carry the grief for you.*

"It is what you came here hoping to find," says Sebastián. "A dark fairy tale you could sell to yourself to help make sense of the unfathomable tragedy that befell you."

"*A place to store my grief*," I repeat. Is that what this castle is? Not just for me, but for all of Oscuro.

Our collective shadow.

I scan my blood on the tablet to gain access to the journal room. Sebastián is at my side as the bookshelf door opens.

He's already reading a journal by the time I make it up the stairs. He sets it down and picks up another before I've even opened one. At this rate, he'll get through the entire collection tonight.

"Here is something," he says after a stretch. "An ancestor your age, Araceli, writes that they see smoke every time bad luck befalls them. A second entry tells of their discovery of a twin sister, Isabel, whose childhood death had been kept a secret. That is all. Araceli did not write again."

I remember how Matilda wrote just the one entry, too. By the time I pick up a second journal, Sebastián has finished reviewing a couple of rows' worth.

"Look," he says, showing me a drawing of a figure standing in front of the mirror in the room with the chandelier. Two other figures stand behind the person, and a speech bubble over their heads says: *No hay luz en Oscuro.*

"That's the memory spell that let me see Antonela's past," I say, reaching down to turn the page.

The next drawing shows the room we're in now. A figure holds a book open. It has a red cover.

"*Manifestation spell*," I read. "*This will bind your twin's energy to yours if they are on this plane.*" I swallow. "That's what I did." The admission comes out a whisper.

Bea was right. I shouldn't have listened to Teo. "Bea's death is my fault."

"No, it is your sister's."

My *sister's.*

The word still sounds strange. My whole life, I would have given anything for a sister. Someone to share the back seat with, fight with over the radio station, play with when we got to a new place—a built-in friend.

But our own family sent her to Hell, where they ruined her. They molded her into a monster who's murdered everyone I love. And now she's coming for me.

I'm just about to give up on the journal I'm reviewing when I spot something on the page I recognize. The drawing of a book with la Sombra's crest on the cover.

"I've seen this before. It's the Book from the thirteenth tale. The one Felipe says his family is hiding."

Sebastián comes over, and I read the entry out loud:

The worst day of my life started like any other.

Abuelo tended the jardín de sangre, Abuela cooked, and Mamá was resting her very pregnant belly in bed. Papá should have been watching me, but he was more interested in reading the newspaper.

My aunts lived with us, but they were vacationing in France.

I was by the dining hall when the lights on the walls started flickering. All of them, all at once. I had seen that happen before, but no one else ever said anything, so I assumed it was normal. Yet now for the first time, it occurred to me that maybe the others could not see it.

The lights seemed to be leading me deeper into the castle, toward the jardín de sangre. Except before I reached the door to the cathedral, something broke through the stone floor, spraying chunks of rock into the air.

I fell back and shrieked as a large shape crawled up from underground, and all the lights shut off.

In the blackness, I could barely breathe as the intruder moved closer. I felt them hand me something—a book*—and they whispered one word:*

"Run."

The lights blasted back on, and the intruder was gone. Yet the book remained.

I opened to the first page, where a note had been tucked inside. It was clear the writer had only a rudimentary grasp of my language, but the message was this:

> *Your ancestor is dangerous*
> *Their plan to share power with your world will destroy it*

> *It is what they did to mine*
> *Now I give my life to end theirs*
> *I have gone far to spell this Book*
> *I hope it can stop the threat when it appears*
> *Give the Book to one not of Brálaga blood to hide*
> *They and their descendants will be its keepers until the right*
> *Brálaga comes for it*

I was only ten, and I doubted my parents would believe me, or give me permission to go. So I ran off on my own to the first place I could think of, the home of a family friend I could trust, and I explained what happened. They agreed to hide the Book and tell no one, but only if I would let them walk me back to la Sombra, as I was young and it had gotten late.

When we reached the castle, the front door was open, and there was a sinister aura in the air that made us both hesitate to enter. The keeper of the Book was too afraid to go inside, but I barreled ahead.

I did not find anyone. It was like my entire family had vanished. Deep down, I knew someone powerful had come looking for the Book.

My aunts cut their vacation short. They kept asking me what happened, but I could not speak of it. It was then they decided to tell me about my twin brother.

They showed me the journal room and shared the story of how they sent him to the other castle. It was only after reading others' entries that I discovered the Brálaga curse.

My aunts had damned us all.

As punishment, I never told them the truth of what happened to our family. I write this entry many decades later, long after their deaths.

Seven years after losing my parents, my twin returned to me. I could feel Franco's presence in the castle, and we found a way to communicate using the mirror. The manifestation spell bound his spirit to me, and he possessed one of our aunts to corporealize and return to Earth.

When her body gave out, he took her sister's. When hers gave out, he possessed people outside our bloodline, but their bodies broke down even faster. The whole time, we searched for a permanent solution to *his problem, some kind of Earthly shell that would last, but we never found one. We barely had six months together before he faded away.*

It has been seventy-one years since that day. At eighty-eight years old, I am the oldest Brálaga in recorded history. I have not returned to this room since Franco died, and I do not plan to come back here again. I record this message for whoever needs to read it in the future.

The keeper of the Book and I never again mentioned what happened that day. Yet, shortly after their death, I received a note:

I am the new keeper of the Book. I vow to keep this secret alive through the generations of my bloodline, so it will not be forgotten.

I have no idea what the Book is or what makes it dangerous for us to behold. I wish I had read some of its pages, but I was a terrified ten-year-old when it was handed to me.

If you are the one for whom the Book was meant, I wish you good fortune.

Your ancestor,
Lala

I read through it to myself a few more times.
Six months.
That was how long Franco managed to hang around. Antonela could cause a lot of damage in that time.

"I need to find the Book," I say to Sebastián.

His face hardens like I've said the wrong thing.

"That will have to wait. Your uncle is here."

CHAPTER 28

"OKAY," I SAY, ONCE WE'RE in the library. "We can stage it here."

I get the syringe from my hoodie pocket and uncap the needle. Then I drop to the floor, my limbs sticking out at odd angles, thigh concealing the weapon in my right hand. A shadow falls over me, and I feel Sebastián's chest pressing down.

"What—?"

"Shh," he whispers, his lips by my neck.

I gasp in pain as his fangs bite down, drawing blood. He doesn't drink, only punctures my skin to make the scene more convincing.

He licks the blood off his teeth. "Delectable," he whispers before vanishing. I let my head loll to the side so some blood trickles across my neck.

"He's almost here," Sebastián whispers. "Take smaller breaths."

I can just make out the sound of footsteps coming up the stairs, but I'm looking away from the entrance so I don't see Teo walk in. But when I hear his sharp intake of air, I know he's seen me.

"¡Pero es de día!" *But it's daytime!*

I open my eyes to see that Teo isn't staring at me.

He's gaping at *Sebastián*.

The shadow beast lifts my uncle by the neck, and I leap to my feet, shouting, "Stop!"

Teo glares at me, seeming more upset by my signs of life than his own impending doom. He looks like he would speak, except his throat is being crushed.

"Put him down," I say to Sebastián. "*Please.*"

To my surprise, the Iron Prince obeys me. Once Teo is on the ground, he stumbles back against a bookshelf.

"Antonela said we would not be able to see or touch each other," he says, staring warily at Sebastián. "What's changed?"

La Sombra's seeds are rewriting the rules.

Neither of us says it, but I know Sebastián and I are both thinking it. He can appear in the daytime. He can step out on the tower's balcony. And he can interact with Teo.

If the plants' healing qualities can curb the sharp edges of a spell . . . maybe they can do the same for a curse. Is that why Bea wanted me to take them?

"You're the one with all the answers," I say to Teo, holding up the syringe threateningly. "You tell us."

"If you keep me here, she will know you're alive," he threatens me back.

"But she *won't* know Sebastián is here," I say, crossing my arms, "waiting to strike as soon as she walks through the door."

Teo's lack of retort exposes his concern, and Sebastián presses him, "Why is she afraid of me?"

"She fears no one," says Teo, squaring his shoulders like defending Antonela makes him more powerful. He looks at me, and I see no love in his eyes. He's Antonela's champion through and through.

"Your sister is going to be the first Earth-born bruja, and our bloodline will be the most important that ever lived." His brown eyes beam bright with Felipe-like fanaticism. "I know it's hard to hear, but she is a marvel. After all she's been through to survive, are you going to let her die, just so you can play house with a creature who doesn't belong here? What happens when you grow old or sick or he gets bored—?"

"*She killed your sister!*" I roar, reaching for any trace residue of love for his twin. "She killed Bea! Your twin who loved you and was willing to give up everything just to save you—"

"But she wouldn't give me the one thing I wanted."

"You mean *magic*?" My eyebrows are at my hairline. "You read the journals, you know the entries better than anyone, and you still don't get it? She was *protecting* you! Don't you see? Look what you've become!"

I shake my head in disgust, and I hate that tears burn my eyes because he doesn't deserve them. "You chose the wrong ally, Teo. Whose body do you think Antonela will use next, after . . . ?"

I can't even finish the sentence.

"Bea may not have accepted it," he says, filling in her name for me. "But from the moment we sent Nela to the other castle, we owed her our submission."

He is unflinching in his devotion. He is Antonela's loyal soldier to the end.

"What about me?" I hear myself ask, and I didn't expect to sound so young.

"You got to *live*." His eyes grow Felipe-like again in their intensity. "You traveled beyond this castle, this town, this country—you got to cross the ocean and grow up free of this place's shadow!"

"So, this is it then?" I ask, my voice still small. "You've chosen sides, you love my sister, and now you want me to die. No pity or help for me. Is that right?"

I hate that it hurts.

This man with my aunt's face, my mother's brother, has yet to express a single ounce of love for me. Yet he's willing to die for my sister—the girl he murdered.

"I'm sorry, Tela," he says, for the first time actually sounding it. "You deserved better."

"I'm not asking you to betray Antonela," I say, boxing out Sebastián and moving in to make the conversation feel more intimate. "All I'm asking for is a chance. I deserve to fight for myself. For my life."

As I say the words, I realize I couldn't say them with the shadow beast's gaze on me. Not with how careless I've been about my life around him.

I came to Oscuro feeling so cavalier about surviving the Subway 25, convinced I was an oversight that could be corrected at any moment. And thirteen days later, I'm fighting for a future I could never have envisioned.

"What is it you think I can do for you?" Teo asks me, and I have to blink a few times to clear the moisture from my gaze.

"Explain to me why my sister can't possess me like she did Bea."

"Magic is inherited in pairs. You share power as a unit and are meant to keep it in balance. Antonela can only inherit your body if you are gone and the body still functions."

Something isn't right.

I think back to what she revealed to me about the spell: *When Bastian drains you, he will return to his realm, and I will be released into your body. Then the same spell that took our parents' lifeblood will return it to me.*

"If Sebastián kills me," I say, frowning, "how will my body still function?"

Teo looks like he's said too much, but I can't let him go silent now. "He doesn't need to drain me then," I theorize out loud to gauge my uncle's reaction, his face close enough to read. "The spell is triggered to send Sebastián back home when he drinks *just enough* of my blood to stop me, but not kill me."

Teo's eyes widen for a flash, just as his twin's did when I exposed her secrets. "There must still be blood in your system for Antonela's regeneration spell to work," Teo admits, and the shininess of his eyes betrays his excitement to share this knowledge.

"Magic that is only possible because she sacrificed my parents' blood," I remind Teo. "She killed *both* your sisters."

"Why is she afraid of me?" Sebastián moves in again, and between us, we're completely blocking Teo's path.

"She's not," says my uncle.

"Lie again, I dare you," says Sebastián, glaring at Teo in a way that makes me nervous. "What happens if I drink Antonela's blood while she is in possession of a body?"

Teo doesn't answer.

"Estela, leave." Sebastián's shadows spread across the bookshelves, his darkness expanding as his stare narrows on Teo's neck.

"Okay," I say, and I step back like I'm going to obey. "Goodbye then—"

I walk toward the exit, hoping my uncle gives us something right *now,* because I trust Sebastián to go through with his threat—

"Wait!"

I stop and turn to see that Sebastián already has my uncle's neck in his jaws. He retracts his fangs and lets Teo speak.

"If—if you drain a body in Antonela's possession, the spell breaks, and you return home."

Sebastián looks at me. *That's* why my sister ran from him.

"She can't risk you leaving," confirms Teo. "You are her only chance for success. If you take that from her, she will take the whole world from Estela. She will publicize Felipe's death, tell everyone where to find the body, awaken la Sombra's bloodlust—"

Teo's head slumps to the side.

I didn't even see the injection go in. Sebastián tosses the empty syringe to the floor, and I guess I should be grateful he stabbed my uncle with a needle and not his fangs.

"Antonela will just use him as another vessel," he warns me. "It is not in your best interest to let your uncle live."

I know he makes a valid point, and he's only thinking of our survival. Yet I can't help wondering if he's also looking for an excuse to rip into a fresh vein and drink.

"I had more questions to ask him," I say. "I wanted to know about the Book—"

"He is not going to help you defeat your sister. He serves her now. We should keep reading the journals to see if anyone else wrote about the Book . . . or perhaps you can reach out to Felipe's family and ask them directly?"

"No way can I talk to them! It was hard enough lying to Arturo today. I kept thinking of Felipe in the forest asking me to forget the black smoke and run. I should have agreed then—"

There's no water in the fountain.

Felipe said those words to me right before Teo struck. I thought it was gibberish from the fear, but what if it was a clue about the Book?

"I need to go to the town plaza," I say, my mind whirring. "I think that may be where the Book is hidden."

Sebastián looks out the window, and I'm sure he's going to tell me it's not safe, my sister could intercept me, I shouldn't leave his protection—

"It won't get dark for another couple of hours," he says. "*Hurry.*"

I nod, glad I've earned his trust. But has he earned mine? I glance at Teo, worried about leaving him here. Sebastián looks at me like he can read the fear on my face. "I will not kill him while you are gone."

I could do without the *while you are gone* part, but I take the small assurance and run.

When I make it to the plaza, I'm relieved to see Gloria feeding the pigeons as usual. Yet as I approach, I feel a punch to the gut because she's Felipe's great-grandmother, and she doesn't know he's gone.

"Felipe no está, angelito," she says to me. *Felipe is not here.* When I get closer, I see the wetness on her cheeks.

My tongue feels numb, and I don't say anything.

"Ha regresado tu tío," she says, one corner of her lip pulling up in a sneer. *Your uncle is back.*

I nod in assent. "Estoy buscando algo. Es un libro." I tell her I'm looking for a book.

"Me imaginé," she says, as if my request makes perfect sense. "Mi marido me dijo que algún día podría venir alguien a buscarlo. Desde que regresaste a Oscuro, me imaginé que serías tú."

Her husband told her that one day someone might come looking for the Book. She says ever since I returned to Oscuro, she imagined it would be me. Her husband was most likely the great-grandfather who told Felipe about Brálaga magic. He must have told his wife, too.

"¿Dónde está el Libro?" I ask for the Book.

She points to the oxidized statue of Brálaga holding the pitcher that should be pouring water. I climb onto the lip of the fountain, and I get as close as I can to the coppery figure, then I reach a hand inside the pitcher.

It's empty.

I glance back at Gloria. Her finger is now pointing down.

I look in the fountain's pool. It's empty save for leaves, feathers, dirt, and other small debris. There are cracks along the inner bowl walls, and some of the fissures are thick enough to stick in my hand. I flop onto my belly and reach down, digging inside the gaps to feel for the Book.

I keep moving around the pool, shoving my hand into each fracture, but I don't find anything. I'm just about to look up at Gloria for another clue, when my fingers close on something hard and thin. I pull it out into the late afternoon light.

The Book.

It's real.

I open the red cover that bears the castle's crest, and I find a wispy, withering piece of paper with a note written in ink too faded to make out anymore. But I remember what it says from Lala's entry. This is the note that told her to take the Book far from the castle and entrust it to someone not of Brálaga blood. It's the reason Felipe's family became the Book's keepers.

I flip through the ancient, stiff pages, but they're all blank. I turn them faster, expecting the paper to cut my skin and my blood to unlock a coded message, but nothing happens.

This isn't magic. It's an ordinary book.

My heart plunges with disappointment as I leaf through empty page after page—until at last, I strike ink.

The message is one sentence long:

Para atrapar un espíritu. To trap a spirit.

I turn the page and find a diagram made of three stacked boxes:

The first contains a small round portrait of a person's face.

The second features two elements, side by side. On the left are five black seeds from the jardín de sangre, and on the right are three red drops that look like they're meant to be blood.

The third box shows two figures with an air bubble above them that says in perfect calligraphy: *No hay luz en Oscuro*.

I stare at the diagram for as long as I dare, until the sun hangs too low in the sky. Then I carefully place the Book back in its hiding place.

"Gracias," I say to Gloria.

"Que Brálaga la bendiga," she says, tears still rolling down her cheeks as she stares in la Sombra's direction.

May Brálaga bless you.

CHAPTER 29

WHEN I GET BACK TO la Sombra, I relay the spell to Sebastián by re-creating the diagram in my journal.

"I think the first drawing represents a picture of who we're trying to trap," I say, seated at my desk. "Then I have to eat a bunch of seeds and sprinkle my blood on the photo." I point to each drawing as I list off the steps. "Finally, we have to resurrect my aunt so she and Teo can chant *No hay luz en Oscuro*."

"Was there any indication of the spell's location?" asks Sebastián, either ignoring or not picking up on my sarcasm.

"Isn't it just the castle?" I ask.

"A trapping spell needs anchoring to an object or a room," he says, standing over my shoulder. "A photograph alone will not possess that power."

Great. Another riddle.

I think back to Lala's journal entry. She wrote that the being who gave her the Book came up from the ground, but where was she ... ?

On her way to the jardín de sangre. I don't think she'd made it to the cathedral yet. Which means she was right above—

"The purple room," I say out loud. "That has to be where la Sombra's gateway to other worlds is located. It's where my sister crossed over, and it's where the being with the Book burst into the castle."

"It's the first space I remember," says Sebastián faintly, like he's deep in thought. "The crossing to this dimension is hazy, but that room stands out to me as the gateway."

"Its power must be why the purple room is hidden in the first place," I say. "I need to lure Antonela there so I can use the Book's spell to trap her."

That's where all this started, and it's where it has to finish.

"We are trapping her *spirit*," Sebastián corrects me. "*Para atrapar un espíritu* means your sister must be in noncorporeal form."

"You mean I need to get her to leave Bea's body?" I ask, and Sebastián nods in assent.

There's only two ways that's going to happen: either Sebastián destroys her current shell, or Antonela has to believe she can move into mine. "We'll have to fake my death again," I say.

"Your sister will not be as easy to fool as your uncle. She risks too much entering the castle prematurely. She will not do so until she is sure the spell has broken."

"Then how do we convince her?" I ask, turning to face him.

"We will have to put on a good performance. I have to drink enough to weaken you, so she will believe the spell has sent me home and I am no longer a threat."

"Unless you *actually* disappear," I say ominously. "We have no idea what amount you need to drink to end the spell keeping you here," I point out. "Not to mention the fact that we're missing a key ingredient for this trapping spell—*my aunt*. And I'm not sure how I'll convince Teo to help—"

"You cannot," says Sebastián matter-of-factly. "He will die before he gives up on Antonela. I will be the one doing the chanting."

I frown at him. "*How?* You're not of Brálaga blood."

"I will explain later. First, we must get you those seeds."

We hurry down the stairs in silence, but as we're crossing the mirror room, I can't hold in the words anymore. "Teo said you can go home without killing me if you drain Bea."

"I know."

We reach the fork in the hallway and cut toward the windowless cathedral. "What do you think about that?" I prod.

"I think I already said I choose you over everything."

His words still warm me, but I can't help saying, "If you're staying because you don't want to hurt me, this is your chance to go, pain-free."

I don't slow down. It's like I can only have this conversation on the move, without having to meet his eyes.

"Estela," he murmurs, keeping pace with me easily. "Look at me."

I don't know why I can't. I quicken my pace as we cut through the string of barren, doorless rooms, toward the jardín de sangre.

"Tell me how you feel," his voice whispers in my ear. "If you want me to go, I will go."

I stop moving when I'm on the red rug, atop the purple room. Sebastián stands before me, his silver eyes piercing mine, fishing for the words that won't surface.

"I love you," I say at last, my voice thick with unshed tears. "And that makes me afraid that I'm going to lose you."

"You will not," he assures me without skipping a beat, "because I love you, too."

His statement is a symphony, and I will my eyes not to well with water.

"Yet at the moment," he says, embracing me, "I am more afraid of losing you."

The walls blur as he transports us to the cathedral. When he sets me down before the stone wall, I search the rocks for the right one. After a few seconds, he points it out to me.

I spill my blood to open the secret door to the shed, and I pull on boots to head out to the jardín.

I can hardly think of the hope I felt sprouting in here just two days ago, when Bea showed me this place. Now that future is gone, uprooted by Antonela, just like my old life with my parents.

Sebastián gives me a handful of seeds before ripping into a blood bag from the small freezer. After swallowing, I use the canister to blood the garden, the way I saw Bea doing.

I approach the plants that resemble legs and arms with toe-like flowers and drizzle blood over them. A wave of dizziness hits me, and I wonder if I took too many of those seeds.

I turn toward the tiny trees with bone-like trunks and tonguelike leaves, when I see the foliage start moving around me.

"Do you see that?" I ask Sebastián.

"Yes."

The garden is rearranging itself, the plants coming together to create a passage that ends in darkness.

"I think it wants us to follow," says Sebastián, and I nod in assent, too awe-struck to speak. I feel the thrill of adrenaline, but I'm not afraid because I can't imagine anyone more powerful than the shadow beast. I feel safe at his side.

As we step down the passage, the foliage begins to entwine, until the lattice of body parts looks more like a cave wall.

There's light up ahead, and we approach a bonfire with the reddest flames I have ever seen. They look like they're made of blood.

"Welcome."

I look up in alarm as a tall hooded figure appears. Yet when I see them, some part of myself relaxes, as if they are intimately familiar to me.

"Who are you?" asks Sebastián.

They pull their hood back, revealing silver hair, and I gasp on recognizing my ancestor. "Brálaga!"

"Estela," they say, beaming. "Prince Bastian. It is an honor to make your acquaintances."

"The honor is ours."

I stare at Sebastián in shock. He sounds and even looks *humbled*. As if he knows who Brálaga is and respects them.

"Happy eighteenth birthday, Estela," says Brálaga. "I have met your twin, and I hoped to also meet you. It had been a few Earthly centuries since the last human crossed over to the other castle, and my curiosity was piqued."

"*Centuries?*" I echo in surprise.

"Your ancestors ended this tradition generations ago, after collecting enough data to determine this path led only to chaos and destruction—in the short run. Yet your uncle understands the need for sacrifice and was willing to continue the experiment."

"You mean he cursed us," I say, crossing my arms.

"From your perspective it seems like a curse. From mine, it is the price of evolution—and his gamble has nearly paid off. Your sister has come the furthest in re-corporealizing on Earth as a human-caster hybrid."

"That's what you want?" I ask. "For her to pass on her power to the next generation of Brálagas? You're trying to colonize humanity with your blood—"

"I already have. Now all that is left is for one of my children to reach up for my fire and bring it down to share with the others."

"You think Antonela is your Prometheus?"

"She has been *most* impressive," they say. "Using a Bleeder to cross dimensions? And of all Bleeders, she convinced the *prince*? The plan itself is quite ingenious, but that Antonela actually executed it merits great admiration."

Their expression reminds me of how Sebastián—*Prince Bastian*—looked at my sister in her memories, and it makes me feel the same way I did then. *Jealous.*

"Of course," Brálaga goes on, "Antonela could not have predicted, nor could anyone, that in lieu of killing you, the starving Bleeder would fall in love!"

They chuckle, and the temperature in the air seems to rise, like they're beaming solar heat into the room. "It is quite a delightful tale."

I look around at the walls, wondering how Brálaga plans to crush us. I get closer to Sebastián to signal him to get us out of here. "If your hopes ride on Antonela's plan," I say to them, "then I assume you have come here to help her?"

"I do not interfere."

"I don't buy that. You could be waiting centuries again for the next human, and they might not even make it this far." I nudge Sebastián, but he doesn't move. I look up at him, and he frowns at me like I'm a misbehaving toddler in a movie theater.

"You assume Earth's linear timeline, and the pressures of a ticking clock," says Brálaga with a sympathetic smile. "I do not experience existence that way."

They come closer, and a bench grows in the center of the cave, large enough for the three of us to comfortably share. They sit first and pat the spot beside them for me to join. Sebastián remains standing, but I take a seat, if only to see my ancestor from up close.

They have a slight glow around them, and I wonder if this is even their real form. If I reached out, could I touch them, or would my fingers go through them?

"I no longer remember my beginnings," says Brálaga once we are side by side. "I do not recall the organism I once was, but by now I no longer think in the self-serving way you assume. I am no longer an individual. I have morphed into a new entity that transcends a physical shell. I am partly this garden, I am partly this castle and the other castle, I am partly all the Brálagas in the world. I am partly you. And constantly, I am expanding. I do not know what I am evolving into, or what happens next, just like any of you. Yet at this moment, I am a grandparent in awe of two human beings—and a Bleeder."

Brálaga looks at Sebastián. "You have surprised me, and that is hard to do."

"What happened to the other twins?" I ask, greedy for answers to my questions. "Matilda and Josefina? Araceli and Isabel? They only journaled once."

Brálaga nods, their expression grim. "Humans are very delicate," they begin. "It is an easy thing to forget when you have been raised in the other castle. Josefina drowned Matilda, thinking she could revive her body, but as drowning is a natural death, Josefina died on the spot as well. Isabel tormented Araceli by possessing and killing those around her, which had an unexpected and devastating effect—Araceli killed herself, thereby also killing Isabel."

I wonder how they will sum up my fate when this is over. "Do you know about the Book?" I ask, and Sebastián moves in, resting a hand on my shoulder. Something about the reaction makes me tense, as if the question has just endangered me.

"There will always be those who fear progress because they cannot see past the sacrifice it requires," Brálaga says, not exactly answering my question.

"The being who delivered it claimed your plan would destroy Earth," I say.

"Growth is death," says Brálaga, without elaborating. "I know you have many more curiosities, but as the hour of your battle nears, I must ask you to limit yourself to a few final questions."

I can barely breathe at the mention of my *battle*. Yet I force my gut to unclench, and I try to focus on this last chance to interview Brálaga. There is something I want to know about that only they can explain, so I ask, "What is la Sombra exactly?"

"A carnivorous castle," they say with a small smile, and the cave walls around us flutter with shadows.

As the animation unfolds, I see hundreds of silhouettes together in what appears to be the windowless cathedral. This looks like a party. As the figures cluster together to converse, dance, and eat, something starts to happen at the far end of the room.

By the back stone wall that leads to the jardín de sangre, the ground begins to dip. A gap widens between the floor and wall that looks like a mouth opening—

The celebration turns to hysteria as guests are sucked into the castle's belly.

"This soil is connected to the other castle, my home dimension, which is constantly trying to expand," explains Brálaga, their tone almost mournful. "If la Sombra were to feed on too much blood, the connection could become so strong that it swallows your reality. Yet that is not my intention for your world. While it is true that many will die if Antonela is successful in corporealizing as the first Earth-based caster, she will also be the mother of a new evolution of powerful earthlings."

"*Will* she be successful?" I ask, not expecting them to answer.

Brálaga's gaze slides from me to Sebastián, lingering on the shadow beast. "Why spoil the ending when it is so near? We will find out soon enough. I will be watching."

"What happens if Antonela and I die and Teo takes off?" I blurt. "There won't be a Brálaga left at the castle!"

"There are Brálagas everywhere, child. See for yourself."

Black veins surface across the cave, and I'm reminded of the other castle's walls. The veins draw a map of Earth's seven continents, and bloodstains pop up across each one, pooling mostly in Europe and the Americas. It looks like some sort of census map.

"Just as you did not know about this place, others are unaware of their Brálaga blood. Yet when I need to call on another branch of the family, I do."

The bench beneath me disappears, as does Brálaga. The cave walls and the census map are replaced with the foliage of body organs. The plants start to grow, until they're crowding our space and about to crush our bodies—

"Time to go!" says Sebastián.

His grip closes around me, and everything blurs as he whisks me away to safety.

Sebastián deposits me in a chair in the dining hall.

In just two weeks, this castle has managed to upend everything I thought I knew about the world.

He sets what's left of Beatríz's tortilla in front of me, and my appetite curdles at the memory of us cooking together. "You knew who Brálaga was," I say to Sebastián.

"Everyone knows Brálaga, the self-made god," he says, passing me silverware. "I still cannot believe we met them."

Self-made god. That's a term I never heard before.

Thinking of the way Brálaga looked at Sebastián when I asked if our plan will work, I ask point-blank: "What aren't you telling me?"

It takes him so long to answer that I almost get upset, until I realize he's nervous. I've yet to see the shadow beast like this.

"Among my kind, there is no stronger bond than the one forged in blood," he says, his voice taut. "The blood-bond is an eternal vow that means you are mine, and I am yours."

I catch a barely detectable quiver in his voice.

"You said it's for procreation," I say, halfway between statement and question.

"Not exclusively," he says. "It is also used when two Bleeders want to bind themselves to each other forever."

My heart seems to triple in size, threatening to crack its cage.

"If you were my blood-bound," he goes on, his voice as deep as a velvet night, "your blood would imprint on mine, and mine would imprint on yours. Bleeder blood will give you a boost of power for facing your sister, and our bond will hopefully keep me with you even if the spell breaks."

My chest feels too full to speak. Is Sebastián *proposing*?

He takes my hand, but my whole body has gone numb, and I can barely feel his grip. "With your Brálaga blood in my system," he says, "I could perform the chanting required for the Book's containment spell. I would also have access to Brálaga-only spaces. Though I do not have a twin, my power more than equals that of two humans."

He's proposing to protect me. "Are you serious?" is all I can think to say.

"Must I repeat it a *third* time?" he whispers, pressing a kiss to my hand. "*I choose you over everything.*"

"But what if—"

"If your life were not in peril?" he injects. "Yes, I would still want you to be my blood-bound."

"Thank you," I say with a small grin. "But I was going to ask, what if I become one of you?"

His smile is like two stars colliding, and I feel blessed by the sight. "That will not happen. As I explained, Bleeders are born, not made. Once your sister believes I am gone and leaves her body to attempt entering yours, I can return and begin chanting."

"Unless the bond doesn't keep you here," I can't keep from saying. "Depends on if our love is stronger than her magic."

"I believe it is." His eyes are still giving off light. "After reading an entire bookshelf of romance novels, I gather this is how your kind does it."

Sebastián drops down on one knee, and I think I'm going to faint.

"Estela Amador Brálaga, will you be my blood-bound?"

The smile on my face is so monstrous that I can barely form the word. "*Yes.*"

His mouth meets mine.

I savor different flavors in his kiss tonight, many of which I've never tasted, and when I open my eyes again, we're standing in the lunar temple, surrounded by the words *No hay luz en Oscuro*. The day's dying light shines through the stained glass windows, illuminating all eight stages of the moon.

He brings my hand to his face. "With this drink," he says, "I seal my vow to honor and protect you."

I wince as his fangs break my skin and sink into my wrist. After he drinks my blood, he brings his own wrist to his mouth and bites.

"Your turn," he says, blood dripping down his chin.

I repeat what I heard him say: "With this drink—"

"Start with my name."

"Sorry, right. Um, Prince Bastian, also known as Sebastián."

He arches a brow as he offers me his wrist.

"With this drink," I say, "I seal my vow to honor and protect you." Then I press my mouth to the puncture wounds on his skin and suck.

New worlds explode on my tongue.

I had been expecting to taste metal, but instead I savor more unfamiliar flavors that are mind-blowing to behold. The kiss was just a shadow of Sebastián's taste, and when I look at him, I feel a shuddering in my body, a yearning to be closer.

Our mouths crash together.

I'm not sure when our shirts come off, but our chests are skin to skin, and I feel every part of him. His body thrums like a supercharged engine, purring with power yet taut with self-restraint.

"Can you take off your pants?" I ask.

He looks at me steadily as he warns, "Bleeders do not wear undergarments."

Blood rushes to my face, and his gaze strays to my cheeks.

"Consider me warned," I say, but when I take in the full breadth of him, I wonder if our bodies are even anatomically compatible.

His fingers stroke my inner thigh, inching higher with every caress, until he's stimulating me where I'm most sensitive. As his mouth finds my jawline, an irrepressible smile overtakes my face, and I reach down with my hand and grab him.

Sebastián's kiss stalls with surprise, and now my mouth overpowers his, enjoying the advantage. But before we get more carried away, I say, "I want you to promise me something."

He must hear the emotion in my voice because he slows down and meets my gaze. "What is it?"

"This could be the last thing I will ever ask of you. Will you do it for me?"

"Anything."

"If by some miracle I survive, and you see any signs of Antonela in me"—I swallow to clear my throat—"kill me."

CHAPTER 30

"WHERE ARE WE GOING?" ASKS Teo when he leaves the bathroom. Sebastián and I escorted him to wash up after freeing him of his ropes and feeding him a meal. "Come on" is all I say, leading him deeper into the castle.

Sebastián and I are in disagreement over what to do with my uncle. He's worried about my sister jumping into Teo's body before we can perform the trapping spell. I want to leave Teo in the tower, which is hopefully far enough away from the purple room to avoid that.

"I will do a sweep," says Sebastián after binding my uncle's wrists and ankles. He's scanning the perimeter for Antonela.

"The vampire is going to kill me," says Teo once we're alone in the journal room. He's bound on the floor, and I'm standing by the door. "You have to let me go."

"He's not going to kill you," I say, but even I can hear the lack of conviction in my voice.

"You fear the same thing," says Teo, seeing past my lie. "That's why you've been keeping me in *these* rooms."

"Which rooms?"

"The ones only you can enter. You're afraid of what he would do with complete access to me."

"That's ridiculous," I say, and yet there's a part of me that *is* afraid of what Sebastián might do to him. "Besides, he already has access," I say, as a reminder to myself.

"What do you mean?" asks Teo.

"Sebastián and I are blood-bound. Sorry you weren't invited to the ceremony."

Teo looks at me blankly. He has no idea what that means.

"Ever hear of the Book?" I prod.

"Lala's journal entry." He's as quick as a search browser, and I can't help but admire his encyclopedic recall. "For years, I searched this town for any hint of it. I asked everyone in Oscuro about the Book she described. I've determined it's not real."

I hear the lack of conviction in his voice as clearly as I heard it in my own. We're both lying to ourselves. I pretend Sebastián isn't a bloodthirsty vampire who's barely restraining himself from making my uncle his next meal. And Teo pretends the Book isn't real because it's one of the few Brálaga riddles he couldn't crack.

That means Felipe never confided in Teo about his family's legacy. He didn't share that they were the keepers of the Book.

I opened up to you more than anyone else in my life, Felipe told me. Hard to believe that was just last week.

He may have chosen Teo, but he trusted me more.

"How did you know?" I can't keep from asking him before I go. "That Antonela would come back?"

"I've always felt it," he says, speaking of her with the same reverence Felipe reserved for la Sombra. "When you alone survived the subway, I knew it had to do with Antonela. I assumed she must be here, waiting for you to come home. So I stayed close to answer your sister's call."

"But you didn't know if she'd forgiven you," I say, reading between the lines. "And you couldn't face the possibility that you had been wrong to light the black fire. That's why you didn't dare step inside the castle before yesterday."

I know I'm right by his silence.

I find Sebastián by the gargoyle staircase, eyes wide and expression grim. He waits to acknowledge me, his senses focused elsewhere. When he looks at me, I know what he's going to say.

"She is near."

Everything inside me grows brittle at those three words.

Mouth parched, I say, "Remember, we need to lead her to the—"

"I know the plan," he says, sounding frustrated, "but I insist that we should—"

"I'm not murdering my uncle," I say, putting an end to that debate.

"Nor should you," says Antonela in Bea's voice.

Sebastián and I whip around.

My sister entered the castle without even the shadow beast realizing. How is that possible?

He lunges at her, grabbing Antonela by Bea's neck. "Big mistake, walking in here," says Sebastián, a gleam of excitement in his eyes.

"If you kill this shell, I will be gone before you realize it," she says, voice raspy, not sounding upset at all that Sebastián is semi-strangling her. "I am no longer tied to la Sombra, so I will move on to the next person in town, and the next, and the next, until I have murdered them all, and the authorities are forced to investigate. Then I will murder them, too. La Sombra will swallow so many bodies, it will no longer be sated with little drizzles of blood. It will demand entire cities. Now take your hands off me."

Sebastián looks lethal, his gaze narrowed and top lip pulled back, and I know he's more likely to snap her neck than let go.

"Please," I say to him. "Let her go." If he kills her body now, her spirit will be gone before we can perform the spell.

He drops his hands after only a slight hesitation.

"This is better," says my sister, fixing the neck of her blouse. She bares all of Bea's teeth in a smile. "A family reunion."

Since she's already inside the castle, Sebastián and I fall back to plan B. "Yes, a family reunion," I agree, flashing her a grin that's just as toothy. "How about a game of hide-and-seek? For old times' sake."

"Sure, why not?"

She speaks with all the confidence she lacked at the other castle. It is truly as Sebastián—*Prince Bastian*—said: Antonela is *fearless*.

"I'll hide first," I say, and before she can react, I break into a run.

I don't hear her following me, and even if she tried, I doubt Sebastián would let her. Not until he's sure I've made it to the purple room.

I run harder than I have my whole life.

When I reach the red rug, Sebastián has already pulled it back for me, and the trapdoor is open. This is our plan B scenario, in case for any reason Sebastián couldn't transport me to the purple room, and I had to make it here myself.

I don't care about closing the door or replacing the rug. For the first time in my history of playing hide-and-seek, I'm not trying to stay hidden.

I want to be found.

I spread my blood on the apple-shaped rock, and I enter the purple room with singed walls.

"I get it, Bast."

At first I think Antonela has beaten me here—then I confirm I'm alone.

"I know what you see in her." My sister's voice is coming through the wall-paper. "*Me.*"

It's as if la Sombra is broadcasting the conversation.

"But remember that it is just a body," Antonela goes on, "and it will be mine again soon."

"You betrayed me."

Now it's Sebastián speaking.

"You give me too much credit, Bast," she says, and now that I'm more familiar with the evenness of her tone, I'm also more attuned to its nuances. There's a gentler tenor when she speaks to him that makes me wonder if she's not altogether indifferent to his opinion of her.

"I did not anticipate much of what has happened," she says. "I knew so little then. When I came before your throne, I understood only survival and leverage and power. You opened my eyes to attraction and sex and partnership—"

"*Partnership?* I understand this word better now than I did in my old life, and this was not it. You acted purely in your own interest."

"I am sorry I did not trust you." Antonela's voice is lower, like she's moved closer to him. "Show me I can trust you now. Drink my sister's blood, and set me loose upon this world."

The seconds are torturous.

"First, you have to find her."

Sebastián is leading Antonela toward me as planned, but it's hard to feel any relief through the terror of knowing this is it. I'm about to face my twin, and whatever happens, I may not survive.

I thought after the subway that I was done with life. I was sure the world held no future for me. Then I fell in love with the instrument of my death. The weapon brought here to kill me.

Now I know there are things worth living and fighting for. I understand why my parents gave up everything and everyone they knew to keep me on the run and off the radar of la Sombra's curse. They knew my life was worth the sacrifice.

For all they gave up for me, I can't let one of their daughters kill the other. That's why the trapping spell is the only way. Maybe over time, Sebastián and I will find a way to help Antonela.

"You were much better at this game as a child."

My sister steps into the purple room, Sebastián behind her.

"Please," I say. "Don't do this."

She doesn't look at me. "Remember you are the prince of the Bleeders," she says to Sebastián. "You belong back on your throne. You said your father would coffin you if he found out, remember? You risk too much staying here longer."

"How would he find out?" asks Sebastián, pretending to care.

At least, I hope he's pretending.

"You disappeared right after a pair of casters visited your castle. No doubt your guard will think magic played a role. If the casters in power want to keep the peace, it is likely they will perform a locator spell to redirect the Bleeders' attention elsewhere."

"It would take a *remarkable* caster to be able to locate me on Earth," he says, his words measured, like the weight of his thoughts is slowing his speech.

"True," she says, with a shrug. "Just as it would take a *remarkable* human to trick you."

They stare at each other.

Despite everything Sebastián has said to me, despite his being my bloodbound, in this moment, I am on the outside. I have no idea what has happened between them. Or how he feels about my sister.

Sebastián turns to me, and I know this is it. He will have to make a choice between Antonela and me, and the one he selects will be the one who survives.

He's already told me three times that he chooses me over everything. And yet Antonela just seemed to make a strong point. Will it be enough to change his mind?

He takes my face in his hands. Then he kisses me.

His lips move all over, down my chin, along my throat, and it feels so good that I barely feel it when his fangs puncture my skin.

I inhale sharply as there's a pull on my insides, like I'm being sucked out of my body.

Sebastián moans, unable to tamp down his enjoyment, and I feel that familiar mix of pleasure and pain, until I begin to grow lightheaded. I try to keep my eyes open a slit to see if my sister has moved yet, but she hasn't.

I'm beginning to feel weak all over, but Sebastián isn't slowing down. Soon I'm going to pass out, and I won't stand a chance against Antonela.

Black smoke flickers in my sister's eyes.

I tap Sebastián on the shoulder to let him know to stop, but his fangs are still hooked in. I can barely breathe. He's taking too much. How will I fight her off if I'm unconscious?

Sebastián leaps back, his eyes wide with horror the likes of which I never thought I would see on his face. His mouth is smeared with my blood, and he opens it to tell me something—

But he bursts into smoke, taking all the room's light with him. Once the air clears, he's gone.

My sister approaches me. She bends down, and I try to move, but my eyes flicker, my body too heavy, heart pounding dangerously slow in my ears. I'm dying.

"Goodbye, sister," she says, and it almost seems like emotion softens Bea's eyes. "I am sorry it had to be this way."

Her corneas are completely black with smoke as she grips my chin with Bea's hand.

I stare at the spot where Sebastián disappeared, waiting for him to reappear. If he doesn't come soon, she will possess me. What's taking so long? He should move faster than this.

Antonela pries open my mouth, and the smoke funnels out of her body to enter mine.

What if Sebastián is gone? That means he has no way to come back.

I'm alone.

My sister dives for my throat—and I try reaching out with my hand to shove her away, not expecting it to work.

To my extreme shock, I make contact. But I have to squint to make sure I'm seeing right.

My arm no longer seems to be made of flesh and bone.

I have become purple smoke.

RAUL'S RULE #12

YOU CAN ONLY SOLVE THE CASE, NOT THE PERSON.

CHAPTER 31

ANTONELA AND I ARE BOTH smoky shadows, our shapes identical silhouettes. I look down at my purple form in awe, my gaze jumping back and forth between it and my body lying unconscious on the floor.

This doesn't feel real. *Am I dead?* How do I get back to myself?

"How is this happening?" Antonela asks me, and I know she's not the one doing this. As she follows my gaze, my body looks vulnerable and unprotected.

The lights flicker, and we look around us.

This is the castle's doing.

La Sombra has been leading me to Antonela since I arrived. The purple room gave me the photos, the letter in the journal room revealed I had a sister, the mirror room showed me Antonela's past, and my dreams shared memories of our childhood together. Brálaga told me they are partly this castle, which means this place is in league with them. It keeps us chained to Brálaga's vision.

This is how the cycle continues.

The blood we've fed la Sombra has made it a real-life member of the family, and it wants what any creature wants—to survive and reproduce.

We are its children. If it wanted to, the castle could eat the whole world—but it doesn't. Because it loves us. And in our own sick way, we love it. This place gives us shelter and purpose.

We are cursed with the castle's love.

"I don't want either of us to die, and I know you don't, either," I say to

Antonela, subtly moving closer to my body to shield it from her. "Today is our eighteenth birthday. We should be celebrating, not fighting. We can figure this out together if you can just have some patience."

I hold out a purple smoke hand to her in an offer of peace.

"There is nothing to figure out," she says, leaving me hanging. "I must have your body in order to achieve my goal."

"You mean *Brálaga's* goal." I start moving toward her to lead us away from my body. When I get too close, she pulls back, keeping a buffer between us. She must've picked up more than a few defensive mechanisms at that school.

"You have been used by Brálaga and Teo, but you're free now," I tell her. "You can do what *you* want. After being alone your whole life, don't you want a family? A *sister*?"

"I want power."

"You told Sebastián that he opened you to new feelings."

She stops moving, the shadow beast a sore spot for her. I shrink the distance between us to three feet, and still she doesn't budge. She waits in silence, as if daring me to come closer.

I stay where I am. "Give me the chance to do the same for you. I can show you how it feels to be *loved*—"

"*Bast* knows what it is like to grow up among monsters, trapped in others' power grids, the prisoner of a fortress you cannot escape," she says, her voice a snarl. "*You* understand *nothing*. You are innocent, gullible, young. The only one of us who has anything to teach the other is me to you, so get out of my body."

Before I can even think to protect myself, she jabs a fist into my gut, and I double over in pain.

My vision goes dark, and I'm in a black space that is pure grief. I feel every bad feeling I've ever had sucking me down, every depressive thought, every betrayal, mad moment, sadness, nightmare—

Only the feelings are not mine.

They're *hers*.

Five-year-old Antonela stands amid black flames as the spell sends her to the other castle. She is terrified, crying, hysterical, as the world spins around her, and then she's in and out of consciousness.

She sees fragments of scenes. A door opens, and hooded giants pull her through.

She opens her eyes to find she is trapped in a coffin. She is being bathed by a tall hooded being.

She finds herself in a space with other young beings, and none of them look like her. They have things like horns, or fangs, or claws, or wings. She has no recollection of anything except for this moment, this home, this family.

Antonela grows with her cousins, brought up by their hooded instructors. Yet she and the others do not age at the same speed, and she gets left behind.

The others are constantly picking on her. They throw things at Antonela, they beat her, they set her hair on fire, they burn her skin—

"Enough!" I shout, breaking free of her memories.

"You cannot even stomach the ghost of what I have endured," she says, sounding almost proud. "You have nothing and no one, remember? What is the point of hanging on when all life has to offer you is pain?"

Before I can block the blow, she pops me again, this time in the jaw.

I'm on the subway, with Mom and Dad and the four girls.

I'm at the center, sobbing into my pillow while my roommate snores.

I'm in front of the media while the FBI director lies to the world.

I'm sitting across from doctor after doctor at the center, each of them trying to get me to speak.

I'm at the Madrid airport, and Lety is telling me to find my voice.

I'm holding Bea's body, begging her to hold on as Antonela takes over.

I'm with Sebastián, and he's saying, "I choose you over everything—"

I blast out of the memory black hole, his love reminding me of my strength. I refuse to retreat into that lost girl again. I will not fade away into my grief.

I will fight.

"We have both had our share of pain," I say to Antonela. "If anything, that should bring us closer, not pit us against each other. We should be looking for a way around this curse—"

"I am not interested in a human life," she says, coming in for another strike. "I have the chance to be something greater than you can ever become. Your fame on this planet comes only at my hand. Yet I can reach heights beyond this realm. I can be the first of a new species. Do you really believe your insignificant life is worth thwarting evolution?"

Insignificant?

I see her smoky hand clenching into a fist, and before she can swing it, I punch her in the face, my chest swelling with some of my happiest memories.

I am nine years old, and after binging R. L. Stine books, I write a short story about a girl whose enemy slumbers inside her and only wakes up if she stops moving, so she must always be on the run. When Mom reads it, her eyes tear up, and I have never felt prouder.

I am ten, and Mom introduces me to one of her favorite films, Back to the Future. *I love it so much that I watch it again and again and again all year long. I tell Mom that on my eighteenth birthday, I want to get a tattoo with the DeLorean's license plate,* OUTATIME. *She promises to get one with me so we match.*

I am thirteen, and Mom is off on a solo camping trip, so I'm alone with Dad when I get my first period. He feels so awkward that he agrees to let me help him on a case for the first time.

I am fifteen, and we are living in an ocean-side motel in Miami, Florida. It's spring break, and the same group of local high school students floods the beach every day. That's how I meet Jair. He's got crunchy curls and gentle eyes. We kiss in the shade of a palm tree. It's the first time I taste a boy's tongue.

I am sixteen, and I'm with my parents in Virginia, lying on the beach at night. The three of us are staring at the stars, and we design a new constellation after ourselves. We Frankenstein our names together and call it Esteliviaul—

"Stop!" Now it's Antonela who can't stand reliving my memories. "Do not try to paint our family to be something they are not. They *sacrificed* me—"

"*Teo* sacrificed you! And the rest of us have suffered for his actions. Losing you destroyed our parents!"

"In all your memories, our parents' only priority was to protect you. But you know what I did not see? I never saw them try to recover me."

There's real emotion in her voice. "It could have just as easily been you," she points out. "If I had been the one hiding. Then they would have abandoned you just as completely. This version of the loving family you have is only because you are the one who got to stay."

"I know, but we don't get to control that," I tell Antonela. "*What-ifs* are worthless. What's real is this moment and each other. That's all we have. And I am asking you, begging you, to give us a chance—"

Her hands close around my neck, constricting my throat and cutting off my pleas.

"*No,*" she says, and her memories blast through me.

Antonela is in the Atrium of the other castle.

She is with Brálaga, but this is not the same conversation I witnessed in her memories. There are far fewer sand grains left now. Antonela must have gone back to see them again. Maybe this is when Red and Cyclops spied her going in.

"They sent me here! I was their sacrifice! Why would I even want to go back?" she's asking Brálaga.

This is a different Antonela. Until now, she seemed cool and untouchable, even in the face of constant beatings. Yet it's clear the memories of Earth stirred something in her for the first time, making me wonder if she's ever been truly hurt before now.

"I have already told you the alternative," says Brálaga pleasantly. "Would you like to live in the castle walls?"

"Then help me," she says, crossing her arms. "Or I will tell my cousins what awaits them—"

"You cannot threaten me. Nor can I help you."

"You told me I needed a body for the crossing to Earth, but you did not tell me I would need a body to live there."

"I told you it is a universe ruled by matter. If you need a body to cross over, it logically follows that you would need one to remain there."

"So I have to take my sister's. If I can even figure out how. That is the only way?"

Brálaga looks at her sadly. "How could you sacrifice if you have nothing left to sacrifice?"

Antonela feels her heart closing toward her family and any hope of reuniting with them. Which leaves her only one goal left: seize power and fulfill Brálaga's vision.

They are her true parent, after all, and she will make them proud.

I elbow my sister in the gut, and her grip loosens enough that I free myself. "We can still be a family, the two of us—"

She tackles me, and we roll around, wrestling each other as two shadows, purple versus black. I knee her, but she twists away in time, and before I know what's happening, she dives for my unconscious body.

"No!"

I race her toward it, but she turns in midair and punches me. One final memory slips in:

"I say you are fearless," Prince Bastian says to Antonela.

"I know," she says, sliding onto his lap. "The question is, are you?"

He makes a grunting sound, and I realize it's a chuckle because he's smirking. "Tell me, how will I return from Earth?"

"You will drink my blood," she says, and he frowns questioningly.

"You want me to kill you?"

"Yes."

He stares at her, and I know she's stumped him yet again, but in a good way. He leans toward her, lips parted and fangs out, and she doesn't move.

"Have you ever been kissed, human caster?"

She doesn't answer verbally, but her body language says it all. Her spine is stiff and her jaw is clenched.

He pulls down her blue mask, and her breath catches. The Bleeder runs a finger across her lips, and she shivers.

"You have no idea what you are feeling right now," he says, his face inches from hers. "It is called desire."

His mouth brushes hers, and she leans into him, ever so slightly. Yet he pulls away before they kiss, sliding her mask back on.

"Perhaps after sating my appetite with others," he murmurs to her, "I will choose to keep you."

I pull out of her head right as Antonela and I crash to the floor.

"You have nothing," she says, locking her hands around my neck. "Not even the Bleeder is yours. This body belongs to me now."

I want to fight her off, but what future awaits me even if I defeat her? At least Antonela has a chance to make a difference in the worlds. I'm nobody. I have nobody.

If I "win," it just means I killed my sister. I doubt I could live with that on my conscience anyway.

"Yes," she says softly, seeing the change come over my expression. "Give in, sister. It is the right thing to do."

Sebastián isn't coming back. He's home in his castle, back in his rightful place, and soon I will be another memory for him, like blue bear.

My parents, Felipe, and Bea all died so my sister might live. The only one left is Teo, and he doesn't love me. At least Antonela will be wanted. Our uncle will care for her, something she's never experienced.

She seems to know it's over because she pulls away and dives for my body. I want to get up and race her, but I'm a vessel without a motor, and there's no breeze to help me along. I tried so hard to find answers for my parents' deaths, and they all led back to me, to this moment, my final sacrifice.

The last thing I have left to lose in this world.

My life.

I let my head roll over, and a tear spills out as I watch Antonela's black smoke hands prop up my head and yank open my mouth—

Then I see him.

Sebastián is sitting by my body. He doesn't seem able to see me or Antonela in our shadow forms. He's holding my hand and Antonela's picture, chanting words I can't hear. But I know what he's saying.

No hay luz en Oscuro.

I stare at my shadow beast in awe, this creature of darkness, remembering how he said I awoke in him a gentleness, something he doesn't want to lose. If there can be softness even in the hardest of iron hearts, then the chant is wrong.

There *is* light in the dark.

I have been missing my parents for months. My grief has consumed me, this curse has damned me, the undead haunt me—and yet, in the midst of all this death, I found new life. I fell in love.

I guess some flowers only blossom by moonlight.

My sister's shadow form is dissipating into a cloud of smoke so she can enter my body, but I vault over and tackle her to the ground before she can shift forms.

A future with Sebastián awaits me. If our blood-bond held, so can I.

"Let go!" she shouts at me, but my embrace of her only tightens.

"Bast will never be human," warns my sister, as I let my love for him invade every inch of my shadowy being, and I feel like I'm transmitting my warmth to Antonela not as memories but as emotions.

"He is a monster, and that will never change!" she says, but her voice sounds weaker, and now I know the power I have that she fears. My hope. My resilience.

She hates that I can see the light in a creature of the dark like Sebastián . . .

or like herself. That I could forgive Bea. That I could fight for my life even when it seems I have sacrificed it all and have nothing left to anchor me.

That is humanity's true magic—our unabashed ability to hope. And Antonela can't kill me without killing that first.

I shove her away from me suddenly and clutch the picture from Sebastián's hand, which has a few drops of my blood on it.

He looks stunned when it disappears from his fingers.

Antonela is already melting into a cloud to make for my mouth again— and right before her shadowy torso scatters, I shove the photograph into her black-smoke heart.

"NO!"

She screams as the fumes that make up her spirit begin to swirl and retreat into the photographic paper, which swallows her presence until there's not even a wisp of smoke left.

I feel a wave of lightheadedness, and when I blink, I'm lying on my back, my hand enfolded in Sebastián's. I'm no longer made of purple smoke but flesh and blood.

"Estela?" he asks as I sit up. I look at him, and he searches my gaze. In a lower register, he asks, "Antonela?"

"No," I say. "Estela."

He pulls me into his chest and embraces me. "It is done," he says, holding me as I cry. "You are safe, and we are together. For the rest of your life, I am yours." He kisses me on the head. "Happy birthday, my blood-bound love."

I blink a few times, sniffing and covered in snot, my heart rate still not settling. It can't really be over, can it?

I look around and spot the bloodied photograph of a smiling five-year-old Antonela baring her chipped tooth. I already know where it's going to stay— hidden under the loose stone in the purple room, until the day I figure out how to save her.

"Does this mean," I say, wiping my nose on my arm, "that now I can live with my monster prince in our cursed castle?"

"Yes, princess," says the shadow beast, baring his sharp teeth. "Welcome to your happily ever after."

1 3 M O N T H S L A T E R

SEBASTIÁN ENTERS THE JOURNAL ROOM at the peak of la Sombra's tower, carrying in a tray of food.

Teo is on the floor, reading a journal. It has only been a couple of months since he started speaking again.

"¿Alguna noticia?" asks Sebastián.

"Not yet," answers Teo in English. He is searching for anything that might help Sebastián loosen la Sombra's leash, so he can travel with Estela.

They mainly keep Teo around as insurance. His and Sebastián's presence at the castle gives Estela the freedom to be gone to pursue a medical degree, as she is taking over her aunt's practice. At first, Teo used to try to escape. He does not anymore.

He has nowhere to go.

"I know you're just trying to keep me busy," says Teo to Sebastián as the shadow beast is about to leave. "Because you need me here more than I need you."

"You better hope so," says Sebastián. "It was you who convinced me you were worth more alive than dead."

A year ago, before he returned to the purple room to perform the trapping spell, Sebastián first went to the tower to kill Teo. He thought it was the only way to keep Antonela from using him against Estela.

Yet Teo convinced Sebastián that keeping him alive would benefit Estela, as it would free her to move around. Teo said if Sebastián killed him, it would be from a selfish desire to keep her as caged here as the shadow beast.

"I am of Brálaga blood now, too," Sebastián relished revealing to him. "She can go as she pleases as long as I am here."

The Bleeder was just about to kill Teo when the man played his final card: "But what if I can figure out how to break that limitation of the spell, and you could travel with her?"

The sky bleeds red as Sebastián meets Estela in the garden at sunset. She is fondling the black roses that just blossomed.

She grins as he approaches, the wind coiling her curls around her neck. There are cuts from the thorns all over her hands.

A ball of blood bubbles up on her finger, and his tongue grows fat with anticipation. He brings her hand to his mouth and sucks it clean.

Thanks to the seeds, he can now walk as far as the castle's iron gate—but he still can't leave the grounds. Given the nature of the spell binding his presence here, it is unlikely he ever will.

One might think the Iron Prince traded one cage for another, except that he has never felt freer. For the first time, he is making his own choices.

He looks down at the small placards Estela placed for her parents. She buried their passports here, along with the leather journal, so that she would have a place to visit them.

"Ready to eat?" she asks Sebastián.

"I do appreciate that you know how much I like to hunt my meals," he says, kissing her arm.

One morning, someone from the ayuntamiento—*local government*—came by asking Estela if she would step in for Bea as interim mayor. She said yes to keep with tradition. Then they looked at Sebastián and asked who he was.

Shocked that they could see him, the shadow beast reached out a hand to shake the person's hand, and their skin made contact. That was how he and Estela discovered the seeds had changed the rules again, and now people could see Sebastián.

It was a month later that Estela came up with the idea for how to feed him.

"He has arrived," says Sebastián, picking up on the faint sound of a car engine approaching, and he vanishes into shadow.

Estela rises and watches as Jake Plunket gets out of the cab and walks up to the gate.

She has a hobby of researching cases around the world in which a criminal got off on a technicality, with a focus on murderers, rapists, and pedophiles. Particularly ones without a big social footprint.

"Mr. Plunket?" she asks, walking down the cobblestone steps.

"That's me," he says with a leer.

"The door is off to the side, can you see it?"

He stares at the gate until he spots the handle, then he steps onto the grounds and sizes up the castle walls. "Holy God, so you're saying this is all *mine*?"

"That's right," she says brightly. "Let me give you a quick tour."

He looks her up and down the same way he did la Sombra. "Yeah, why don't you give me a tour? I have a feeling this is the kind of place one can get lost in, you know?"

He chuckles to himself as she smiles even wider, making herself look more innocent.

Once Estela finds the right criminal who meets her criteria, she contacts them, claiming to represent an estranged relative who's left them an inheritance, and she asks them to sign a confidentiality agreement in exchange for a one-way ticket to Spain.

Jake whistles when they enter the castle. "Damn! I had no idea I had Spanish ancestors. This is wild!"

"This way, please," she says, leading him past the entrance hall.

"We alone here?" he asks her.

"Yes," she answers with a friendly smile over her shoulder.

Estela feels his hand on her backside as soon as she turns around. "You wanna stay here with me, honey?" he asks, voice breathy.

"Sure," she says, facing him again. "Mind if my boyfriend stays, too?"

Jake's face falls. "What?"

"I should warn you, he's the jealous type."

All the lights go out, drowning la Sombra in darkness. "Hello?" Jake calls out. "What is this? Where'd you go, you little—?"

The lights blast back on, but Estela is gone.

Standing in her place is a demon with silver eyes and sharp fangs and sinister shadows. "Welcome home," says Sebastián.

Jake screams and turns to run, but the shadow beast swoops down and carries him deeper into the castle.

Estela goes to the kitchen to eat some dinner of her own while Sebastián plays with his food. When he is finished, getting rid of the corpse is easy, since the house is always hungry. The jardín de sangre is blooming year-round.

Estela has been studying for medical school entrance exams, but more and

more she finds herself drawn to her moonlight gig as Sebastián's food pro-
curer. She much prefers investigating people and cases.

When he shows up at the dining table, Sebastián's eyes are bright, his skin
glowing.

"At least you wiped the blood off your face," says Estela with a grin.

"Thank you for dinner," he says, grinning back as he comes over and kisses
her. "I love you, Estela."

A curl of black smoke floats across her eye.

She blinks, and it's gone.

"I love you, too, Bast."

ACKNOWLEDGMENTS

As always, thank you so much for reading! It's because of you, my readers, that I get to do what I love, and I am forever grateful to you.

Additional thanks go out to:

- Eileen Rothschild, for taking another chance on me. Your brilliant feedback is what brought this ~~castle~~ story to life.

- Kerri Resnick and Borg, for a gasp-worthy cover that transports me to la Sombra.

- Lisa Bonvissuto, Melanie Sanders, Meghan Harrington, Rivka Holler, Gail Friedman, Jonathan Bennett, and the rest of the teams at Wednesday Books, St. Martin's Press, and Macmillan, for turning this story into a book and sharing it with the world.

- Laura Rennert: after a decade of literary adventures, I still feel so lucky that I get to do this with you. As always, your notes were pitch-perfect.

- Nicole Maggi, my dear, you're what I miss most about the West Coast. I feel immeasurably fortunate that everything I write gets to go through you first. *Oy with the poodles already!*

- Sofía Rhei, muchas gracias por tu ayuda editando mis frases argentinas para que suenen más españolas. ¡Espero viajar a visitarte pronto!

- Lisa Novoa, Noa Freiman, and Corinne "Galaxy Girl" Farkash: everything has changed, but the things that matter have stayed the same. Luv u 4-eva.

- Caden Armstrong, for being as excellent an editor as you are a friend. Hugs also to Robin Potts, Will Frank, Lizzie Andrews, Alexandra Monir, Gretchen McNeil, Leslie Pope, Richie Segal, Aurora Lydia Dominguez, and an extra hug to Courtney Saldana, who shared her light with me in dark times.

- Leo's family, for welcoming me so lovingly. Ana, Roberto, Anita, Heidy, Iraida, Andy, Andrew, Alexis, Alex, Pedrito, Mamulia, Pepo—los quiero mucho.

- Andy, for always having my back and being a great brother.

- Mica, for being my unicorn rainbow princess and the best niece ever.

- Meli, for being my inspiration. The best thing about my childhood was that I got to share it with you.

- Our wedding guests, for helping fund ~~my research~~ our honeymoon in Europe. Leo and I visited ancient castles in France and Spain and explored the vibrant towns tucked in their shadows. Thanks to our family and friends who contributed—and to my amazing dad, who was our tour guide.

- Pa, gracias por la boda de mis sueños y una luna de miel llena de castillos.

- Ma, gracias por ser mi primera lectora y la mujer más fuerte que conozco.

- Leo, I love and admire you so much. Thank you for being my happily ever after.

ROMINA GARBER (pen name Romina Russell) is a *New York Times* and internationally bestselling author. Originally from Argentina, she landed her first writing gig as a teen – a weekly column for the *Miami Herald* that was later nationally syndicated – and she hasn't stopped writing since. Her books include *Lobizona* & the Zodiac series. She is a graduate of Harvard College and a Virgo to the core. For more information, please visit www.rominagarber.com.